'Meticulously plotted and UTTERLY chilling – everything you want from a contemporary thriller' PAULA HAWKINS

'I cared desperately about these characters and turned the pages frantically, praying for their survival. Clever, compassionate and completely compelling' ERIN KELLY

'A deliciously disturbing thriller' ANN CLEEVES

'I can't remember the last time I was so invested in a book' SATHNAM SANGHERA, *THE TIMES*

'An unsettling, compelling story. Mel McGrath has a unique skill for drawing flawed yet fascinating characters who captivate the reader' RACHEL ABBOTT

'Mel McGrath tackles hard-hitting issues in a thought-provoking way... A book-club novel ripe for discussion' ADELE PARKS, *PLATINUM*

'I was completely drawn in... A timely addition to the academic noir genre, as #MeToo finally starts to catch up with universities in a long-awaited reckoning. Highly recommended' HARRIET TYCE

'A gripping exploration of consent and power play, this is all too timely' *HEAT*

'A clever and compelling storyline, with complex characters you really care about. *Two Wrongs* is the perfect read' B A PARIS

'Mel McGrath skilfully controls the drip-feed of information in a complex and painfully topical mystery' *TIMES CRIME CLUB*

PRAISE FOR MEL McGRATH

'McGrath excels in creating believably flawed characters, and her masterful control of suspense and pacing make for a psychological thriller that is both perceptive and disturbing' *GUARDIAN*

'Dark, clever, terrifying' PAULA HAWKINS

'Absorbing... McGrath asks: should it be a crime to witness a violent event, and say nothing?' *THE TIMES*

'A scorching, clever thriller' TAMMY COHEN

'Chilling, fiendishly plotted and surprising, this stayed with me long after reading' *WOMAN & HOME*

'This roller-coaster read will have you hooked' *CLOSER*

'Psychologically acute and deeply satisfying' *TELEGRAPH*

'Perceptive... McGrath is a thoughtful writer' *DAILY MAIL*

'A dextrously written thriller and examination of guilt and innocence... [McGrath is a] diamond-hard talent' *FINANCIAL TIMES*

'Unsettling, disturbing and vital. 5*' *HEAT*

'A psychological tour de force with a superb plot from one of the UK's most gifted crime writers' KATE RHODES

'Disturbing and dark yet very compelling' MEL SHERRATT

'Utterly compelling right from the start' *CRIME MONTHLY*

Mel McGrath is an Essex girl, co-founder of Killer Women, and an award-winning writer of fiction and non-fiction.

As MJ McGrath she writes the acclaimed Edie Kiglatuk series of Arctic mysteries, which have been optioned for TV, were twice longlisted for the CWA Gold Dagger, and were *Times* and *Financial Times* thrillers of the year. As Melanie McGrath she wrote the critically acclaimed, bestselling memoir *Silvertown*. As Mel McGrath she is the author of the bestselling psychological thrillers *Give Me the Child* and *The Guilty Party*. *Two Wrongs* is her latest novel.

Also by Mel McGrath

The Guilty Party
Give Me the Child

TWO WRONGS

MEL McGRATH

ONE PLACE. MANY STORIES

HQ
An imprint of HarperCollins*Publishers* Ltd
1 London Bridge Street
London SE1 9GF

www.harpercollins.co.uk

HarperCollins*Publishers*
1st Floor, Watermarque Building, Ringsend Road
Dublin 4, Ireland

This edition 2021

1
First published in Great Britain by
HQ, an imprint of HarperCollins*Publishers* Ltd 2021

Copyright © Mel McGrath 2021

Mel McGrath asserts the moral right to be
identified as the author of this work.
A catalogue record for this book is
available from the British Library.

ISBN: 978-0-00-848778-2

MIX
Paper from
responsible sources
FSC™ C007454

This book is produced from independently certified FSC™ paper
to ensure responsible forest management.

For more information visit: www.harpercollins.co.uk/green

This book is set in Sabon by Type-it AS, Norway

Printed and bound using 100% Renewable Electricity
at CPI Black Print, Barcelona

To those who continue to listen.

Prologue

The lights on the Clifton Suspension Bridge are dazzling in the thin Bristolian rain. The woman walks across it all the time on her way to and from her shift cleaning at the Royal Infirmary and even though it is a notorious suicide spot she has never yet seen anyone fall. But there is a first time for everything and as she spots a young woman clutching the railings of the suicide fence, the thought zips through her mind: this might be the time.

She hears herself call out reflexively – Hey! The young woman clutching the fence looks her way and for an instant hope surges in the woman who has just come off shift until the younger woman, turning back to face the gorge, reaches out and begins to climb the fence. There is a terrible purpose in the way she moves. The woman who has just come off shift knows that whatever she does now could make the difference between life and death, and knowing that, sensing it, makes the hairs on her skin lift and her heart hammer and her legs surge forward.

Still the young woman clambers upwards.

'Hey!' The woman who has just come off shift feels her breath quit. She is so tired. It was a long day at work and she cleans the A&E department and there is always so much blood and grease and body fluids and so many cups and snack wrappers to clear up. She is accustomed to seeing bodies and knows what that three-second flight from the bridge through the air and into the water can do to flesh and bones.

The young woman lifts one arm and shouts, 'Go away!'

The woman who has just come off shift stops in her tracks, three or four metres from the figure making her way up the fence. It is all in this moment. Life, death. She hears her own voice bark back, 'Please, stop!' The young woman freezes and shouts down.

'Stay where you are,' the young woman screams. 'I don't want your help!'

'OK, OK,' the tired woman replies, holding up her hands as if in surrender. 'But talk to me!' She has no idea what she is going to say but she knows that she must find a way to connect. The tiredness has drained from her. Her mind is razor sharp. If I let this happen, she thinks, what will I tell my kids? How will I live knowing I have let a woman die?

She wonders how the young woman can think of leaving this city that she loves so much, this wonderful, stone city with its dark history, its independent, almost feral people and its brilliant, hopeful bridge? She wonders if the young woman knows that this bridge was first conceived of by a woman with six children who drew up the plans and gave them to a man and refused to take any credit because women 'shouldn't be boastful'. Women are always building bridges, linking things, people, moving between worlds not made for them, always thinking up new ways to reach across the darkness, to connect.

She wants to ask the young woman why she is doing this,

2

how can anything be this bad, but she knows enough not to. Instead she shouts out, 'I'm Sondra, what's your name?'

The young woman turns her head. 'Satnam.'

'We've all felt like you're feeling now, Satnam,' the tired woman says. 'I'm older than you, so I know. But the feeling passes. It always passes.' They are more than strangers to each other now. Each has made her way indelibly into the other's experience, their history, the story of their lives.

Satnam shakes her head. 'I can't, I just can't.'

Her words are slurred. She's not in her right mind, Sondra thinks. 'Please, Satnam, come down from the fence. If we stand here any longer, we'll both be wet through. I live just the other side of the bridge. We can go and have a cup of tea. I've got chocolate chip Hobnobs! We can talk.'

Sondra reaches for her mobile phone to call the emergency services but, guessing at her purpose, Satnam shouts, 'No, no police!'

'OK,' Sondra says. 'No police. But let me call the Samaritans. You don't have to speak to them. You can just let me do the talking.' She'd love to call the Samaritans right now. They would know what to do and the tired woman has absolutely no idea.

Satnam's head is bobbing. She's mumbling, trying hard to remain conscious and on the fence. The wind is up, the bridge swaying minutely underfoot. Bristol is such a blowy city. The tired woman loves that about it. Every day is a bad hair day in Bristol. You can't be a Bristolian and be fussy about your blow-dry. What odd thoughts come unbidden when you're up against it. Sondra scopes around in her head for some better ones. 'I don't need to call the Samaritans. I can call anyone,' she says. 'Just give me a number.'

3

Satnam is looking at her now. She is so young and beautiful, with delicate, even features and long, black, unruly hair. 'I don't know any numbers. My phone...' She's losing focus, slurring her words. Sondra can't tell if this is a good thing or not. She takes a step closer. It's the wrong move. Satnam resumes her grip on the fence and climbs higher, balancing herself by bracing on the upright.

'OK, OK, I won't move. Is your phone here?'

Satnam nods. She's pointing away, towards the bridge tower. 'You left it over by the tower?' Satnam moans in response. Sondra says, 'Promise to stay there and I'll get your phone.' She walks backwards towards the tower, slowly, one step at a time. In a minute she's reached the spot where Satnam was pointing. One eye scouts about under the lights, the other remains on Satnam. It's hard to see. The rain is on her glasses and so much is in shadow. She wants to ask, What does it look like? What colour is it? But those questions will be wasting time and there is no time to waste. Besides, the young woman is growing more and more incoherent. Soon, she thinks, Satnam won't be able to say anything at all. Sondra's eyes sweep the paving on the walkway. Just as she is beginning to feel desperate, her foot makes contact with something. She bends and gropes at the pavement and there it is. An iPhone. Oh, what a relief! She has found it and it's an iPhone. Sondra also has an iPhone so she knows how they work.

'You need to tell me the passcode.' She thinks she hears one oh four oh but it's so slurred that might not be it. Hurriedly, she plugs in the numbers. And thank God, thank God, the homescreen appears.

Satnam says, 'Call Nevis.'

Nevis? Is that a last name or a first? Will Sondra find it in the contacts? Maybe, but it'll take too long. Another better idea bubbles up. She pushes the menu button and waits for the tone then speaks into the phone as clearly as she can. 'Siri, call Nevis.'

The phone speaks. 'Calling Nevis.'

At that moment the eye that is on the young woman registers movement. Sondra turns her head and sees that the young woman has jumped down onto the walkway and is dragging herself towards the gap in the fence where the suspension wire attaches to the bridge.

Oh God, thinks Sondra. I shouldn't have walked away. I shouldn't have left her. She's going to go and I'm not going to be able to pull her back. She feels herself take a leap forward and closes her eyes.

Chapter 1

Nevis

Nevis Smith, student mathematician, bird lover, and keeper of secrets, is lying on her bed in the flat she shares with Satnam Mann trying to finish a tricky piece of coursework on deep vent modelling when her phone bleeps with Satnam's ringtone.

'Hey, I thought you'd gone to bed already.' The door to Satnam's room was shut and the light was out when Nevis came in late from the library.

An unfamiliar voice replies. 'My name is Sondra. I'm with your friend Satnam on the Clifton Suspension Bridge. She wants you to come *straight away*. Please come, right now.'

Nevis says, 'Is she hurt?'

'Not yet, not yet, but she's in a bad way. Oh please. Don't call the emergency services. She's says that if she sees a blue light she'll jump. Please, I don't know what else to say to her, just *come*.'

The words hum and hiss and swirl around in Nevis's head. Is this some kind of joke? Or a scam? Someone playing a sick prank. What would Satnam be doing on the bridge past midnight? Why would this woman be calling? In any case what Sondra is saying is impossible because it's after midnight and Satnam is asleep in her bed.

And yet the urgency of the voice is unmistakeable. Nevis rushes into the hallway and throws open the door to Satnam's room. In the murky light she picks out the shape of an empty bed. There is something rancid in the air which she has never noticed before. Is she imagining things? She can hear her head drumming or is it her heart? What is happening? Nevis, who prides herself on thinking straight, can hardly think at all.

She reaches for the light switch and flips it on as if that might illuminate the inside of her head. But no. The bed remains empty. She walks around it and opens the wardrobe. She calls, 'Satnam?' and hears traffic outside and the clamour of her pulse. What is going on? As she turns to leave, her eye catches a bottle of vodka on the bedside table. How could she have missed it? She hurries over, picks it up, shakes the few remaining drops inside the bottle, puts it back down and feels the moving parts of her brain clicking into place at last.

Is this *The Moment*? she thinks. Has it come?

Honor always told her that in every life there is The Moment. It might be very small, like holding out a hand to stop a child stepping over a pavement, or very big, like giving the go-ahead for a doctor to flick the switch on a life-support machine. It may be saying yes or saying no. It might be as simple as making or taking a phone call. The Moment can steal up on you and arrive in the most unexpected minute of the most unexpected hour. It may hit hard or be so soft-footed that you may not hear it coming. Your life can be defined by it. It can be your making or your ruin.

Satnam is on the Clifton Suspension Bridge with Sondra. Satnam is... oh it's too horrible to think about but Nevis must steel herself. Satnam is in deep, deep trouble. This is my

Moment, she thinks. This is my time. Whatever decisions she makes, whatever action she takes now will be etched on her soul. She cannot escape this; she can only move towards it.

Nevis's hand is trembling so hard now that she can hardly hold the phone. 'Let me speak to her.' She can feel her adolescence receding. So distant now. Adulthood coming at her like a rocket.

'She won't let me approach. Please just come,' Sondra says.

Nevis thinks. Can I do this? Do I have a choice? She takes a deep breath. You always have a choice, Nevis. The right thing or the easy thing. Step up. Stop asking questions. Control yourself. Take a breath and quiet your heart. This is The Moment.

'Tell Satnam I will be there in fifteen minutes.' Her voice sounds weirdly distant, Nevis thinks, as if it belongs to someone else. She grabs her phone to summon an Uber and throws on clothes. A different person from moments ago. A crisis will do that. In seconds she's rushing down the stairs and into the street, one eye on her screen to follow the progress of the taxi, willing the driver to go faster. Farok in the black Prius, *come on*. Three minutes, two, one. The longest one hundred and eighty seconds in history. There's a moment, maybe a second or two, when she loses heart and thinks, how can I do this? But how can she not? Satnam is her best friend, her only friend. Nevis owes her this.

The Prius has barely come to a stop at the side of the pavement before Nevis is throwing open the door and hurling her body inside. Farok whips his head round, meets the expression on her face with a look of alarm.

'Nevis, Clifton Bridge?'

'Yes. It's not what you think. Or it is what you think, but it's not me, it's my friend.'

8

Farok hesitates for a second as if trying to decide whether this ride is way above his pay grade. He turns back to the dashboard and glances at her in the rear-view mirror and – miracle – a look of resolution is on his face. He's decided this one is worth doing.

'OK,' he says. 'We'll go very fast.'

As they speed up the hill towards Clifton she calls Satnam's number again, but the device goes to voicemail. What if it's too late? Oh God, please no. This is like solving an equation, Nevis tells herself, perhaps the most complicated, challenging equation you have ever been asked to solve. There will be a point where you can take one of several different pathways. Only one of these pathways will lead to the correct solution. You have to think it through. You have to get it right.

But how? She does not have all the parameters. This isn't the Satnam that she knows. This is not the friend who sits on her bed and watches crap telly or the friend who called out the wanker who thought it was funny to spray-paint 'Mentalist' on Nevis's daypack. This isn't the friend who dreams of becoming a medical researcher, the girl who is determined to marry for love whatever her parents might think. It's not the girl who jogs even when it's raining and is always happy to share her chips. But perhaps the Satnam on the bridge is the same Satnam who says she's going to the library but never seems to be there, the friend who has lost weight recently but says she hasn't, the one who cries in her bedroom and once – recently – threatened to leave Avon University. Perhaps this Satnam has secrets.

People are complicated. Satnam is complicated. If only people were as simple as mathematics.

'I don't know what to do,' Nevis says, to no one in particular.

The person she would normally ask in a situation like this is Satnam. Because Satnam has everyday, ordinary, practical smarts. Nevis has maths smarts as well as knowing a great deal about river birds. But Nevis has no people smarts. I am useless, she thinks.

Farok doesn't answer. He doesn't know either. Of course he doesn't. He has no idea. In any case, he's doing what he can, which is driving really very fast across the northern edges of the city towards Clifton. Farok is looking at Nevis in the rear-view mirror. He also seems terribly concerned.

I can't speak, Nevis thinks, the words have gone. There is just wire wool in my throat where sentences should be. Who can I text to help me?

She pulls out her phone. There are so few numbers in her contacts. There is Honor of course but they haven't really spoken in months, not since Nevis found the letter.

Chapter 2

Honor

Honor is asleep when the call comes from Nevis. At first she doesn't realise what has woken her and thinks it must have been Zoe, who is sitting at the bottom of her bed, doing what she has always done since she died, staring into the middle distance. Is it morning or is Zoe playing one of her tricks? Perched on her elbows now, Honor scouts the darkened room. The slice of window left visible after she shrank the curtain in the wash is still night-black. She listens out for birds but hears only the usual distant hiss of London traffic making its way along the A12 at Bow and the murmur of the boat on the water. Her brain, which feels as thick as toothpaste, is demanding more sleep. It's tempting to ignore Zoe. Over the nearly two decades since Zoe's death it has become Honor's principal survival technique to pretend there's no trouble in life so pressing you can't turn your back on it and hope it will go away. Then again, Honor also knows that Zoe will not go away until she's said what she's come to say, which is tricky, given that she never speaks.

'What's up?'

No reply.

Her phone buzzes and throws out its tinny blue light. So this is why she woke after all. There are only two people who ever text after work hours: her daughter Nevis and her neighbour Bill and it's too late to be Bill.

Honor reaches over to the bedside table where the phone is sitting on its charger and reads Need speak now. The breath catches in her throat. Her pulse thrums. Nevis was always scrappy about keeping in touch. She's never been one for the long, intimate conversations that Honor knows other mothers have with their daughters. In the last few months they've barely communicated at all. Something Honor did or said. Nevis won't say what. It's gone midnight. There's a hammering at the front of her brain. Her chest pops and splutters. All the old, long-buried anxiety comes rushing back as though the dam that had kept it back all these years has just burst its banks. She can feel it rising in her legs. She presses callback, the pad of her finger sliding on the screen, leaving a tiny slick of sweat. Holds her breath while the call connects and when Nevis doesn't pick up, feels a terrible sinking. She cuts the line and bashes out a text.

I'm here. Call me.

She waits a few seconds and when there's no response, tries again. The cold damp inside the narrowboat hits her. The *Kingfisher* is always chilly on the canal, even in summer, but March cold is particularly penetrating. On another night she might throw on her poncho but there are more pressing things. A moment or two later she tries Nevis for a third time and gets no response. She takes a breath, checks the sender and re-reads the text in case she has got it wrong.

Need speak now.

Honor thinks about calling the police but what will she say? A nervous tic starts up behind her eyes, like the ignition on the gas burner. Again she calls and again, nothing.

She's up now and in the saloon, plucking her puffa jacket from the hook beside the steps to the deck. There's a sudden tiny shock of fur as Caterine the Great, disturbed from her usual routine, weaves herself around Honor's legs. Any other time the cat would be a comfort but tonight she steps round the animal and clambers up the steps onto a deck already slippery with rime. Frosty cobwebs sit on the glass windows, reminding Honor, unexpectedly, of a day, a few years ago, passing a happy hour or two on a school science project with Nevis to make ice from supercooled water, the seed a grain of rice thrown into the water bottle, the instant transition of water to ice, the cracking as it shattered. There is a bright moon and over the marshes a pink London sky. From somewhere far away comes the tinkly laughter of people partying on the water. A distant siren blares.

She runs up Sugar House Lane towards the van. Beside the old warehouses, newly converted into 'luxury apartments', a fox crosses her path, its breath pluming the night air. The driver's side door of the orange 1999 Ford Connect – which Nevis christened Gerry – gives with a 'thunk' and a musky blast. A pool of stagnant water sits in the passenger side footwell, the result of some leakage whose source she has never been able to locate. Moss grows on the interior seals. She hopes the cold won't prevent the engine starting. The key hasn't been turned in weeks. Time was she needed a vehicle to haul boat supplies – timber, marine varnish, engine and pump parts – from the chandlers in Essex, but these days everything's available online for delivery and most of her work is now fixing and repairing other boats on the canal. Gerry remains hers out of sentiment and to haul Nevis's things to and from university at the beginning and end of each academic year, though now Nevis is no longer living on campus that's probably not so necessary either. Day trips to visit her daughter are easier by train. An hour and forty-five minutes and not too expensive if you book early enough, though this year she hasn't made any of those. Hasn't been invited. Nothing has been the same since the week before Nevis started back at Avon University in September. Nevis did not come home at Christmas. They have barely spoken in months.

Need speak now.

The key turns and the van, which she bought second-hand only months after Nevis's birth, chugs into life. *You beauty!* Honor pats the dashboard as a thank you, puts the gearstick into first and pulls out of the parking space into the street.

Chapter 3

Nevis

Nevis is feeling queasy, though she knows it's only nerves. They are in Clifton now, the tyres of the Prius tocking wildly across granite setts. True to his word, Farok is driving like a man whose wife is about to give birth in the back. Or a man trying to prevent a death. She checks the time remaining on Google Maps and notices the missed calls and messages from Honor. She will have to call or text later. For now, it is more important to prepare herself for whatever she is about to face. Why has Satnam asked for her? Has she kept something from her? What can be so bad that she has never mentioned it to Nevis? Weren't they supposed to be best friends? What can she be wanting to say that Nevis doesn't already know? Why did Nevis never think to press her about the weight loss? Why didn't she probe when Satnam talked about leaving uni? Why did she allow herself to be soothed by Satnam when she said her tears were PMT? She sees now that these things might have been cries for help. Why didn't she see it then?

I'm stupid, she thinks. I'm a bad friend.

At last the Clifton Suspension Bridge looms up ahead, dimly lit by a thin moon. The lights are customarily switched off at midnight and it is now gone half past. The journey has taken one minute fifteen seconds less than the prediction on Google Maps, but it's been the longest journey of Nevis's life.

And there is still further to go.

Directly ahead on either side of the slipway onto the bridge stand the two toll houses, each illuminated by a night light, and beyond them the looming mass of the first tower dimly lit by the moon. No one is visible. Where are the toll house attendants? She'd read somewhere that after midnight, when the lights on the bridge switch off, body heat cameras are able to detect anyone climbing the suicide barrier. Perhaps the attendants have picked up Satnam's image and are on the bridge with her now. Perhaps they have called the police? A shocking thought bubbles to the surface. What if she is too late?

The thought stops her in her tracks. Wouldn't she be able to tell if something terrible had already happened? Wouldn't there be a sign? They say you can sense the presence of the dead if you put your mind and your body to it. Nevis has experienced this herself: sometimes, in the quiet of the night, she has sensed her birth mother, Zoe, as if she were waving to her from behind a closed door.

Stop thinking, Nevis, you are wasting time! Just move. Shouting a thanks to Farok, she feels her limbs breaking into a run, the soles of her feet thudding onto the pavement, propelling her past the toll buildings towards the tower and, reaching it, into the cool darkness beneath and then out again onto the span of the bridge. There, just beyond the first tower with her back to Nevis, she sees a figure standing in the moonlight. Too tall to be Satnam. The woman is unaware of her presence and there is no one else to be seen. Could this be Sondra? Does

Sondra even exist? Her belly pulses, stomach churns. What if this whole thing is some kind of sick joke, or a scam? She'd been scammed before, more than once. Satnam says it's because she's not very worldly for which Nevis reads, not very good at reading people. To Nevis human hearts and minds are like jewels sitting in a locked box for which she has no key. She knows they're there. If she picks up the box and shakes it, she can hear shuffling and the sound of soft cries and laughter whose origins she will never understand.

She shouts: 'Hello?'

The figure on the bridge wheels about and shouts back.

'Are you Nevis?'

'Yes.'

The woman beckons her with frantic hands. Nevis takes a step forward then two and in a few moments she has caught up to her.

'Look,' Sondra says, pointing a few metres ahead, to where Satnam stands, spectral in the moonlight, on the edge of the bridge where the fence meets the suspension rail, facing the abyss and unprotected by the fence. There's a gap in the barrier here. At any moment Satnam could squeeze through it and step out into the air.

Never in her life has Nevis seen anyone more lonely.

'Just talk to her,' Sondra whispers, but how? She thinks, I'm no good at talking, there's a wire loose. Some connection between mouth and mind is broken in me. The fear is choking. The terror of getting it wrong, of saying the one thing that sends Satnam over the edge. She can feel the ribs rattling in her chest.

'Speak! Tell her you love her,' says Sondra. And so she does, faltering at first and then finding her voice all of a sudden, crying, 'Satnam, it's me!'

It's as if a great wave has rushed to the shore and caught her unawares. How did I not see this coming?

Satnam's face whips round. In the moonlight Nevis can just make out the faint gleam of her teeth. Is she speaking? What is she saying? The wind is taking away her words. Once more Nevis calls her friend's name, then gathering herself she advances a step.

'Stay back!'

'Whatever the trouble is, we can fix this, Satnam.' She thinks, you called me. You want me here. Please, let me come closer. Let me come to you.

Her friend is shaking her head now.

'Please, Sat, it's going to be OK. I promise.'

The girl is sobbing and speaking. As the wind dies most of what reaches Nevis is incoherent, a slurred stream of words not meaning much. The odd sentence makes its way to her. *You don't understand. I've had enough. I can't live with myself any more.*

Nevis takes a step forward. Her heart is a drum roll, pulse drilling her brain. She thinks, why did you ask for me? Was it to ease your soul or to be a witness to your death? She stops, dizzy with fear, clutches her head and in that instant something soft arcs across her field of vision. A shout. 'Oh God, no!'

She turns to see an owl banking over the gorge.

An owl means wisdom.

An owl means endurance.

An owl means new beginnings.

The owl is a sign.

'Satnam!' No answer. Nevis is close enough now to see her friend's face, dazed and expressionless, the head unsupported and wobbly, shaking on legs that don't seem to belong to her, hair pasted by the rain against her cheeks, speaking without making sense. She feels herself surge forwards calling, saying 'No!' and 'Please!' and finally, 'I love you!'

Satnam lifts her right foot. Nevis can no longer look, feels the breeze against her cheek as she turns away. The world goes to black and one by one the tracings of the retinal veins appear like red comets. The wind whips up again and sings through the wires of the barrier. Nevis braces herself. Behind her Sondra cries out.

Chapter 4

Honor

Honor is heading west out of London. At this time of night the traffic is light and flowing freely over the Westway and on through the outer suburbs towards the M4 and she's thinking about how quickly the years have flown by since she first decided to quit the Welsh Marches and begin life afresh with Nevis on the canal in the eastern fringes of the capital. Was that the best decision? It seemed important, no, vital, then to leave everything behind, to be able to say goodbye to the painful memories and the dreams of revenge. Zoe's death still felt so raw then. She would never break free, she knew, not while the man who was responsible for Zoe's death was out in the world. Every patch of woodland reminded her of their foraging days, every passing caravan spoke of their life together, every bridge brought back agonising memories of her best friend's death. Zoe haunted her every waking hour and came to her in her sleep. The only thing that thrived inside her during those first months was hatred. Here she was, at nineteen, with her best friend dead and Zoe's baby to raise and no idea whether she had the strength to survive any of it. She'd lived like a zombie, warming Nevis's bottles and changing her nappies on autopilot.

Becoming the best mother she could be had taken second place to her all-consuming grief and the naked, desperate desire for revenge. And then she woke up one day and realised that love, a simple mother's love for her daughter, had crept up on her and grown so fierce and hot that it burned out all the bad.

Nevis, you saved my life. Why have I never told you that?

The van tocks across the concrete panels of the road.

Need speak now.

Has Honor ever known Nevis *need* to speak before? She doesn't think so. Nevis doesn't like talking. She can go whole days and barely say a word. Even as a young child speaking came hard to her and as she grew older she opened her mouth less and less. Honor got the impression that she had secrets and liked to keep them. A legacy of her birth mother. By the time Nevis reached adolescence she barely spoke unless there was some information to impart. With Nevis it was more than the casual teenaged sullenness for by then she had discovered her own true language. Mathematics. For Nevis the turns of algebra and rhythmic shapes of geometry were more eloquent than spoken language ever could be. And so for her to need to speak now, in the middle of the night, to Honor who she hasn't properly spoken to in months, something very important and very urgent must have happened. But what?

Pulling the van into a layby just before the junction onto the M4 at Chiswick, Honor speed dials Nevis's number, gets her voicemail, leaves a message just to say she is on her way and about to get on the motorway. She won't be able to call for a while – nothing as sophisticated as a handsfree set – but Nevis should call or text her if she needs to and Honor will pull onto the hard shoulder and call her back.

Something has happened. Obviously. The flat has been burgled or Nevis has been mugged or, God forbid, worse. She is unwell. Or pregnant. There has been an accident. She has had a fight with Satnam. Female friendships can be scarily intense at that age. Honor knows that as well as anyone. And Nevis is sensitive and prone to misunderstandings. Growing up, all Nevis wanted was to eat chips and absorb herself in maths or birds. Most kids didn't want to do maths or look at birds or eat chips all day and Nevis didn't really want to do much else. The kids would go off topic and Nevis would become confused or withdrawn. Kids who were weak in maths would befriend her then get her to do their homework. At school some girl would take Nevis under her wing for a while then drop her, saying she was weird. She would go over to a new friend's house for tea and would not be invited back. The quick allegiances and casual betrayals of teenage girls left Nevis bewildered and out of her depth. She grew more wary and lost her confidence until she arrived at Avon University to study mathematics and biosciences and met Satnam.

The van is screaming along in the slow lane of the motorway now as if it's being tortured. A presenter on the radio, which is set to the BBC World Service, begins a lecture on Greek mythology. It has begun to rain and she is somewhere near Slough, and these facts would be depressing if Honor had the mental space to think about them. Nevis used to tell her that she drove as if she were set on murdering the engine. They would laugh about it. Like you could murder a fly, Mumtoo, Nevis would say.

Flies are safe from Honor. People are another matter. One person.

The van bumps over the rumble strip and onto the hard shoulder then growls ominously as Honor makes a correction with the steering wheel and the tyres come to land squarely in the slow lane once more. Shit, she thinks, I lost concentration. I must stop thinking about murder before it kills me. A coffee would help. Honor remembers seeing a sign for a service station in eight miles. Better lose ten minutes on the road and get there safely. At Leigh Delamere services she buys a flat white ('We don't do just normal white') and tries Nevis again, this time leaving an estimated arrival time while the server – didn't they call them baristas these days? – an exhausted-looking young woman in a T-shirt with an unconvincingly perky slogan leans her forehead on the coffee machine and takes a micro-nap while waiting for the dark liquid to trickle into the corrugated paper cup.

It is 1.45 a.m.

Honor takes the coffee back to the van and gulps it down in the service station car park. The lecture on Greek mythology is over and the radio is now playing soothing light jazz. It is gone two o'clock when she turns off onto the M32 approach into Bristol and the effect of the coffee seems already to have worn off. She winds a crack in the passenger window to catch the breeze but the air smells cloyingly of diesel fumes. Or maybe this is just a reflection of Honor's mood. Of her state of mind in general. She hums along with the jazz but the voice in her head sings an altogether different tune. *What has happened to Nevis and why hasn't she called me?*

Chapter 5

Nevis

The hour between 12.30 and 1.30 a.m. passes in a blur. One moment Nevis is standing on the bridge, the next she is slumped beside a retaining wall, with a stranger's hand in hers. Her whole body is shaking. A police car arrives, its siren silenced, then another. The police close the bridge and station uniformed officers at either end to divert traffic, though it's so late that there isn't much. A few moments later someone lays a space blanket over her shoulders. She is aware of a policewoman imploring her to speak but the words have flown away. She watches Sondra talking to the policewoman but she cannot hear what is being said. Something has gone wrong with her brain. At that moment an ambulance arrives and two paramedics hurry along the bridge. One of them is a young woman not far off Nevis's age. There are blinking lights and flashing torches everywhere and a rank smell which could be fox, but is actually, Nevis realises only after the fact, the stench of human fear. The scene is so upsetting and so chaotic that one minute Nevis feels as if her head is exploding and then, moments later, as if it's happening to someone else far away. The female paramedic rests a hand on her arm. Nevis hears herself say, 'I want to travel with Satnam' and with a hand around her shoulders the paramedic leads her to the ambulance.

As they make their way through the city in a tunnel of blue light, the paramedic keeps up a flow of chatter. All Nevis's focus is on why this has happened but she still can't make head or tail of it. Satnam is her best friend. *Shouldn't* she know? Is this because her head's not quite right, or different anyway? Wouldn't a real friend have guessed? Shouldn't she at least have had a clue?

At the hospital she doesn't want to leave Satnam but they don't give her a choice. A nurse leads her away to a waiting area in A&E and fires questions. How is she feeling? Does she think she might faint? Would she like a cup of tea? A sandwich? No, no and no. Does she have any idea why this happened? Another no. Did anything happen leading up to this? No, yes, Nevis isn't sure. The questions fade into the background and a voice that Nevis knows is hers even though it seems to be coming from outside is asking over and over, 'Is she going to be all right?'

'We don't know, but we're doing our best,' the nurse says simply. 'It's a good job she collapsed before she could jump. There would have been no coming back from that.' The nurse moves to lay a hand on her arm. Nevis shifts just out of reach and the nurse makes no attempt to touch her again, instead in a soft kind voice, asking, 'Would you like me to call someone?'

I should call Honor myself, Nevis thinks, instead of allowing a nurse to do it. But she feels helpless and almost paralysed, completely lost for words. Tapping the passcode into her phone, she blinks at the blizzard of notifications and missed calls from Honor, then passes the device to the woman beside her. She has become like an infant, floppy and unable to make a coherent decision. The nurse initiates the call and speaks for a few moments. Nevis doesn't listen. Finally, the nurse cuts the call, and, patting her hand, in a cosy, woolly voice, says, 'Your mum says she'll be here soon.'

She wants to say Honor isn't her real mum but she doesn't know how to explain. And now would probably not be the time. The nurse is still asking questions, this time about whether Nevis has a contact number for Satnam's parents. Does she know the names of Satnam's parents? Yes, yes, at least she does know that. Bikram and Narinder.

'Do you have a number for them?'

She checks in her pocket, pulls out Satnam's phone. Sondra said she should take it in the ambulance. 'Oh, but I don't know the passcode.'

'Don't worry, we can find the number.'

'Wait.' She remembers now. 'I do have it.' Dropping Satnam's phone in her backpack she reaches for her own. Satnam's mother Narinder had given her their home number last year when they were on better terms, before Narinder found out about Luke. She reads the screen, memorising the integers as she goes.

The nurse promises to place the call and turns away. For the first time since getting into the taxi what seems like a lifetime ago, Nevis finds herself alone, her mind emptied of everything but Satnam.

*

Not long afterwards Sondra arrives in the company of a police-woman, who tells Nevis they've taken Satnam up to the ICU.

'A quick word?' the officer says to her, in a tone that suggests it's not really a question. Sondra shoots Nevis an encouraging look.

It's difficult, especially now, for Nevis to do much talking. Part of her is still standing in the thick, reflected light from the bridge's lamps, watching the figure pressed against the barrier, hands clinging to the wires. Another part is with Satnam in the ICU. There's not much left for speaking. Besides, hasn't she already said everything? What else is there to talk about?

'Can we go somewhere else?' No point in being in A&E and the waiting room feels oppressive.

'If you like,' the policewoman says. 'How's about a cup of tea at the caff?'

The three of them walk through the hospital. More corridors, more noise and confusing signs. The cafeteria sits near the entrance. A pod-shaped room, lit with white, fluorescent tubes. A few exhausted-looking people sitting at tables. Food service has not yet opened for the day but a bank of vending machines hums on a far wall. Sondra reaches out and squeezes Nevis's hand, trying to be comforting, but Nevis doesn't like to be touched. Not by strangers. Not by anyone except Satnam.

They take a table and Sondra volunteers to go and get coffee from the vending machine. The policewoman wastes no time in small talk. She wants to know how Satnam seemed last night.

'I already told the other officer.'

'Just once more if you wouldn't mind.' There's a beep from the policewoman's phone. She holds up a finger and is soon engrossed in conversation.

'Is everything all right?' Sondra says, returning with the coffee.

Well no, *obviously*.

The two women sit in awkward silence for a few moments, before Sondra pipes up with, 'Nevis is a nice name. As in the island?'

'As in the mountain.'

As the policewoman finishes up her call, Sondra excuses herself to wait out the conversation at another table.

'Sorry about that. So, you were saying, does Satnam usually drink and take drugs?'

'That's not what I was saying.'

The policewoman stiffens, checks her pad, and pastes on a professional smile. 'We're not looking to get either you or your friend into any trouble. We're just trying to get to the truth.'

The truth. Well, yes, obviously, not least because Nevis is very bad at lying.

'She drinks wine sometimes.' Nevis wonders if she should mention the bottle of vodka in Satnam's bedroom and decides not to.

'I see.' The policewoman writes something down. 'What about drugs? Something for those essay deadlines? A little smoke to relax?'

'Nothing that I know of.'

'The initial toxicology report apparently suggests Ritalin. Is that something you've ever seen Satnam using before?'

'No.'

'And can you tell me exactly what happened last night?'

'No.'

The policewoman cocks her head and grimaces. 'I think you told my colleague that you ate chips together then Satnam went to bed and you went back to the campus library. Is that correct?'

'Yes.'

'Sooo... you *can* tell me.' There's a familiar look on the woman's face that Nevis has learned to read as frustration.

'I only know what happened to *me*.'

'Yes, I see. Well, OK then, so did Satnam seem her usual self... to *you*? Did she say anything out of the ordinary, anything that seemed odd, again, to *you*?'

Nevis takes a deep breath. Her mind turns and quickens then fizzes like a firework. The space behind her eyes is heating up and she wonders, suddenly, if she is going to cry.

From somewhere far away she hears the policewoman repeating the question. A hand lands on her arm.

'You need a moment to think about it?' asks the policewoman.

'No.'

'So, nothing strange.' The policewoman is staring at Nevis now, trying to work her out.

'We've checked out her social accounts, obviously, but there doesn't seem to be anything there to...'

A familiar face appears. The nurse who led Nevis from the ambulance.

'A quick word? Nothing bad, just to let you know that the doctors have managed to stabilise Satnam. She's still very poorly and the next twenty-four hours will be crucial but for now she's stable.'

'Can I see her?'

The nurse, whose name is Becky, Nevis remembers now, grimaces. Nevis is not sure what this is supposed to mean. 'Not right now, sweetheart. She's in good hands. Her parents are on their way.'

'They don't like me.'

'Why wouldn't they like you?'

'The usual reasons.'

Becky flashes the policewoman an odd look.

The policewoman goes on talking once Becky has left but Nevis has switched off. She checks the time on her phone. She's thinking about Honor now, hoping she gets here soon. Normally she would have timed the drive from the exact minute Honor set off. She wishes now she had because not knowing is anxious-making. An oversight. Her legs begin to jig up and down. She is longing for Honor to arrive but also afraid of what she might feel when she does. The hurt from the summer has not gone away.

The policewoman's hand lands on her arm once more and a voice says she needs Nevis to focus on the question. The police need to find Satnam's phone. 'Sondra told us she gave it to you in the ambulance. Is that right?'

'Yes.'

'So, do you have it on you?'

'No,' Nevis says. This is not a lie. It is merely not the whole truth. The phone is still in Nevis's backpack.

'Maybe you left it in the ambulance?'

'It's possible.'

Shortly afterwards the policewoman stops talking and leaves Nevis in the company of Sondra once more. Hours pass or seem to. She watches traffic accidents being stretchered in, ashen-faced elderly folk, worried-looking parents with their subdued or else screaming kids, all rotating in and out, in and out in the early morning churn. She takes out her phone and checks Satnam's social.

In the few short hours since she left for the library Nevis

Smith has changed, some small, bright part of her gone, perhaps forever. The alteration became clear to her in the conversation with the policewoman. The old Nevis Smith never once in her life told a lie. This new, sadder, Nevis is surprisingly good at telling only part of the truth.

Chapter 6

Cullen

Christopher Cullen is pulling on his still-damp jacket and trying not to allow Veronica's complaining to get to him. He knows how much his wife hates it when he drops everything for his mother. The calls usually come at night, often from the care home, sometimes from Amanda herself. When it's the home it's usually because Amanda has done something unconscionable to one of the other residents or is refusing to let anyone in her room. Amanda will then call to deny the accusations and counterattack with a list of grievances about the facilities or the food or the carers and to demand her son come over *immediately*. This time it's the care home. Amanda, or the Dalek as he calls her in private, on the grounds that she is capable of exterminating everything in her path, has called the police again, this time claiming to have been kidnapped.

'Do you really have to go?' Veronica says, watching him from the doorway to the living room. His wife has no idea of the hold Amanda has over him and Cullen wants to keep it that way. A few loose words and his mother could ruin him, ruin *this*, the beautiful house, the glamorous, prestigious wife, his future prospects. And if it came to it, if he crossed her, if he displeased her, she would. Cullen is in no doubt about that.

'It is what it is,' he says, blandly, relieved to have an excuse to get away and not be called upon to service his wife who, he suspects, might be ovulating.

'Don't tell me you've forgotten!' she says, affronted.

Whumph. There it is. The demand, the judgement and, oh God, his wife's more-in-sorrow-than-in-anger look, similar enough to Princess Diana's doe eyes to make him suspect Veronica of practising it from old clips of the princess on YouTube. 'Can't it wait till tomorrow?'

'No,' Veronica says, determinedly. 'My OPK checked positive yesterday. Sorry, darling, but the old ovavavooms are primed and ready. It's time to muster the troops.'

Most of the talk between them these days seems to be about ovulation prediction kits and luteinising hormone surges. Cullen's not even sure he wants a baby. Until recently he and Veronica were of one mind on this but when she hit thirty-five, the clock didn't just start ticking, it began to beat out a desperate kind of alarm which Cullen found at first bewildering and then just plain terrifying. Veronica became obsessed with the mechanisms of reproduction, forever taking her temperature and monitoring her cycles, taking no sexual interest in Cullen whatsoever until the indicators told her it was time, and then laying siege upon his seed. For a while Cullen pushed back, but soon discovered that only led to rows. Surrender seemed easier. That and looking elsewhere for the satisfaction of his needs. He told himself that this too would pass and until it did, he had a right to his extra-curricular fantasies, his own particular obsessions.

'A quickie will do,' Veronica says now.

Cullen briefly considers his options which boil down to servicing Veronica now or later. I'm having an off day or I've got a headache won't wash. Later only means putting off the inevitable and there's something about seeing his mother which stops the old troop carrier in its tracks. Dr Freud would have a field day with that! It had better be now.

'Kiss me, darling,' Veronica says, smiling and with a gleam in her eye.

All right, all right, he thinks. His eye lands on the handle of the cupboard under the stairs where he keeps his Browning game gun and a strange thought crosses his mind for a moment. Blinking it away, he turns his brain to conjuring images of long ago until, thank God, his groin automatically begins to rustle and stir.

Afterwards, he helps Veronica prop herself on the sofa with cushions and returns to his still-damp jacket in the hallway. At the door he notices that the cleaner has picked up the post – Veronica always leaves it where it falls, on the grounds that it's 'boy stuff', by which she means bills – and left it in the letter rack. He leafs through, stuffs a couple of items in his jacket pocket and heads out of the front door, past Veronica's brand-new top-end Mini to his own ten-year-old Volvo S60. He lets himself into the driver's seat, removes the mail from his jacket pocket and stuffs the envelopes in with all the others in the glove box. Eventually, he'll have to empty it, but for now, it's out of sight, out of mind.

On the way to Wychall's, Amanda's home from home for the past year or so, he stops briefly at the twenty-four-hour shop on the northern fringes of Clifton to look for her favourite petticoat tail shortbread and, finding only shortbread bars, picks up a pack and makes his way to the till. Outside it has started raining hard and on his dash to the car rivulets of ice-cold water make their way down the back of his neck, adding to his general resentment. Caught between two demanding and unreasonable women. He turns the keys in the ignition. Terrible, jarring music blares from the radio. Hadn't he left it on a classical station? He presses buttons until he reaches someone talking on the BBC World Service about Greek myths which gets him pondering which of the women in his life is best described in which myth. He decides that on a good day Veronica is Helen of Troy but on a bad day she can turn into an absolute harpy. Amanda is a Furies-slash-Sirens-slash-Medusa mash-up. He tries to picture her with snakes for hair and the thought makes him laugh out loud.

On the drive over he has to pull in for an ambulance, lights flashing, but no siren at this late hour. He taps on the dash-board, watching it go before gliding out into its slipstream. At Wychall's, he pulls into a parking spot, makes his way to the locked entrance and rings the night bell. One of the nightshift carers (Maura?) bustles over and opens the door.

'Oh, Professor Cullen! We were expecting you a little earlier,' Maura says, with a smile.

'Yes, of course, I'm so sorry. Admissions season at the university. Horrible workload,' Cullen says now.

'She refused a sleeping pill. She's still saying she's been kidnapped.' Maura smiles kindly. 'She's in her room. I'll bring you both a cup of tea.'

Cullen creeps along the peach corridor to room 24 where he finds Amanda sitting up in bed with a scarf tied around her

35

head. There has been an attempt at make-up, which gives her the air of a panto villain. He goes over and takes her hands. The skin is papery thin with plum-coloured patches.

'I am very unhappy, Christopher,' she says, as though stating something momentous, the discovery of a new planet, or the start of World War Three. 'This is not the sort of hotel I'm used to. I've complained but they've kidnapped me so they won't do anything.'

Cullen lets go of her hands and settles himself into the winged armchair opposite the bed.

'Who exactly has kidnapped you, Mother?'

'Never you mind. I'd like you to take me home.' Her voice falls to a whisper. 'Have you brought the money? Otherwise I've no idea how I'm going to pay them to let me go.'

'Funny you should say that, Mother. I have no idea either. You might just have to stay here,' he says, spitefully.

He watches Amanda's nostrils flare and a tiny tear appear in the corner of one eye as she looks away, and hates himself a little.

'There, there, it's all right. I'm only joking. I've got it, don't you worry.'

When she turns back to him, all trace of upset is gone. How much of this is early dementia, he thinks, and how much is Amanda yanking his chain?

'Oh but I *do* worry. I've always worried about you, darling.' A faraway look appears on her face. He's no longer sure whether she's talking to him or to his long-dead father. Perhaps there will come a time when she forgets about him altogether. Liberation day. 'Where will you sleep? Not in here. You snore dreadfully. Do they have another room?'

To his relief, Maura bustles in carrying a tray on which are balanced two canteen-style cups and saucers.

'Here, let me take it,' Cullen says, thankful for the interruption but eager, too, for the visit to be as truncated as possible. He puts down the tray, picks up both cups and hands one to his mother. He watches Amanda rising up against her pillows as if she's about to storm the battlements. His battlements, inevitably.

'My son was very clever,' she says to Maura, as if he were no longer in the room.

Here we go again.

'I'm still very clever!' he says. Maura shoots him a sympathetic little smile. His mother closes her eyes and doesn't respond. Why does he let her get to him? His mind has slipped back a quarter of a century to a drizzly afternoon in his uncle's static in Llandudno, his mother fussing over the salty wind ruining her hair, his ten-year-old self doing his best to demonstrate the Golden Spiral using a shell from a rockpool, and his uncle, patting him on the head like a beach donkey, saying, 'Another time, lad.' And later, his mother lying beside him in the tiny bed, stroking his head and saying, 'My darling little boy, if you show your uncle up again, he won't invite us.'

'I brought you some shortbread,' he says, pulling out the packet from his jacket pocket. He puts down his tea and comes over carrying the packet before him as if it were some treasure and he a courtier currying favour at a medieval court. He is willing her to open her eyes and respond to him now but they are if anything more tightly shut and she's humming a tune under her breath.

'I am wondering what we can do to make you feel a bit more

settled,' he says, 'only I do have a rather early start tomorrow.' He checks his watch – nearly one o'clock.

'Petticoat tails?' she asks.

'No, they only had the bars.' He watches Maura retreat and feels a stab of envy.

'Oh,' Amanda says, turning her face away, 'I won't bother then.'

'It's the same stuff, Mother, just a different shape.'

Amanda blinks. She takes a sip of tea. He watches her throat rise and struggle a little in the swallowing.

'Come and give me a kiss,' she says.

He goes over and, kneeling beside her, presses his lips into her cheek. In turn she strokes his hair, a dreamy smile on her face.

'My darling little boy. If only you hadn't grown up.'

He closes his eyes and tries to think himself back to his early childhood without Llandudno or his uncle getting in the way. He wants the moment to last forever and knows that is impossible. How can it be that he still longs for his mother to be someone else, someone he once thought he knew.

'I'm still your little boy,' he says.

Instantly, he feels her stiffen, her hands cease their movements. 'When did you last wash your hair?'

And there it is. He is Adam being expelled from the garden all over again. He pulls away and rises, brushing down his trousers.

'I'll be off then.'

Maura meets him in the hallway. 'Before you go, management asked me to tell you that we're still waiting for your payment for February.'

The phone in his pocket buzzes. He lets the call go to voicemail.

'Of course. Just an oversight.' This is not the truth. For a while he paid Wychall's fees from what remained from the sale of Amanda's home once her debts were cleared but that money has long since gone. He's talked about moving her to a more affordable facility – more convenient was the way he'd put it to her – but she refused to countenance the move. There's nothing he can do to force her. She has him exactly where she wants him. What she holds over him, what she knows.

He sits in the car in Wychall's car park gripping the steering wheel and shouting, 'Fucking fuckety fuck' at the windscreen, before heading back to the house he can't afford, most likely soon to be occupied by a child he has no idea how he's going to support.

Chapter 7

Honor

Honor spots Nevis's pixie crop and Breton tee from the hospital entrance. There's the old, familiar echo of Zoe, the friend she'd loved like a sister, in the way Nevis holds herself, as if she were not quite there. A woman she does not recognise sits beside her daughter. They don't appear to be talking. She approaches without being spotted and lays a hand very gently on her daughter's head. Nevis starts and twists to look at her mother. Her face is shockingly white, the green eyes drained of all colour, the expression fixed, like that of someone startled in death. It has been months since they have seen one another, months in which Honor has agonised over what she has done to hurt her daughter. Now is not the time to ask about such things.

'What happened?' A text had arrived from a number Honor didn't recognise saying that Nevis was not hurt but to meet her at the Bristol Royal Infirmary. The number, she guesses, belongs to the woman sitting beside them whose name, she discovers, is Sondra.

'I'm so glad you're here,' Sondra says. She glances at Nevis, inviting her to speak, and when she does not, she goes on. 'Nevis's friend Satnam collapsed on the Clifton Suspension

Bridge tonight. We thought she was going to...' she stops and flashes a look at Nevis, '...well, you know, but she collapsed before she could do anything drastic.'

The news is bewildering and for a moment Honor doesn't know what to think. The Satnam Honor knows, the one who came to stay on the boat last summer with Luke, is full of life, kind, loyal, joyful and, above all, stable. The last person you would expect to do something so self-destructive, so *dramatic*.

'How is she?'

'Upstairs in intensive care. The nurse said she's in a coma. That's all they've told us.' Sondra fills Honor in on the events of the evening but still it seems so abstract and unlikely. 'Had she been drinking or taking drugs?'

'Both, according to the police, but I'm not sure what,' Sondra says, craning to look at Nevis who is sitting beside her with her head hung low. 'Perhaps you know more?'

Nevis's jaw begins to wobble and the sinews in her neck flex and pulse. A tic starts in her right eye. She is biting her lip so hard that a bead of blood appears. Honor takes her daughter's hands. The palms sit limply in her own for a short while before Nevis withdraws and angles herself away, arms clutched tight around her chest.

'Now you're here I should go,' Sondra says, rising. 'I have to get my kids off to school. It was me who texted you so you've got my number. I don't think there's anything... but feel free to call me any time.'

Honor thanks her and waits for her to leave before turning to Nevis. 'How are you, darling?'

Nevis meets her eye then looks away. 'Did you drive Gerry here?'

Sometimes, when Nevis was small, Honor would empty out the van and stick a mattress in the back of Gerry and they would go out to the countryside and wild camp on the edge of some wood, as far away from people as they could get. Whenever they had a falling-out or Honor got too sad about Zoe, and Nevis was old enough to leave the boat on her own, she would take the keys and clamber inside Gerry, perching among the machine parts and offcuts of marine timber. Nevis had always found things more comforting than people.

'You want to sit in the van?'

'Maybe. In a bit.' She rubs her eyes.

'You must be exhausted.' Stretching out her hand so their fingertips just meet. 'Shall I drive you back to the flat?'

Nevis turns her head and blinks. 'Why are you wearing pyjamas?'

Honor pulls her coat tightly around herself. 'I left in a hurry. It's OK, Nevis, it's not a problem, I promise. Half the people here are in pyjamas.'

How she wishes she could just hold Nevis in her arms right now, but Nevis will not like it, would not have liked it even when they were on better terms.

'I'm struggling to understand why Satnam would have done this.' Nevis's response to Sondra's question leads Honor to believe that her daughter knows more than she's saying. 'Is Luke still in the picture?' Satnam's boyfriend came to the *Kingfisher* a couple of times last summer, when Satnam was staying with them. For the most part these were happy visits. They cooked spag bol and laughed and Luke and Honor shared a spliff on the towpath. The shadow of Satnam's parents' disapproval hung over the young couple but it was evident that they were in love. But Nevis insists that Luke ended the relationship in November. It can all be pretty intense and erratic at that age, she supposes. Not that Honor knows this first-hand because romantic love isn't something she has allowed herself to feel. Loss will do that to a person. So will dealing with all the busyness of bringing up a kid alone.

'And how did Satnam feel about that?'

'Fine. She said it was for the best.'

To Honor, the chances that a young woman who has already faced the disapproval of her parents in order to carry on a relationship with a man she loves feels 'fine' about being left seem pretty slim. But Nevis can be quite literal in that way. If Satnam said it was 'for the best' then Nevis would have believed her.

'Maybe they'll let us see her now. Shall we go and ask?'

Nevis shakes her head.

'Do you mind if I go and report back?'

Reaching the second-floor corridor Honor is momentarily blindsided by the smell of illness. Checking the signs on the wall she turns left through a set of double doors and down a corridor towards the intensive care unit. There, a tired-looking woman with a scraped-back ponytail and a smile left over from the start of her shift explains that Satnam's parents have not long since gone and they are restricting visitors to close family 'for the time being'. Honor has no desire to run into Narinder or Bikram Mann and the feeling is almost certainly mutual. When Satnam came to stay on the *Kingfisher* last summer, Honor had found herself caught in the midst of a family dispute, with Satnam refusing to speak to her parents and Bikram accusing Honor of turning their daughter against them. Not long afterwards Nevis received a call from Narinder asking her to reconsider sharing a flat with their daughter on the grounds that Nevis was 'unsuitable' and Narinder found her 'strange'.

The last part stung, not least because Honor had heard it so often and because she knew that this was part of the reason Satnam liked her. So much so, in fact, that one evening last summer on the boat, Satnam had found Honor alone and told her that Nevis 'might well be the best person who ever lived and it is the great wish of my heart that we'll be friends for ever'.

The great wish of my heart.

How could you not love a girl who spoke like that? And how could you not worry that such a girl found so little in her life to love that she was prepared to end it?

When Honor persists the tired-looking woman blinks then sighs and, calling her colleague Becky over, explains the situation.

'Very very quickly, then,' Becky says. 'Follow me.' They move through the waiting area to a corridor and from there to a smaller wardroom labelled 'Pine'. At the door Becky turns and says, 'Satnam is unconscious. We've intubated her so the respirator is doing her breathing for her. Five minutes max, please.'

At the cubicle curtain, Honor hesitates, her mind tunnelling through time, to a memory, a single point inhabited now only by darkness and by Zoe. Steeling herself she raises her chin and slides between the curtains. The young woman looks dreadful, her skin grey-brown, her face and arms such a tangle of pipes and tubes that it gives her the appearance of something not quite human. Someone, one of Satnam's parents, Honor supposes, has left sweet pastries on the table, a gesture whose tender optimism moves her so much that she finds herself having to bite back tears. It's not going to end like this, with sweets and sympathy. Whatever happens to Satnam now, the Mann family will never quite recover. Nevis will never quite recover. No one will ever be the same.

At that moment the curtain parts and Nurse Becky appears. She takes a step into the cubicle, acknowledges Honor with a hurried smile, pulls the curtain and goes over to the figure on the bed, where she checks the tubes and the stats on the machines.

'The breakfast trolley won't be round for a couple of hours but I can get you a cup of tea if you fancy?'

'Thanks but don't worry.' She watches Becky going about her business. 'Is she going to be all right?'

Nurse Becky presses her finger against her lips and gestures for Honor to step outside. Once they are beyond the cubicle curtains, she whispers, 'People in comas can often hear voices.'

'Of course, I'm sorry.'

'The situation is really unpredictable. She's stable for now, but the combination of alcohol and drugs is… If the organs begin shutting down it's really difficult to reverse. And she could go into cardiac arrest. Terrible really. Such a lovely young woman.'

The nurse bites her lip then reaches out and rests a hand on Honor's arm. 'You might keep an eye on your daughter for a week or two?' Nurse Becky glances at her watch. 'Now, I'm afraid I'm going to have to ask you to leave. We need to run some tests.'

Downstairs, the café counter has opened and breakfast is being served. Nevis is sitting at a table, eyeing her phone.

'How was she?'

'Peaceful.' Honor touches Nevis very lightly on the hand, 'I know things have been difficult between us. I've done something to upset you and I wish you'd tell me what.' Her eye is drawn to the double doors leading into the kitchen. A trolley appears and, following it, a woman in a hygiene cap and overalls.

'Not now,' Nevis says, withdrawing her hand and turning her attention to the kitchen porter as she stacks the trolley with used cutlery and crockery.

Honor wants to say, 'Turn back to me,' but her courage fails her. And besides, Nevis is right. Now is not the time.

'I want you to know that I'm sorry. And whatever it is, we can fix it.'

Honor watches the double doors swinging back, the force of momentum creating a tiny pendulum motion before they finally close. 'We should get something to eat.'

At the counter she orders Nevis poached eggs and one of those expensive coffees everyone seems to swoon over, and contents herself with tea and toast. She puts the tray on the table and puts the eggs and coffee in front of her daughter.

They eat in silence for a while, then Honor says, 'I'd like to remain in Bristol for a bit just till you get through this. I wouldn't have to stay with you. I could find somewhere to crash for a few days.' Where, though? she wonders. Bristol is an expensive city and Honor has no money. Still, she will have to find a way. Get in touch with the bargee community, pick up some work readying boats for the summer season. Whatever.

She watches Nevis's face for a reaction and gets none. Of all her daughter's quirks this habit she has of pulling down the blinds is the most puzzling. What are her thoughts? What

46

feelings are passing through that sweet head? Honor watches her turning her phone over and over in her hand. Eventually, Nevis frowns and says, 'You're not even dressed.'

'I'll pick up some clothes in a charity shop.' Honor gets all her clothes this way.

Nevis's right hand reaches across her body and pings at the elastic worry band hanging from her left wrist. 'I'm not going to kill myself if that's what you're thinking.'

Honor's chest tightens. For a moment she finds herself too shocked to speak. The thought has not occurred to her. Why would Nevis suppose that it had?

'Why on earth would I be thinking that?'

'Because you don't trust me. You've never just *trusted* me.'

And with that Nevis gets up, reaches around the chair for her peacoat and sweeps across the floor of the café. Honor watches her go, her heart telling her to follow, her head keeping her in her seat. She sits there for what seems like the longest time, fixed in place, immovable. Eventually Nevis reappears, embarrassed and with an odd, forced smile on her face.

Planting a small, lukewarm kiss on her mother's cheek, she says, 'Sorry about that. Bit of a stressful night. Thanks for coming and everything, but I'm OK, really. I've got a shift at the chippy later. And a ton of coursework. If things take a downturn with Satnam...'

'I hope they won't.'

'But if they do...'

'I'll be here – so long as you don't mind me staying in Bristol for a bit?'

Nevis considers this and gives a shrug. It's a deal then.

'Well, I'll be off,' Nevis says, pointing to the exit.

'Let me at least give you a lift.'

Honor notes her daughter's hesitation, as if Nevis has something else to say and can't find a way to say it. 'Darling, if there's something you're not telling me, please, you know I won't judge you whatever it is?'

There is a brief split second when Nevis seems about to speak, then thinking better of it, she rolls her eyes, puffs her cheeks, lets out a long, exasperated sigh and heads, once more, for the door.

Chapter 8

Cullen

The news that a student in his department has attempted suicide reaches Cullen at a Monday morning community liaison breakfast at the university, whispered into his ear by the head of student welfare, Lea Keane. Cullen takes a breath and closes his eyes briefly to collect himself and pastes on a thin smile for the benefit of the others gathered around the table before rising from his chair and apologising. Urgent business. He doesn't say what, obviously. There are outsiders present. He waves Keane through the door and they make the short walk to the Deanery without speaking.

Going round to the business side of his desk, he waves Keane to a visitor's chair but doesn't offer her a coffee. He's never liked Keane. Is it the moustache or the busybody air or the taste for garish clothes featuring big blooms which reminds Cullen uncomfortably of his mother? Probably a combination of all three. Plus, he doesn't believe in counsellors or therapists; considers them archaeologists of human misery, forever disturbing feelings that are best left buried.

'Were you notified by the parents?' Cullen asks, lowering himself into his ergonomic office chair. He finds knowing the exact sequence of events soothing. It's the mathematician in him. First this, then that, feeling the ground beneath him.

'Not exactly, though I have spoken to the parents this morning. I found out in the wee hours. My daughter Jackie was one of the attending paramedics and she phoned me when she got off shift. I did call you but you must already have gone to bed.'

Oh, he thinks, so that was the unanswered call. It had slipped his mind.

'So,' he says, leaning on his elbows and steepling his hands on the desk. The timing couldn't be worse with the university about to go into admissions. 'Who is this about?'

'One of your second years. Mathematics and biosciences. Satnam Mann?'

Cullen's brain stops turning over. A moment passes before a question floats out from under the white noise in his head. Can Keane really have said Satnam Mann? He notices his hands shaking and jams them under the desk before Keane spots them.

'Is she conscious?'

'The hospital won't speak with me directly, but the parents told me she's in a coma. They didn't seem to know whether that was medically induced or not. It was hard getting anything out of them at all, to be honest. Jackie told me a passer-by came across Satnam trying to climb the suicide barrier at the bridge, but she collapsed before she could, well, you know.'

'I see,' Cullen says, with some relief.

'The parents are saying it was an accidental overdose. In their version, Satnam took a couple of pills so she could stay up late to write an essay and had some sort of reaction to them. I got the impression that they couldn't bear to bring themselves to accept that their daughter might have tried to kill herself.'

'It *could* have happened like that, though, couldn't it?' Cullen says, hopefully. An accident could be made to go away. A confirmed suicide bid would have to be looked into. And that would bring all kinds of trouble.

'I suppose so, but there was a lot of alcohol and Ritalin in her blood so I'd say the chances are pretty slight. I googled Ritalin overdose. It can be fatal, not immediately, but after a few days or even weeks. The heart goes into overdrive and the organs eventually fail. Once that starts, it's only a matter of time.'

'I see,' Cullen says, wondering now if it might actually be easier if the Mann girl did die. It might solve a few of his problems. 'Does she have any record of mental ill health?'

'Obviously, I can't access her medical records but she's never engaged with student welfare. No time off. No red flags at all. When Jackie quizzed her flatmate in the ambulance, she said they'd spent the early part of the evening together and Satnam was her usual self. I looked through her file. It seems she was struggling academically in the first year, but she must have knuckled down because her grades this year have been excellent. I suppose she might have been feeling under a lot of pressure.'

'A couple of students did some remedial maths with me last summer. She was among them, but there was no sign that she wasn't coping,' says Cullen. 'In fact, as you say, the opposite. She's been doing extremely well. Have you informed the Vice Chancellor yet?'

'No, I thought you would probably want to do that.'

'Right,' Cullen says, relieved that Keane has remembered the correct chain of command. Cullen and the VC, Madeleine Ince, go back years and he'd much prefer to have this conversation with her himself.

'I could use a coffee. Can I get one for you?' Cullen says, relenting on his previous decision, but only because his head is banging from lack of sleep.

'I've already had too many this morning.'

As Cullen goes over to the coffee machine in the corner of his office, an uncomfortable thought comes into his mind. 'Is the flatmate one of ours too?'

'Yes. Nevis Smith. Same year and subject area as Satnam. You know her too presumably.'

As Keane carries on talking, Cullen stares at the coffee machine. The flatmate's name rings a bell. Ah yes. The quirky, quiet one? Always wears the same uniform of striped tee and jeans. Aware, suddenly, of the silence in the room, he says, 'Biosciences can be a very challenging degree.'

'We can't have undergrads trying to take their own lives.' The shocked tone in Keane's voice suggests rebuke.

'No, no, obviously not,' Cullen says, holding the cup precisely under the coffee spout. His hand is shaking, just a little. All it would take is a quick snifter to make it stop. He reaches around the back of the coffee machine where he keeps a sneaky quarter bottle of Famous Grouse, then decides against it. The risk of Keane spotting him doing it or smelling the booze and telling the higher-ups is too great. Instead he drops a sugar cube into his cup and watches the tarry liquid seep into it, his mind automatically turning back to last night with Veronica, the whole business not that much different from inserting a capsule, pressing the on button and waiting for an espresso to be expelled. He takes a sip from his cup and is relieved by the sense of the scattered fragments of his mind gathering back in.

'I'm not sure we're getting the whole story at this point,' Keane says.

He feels his hand slip on the cup. 'No?'

'Well no, obviously, there's a reason why Satnam decided to do what she did, we just don't know what it is.'

Taking the coffee to his desk and resuming his seat, Cullen clears his throat and does his best not to sound alarmed. He doesn't like the way this sounds. 'Has somebody checked her phone?'

'It seems to have gone missing.'

Cullen's heart skips. 'Temporarily missing or permanently missing?'

'According to the flatmate, it got left in the ambulance, but the crew couldn't find it so I'm guessing it must have fallen out when they opened up the ambulance.'

Cullen is weak-kneed with relief. 'Naturally I took a look at her social media timelines and so on. Nothing alarming or untoward. In fact, she hardly seems to have used social media this academic year. The most recent post was a picture of her at a Valentine's Day party with three other girls and she looked perfectly fine. But then I don't know her, so...'

Cullen sits and blinks and wonders how best to make this all go away. Too many disordered thoughts swirling around. Probably shouldn't have had that third coffee.

'Perhaps it *was* just an accident. Students buy prescription drugs on the street all the time, drink too much, get wasted,' he says, hoping to sound rational and steady, neither of which he really feels.

Keane blinks, her face registering surprise. 'I'm not sure anyone takes as many pills as Satnam evidently did by accident.'

Irritation snakes up Cullen's spine. It would be easier just to go with the parents' version, wouldn't it? Why is Keane so insistent on picking at the scab? The hairs on her moustache glisten in the light from his desk lamp and he is suddenly overwhelmed by the urge to be alone.

'Do we *know* how many pills Satnam took?'

'It says on the internet that you have to take a lot to overdose.'

Cullen snorts. 'Oh, well, if it says on the *internet*...' He holds up a hand to discourage Keane's response and stands to signal that the meeting is at an end. Surprised when Keane makes no move to leave, he pastes a weak smile on his face and says, 'Is there something else?'

'You're *not* serious, are you? About it being an accident.'

Cullen feels stumped. He takes a step away from his desk towards the door and hovers, desperate for Keane to leave.

'I'll let the Vice Chancellor and the department know. Sooo...' He goes over to the door and holds it open now. Keane's ample behind remains in the visitor's chair. He wonders for a second if she's wedged in. A vision comes to mind of having to wheel her out still stuck to her chair.

'In my opinion, a team meeting would be a wise precaution,' she begins. 'The senior directorate: welfare and pastoral, academic and administration need to discuss how the university is intending to respond. We don't want to do nothing and find we have a suicide contagion on our hands.'

Cullen allows his smile to fade and openly checks his watch. The thought of a meeting makes his heart sink. He is drowning in meetings, most of them useless.

'So here's the thing, Lea. As you know, we're about to go into admissions for next year. As you'll also be aware, competition for the top students in STEM is the stiffest it's ever been. Every university in the country is after them. The last thing we need is to stir up any adverse publicity. No one died...'

'Not yet...' Keane says pointedly.

Cullen suddenly feels exhausted and it's not yet ten o'clock on a Monday morning. What will it take to get the harpy off his back and close this thing down?

'You've been very clear, but as Dean...' and your *superior* he thinks, but is wise enough not to say, 'I'd say that we have no reason not to respect the parents' view. That's what I'll be recommending to the VC. If anyone other than the parents gets in touch about this, I suggest we shut them down. We're investigating an unfortunate incident, we're not making any public statement right now, please respect the party's rights to privacy, blah blah blah.'

Keane compresses her lips as she gathers her things and pushes herself up from the chair. At the door she meets his eye with a concerned look on her face and says, 'I just feel...'

Cullen pulls the door open and swings it in Lea Keane's direction. He watches her step back, a look of alarm on her face, and rearranging his features into what passes for a smile, says, 'If only everything was about your feelings, Lea, what a marvellous world this would be. Now, if you'll excuse me...'

Chapter 9

Nevis

Having no desire to go back to the flat, Nevis heads up towards the Downs and the university, where she intends to remain, telling herself that in the library she'll find peace and calm and even a nook in which to nap, until it's time to leave for her shift at the chippy, where the familiar routines of floor washing, loading potatoes into the peeler, and emptying and cleaning the batter mixer might help keep her mind off the incident on the bridge for a while.

It is a bad business having to lie to Honor, or not lie exactly, but to avoid telling the truth. There was plenty she wasn't telling, obviously, but that's because Honor is the wrong person to tell. After all, Honor has kept so much from her.

The walk takes her through St Michael's, named after the huge grey church in its midst, and up steep hills into the eastern parts of Clifton, though she is too busy in thought to really notice how the church looms like an eye over her, how the hills snatch at her breath. You overthink, Satnam would say, but there is so much to think about. As soon as she can she turns off the main road into the smaller side streets to avoid the blare of traffic and people.

'Bristol's too busy? What are you talking about? You're from London!' Satnam said, when they were freshers, newly arrived in the city, and Nevis made her views known. What she wanted to say was, no, I was born in the Welsh Marches, which was true, but not relevant somehow. Satnam couldn't know that until a few years ago, when the Olympics arrived nearby, Hackney Wick, where Nevis had spent most of her life, was a real backwater, otherworldly and remote, a dead zone of abandoned factories and offices squatted by artists and eco-warriors. There was a particular peacefulness to be had on the water, away from the shops and the press of people. The marshes, from where you could walk along the banks of the Lea almost as far as Epping, lay only ten minutes away. There was no reason for anyone other than the occasional dog walker to come to Hackney Wick, and the anarchists and artists, the boaters and the hippies, were left to their own devices. By contrast Bristol seemed unmanageably loud and busy but a person can grow used to just about anything and by the end of the first year, she had come to love the grand, melancholy buildings, the fine rain and blustery winds, the graffiti, the waterside cafés selling artisan coffee and delectable cakes and the bridges spanning the canals and the navigations and the brown waters of the River Avon.

Now, reaching the security gates onto the campus, she swipes the ID card she keeps in the pocket of her peacoat and wanders along the path that runs alongside the car park towards the bank of lifts to the library on the second floor. The University of Avon hadn't been her first choice. She'd been hoping to find somewhere in London that she could commute to from the boat. It was Honor who'd persuaded her to look further afield and made it possible by putting aside some of the money that Zoe had left her. They'd done some googling and found the course in mathematics with biosciences at Avon. No other university was offering anything similar and the student feedback was phenomenal.

'This place is perfect for you,' Honor said. They were standing in the foyer of the biosciences building. An almond-eyed girl stood beside them, flicking through the course prospectus. Honor asked if she was applying for the same course. The girl confirmed as much, and that would have been the end of the conversation were it not for the fact that Honor went on, remarking, 'You look like someone I used to know,' and Nevis knew she was thinking about Zoe because the girl did bear a striking resemblance to Nevis's birth mother.

'Is that a good thing?' the girl asked.

Honor told her that it was and the girl said, 'Maybe it's a sign then,' and turning to Nevis and holding out her hand, added, 'I'm Satnam. I hope we both get in so we can be friends.' Which was the best thing any stranger had ever said to Nevis before or since.

At the second floor, Nevis switches her phone to silent. Swiping in to the library, she makes her way directly to her usual seat – K14 – and accessing her coursework, a mathematical model of the movement of seawater in deep ocean vents, due at the end of the week, on her phone, begins to check the equations. She won't make the deadline. Her tutor on that project is Dr Ratner who has seemed cool about other students' late submissions, though she supposes she'll have to run it by him.

For the next hour or so she does her best to focus. Before

long, her mind is toggling between Satnam and Honor. Eventually even those worlds blur and her eyelids give in to the gravitational pull.

She wakes, some time later, disorientated and anxious. Inside her a bird still flutters its blue metallic wings, the remnant of a recurring dream, then fades. The bird is *Alcedo atthis*, one of the world's 114 species of kingfisher, and her favourite of all the water birds. In the Bible kingfishers are the first animals to leave the Ark after the flood. In Greek mythology they are Alcyone and Ceyx, a pair of star-crossed lovers who are punished by the gods before winning their pity. For as long as she can recall the birds have appeared in the watery realm of her dreams.

She lifts her head from her arms. Sitting opposite is Daniel something or other, a student she hardly knows, who catches her eye and makes a sad-emoji face. A moment later an email notification appears on her screen via the university's intranet. Is Satnam going to die? Daniel xoxo.

It's only been a few hours since the incident on the bridge and the gossip mill is already churning. Wanting no part of it, Nevis is rising and gathering her things to leave when there comes a tap on her shoulder and she turns to see a tall woman, about her age, with straightened dark-brown hair and too much make-up.

'It's Tash,' the girl says in response to Nevis's blank expression.

Nevis searches her mind. The name Natasha Tillotson pops up. One of the girls in the Valentine's photograph on Satnam's feed. Something odd about that photograph, though her mind can't quite organise itself to work out what. The expression on Satnam's face?

'What happened?'

'I don't know.' Tash blocks her way, her face darkening. Nevis protests but still Tash does not move.

'You were there on the bridge, weren't you? That's what everyone's saying.'

'Get out of my way, Tash, *please*.' She puts her arms out and gives Tash a hard shove, then finds herself running. A handful of students she does not know are standing waiting for the lift. She runs towards the stairs. On the ground floor she pauses to catch her breath.

There are things she knows, things she has kept from the police, from Honor, from everyone. The conversation that evening when Satnam reached for the TV remote and, switching it to off, said, 'I'm thinking of leaving Avon.'

'Why?' Nevis asked, puzzled. Satnam had never given any hint that this was on her mind.

'I've had enough.'

'But you've been doing brilliantly.' This was true. Satnam had struggled towards the end of the first year but since the autumn her grade average had shot up.

'There are things you don't know about, Nevis. I wish I could tell you, but I can't.'

A sharp stab of rejection hit Nevis between the eyes. She said, 'I thought we were best mates.'

Satnam reached out and took her hand. 'We are, and that's why I can't tell you.'

Nevis felt herself pull away. The pain between her eyes reached around her head like a badly fitting hat. Rising from the sofa then, she'd said, 'I'm going to the library.'

She moved out into the hallway and grabbed her backpack

from her room. When she returned, Satnam was standing by the door, her hands pressed together in a pleading gesture. 'We could leave Avon together, transfer somewhere else.'

But Nevis's legs were already moving from under her, propelling her away from the source of her anguish. Sweeping past Satnam she swung open the front door and tumbled out of the flat onto the landing. She had already reached the bottom of the stairs and had her hand on the door when she heard Satnam cry out, 'Nevis, come back, *please*.'

The phrase haunts her now. The desperation in Satnam's voice. The cruel way she had ignored it, selfishly caught up in her own muddled feelings of rejection, her fear of having to expose herself. Satnam had been about to confide in her, to share her secret and all she could think about was the secret that she, Nevis, was keeping. If she'd only turned and climbed the stairs, they could have sat back down on the sofa and finished their chips and they could have talked. But there was no way back from her wounded pride. Her stupidity. That pain which clutched her skull. She saw now how much keeping her own secret had twisted her, how it had crept in and poisoned the only real friendship she had ever had. Satnam had offered her a chance to break away from all that but when it came to it, her courage had failed her and she'd abandoned her friend when Satnam had most needed her support.

She makes her way home, climbs the damp, greasy staircase to the flat which, until the early hours of this morning, she shared with Satnam. At the top of the stairs she stops and fingers the keys in her backpack and alights on Satnam's phone. A bloom of relief that the police had believed her when she'd said she didn't have it. The desire she had only moments ago for a cup of tea and some Marmite toast has gone now. She feels dirty, itchy. Making her way to the tiny bathroom, she pulls off her clothes, dives in the shower with the water on its hottest setting and scrubs herself with a nailbrush until her skin hurts. Afterwards, she opens the bathroom door and takes a step out. The door to Satnam's room which remains half open from when last night, in a panic, Nevis rushed in, hoping against hope that the woman on the other end of the phone was wrong, that there had been some mistake and that the Satnam she knew and loved was fast asleep in her room. Inside the room empty air stirs. On the bedside table sits the opened bottle of vodka Satnam must have thought would give her courage. Nevis wonders now if she should have told the police everything she knew and whether not telling them had simply added to her betrayal but it is too late now. She has lied to them, or, at least, failed to tell the truth and there is no way back from that.

She shuts the door to Satnam's bedroom and moves through the hallway to her own. Shaking out the coverlet and laying it over the bed, she picks up the lamp and bends the dent in the lampshade strut back to the perpendicular, straightens the poster and replaces the socks in their colour coded pockets in the drawer. Finally, she puts her own phone and Satnam's on to charge. Her shift at the chippy starts in four hours. Till then, what's called for is sleep. She falls into bed naked, screws her eyes shut and waits. From two floors down the rumble of traffic makes its way into her bones before it reaches the ear. Twenty minutes later her head is still swimming. Getting up, she pulls on fresh underwear, a clean pair of Levi's 501s and one of her several identical long-sleeved Breton tees. In some corner of her mind a small, angry red top spins. How strange that she should be angry. But perhaps in the circumstances anger is forgivable or even normal? Or perhaps it's just a defence to make the guilt endurable.

There are things you don't know about, Nevis.

She wonders if all this will make her crazy.

Unplugging her phone from the charger, she half hopes by some miracle to see a message from Satnam, whilst knowing that miracles only happen in films. Satnam's phone sits charged and locked. She tries a few number combinations and, failing to open it, slides the device into her pocket. In the kitchen she puts the kettle on to boil. Digging out a filter from the drawer beside the fridge, she measures two scoops of ground coffee onto a scale, then tips it into the AeroPress, taps the dead silverfish from an old *Games of Thrones* mug and sets the press over the lip. Scenes from last summer in Hackney flicker in her mind: Sat and Luke and Honor sitting under the cratch cover at the ship's bow eating Honor's spag bol, watching the swifts swooping to catch mosquitoes dancing above the water. Sat and Nevis sitting on the bank of the canal spotting kingfishers while Luke and Honor shared a spliff on deck. Returning in the dimming light and accidentally disturbing a troupe of cygnets bracketed by their anxious parents. What else can she recall? Satnam was struggling academically back then. There was coursework over the summer which Nevis helped her complete. Her grades weren't disastrous but she had twice flunked maths and had just completed a remedial course. Satnam hadn't told Narinder and Bikram that. She said once that if she failed to shine academically, her parents would put more and more pressure on her to drop out and get married. They had picked a suitable candidate. Their discovery that she was seeing Luke most likely exacerbated the situation. She didn't talk about it much, but Nevis knew that Narinder and Bikram didn't like Satnam dating period, let alone dating a *gora* from outside the culture. When she'd said she'd had enough, did she mean she'd tired of fighting her parents, grown weary of having one foot in each culture and forever being caught between the two? Had she told Luke that their relationship had no future? Is that why Luke had dumped her back in November? Had she decided to go back home and marry? Is that what she meant when she'd said she was thinking of leaving Avon?

If that was so, then why had she made such an effort to improve her grades this year? Why had she told Nevis that as a result her parents had eased up on her about getting married and begun to be more focused on seeing her graduate and getting a good job? And why had she drunk a bottle of vodka, downed a bunch of pills and taken herself off to the Clifton Suspension Bridge?

Was she feeling the loss of Luke? Had she tried to get back together with him and been rejected? Or had her parents changed their minds and started pressuring her to leave Avon and marry? What did she mean by saying there are things Nevis doesn't know? What things and why had she kept them to herself? Didn't they share everything? Had Nevis done something to kill their friendship? Was that what she was going to tell her when she called her to the bridge?

The coffee trickles into the cup. She adds some water from the kettle, sits down at the tiny table and checks her texts and voicemail inboxes. A couple of messages from Honor. On Satnam's social, Daniel and a few others have written sentimental or otherwise morbid get-well messages. She finishes her coffee and checks her student email but Dr Ratner has not yet responded to her request for a deadline extension. She's about to leave the system when she sees another notification. She clicks. An email from Tash Tillotson pops onto the screen.

You know, don't you?

Her eyes slide across the words. She reads again, desperately searching for another meaning but the words remain the same. She feels herself fall and wobble. In her stomach something bitter churns. She just makes it to the bathroom in time before the sickness rises.

Chapter 10

Cullen

Cullen comes off the call with the Vice Chancellor feeling uneasy. The pain in his head has gone south into his neck. He calls out to Tina in the departmental office to fetch him some ibuprofen and thinks he should probably get a better office chair. The university will never pay for it, of course. Another thing to find money for.

He's knocking back the pills with a slug of Famous Grouse when Veronica calls.

'I've just got back from shopping,' she says, ominously. She has a way of saying the most unwelcome things in such a lovely, mellifluous tone that it catches you unawares. She's been catching Cullen unawares for years. He really should have spotted from the moment he met her, he close to finishing his PhD, she a new graduate, that the Hon. Veronica Fanshawe-Drew would prove to be a money pit. Even then he saw that she was a daddy's girl, dreamy and fun-loving but also spoilt and hopelessly impractical. One time, he remembers, she spilled hot sauce on her dress and, rather than wash it, threw the thing away. He should have read the runes right then. But he'd had so little experience with women, he was so completely naïve, and God, Veronica had such energy, she was so absolutely charming and so physically beautiful whilst being so completely unlike *her*. More to the point, she seemed so impressed with him, that he couldn't help being won over. She appeared to have it all. A beautiful loft apartment in central Manchester, a paid internship in an art gallery and family with money. She was the only person Cullen had ever met who bought art. The thought she might be the sort of woman who would require financial upkeep didn't occur to him. Within months Cullen had moved into Veronica's loft apartment. Fourteen weeks later the Fanshawe-Drews lost everything in the financial crash and Cullen discovered that the flat was heavily mortgaged. Still Cullen thought everything would be fine. He and Veronica were happy and, with his newly minted PhD and the offer of a lectureship at Manchester Metropolitan, he felt secure enough to ask her to marry him. After they returned from honeymoon Veronica began to complain that the funding cuts made her job impossible and she wanted to leave. Cullen focused his own energies on finding a better paid job. A senior lectureship came up at Avon, Cullen applied and got it. The pay was modest but Cullen didn't tell Veronica that. They moved to Bristol and Cullen was shocked by how much more expensive than Manchester it was. Veronica drifted for a while then managed to use her contacts to swing a part-time job at the Bristol Art Gallery. Everything seemed to settle until Veronica came home one day to say she'd spotted her dream home, a Georgian villa on the northern fringes of Clifton. It was way more than they could afford but Veronica wouldn't be persuaded out of it. Her father called in a few favours to secure the couple a mortgage and seven weeks after Veronica had first spotted it in the estate agent's window, the house was theirs, or rather, it was mostly the bank's. Perhaps only the study and the downstairs cloakroom truly belonged to them, but over the years that would change as the mortgage was paid. With two salaries it would be manageable but they couldn't afford to be complacent. A year into the job at Avon Cullen vaulted over Mark Ratner to take the position of head of department and increased his salary by twenty per cent. A year after that he was promoted to dean. It was around that time Veronica started complaining of stress and before long she'd left the gallery with no plans to work again. So far as Cullen could tell, she now spent much of her time at the gym or in the café inside the gym or window shopping. He'd wanted a lover and a wife but it seemed to him increasingly that he'd become the keeper of a very expensive exotic pet. That's when, for him, the loneliness set in. Her desire for a baby only made things worse. Strangely, he still loved her, though it would have been easier if he didn't.

'Is that why you're calling?' he asks now.

'No, darling, of course not. I'm *calling* because there was a man in the drive when I got back. He said he needed to talk to you. I offered to give him your number but he said it would be best face to face so I told him to come back when you're in. I wouldn't have bothered you with it but he looked a bit of a thug so I was worried.'

Cullen blinks and swallows. He doesn't recall giving out his address. On the other hand, people like that, thugs, they can find that stuff out pretty easily these days.

'Don't worry, I'm sure it'll be nothing.'

'I won't then. You'll be home in good time tonight, won't you, darling? I'm still ovulating.'

'One of my students attempted suicide last night so probably not.' In fact the incident on the bridge is unlikely to keep him late but he has no desire to encounter the man on the driveway or, indeed, Veronica on heat. He could do with a night on his own. A few drinks in the pub and a nice supper somewhere. Maybe even a film. Return once Veronica is asleep. 'I'm sorry, darling,' he says.

'Don't tell me any of the details, I can't handle it. The man in the driveway was bad enough. Now we're trying to get pregnant I need to stay centred.'

A sour feeling rises from Cullen's belly and settles in his mouth. Veronica's use of the plural subject pronoun displeases him. *We* are not trying to get pregnant. Veronica is trying and Cullen is going along with it for the same reason he always goes along with his wife – for the sake of an easy life and because being married to the Honourable Veronica makes him feel a little less like the dishonourable Christopher. He switches off the pregnancy monologue and allows his mind to focus on more immediate things, like the conversation he's just had with his old flame, the VC, Maddy Ince. He did not, for a minute, believe what he had told Keane, that it was possible that what had happened to Satnam Mann was an accident, and he told Maddy so. Nonetheless, he thought that if the parents were willing to believe it *was* then they should go with it, not only out of solidarity but also because the accident theory offered the university – and himself – a get-out clause. An unfortunate accident. End of story. His advice to Maddy, therefore, was to allow the whole thing to blow over, which was precisely what he sensed Maddy wanted to hear. Not that he was ever likely to disagree with Maddy on anything of substance. She'd made

69

sure of that. He was OK with the fact that he was, at least to some extent, Maddy's creature. It was she who'd helped him leapfrog over Ratner and secure the position as head of department and, before long, dean. They went way back, knew one another's secrets.

A part of him feels oddly admiring of Satnam Mann. Envious almost. Isn't suicide a rational response to unbearable pain? When you look at it like that, doesn't it seem perfectly reasonable, courageous even? Who hasn't wanted to be free of the bewilderment of being alive at least once? For some people, people like him, and, he knows now, like Satnam, the feeling that you could take your own life at any time is just an extension of everyday existence. More than that, it's a freedom knowing you've always got an out. Funny, Cullen usually has a gift for detecting that small, insistent bead of self-destruction which lurks inside more people than are willing to admit it. Like dogs trained to scent out cancer, Cullen has a nose for a death wish. Which makes it all the more surprising that he missed it this time round.

He swallows another coffee, asks Tina to take messages if anyone calls and heads down the corridor and then down two flights of stairs and through a series of fire doors to Mark Ratner's office in the biosciences building.

'Bit busy right now. Can it wait?' Ratner says.

'I wouldn't be here if it could wait.' Has Ratner gone mad? He might be a decade older but Cullen is his senior. He doesn't have to wait for Ratner any more. Ratner has to wait for Cullen.

Ratner hasn't heard the news so Cullen relays as much as he knows. 'I've just spoken to the VC. She's keen for us to lie low on this but in private wants an audit of the bioscience modules.'

'Why?' Ratner says, looking alarmed.

'She's just being cautious. Wants to make sure we're not putting undue pressure on the students.'

'Biosciences is a challenging subject,' Ratner says.

'Do you have a pen? I'd like to write that down.' Cullen watches Ratner go red then recover himself. 'Look, Mark, I think you know what I'm going to say.'

'Yes. All eyes on the department for a while. Best behaviour.'

'Something like that.'

'Well you don't have to worry about me. I've been a good boy for months now.'

Cullen looks him up and down slowly, carefully, hoping to lock eyes but Ratner continues to gaze doggedly at his keyboard. He's lied so many times about this stuff before. He's probably still lying. Damn him for being so good at it.

'This is serious, Mark. Maddy is watching and she has a beady eye.'

'You have my word,' Ratner says.

It's as much as Cullen can do not to laugh. He'd quite like to punch him now, force him to admit that he's lying, but that would give him the upper hand. Other than keep an eye on him there's not much he can do.

Cullen gets up and turns to leave and, as he does so, he spots a small, urgent figure making her way across the car park. From some obscure part of his memory the name Nevis Smith arises. The girl who was Satnam's flatmate. He makes a mental note to call her, fix a meeting, see if she can cast light on the incident on the bridge. He'll need to keep control of the situation, make sure to keep himself at the centre of the information flow, be watchful and take action if necessary. Satnam, Nevis, Maddy,

Keane and Ratner, from now on they need to be on his radar at all times. He can't afford to let anything slip.

Returning to his office in the Deanery, Cullen finishes up some administrative work, emails Nevis Smith to request a meeting, then makes his way down to the car park. It has started raining now. Bristolian rain, which he thinks of as West Country Wet, not really rain at all, more like mist. He pops the lock on his blue Volvo, gets in, turns on Classic FM followed by the windscreen wipers. Putting the car into reverse he cranes round to reverse out of the space and, when he turns back, he sees in the periphery of his vision the right-hand wiper brushing something small and drenched off the windscreen and onto the tarmac.

A leaf, he thinks, then realises it's an insect drowned in the tiny tsunami created by the wiper. Alive one moment, dead the next.

Chapter 11

Honor

From a café near the museum on Harbourside Honor calls Bill, her neighbour on the water in Hackney, explains the situation and asks him to look after Caterine the Great until she gets back. Right now, she doesn't know when that will be. It depends on how the Satnam situation plays out; not that there's much she can do, but her gut tells her that this isn't the time to leave. The past is stirring, like a great bear waking from hibernation.

Nevis has no idea how vulnerable she is.

They say a baby can tell if she isn't wanted, even in the womb. Honor has read that somewhere. And in spite of everything Nevis *was* wanted. So much. If Nevis knew how hard Zoe had to fight to bring her into the world. Zoe's parents begged her to book a termination. When that didn't work, they threatened to cut off contact if she went ahead with the pregnancy. They said the baby would be tainted and that, however hard Zoe tried to protect the child from discovering her origins, she would inevitably find out one day and, when she did, the knowledge would destroy her. Better that she never be born. Kinder. At first Zoe argued with her parents then she closed her mind to them. She never stopped wanting Nevis, even when Dan and Judy made good on their threat to walk away. Then, after Zoe died, they tried to get custody. Didn't succeed, thank goodness. Zoe was quite specific in her will. Dan and Judy didn't deserve Nevis. Sometimes, in her darkest moments, Honor wonders whether she deserves her either.

As the waitress approaches to take her cup she remembers one more thing Bill can do. 'I'm going to need to find a place to stay in Bristol. I don't suppose you have any bargee friends down here who need their boat de-wintering or a bit of maintenance in exchange for a bed?'

'I might actually. Leave it with me.'

'Thank you, Bill. And don't let Caterine wrap you around her little paw. Don't be fooled by her good looks. She's a monster.'

She ends the call and checks the time. It seems like only minutes since she arrived at the hospital. She hopes Nevis is fast asleep in her flat. Back in the day, driving from rave to rave, Honor would often be up thirty-six hours straight and hardly feel it. Those days are long gone. If she can remember where she parked Gerry, she'll take a nap in the back later, but first it's time to make a call. She taps in the number and a female voice answers: 'University of Avon, how can I help you?'

'Can you put me through to the head of student welfare?' The call goes to tinny muzak. She wonders whether the whole truth, even the parts Nevis doesn't know, is what is needed here. Or perhaps she should simply say that her daughter will need extra support and may not know how to ask for it? After a few minutes a velvety voice introduces herself as the departmental secretary but does not give her name.

Honor explains who she is and asks to speak with the head.

'What's it regarding?'

'I'm worried about my daughter, Nevis Smith.'

'Worried how?'

Honor explains.

'One moment.' The line returns to muzak then back to the departmental secretary.

'I'm very sorry, Dr Keane isn't available right now. I can leave a message for her.'

'Then I'd like to make an appointment to come in.'

'One moment,' the voice says, 'I'm looking at your daughter's records but I don't see any statement of special needs.'

'Well no, but...'

'Your daughter is legally an adult, Ms Smith, so Dr Keane would need Nevis's authority to talk you. I'm not sure what else you'd like me to do.'

There is whispering in the background.

'I just want to know she's being looked out for.'

More muzak. A long pause this time before the voice comes back on.

'Dr Keane says she won't be able to discuss Ms Mann's accident or your daughter specifically without her permission, but she's happy to have a general chat.' The secretary's voice is strained as though she is delivering lines, pausing momentarily just before the word 'accident' as though having to remind herself exactly what to say. They agree on a time. After the call ends Honor decides it's a good thing she didn't get to speak to Dr Keane after all. This way she'll be able to catch some shut-eye before going in and have time to prepare properly for the encounter.

*

From Harbourside Honor wanders along the city's watery arteries past the dark glamour of Narrow Quay to Pero's Bridge and heads towards Broadmead. It is past the commuter hour now and the streets are relatively quiet, the shops shut or shutting, the office buildings empty and still lit, the pavements swept, rubbish collecting in the bins. But there is something feral about the city too, some dark and buried rot, as if beneath all the respectability, the grandeur even, lurks something sinister. In a narrow street just shy of Broadmead she spots a charity shop sign. A young man with a kind face appears at the door to signal they are about to close. Honor opens her coat and points to her pyjamas, mouthing, 'I haven't got a stitch to wear,' and the young man, amused, lets her in.

'Forget to get dressed this morning, did we?'

'I'll be quick, I promise.'

From among the bric-a-brac and musty assortments she picks out a pair of harems, some jeans and a purple fleece, then, bearing in mind her scheduled meeting with Dr Lea Keane, scouts the racks for something more business-like. It has been years and years since she had any cause to wear anything smart or even look presentable. Nevis always says she looks like a New Age traveller on her way to a rave in a field. The young man watches her struggling to choose and pulls out a trouser suit, saying, 'Try that one on. About your size and no visible body fluids, which is always a plus.'

In the privacy of the changing room she slides off her pyjamas, pulls on the suit and glances at herself briefly in the mirror with one eye. What happened to her youth? The years fill up your heart and break down your body. Nothing fits quite right but it'll all do. She bundles up the pyjamas she was wearing when she left London, and hanging the jeans, tops and trouser suit over an arm, pulls open the curtains and heads across the stale-smelling shop to the till.

'Purple is so this season,' the young man says, folding the fleece into a carrier bag and, pointing to the pyjamas hanging over Honor's arm, 'I could put those in the recycling bin? They can process the fabric and turn it into something new.'

'Wouldn't it be great if that worked on people,' she says.

Back outside in a light ashy rain she texts Nevis and tries to recall where she left Gerry the van.

Chapter 12

Cullen

The 'Sono andati' aria from *La Bohème*, Mimi's death scene, accompanies Cullen as he drives through the darkening streets of Clifton. He hums tunelessly along, looking forward to his solo pint and his solo dinner. A car hoots behind him. It's commuter hour, which here in Clifton means a flow of traffic out towards the bridge. He checks his speed and, realising he's been doing twenty in a thirty-mile-an-hour zone, opens the window on the driver's side, slows down to a near stop, leans out and screams at the driver behind. 'Fuck you too!' When the driver attempts to overtake, he pulls the Volvo out into the middle of the road to block him. At the next junction the road widens into two lanes and the driver pulls alongside. He's staring intently ahead, not wanting any trouble. Well, too late, mate. Cullen keeps pace then all of a sudden accelerates, cuts him up and brakes hard at a red light. Fellow behind has to swerve to avoid hitting him.

Haha, that feels better.

He checks the light and accelerates away from the junction. The rain continues to blur his view. Shop window lights flash past him like a series of cheap fireworks, their colours fading into his peripheral vision. His route takes him past a group of young women heading out for a night on the town. How young they look and how full of hope and glossy optimism. Staring makes him feel old and worn out, like a vampire circling his next meal, but also rather wonderfully powerful. They are behind him now, but his gaze still flicks up to the rear-view mirror, a distant note of disgust sounding in the symphony of desire playing in his head.

It is a relief when he can no longer see them. Up ahead the lights of the Clifton Suspension Bridge pinken the skyline. He imagines Satnam Mann poised at the barrier, pictures the bridge, with its suspension cables slung across the gorge like tightropes. There's only one rule if you find yourself on a tightrope and that is to keep moving forward and don't look down.

Cullen parks at the rear of the Saracen's Arms and orders a pint with a whisky chaser and a chicken pie and stares vacantly at the big screen showing a Premier League match, relishing the luxury of not having to think for a while. He's just finishing the pie when his phone lights up. Amanda. If only he had the strength to ignore her.

'Hello, Mother,' he says.

'Christopher, they wouldn't let me see the hairdresser today.'

'I'm sorry about that,' he says, closing his eyes and doing his best to take his mind back to the sublime moment in the car with Puccini playing and his evening ahead of him.

'You'll have to come.'

'I will?' His heart sinks into his shoes.

'Yes. I've told them I won't eat dinner until they bring the hairdresser back. I am not going into that dining room looking like something the cat dragged in.'

Twenty minutes later he pulls into the driveway at Wychall's Nursing Home, shuts off the engine and does his best to compose himself. On the short walk to the entrance the rain whips his face. He keys in the entrance code he's not supposed to know and lets himself inside the home. A riot of strange smells and odd, echoing cries hits him. Floating above it all is the smell of kitchen grease. How much more of this? At the door to the meeting room he catches himself thinking how much his mother's illness has drained the life out of him.

Keep moving forward and don't look down.

He's moving through the lounge when a hand lands on his forearm, one of the relatives, a middle-aged woman who was at the last relatives' meeting and whose name he has already forgotten.

'A quick word?' the woman says.

Cullen feels himself stiffen. Here we go again. He takes a step to one side to loosen the woman's grip on his arm.

'This is a bit delicate so I'll just come out with it. Your mother has been threatening my father,' the woman says. 'I've told the staff but she's still doing it. She goes into his room at night and says all kinds of wicked things. Can't you have a word with her?'

Cullen smiles, holding the woman's eye. 'I've never known my mother to say anything that wasn't true.'

He watches his antagonist redden before slinking away shaking her head.

After some considerable effort, he's able to persuade his mother to go into the dining room wearing a headscarf. They take up two seats recently vacated by other residents and the care staff bring Amanda a plate of dainty sandwiches and a large glass of sherry. He takes the opportunity to go to the nurse's office to enquire about the hairdresser. It's a payment issue apparently. He is astounded by the sum. Over the past month Amanda has spent more having her hair dressed than Cullen has spent on getting both cars serviced and paying for their MOTs.

'Your mother does like her extras,' Maura says, giving him a soft, sympathetic smile.

'I'll sort it,' he says, wondering how and when it will end.

He returns to the dining room to find Amanda's meal untouched but Amanda herself demanding more sherry.

'These dreadful people won't help me out with another tiny drink,' Amanda says then, lowering her voice to a whisper, 'I've got a bottle of brandy in my room. Let's go!'

He wheels her back to her room, on the much-coveted corridor on the ground floor, where many rooms, Amanda's included, have French windows out into the garden (for another £200 a week). He locates the Courvoisier she keeps in a cabinet on the wall, pours two snifters then comes to sit beside her. She taps her fingers on his hand in a musical rhythm and hums something tunelessly.

The scene puts him in mind of long nights on his own in his room as a child scarcely daring to breathe lest the sound disturb Amanda during one of her migraines. On good days, when Amanda was cheerful, he remembers her arranging his food into pleasing shapes and patterns. One time, he must have been five or six, she made his pasta into a face and when he cried and protested that he didn't want to eat a person, she tipped the meal over his head.

He sits with his lips pressed together, waiting for the back-hander that is surely about to come. As she downs the last of her brandy, he watches her mentally sharpening her knives.

'I always think it's such a shame...' she says, at last, withdrawing her hand. Cullen knows what's coming. It has been nearly twenty years but she never passes up an opportunity to bring up the scandal at St Olaf's and her part in rescuing him. He braces himself. '...that you let yourself down so badly. If I hadn't...'

'I know, Mother, but I do wonder why you need to be such a broken record about it.' The instant the words leave his mouth he regrets them. Why does he always take the bait? He watches as Amanda's face stiffens into a gorgon mask and waits for the retaliation he knows is about to come.

'Speak to me that way again, this "broken record" will break you. Don't think I won't.' The words 'broken record' come out crackling with venom.

One day, Mother, he thinks, I am going to kill you.

Chapter 13

Honor

It is early evening as Honor pulls into the car park of the Bristol Royal Infirmary. She finds a space and sits quietly for a moment, gathering herself in the yellow light. Earlier, after the charity shop, she'd driven at random through the city and by some unconscious process had found herself at the Clifton bridge. She left Gerry parked along a slip road on the Clifton side and took herself off along the walkway, past the toll buildings and onto the bridge, feeling the wind bluster as it swept up from the river, bringing with it the smell of mud and more distantly the saline tang of the sea. She has no idea exactly where on the bridge or on which side Nevis came upon Satnam, but that did not matter now. For a long time she stared across the wide chasm of the gorge to the craggy cliffs beyond, watching gulls rise up and bank through the blustery breeze. The other side seemed like another world and it almost was – only a few miles away lay Wales. How she missed the Welsh Marches – Y Mers as the Welsh called them – and the rolling hills around Llanerch, to where she and Zoe had retreated after they'd left Ludlow. All those places – Llanerch, Ludlow and a string of quaint towns and the soft hills of Y Mers – are ruined for her now.

She stands by the suicide barrier and looks over into the wide brown ribbon of water, thinking of that other bridge, spanning the Teme at Llanerch, which, in the early days of her and Zoe's life together, cast such a spell in her mind and now, for quite other reasons, would never leave it. The Llanerch bridge had none of the grandeur of Clifton but it was ancient and beautiful all the same, the stone blocks of its low-slung arches speckled with red and orange lichen. She'd been standing on that bridge when she spotted a lifeless hand caught in the water weeds and saw the silver ring that Zoe wore on her right thumb flashing in the water.

With a shudder she pulls herself back from the barrier, thinking about what it must have taken for Satnam to have made her way here and what recklessness or courage or despair that had taken. It had been gone midnight, Nevis said, after the bridge lights switch off, when anyone climbing the barrier is less likely to be spotted and persuaded out of jumping. Did Satnam know that? What went through her mind? Had the drugs played havoc with her head? Was it a cry for help or a howl of despair, an act of defiance or punishment or a revenge move? Was it rash or rational, impulsive or meticulously planned?

Satnam told Nevis she had had enough.

And, for now at least, so had Honor. Fatigue threatened to overcome her. She walked back to the van and got into the back. Within minutes she was sound asleep. She woke to the sound of her phone and was relieved to see Bill's name on the screen. No bad news from Nevis then.

Stretching herself she rubbed the damp cold from her legs and took the call. Bill had spoken with a bargee friend named Alex Penney who might be able to offer a place on a boat down at the Harbourside in exchange for maintenance work.

'It's not his boat. He's watching it for some friends, said he'd need to check with them. If you drop by the *Helene* tomorrow morning he said he might be able to sort something out. She's in the Floating Harbour near the Arnolfini Theatre. They call them longboats in that part of the country, by the way, but you probably already know that.'

'Yeah. Got caught out by that when I bought the *Kingfisher*.' She'd answered the advert for a longboat in the local press in Ludlow when the money from Zoe's will had come through and asked Mike, the *Kingfisher*'s previous owner, if she was a narrowboat as well as being long. Mike had had a good time with that. 'Thanks, Bill, you're all the aces.'

There's a pause before a hopeful sounding voice says, 'I am?'

They've been round the houses on this over the years. 'My brilliant *friend*,' Honor says.

'Ah yes,' Bill says, sounding crestfallen. 'Of course.'

She checks the time on her phone. It is 6.45 p.m. Nothing from Nevis. She taps out Any news? An answer comes back. Texted N&B twice at 15:12 and 18:23. No reply yet.

It's hard to imagine how Narinder and Bikram must be feeling. Your own daughter, your darling child. The thought brings a sickening churn of the stomach. Doing her best to shake it off Honor makes her way round to the driver's cabin, turns the key in the ignition, fires up Gerry and, making a three-point turn in the street, heads off in the direction of the city. Though it's not quite sunset yet and she drives with the last gloaming in the rear-view mirror, the only bright light comes from the lamps strung across the span of the gorge.

Now here she is, in the middle of the hospital car park,

fumbling for coins to feed the parking meter. The time on the bridge has left her with more questions than answers. For the second time that day she walks through the swing doors into the warm fug of the Bristol Royal Infirmary, following the signs to the lifts and from there up to the second floor, left down the corridor towards the ICU. It is quiet now, in that soft, certain way that hospitals at night always are. Over at the nurses' station a group of nurses and orderlies in various uniforms mill about attending to banks of screens and papers. There's no one she recognises from the morning but that's not surprising given that more than twelve hours have passed and the staff must have changed shift. Approaching the desk she waits, hoping to catch someone's eye. A young woman with her hair pinned into a ponytail turns and smiles and comes over.

'Can I help?'

Honor explains who she is and asks to look in on Satnam. She watches as the young woman's face closes up like the petals of a daylily once the dusk sets in.

'A minute or two is all I need.'

'And you are?'

'Yes, I'm sorry. I'm a friend. The mother of a friend.'

Honor watches the young woman bustle off to the nursing station and return moments later. 'I'm sorry, but the family have said no visitors except immediate family and representatives from the university.'

'Not even for a few seconds?'

The young woman shakes her head softly.

'Can you at least tell me how she is?' Alive, evidently.

'I'm really sorry.'

'Please give her a message then. Please tell her that Honor and

Nevis…' she stops, thinking that the nurse will never remember that '…will you tell her that the crew of the *Kingfisher* is looking forward to welcoming her on board again?'

'The crew of the *Kingfisher*.'

'You will tell her, won't you?'

The young woman smiles softly and turns away.

In the lift on the way down Honor resolves to call Narinder and ask her to change her mind. The two spoke briefly last summer, when Satnam was staying on the *Kingfisher*. The exchange was tense but civil. Narinder wanted her daughter home and was hoping Honor might persuade her. She also wanted to be sure that Satnam and Luke weren't sleeping together. They were, of course, but Honor didn't see it was her business to say one way or another. Satnam was an adult, entitled to do whatever she wanted.

A few weeks later, at the beginning of the academic year, when Nevis and Satnam were moving into the flat, the two women had another encounter. Narinder wanted to know from Honor whether Nevis went out with boys.

'Not that I know of,' Honor said.

'Well at least that's something. Satnam tells me she's a very good mathematician. We are expecting her to help Satnam with her coursework.'

They haven't spoken since.

Honor steps out of the lift at the ground floor and makes her way back to the entrance hall. The smell of food from the café is a reminder that she hasn't eaten since the very early morning breakfast with Nevis what seems like days ago now. Checking her watch, she sees that there is still time on her ticket in the hospital car park. Might as well be now.

At the food counter she orders a baked potato from a small, round woman with her hair in a hygiene net.

'Long day?' asks the woman.

She goes over to the same table where she found Nevis and Sondra sitting more than twelve hours ago. The potato is microwaved not baked, though not bad. Tomorrow is her appointment with Dr Keane at the university. She will raise the question of whether Satnam is allowed visits from friends with Dr Keane. Maybe she has some sway.

She dials the Manns' home number. Narinder answers the call. 'Hello, Honor. I thought you would phone me.'

'Yes. I'm so sorry about Satnam.'

'A terrible accident.'

Accident. That word again. There were some people who believed what happened to Zoe was an accident. Zoe's own parents. In the face of all the evidence that a crime had been committed and the perpetrator remained at large, Dan and Judy continued to insist that Zoe's death was a simple tragedy. As if any tragedy could be simple.

'How are you and Bikram holding up? You've both been in my thoughts.'

'We are praying. Prayers are bigger than thoughts.'

'Yes.' She pauses. 'I'm at the infirmary. I was hoping to see Satnam.'

Silence. A few excruciating moments pass before Narinder says, 'We don't want anyone to see her. Only family.'

'I understand, but...'

'What do you understand?'

'Nevis and I would really love to see Satnam. It might bring her a little comfort.'

'Daughters are supposed to be the comfort. Where is our comfort? The boy we found for her has gone away. He was an extremely suitable boy from a very good family. Now they don't want anything to do with us.'

'That's unfortunate.'

'You understand nothing of any of this. When our daughter is better we will never speak of her accident. Or of you or your daughter. I want you to go away now and not bother me again.'

Honor is left with a blank screen in the palm of one hand, the other pressing her forehead. Narinder's hostility has come at her like a dark tornado. It's a shame about Satnam, unfair on her and Nevis, but perhaps Dr Keane will be able to talk her round. She starts Gerry and pulls out of the infirmary car park. At the exit she hesitates then makes a left. The drive to Nevis's flat takes only a few minutes from here. She won't call. Nevis doesn't like surprises. But it will reassure her to see Nevis safely at home.

She pulls into a space opposite the flat and cuts the engine. In the living-room window a light shines through the cheap curtains. Two figures mill about, both silhouetted but one is recognisably her daughter, the other someone taller and with a man's gait. A friend or perhaps even a lover. For a few minutes she watches as the two figures cross the room then settle before she starts her engine once more and moves back out into the traffic and away.

Chapter 14

Nevis

'I can't get my head around it.' Luke flips the ring pull from a can of Stella. Nevis had seen him earlier, when he'd come into the chippy anxious and keen to talk. She was glad he'd reached out. It had been on her mind to contact him. She'd told him to come to the flat after her shift. Now here he was.

'What the hell got into her?'

'I was going to ask you the same question,' Nevis says. She moves over to the curtains, peers outside at the dying light and draws them closed.

'I haven't seen her to speak to in months,' he says, his voice agitated and tremulous. In the months since he and Satnam split Luke has grown a goatee and he's lost weight. His skin has taken on a strange pallor.

'I've got her phone. I was hoping you might know her passcode.'

He picks up the can and begins bobbing his legs. 'Isn't that a bit, I don't know, invasive?'

'It might give us some answers.'

'Maybe it was just, like, a spur of the moment thing?' Luke asks, taking another swig from the can. She can tell he is genuinely upset. His hand is shaking as he raises and lowers the can. 'I can't get my head around it to be honest.'

'There was an empty vodka bottle on her bedside table. If that had been there for long, I'm sure I would have seen it. We were always in and out of one another's rooms.'

'I remember.'

Nevis had burst in on Satnam and Luke in a private moment once. After that Nevis didn't go in when Luke was around.

'The hospital says she'd taken Ritalin. That's why she collapsed before she could jump. I was just wondering if you ever saw her using.'

'Not really. I mean, I saw her take something a couple of times, last year, when she was struggling with her coursework but everyone does Ritalin or speed or whatever from time to time. It's no big deal. She must have taken a shedload to OD on it. I didn't even know you could get addicted to that stuff.' He shakes his head.

'She said she was working really hard and her grades were much better. When they were bad, she was scared her parents would make her drop out.'

'Have you spoken to them?' Luke puts down his beer and blinks hard. 'I thought about getting in touch with them but they hate me. I mean, they don't know me, but they hate the fact that I slept with their daughter.'

'I think they had someone in mind that they were hoping she'd marry.'

'Maybe that's why she wanted to kill herself then. She always told me she didn't want an arranged marriage.'

'The family are saying it was an accident apparently.' She'd been on Satnam's social, seen a post her brother had left asking for the Sikh community to say prayers for Satnam's recovery.

'Maybe it *was*. If the stuff was mixed with something, you know, weird or, like, toxic,' Luke says.

'No one drinks a bottle of vodka by accident. Or takes that many pills. You got any idea where she might have got them from?'

Luke frowns and blinks and shakes his head. 'Why would I know?'

'She told me there are things I didn't know about her.'

'Things? What things? Did you ask her?'

Nevis shakes her head. How she wishes she had.

'It's all so fucked up,' Luke says.

Silence falls. Then bringing up the picture of Satnam she'd found on her feed, the one taken on Valentine's Day, Nevis says, 'Luke, can I show you something?'

Luke stares blankly at the photo.

'Satnam's unhappy.'

Luke peers more closely.

'Really? She looks OK to me.'

'The smile doesn't go all the way up to her eyes. The morning after, I found her in the kitchen crying but she wouldn't tell me what was wrong.' Nevis relays the encounter with Natasha in the library. 'What did she mean, "You know, don't you?" Know what?'

Luke shrugs. 'Maybe they had a few words. Natasha's a hothead. Drinks too much, comes out with a lot of shit. But if you think she knows something, why don't you go and have it out with her?'

'I thought, maybe, since you know her…?'

'Who, Tash?' Luke raises his hands in a gesture of surrender. 'Look, Nevis, I'm gutted about Satnam, I really am, but a part of me thinks I shouldn't really get involved. It's a bit weird even being here to be honest.' He gazes into his can as if studying something there and a mottled redness spreads up from his neck. 'She dumped me, remember?'

'She dumped you?' Satnam had always told Nevis it was the other way around. She watches his lips press together tightly, and the redness finds its way to his eyes. He coughs. 'Uh *yeah*. She cheated on me then said she couldn't live with herself or something.'

Nevis is winded by this news. Satnam cheating?

'I know. Doesn't seem like her at all,' Luke said, off Nevis's expression. 'But I swear that's what she told me.'

'You don't know who with?'

'What fucking difference does it make?' He looks up at Nevis from under his eyelids. The effect is faintly menacing. 'I didn't mean... I'm upset.'

'No, I'm sorry. It was a stupid question. It's all a lot to take in.' A day ago she would have sworn that Satnam had never lied to her or kept secrets. And now, it's become evident she's done both.

Luke drains the can and bites his lip. Then putting his hands on the table in a gesture of finality, he says, 'Look, I should be going. But, you know, keep me posted, OK? And if there's anything I can do, just ask.'

Later, after Luke has left, and Nevis is in her room getting ready for bed, an email pings into Nevis's inbox. Thinking it's from Luke, she picks up her phone, taps through and sees Tash's name and below it her message:

So which of us is next?

Chapter 15

Cullen

On his way home Cullen very nearly runs over a fox. He's not his usual self at all. Turning into his road he spots a man walking out of his front gate and manages to pull the car to the kerb and turn off the lights without being seen. He waits until the man has got into his own vehicle further down the road and driven off. The same joker who was round earlier, no doubt. He dodged a bullet there. For a while anyway. He had hoped to be able to sit on his own in the living room and empty a generous four fingers of scotch into his belly but he can see now that the living-room lights are still on. Not only is Veronica awake, she's lying in wait, determined to get her claws into him before he'll be allowed to get some sleep.

'How was your mother?' she says, the silk of her dressing gown sliding across the polished surface of her thigh as she turns to look at him from her place on the sofa.

'Oh you know, annoying.'

She's not listening. She says, 'That man just came round again, the one who was on the driveway before.'

'Did you speak to him?'

'Of course not! I didn't even open the door. He was quite

persistent though.' She swivels her neck and shoots him a narrow-eyed stare. 'You're not in any trouble are you, darling?'

Cullen wonders if he can get away with ignoring Veronica's ban on hard drink while 'they' try to get pregnant and decides against it. He helps himself to a bottle of wine lying opened on the coffee table. 'No. It's just a...' Cullen roots around in his mind '...new broadband service. He doesn't seem to want to take no for an answer.'

'OK,' she says, unfurling her long legs, the soft blonde down on her upper thigh just visible in the lamplight.

He takes another gulp of the wine then sniffs it. 'What the hell is this?'

'That clever non-alcoholic stuff,' Veronica says. 'We don't want to put the troops off, do we?'

Afterwards Cullen drifts off to sleep and dreams about being alone on the bridge. He wakes with his heart ticking and his mind first on Satnam then remembering a conversation with Ratner not long ago when Mark admitted to sneaking out for early morning trysts under the guise of marathon training while his wife was fast asleep. Cullen doesn't trust the bastard one bit. The sly look on his face when Cullen asked him to be more discreet. He thinks about how the fucker lied to him. It takes a bold man to do that to another man's face when they both know that's what he's doing. Cullen wishes he'd read him the riot act when they last spoke. Why was he so moderate, so polite? What a dickhead I've been, he thinks. A man like Ratner needs dealing with.

Beside him Veronica sleeps on. He edges out of bed, careful not to disturb his wife lest she demand another tour of duty, grabs yesterday's clothes from the chair and slips out of the room. By 4.30 he's in the Volvo.

In a moment of inattention, he narrowly avoids zooming through a red light then finds himself speeding across a junction without looking, a truck driver angrily sounding his horn as he jams on the air brakes. Something dark and dormant is awakening in him. The old death wish blinking itself out of hibernation, he thinks, the seed of self-destruction pushing out a thin white shoot. For the remainder of the journey he does his best to focus his energies on driving.

I need a drink, he thinks, leaning over the passenger seat and opening the glove box. Pressing the mess of envelopes and bills to one side, he feels around for the quarter of Famous Grouse he always keeps for just such emergencies and, finding it, closes his fingers around it, rotating the metal screw-top between his teeth until it comes away and he can spit it out and hold the neck of the bottle to his mouth. A single drip makes its way onto his tongue. He holds the bottle out and shakes it, as if by doing that he could fill it up, but it remains empty. At a traffic light stop, he presses the window button and heaves the bottle out onto the pavement, finding solace in the crash of the glass as it splinters on the tarmac.

Sometimes, he thinks, I'd like to smash the whole fucking world.

Two men walk by, drunk, holding on to one another.

What the hell am I doing here, in the middle of the night? Then the light turns green and his foot jams the accelerator, leaving the question stranded at the lights for the next poor bugger to ask himself.

If only it were that easy to leave the moment of discovery

behind, but the event is tattooed on his brain. The awful humiliation of discovering Ratner and … well, her name hardly matters … in *his* lab in that … unmistakeable condition and him not having had a clue. Then, after the girl had fled, having to listen to Ratner's lies. It had never happened before, would never happen again, he loved his wife and kids, blah blah blah. Naturally he'd gone straight to the girl's records and there it was. The numbers never lie. Incontrovertible evidence that not only had Ratner been fucking the girl, but he'd been paying for her services. Natasha Tillotson was a poor student; Cullen had taught her in a remedial maths group last summer in which she'd had to be reminded of the basic principles of probability. But in every module run by Ratner she'd come out with a good 2:1. Combing through past examination results Cullen had picked up on a pattern of misbehaviour: perfectly unremarkable students – all female – who'd graduated with surprisingly high marks. He'd been head of the department for five years at that point and it had taken the encounter with Ratner for him to wake up to what had been going on under his nose. A terrible failure of oversight. It was his job to spot anomalies and extra-curricular activities. But he'd missed Mark Ratner's affairs, the uplifts in his favourites' grades, along with clear evidence that this had been going on for years. Why? He knew the answer to that too and it was another failing of his, he realised – a tendency to pay attention to the academic performance of only the really gifted students; boys (and it was, in his estimation, mostly boys) who reminded Cullen of himself.

He wonders if he should have moved against Ratner the moment he stumbled on him *in flagrante delicto* in his lab. He'd considered it. A decade ago, five years even, this would hardly have mattered. Faculty affairs with undergraduates were almost a perk of the job. But the landscape has changed post #MeToo. It would all calm down, of course, and revert back to normal eventually, but right now was not the time to be flagrantly flouting the rules. If he'd gone to Maddy back then she would have supported him so long as he had not put her own position in jeopardy. She would still support him now, but he wasn't convinced that she wouldn't report the infraction to the Board of Governors, if only to save her own skin if it all came out. The Board might well take a dim view of Cullen's management of his team and his failure to spot the anomalies in his students' grades.

Damn Ratner for putting him in this situation! Why doesn't he understand how serious it is? It's been going on so long he probably thinks himself invincible. A third possibility also comes to mind, more alarming than the other two. Maybe Ratner understands all too well the gravity of it and is working it for his own ends. From the moment Cullen got promoted above him, Ratner's resentment has festered like an open sore on an old dog. What if all this is part of an elaborate ploy to take Cullen down? Could Ratner be capable of such a thing? He'd ruin himself in the process but perhaps that would be a price he was prepared to pay in order to exact his revenge?

That can't happen. Cullen cannot allow that to happen. Especially not now. Not with Veronica hell-bent on starting a family. A voice in his head says, go home, you're tired and overwrought. Even if you do catch Ratner sneaking back from some early morning side hustle, no good will come of confronting him at home. But there's another voice in his head, reaching

98

up and out from the deep recesses of Cullen's past. The closer he gets to Ratner's house the louder it becomes until, turning into Ratner's road, it has become a raw, red scream.

Cullen sails past the corner shop and pulls up beside Ratner's driveway. His hands are shaking on the wheel. I must calm down, he thinks, or I'll run the risk of making a fool of myself. He turns and checks the house. Ratner's silver VW in the driveway. A light on in the porch, another in the hallway. All the upstairs curtains closed. He braces himself, takes a few calming breaths, but instead of feeling more resolute he experiences the heat draining out of him. I am so tired, he thinks. Perhaps a nap will help.

He wakes some time later, blinded and skewered to his seat. He blinks and turns into the light, which, he sees now, is coming from the headlights of the VW as it pulls out of Ratner's drive. Befuddled with sleep, he checks his watch. He's only been down for twenty minutes. It dawns on him that Ratner is on the move. In that instant the VW pulls forward and, fearing he'll be seen, Cullen ducks and at the same time reaches for the ignition key. The VW turns and moves down the street. Cullen follows at a distance, pressing himself into the seat so that his face is in shadow.

Ten minutes' drive away, Ratner turns down the steep slope of Marlborough Hill and makes a left onto one of the cul-de-sacs running parallel to the ridge. From here the only way out is for Ratner to come back the way he came. Cullen pulls the Volvo to the kerb, cuts the lights and the engine and gets out. The silver VW draws up to an ugly block of flats half-way along the street, a cheap piece of 1950s infill built to cover a former bomb crater, he supposes. In Cullen's experience the only real way to disguise a wound is to pretend it doesn't exist. That way no one else sees it either. Exposed and poorly dressed wounds make people vulnerable and Cullen doesn't like to be vulnerable. A light rain is falling now. Cullen ducks behind a hedge and watches. He doesn't have to wait long before a girl he recognises emerges from the flats and, pulling her coat over her hair, runs on heels to the waiting vehicle. The passenger door opens and the interior light goes. He sees Ratner lean over and fold the girl into an embrace.

Chapter 16

Nevis

The early morning rain has dried up. It is now clear and crisp and the streets smell of traffic fumes and coffee as Nevis makes her way towards the flats in Kingsdown where Tash lives. She'd asked Luke for Tash's address and he'd texted back immediately. He'd Ubered to a party there once so the address was still in his phone.

Nevis realises that Satnam has other friends. Obviously. From time to time she has brought them back to the flat for chips or pizza and Nevis would make a stab at joining in with the chit-chat or otherwise slink off to the library or to her room. But she has never got to know any of them well and had always assumed they were casual mates, fellow students whose company Satnam occasionally enjoyed. Nevis herself never felt the need to be friends with anyone but Satnam. Other people are too complicated. Until the night on the bridge she'd assumed that no one knew Satnam better than she did, but she's now wondering if Satnam has hidden corners that only her other friends have seen into.

She hikes up Marlborough Hill rehearsing an ideal script of the upcoming conversation in her head. It helps calm her nerves. The truth is she's a little afraid of Tash Tillotson. At the library she'd got the feeling that she was standing beside a death star or a black hole, something vast and scary that was in the process of collapsing in on itself. And then there was the email or, rather, both emails. What did Tash mean by saying she bet Nevis did know? What did Nevis supposedly know? And why would Tash imagine that someone could be next? Why would anyone be next? The girl was a mystery and mysteries of any kind set Nevis's teeth on edge.

Three-quarters of the way up the hill she takes a right and walks along a street of small stone houses to a block of flats. She makes her way through a riot of weeds to the main entranceway and presses the top bell. Moments after ringing it she hears a door swinging open upstairs. Then the hall light comes on and through the panelled glass of the front door a shadowy figure makes its way towards her. The door opens and in front of her stands Tash, smelling of weed and looking slightly flustered, her long brown hair tied in an unruly bun on the top of her head, looking as if she hasn't slept in days or, conceivably, weeks.

'I thought you were someone else or I wouldn't have come down,' Tash says, scanning the street this way and that.

'Do you mind if I come in?'

Hands on hips, eyeroll: 'If it's about those emails, I was drunk, OK?' A lip-suck followed by a repentant sigh. 'I shouldn't have sent them, sorry.'

'I'm trying to understand about Satnam. Why she did what she did.'

'What difference does it make?'

'Maybe none. But I like to be able to understand things.'

Tash's chest heaves but she stands aside for Nevis and leads her into a damp hallway and up the stairs to a small, messy flat with sad walls, undecorated except for a few band posters and a couple of incongruous landscape prints. The kitchen is a few worn cupboards, an old cooker and a cheap, half-sized fridge along one wall of the living room. The air smells of weed and bottled pasta sauce. Three empty cans of cheap lager on the coffee table in the living room suggest that others were here a while ago, but they are alone now. Music is playing on a Bluetooth speaker, something grimy. Not Nevis's bag.

Tash gestures to a chair and says, 'Want a beer? I'm having one.' Nevis sits and, blinking at the mess before her, says, 'Coffee, if you have it?'

'Oh, OK,' Tash says, sounding surprised, like drinking coffee in the late morning is an odd habit. She moves over to the kettle, fills it with water and takes a bottle of beer from the fridge, prying it open using the counter ledge as a bottle opener, then perches herself among the detritus on the sofa.

'My flatmates are still in bed so…' She tails off, leaving Nevis unsure what to make of the information. 'How's Satnam?' Tash says, peeling at the foil on the beer bottle.

'Probably still in a coma. I think I would have heard if anything had changed.' As she says this, Nevis wonders if it is true. Surely Narinder didn't hate her so much that they would keep all news of their daughter from her? But anyway there was evidently a mole at the hospital since it now seems to be general knowledge that Satnam had taken Ritalin.

Tash has stopped fidgeting and is looking genuinely shocked now. 'OMG, I didn't realise. I mean, on social it was just like, she took an overdose of Ritalin but she'll be OK.'

Nevis watches her face, wondering how you're supposed to

know whether or not you can trust people. She feels so heavy right now, like a rock.

Tash says, 'I don't know her that well. You realise that, right? We were both in Mark Ratner's seminar group last year but that's about it.'

The coffee tastes bitter and muddy and, above all, of sour milk.

'I didn't like that last email you sent me. I didn't like either of them, but I especially didn't like the last one.'

Tash's legs begin to jiggle. She takes a sip of her beer. 'I already said, I was drunk, OK? I was upset. It didn't mean anything.'

'Then why are you sending meaningless messages that upset people?'

'Jesus, Nevis, did anyone ever tell you you're a fucking pain?'

'Yes, at school, all the time.'

Tash's nose wrinkles. She sighs and meets Nevis's eye. Something there Nevis cannot read. Sympathy perhaps? 'That sounds shit, I'm sorry. Truth is, the thing with Satnam set off bad memories from something that happened back when *I* was at school. Like, at the end of year nine. In the summer holidays. My sister Alice had just finished her A levels. She was down at the lido every day with her mates. There was a big group of them. Jason, Sam, Fran, a few others, I can't remember all the names. After the lido closed they used to come round to our house 'cos my mum didn't care if they drank and smoked. Anyway, one morning the caretaker at the lido went in early to open up and found Jason at the bottom of the pool. He'd tied a gym kettle to his ankle. The next day Sam's parents find Sam hanging from a tree at the bottom of his garden. Then

Fran turns up in a local picnic spot having taken a load of pills. It was just like a hurricane hit or a tsunami or something. Alice broke down. She didn't go to uni that year, she didn't do anything for months except watch TV. She's still a lost girl.'

'That's awful. Did they ever get to the bottom of it?'

'Suicide contagion.'

'Like an epidemic?'

'I guess. They've always happened. Sometimes they call them copycat suicides. It's young people mostly, you know, after some rock star or celebrity or whatever kills themselves, or sometimes just randomly, like with Alice's friends. Nobody really knows why.' Tash puts her beer down on the side table.

'Like a cult?'

'One that no one realises they're in until it's too late.'

'But there's no evidence anyone else is going to try to kill themselves, is there?'

'No, no, I just… I suppose I thought you and Satnam are really close so she might have told you…' She tails off.

'Told me what?'

'Forget it.'

Nevis sits back in her chair, her hands grinding together in her lap. On the chair beside her, Tash, yawning and fiddling with her hair, says, 'Look, I really need to get some sleep, so…'

Determined not to leave until she has what she came for, Nevis brings up on her phone the Valentine's Day picture of Tash with Satnam and another girl. Tash peers at it for a moment or two, her breath quickening.

'Is this what you thought Satnam might have told me about? It was taken here, wasn't it?' Nevis says steadily. The moment she entered the living room, she'd spotted the sofa in the picture.

'One of my flatmates had a Valentine's Day party. So what?'

'That's Jessica with the two of you, right?' Tash peers, too obviously wanting to get it right. She knows more than she's saying, Nevis thinks.

'Yeah. Jessica Easton. She's in the year above us. I hardly know her either.' Biting her lip and turning her head away, Tash says, 'Look, I'm pretty tired, so...'

'The morning after that I found Satnam at the kitchen table, crying.'

Nevis watches Tash's expression change. Untucking her legs and rising from her seat, she says, 'I told you, I hardly knew Satnam. How would I know why she would have been crying?' There's a pause. 'Why are you looking at me like that?'

'I just thought...'

'Well don't,' Tash snaps. 'You're shit at it.' But she sits back down and taking out a clump of tobacco, dumps it into a paper. 'Sorry. I didn't mean it like that.' Nevis watches her elegant, manicured fingers roll herself a cigarette. 'You want one? It's only tobacco.'

'No, thanks.'

'Sunday night, before she... went to the bridge, she said she was thinking of leaving Avon. Later, at the bridge, she told me she'd had enough.'

Tash frowns and reaching over the table taps her rollie of ashes. She leans forward, the frown disappearing and the eyes turning inward, as if on the brink of some revelation, then, leaning back, she says, 'We've all felt like that sometimes, haven't we?'

'Did something happen at that Valentine's Day party?'

Tash shrugs and in a flat, empty voice says, 'Like I said, I was pissed.'

'You didn't say that.'

'Well, I'm saying it now.' She raises her eyes and sees Tash watching her, flushed and a little flustered. 'You think Satnam is some kind of mathematical equation and all you have to do is solve her and she'll wake up, is that it?'

'Yes,' says Nevis.

A peal of laughter escapes Tash's lips. 'You're hilarious.'

She takes the smoke into her lungs and holds it there for a moment before letting it out in rings. 'You've looked at her phone, obviously.'

'I don't know the passcode.'

'Bummer.' The rings grow smaller.

'We had a bit of a spat on Sunday evening and I left and went to the library. If I hadn't gone...'

Tash tilts her head and narrows her eyes. A frown appears on her otherwise smooth forehead. 'It's not your fault.'

'I was upset that she was saying she wanted to leave.'

'She probably just meant she was looking forward to graduating.'

'Maybe.' Perhaps this is all just about me, Nevis thinks, the way I don't seem to be able to understand people. 'But she also told me Luke broke up with her... but Luke said it was the other way around. She cheated on Luke and then dumped him.'

'One of them was lying, obviously. People lie all the time, Nevis.'

'I don't.'

Tash puts out her cigarette and begins to roll another and Nevis feels very young in her company. 'Anyway, none of that makes it your fault.' She catches Nevis's eye then looks away. Her jaw begins to work up and down on some gum. Silence falls. Nevis opens her mouth to speak but the words don't arrive in time. Tash rolls her eyes. 'Whatever you're about to say, just say it.'

'About that picture, the one at the Valentine's party.'

Tash spits the gum into her hand and sticks it under the table.

'If you must know, Jess and I had words. Satnam played peacemaker. That was all. It was about nothing. I can't even remember what it was about.'

'Why didn't you mention that before?'

'I've just said, it was nothing.'

There comes a ping. Gathering herself, Tash reaches for her phone and reads, her eyes growing bright, a half-smile appearing on her face. She taps a couple of words in return and, turning to Nevis, says, 'Listen, good to talk and that, but I need to be somewhere.'

'Now?' Nevis says, unable to hide her surprise.

'Yes, now, as in right away,' Tash says, hurriedly, rising and bidding Nevis to do the same. Nevis stands and, slipping on her coat, reaches for her backpack.

It's still clear and crisp outside now. A pair of Canada geese fly over, cackling, then disappear. At the street corner Nevis feels her legs break into a run and she does not stop until she reaches the entrance to the flat above the chippy. She plugs in the entrance code. The door lock clicks and there is an instant when she thinks she can see the figure of a woman standing in the hallway. Then it's gone and all that remains is a faint smell of something Nevis recognises but cannot place.

Inside the flat, she moves over to the sofa, picks up Satnam's pink throw and wraps herself inside, letting it warm her body. The strong sense that neither Luke nor Tash have been quite straight sits with her. Perhaps she too might learn how to lie. Just as she did to the policewoman at the hospital but better, more complete. The time may come when she needs to. Something is shifting inside her. It began six months ago when she stumbled across a secret held inside the pages of the *Children's Book of Greek Myths* which Honor had kept on her bookshelf all those years. Back then the understanding woke in her that all the old stories Honor had told her and that she had told herself would require revisiting and that nothing was as it had once seemed.

People lie all the time, Tash had said.

Well isn't that the truth?

Chapter 17

Cullen

Ratner pokes his head around the door of the Dean's office. 'You called?'

'Come in and close the door.' Cullen has stationed himself in his office chair so he's partially obscured by his computer monitor. His face has come out in blotches and he doesn't want Ratner to see.

'You all right? You look a bit sweaty,' Ratner says, taking a seat.

'As it happens, I am not all right. Nor are you, by the way, because *my* shit is about to hit *your* fan.' He watches as Ratner's eyes float across his desk to the Airblade in the corner. Not the sharpest tool in the box, Cullen thinks to himself, but most definitely a *tool*.

'Perhaps you think that because I'm ten years younger than you I'm a decade stupider, in which case I might remind you that you're in the office of your superior.'

'I'm well aware of that,' Ratner says, stiffening. Evidently, he is surprised by Cullen's tone.

'What did I say about your sordid little activities?'

Ratner lurches backwards then gathers himself and says, 'You said to be careful.'

'I told you to knock it off. Completely, I said. You think you can lie to me, you little fucker, but you're spectacularly mistaken. And very, very stupid. Am I making myself plain?' Cullen is aware that his face is now scarlet but he doesn't care. He has never spoken to anyone like this before and it feels good. Primal. Powerful. Like taking a piss in the long grass. In the visitor chair on the other side of the desk Ratner blinks and clears his throat, the look of bewilderment transforming bit by bit into indignation, the way a chameleon's skin switches colour.

'Hang on a minute...' Ratner says, raising his hands in a gesture of surrender.

Just then Tina pops her head through the door. Cullen looks her way and raises his eyebrows questioningly. 'Professor Cullen, your next is in ten.' She smiles and with a nod disappears round the door. He waits until he hears the latch click into its keeper.

'Tell me, is a blow job in the back of the car worth losing your marriage over? Your reputation? Your career?'

'*What?*' Ratner says, outraged. Cullen lets out a bleak laugh as he sees light dawning on Ratner's face. 'You were *spying* on me?' Ratner gasps. A hand goes to his mouth.

'A little airless up there on the moral high ground, is it?'

'Look...'

'I suppose you've considered what's likely to happen if your paramour blabs?' Cullen says.

'She won't,' Ratner blusters. 'Anyway, *she* came on to *me*. She keeps her trap shut about this and she graduates from Avon without any scandal hanging over her. She doesn't throw thirty grand of student debt down the drain. She's no Einstein but she's not stupid. So she and I had a fling. No one cares.'

'Your wife might, if I told her.'

Ratner swallows, hard.

'And the Board of Governors might be prepared to overlook an affair, but they'd have something to say about you inflating a student's grades in return for sexual favours.'

He watches the colour drain from Ratner's face. At last, in a quiet voice, he says, 'How did you find out?'

'Let's just say I'm not stupid, shall we?'

'OK, OK.' Ratner is shocked now, Cullen can see, and a hint of resignation has crept into his voice, but he isn't quite out yet. Any moment now he's going to rally and try to make a case for himself. It's like watching a bull in the ring, half broken and bloodied with banderillas, taking a deep breath before going in for the final charge.

'And Mark?' he says, intimately.

'Yes?'

'I have a wife and mortgage to support. I also happen to like my career. I want you to consider that everything you do reflects on me. So if you don't stop, and I mean completely cease, seeing that girl, I will kill you.'

Chapter 18

Honor

Honor blinks into the dark, puzzled by the unfamiliar surroundings, remembering moments later that she is lying on the mattress in Gerry the van. That explains why she can't feel her fingers and toes. Even the boat never gets quite this cold. She checks her watch. It is still early, but going back to sleep now will be impossible. Sliding out of her sleeping bag, she clambers into the driver's seat and starts the engine, watching her breath condensing on the windscreen. Pressing her palms against the air grills she waits for the hot air to blow away the night chill and hopes that Bill's contact comes good with his offer of a place on a boat. No way could she stay in the van for long in this weather.

At a nearby McDonald's she pays for a coffee and a McMuffin with what little remains in her purse and uses the toilets to wash and change into the charity shop formal tweeds and green shirt. Emerging from the cubicle, she checks herself in the mirror. How is a thirty-nine-year-old woman supposed to present herself? It's so long since she's had to make a good first impression. A few parent–teacher days and the odd meeting with the school head to talk about Nevis's progress and her eccentricities. She rarely goes out socially and when she does it's only ever with other bargees, who are a casual to casual-scruffy bunch. Most of her business in the very specialised world of narrowboat renovation and repair is repeat custom so no clients to impress and no requirement to dress up when you spend most of your day covered in engine grease.

Leaving the van in the McDonald's car park she walks a few metres down the road to a supermarket, checks her bank balance at the ATM and takes out her last £100, using some of it in the store to buy toiletries, underwear and a bottle of hair tamer that promises to ease her frizz. She takes a bus towards the Harbourside, exiting beside the M-Shed Museum. Unlike the canalside in Honor's part of Hackney Wick, which has steadfastly resisted gentrification, at Harbourside you can barely move for artisan coffee shops or vegan bakeries selling four-quid loaves. The things that give harbours their proper quality – namely boats – have been relegated to a section on the eastern side of the Floating Harbour near Redcliffe Bridge. Heading east she soon leaves the cafés behind and the further she goes, the scruffier and more anarchic the view becomes. Ten minutes' walk from the M-Shed the towpath narrows, its tarmac coat split and pitted and charming in a rackety way, like an old man in a ragged overcoat sunning his face on a bench, and a modest tent city reveals itself, the bivvies lined up along the walls of an abandoned factory. There a handful of inhabitants warm themselves on a giant brazier. How inviting it looks! A sudden reminder of the magical parts of her child-hood. Push comes to shove, I can buy a cheap tent and stay here, Honor thinks.

The *Helene* sits at berth not far from the bridge,

a forty-five-foot steel huller of pre-credit-crunch vintage, with a semi-trad fit-out. It is 8.45 a.m. and smoke is drifting up from a wood burner below deck, the chimney liner worn from many years of use suggesting the *Helene* is a proper live-onboard, not a hobbyist vessel or a rich person's plaything. She calls out. A moment later a tousled head appears in the hatch and a windburned face looks up at her and smiles, exclaiming, 'You're Bill's friend!'

Honor introduces herself, wishing her hair looked better and that there were no stains on her clothes and that they weren't so obviously from a charity shop.

The man introduces himself as Alex Penney, and making a sweeping motion with his hand, says, 'I've just put the kettle on *and* done the washing up. Come aboard and we'll celebrate with a cuppa.'

They chat about boats for a while. Alex is perhaps late forties, fit, with an air of playfulness and a bargee's hard-working, sausage-fingered hands.

'She's a beauty,' says Honor, looking around. 'You named her after Helen of Troy?'

He smiles and raises his eyebrows.

'The classical education didn't go completely to waste then. I'm a bit rusty, now, though,' Honor says, taking the seat Alex offers her, folding her arms across her chest to make the egg stain on the shirt less visible.

'Aren't we all?' Alex says cheerfully. 'Bill told me you need somewhere to crash for a while.'

'Yes, I have a ... project,' she says, and realising immediately how vague and evasive that sounds, adds, 'Research.'

'Aha. Anything interesting?'

'Maybe. I've a way to go yet.'

'There's a boat a little further down the Floating Harbour. *Halcyon Days*. The owners had a sitter lined up but they were let down at the last minute. They'd rather have someone there for security.'

'*Halcyon Days*. What a coincidence!' When Nevis was young, Honor would read to her from a children's book of Greek myths. Her favourite was Alcyone, daughter of the god of the wind, whom Zeus turned into a kingfisher after her husband Ceyx, son of Lucifer, was drowned at sea. 'Our boat up in London is the *Kingfisher*.'

'Our...?'

'My daughter and I.'

'Oh.' She watches a smile appear on his face, the lines at the corners of his eyes deepening.

'Do you have kids?'

'A son. He's grown up now.' There's a pause during which words fall away, then patting his thighs as if about to stand up, Alex goes on, 'The boat is a minute's walk away. Why don't we go and take a look at her?'

They make their way along the waterfront past mostly unoccupied boats and arrive at a sixty-footer trad with a cratch cover and a smart red trim, the name painted in black and gold.

Alex jumps aboard and holds a hand out to Honor who, surprising herself, takes it. 'They winterised before they left, but I assume you can deal with that...?'

'Fresh fuel, coolant, water.'

'Check the batteries.'

'Radiators?'

'Burner only.'

The fit-out below deck is less Halcyon Days and more Has Seen Better Days, but there is a dual-fuel stove and a kitchenette, the master bedroom is at the stern, a configuration Honor prefers, and someone has fitted cupboards in the engine cubby. It feels right.

'As you can see, she needs some TLC. The bulkhead panelling could do with a strip down and revarnish. And there's a couple of other bits and pieces, depending on how long you need to stay. The owners said they'd waive rental in return for maintenance. How does that sound?'

Alex throws the keys in the air and catches them again.

'Brilliant,' Honor says.

'Want to think about it?'

'I don't need to.'

Alex looks pleased and relieved. 'So when would you like to move in?'

'No time like the present.'

He laughs and, teasing the keys from his ring, hands them to her. 'I'll leave you to settle in. I'm usually on the *Helene*. Drop by and let me know how you're getting on.'

Once he's gone, she calls Bill and passes on the news.

'Alex seems nice,' she says.

'Oh does he?' Bill says. She decides to ignore the edge in his voice.

'Listen, Bill, I'm going to need to rent out the *Kingfisher*. Not for cruising. Just for someone who wants to stay put for a while. A fellow bargee. I don't suppose...'

'Consider it done. How long for?'

'At least until the end of the university year, say three months?' Whatever happens to Satnam she has to be here for Nevis.

It takes her a few hours to do the basic de-winterising of the *Halcyon Days* then another couple to give the place a good clean. By lunchtime she is more or less done. She sits at the little table in the saloon and thinks about texting Nevis then decides to wait until she has been to see the head of student welfare at Avon and has something concrete to say.

At two she sets off walking. Outside the sun has emerged pale and lovely. The Avon campus lies just northwest of the city centre in Redland, beside the Downs, a good forty-five-minute walk from the Floating Harbour.

At the student welfare office, an administrator shows her to a seat in a small waiting area. At three precisely, a woman in her fifties, salt and pepper hair, bright patterned dress, big artsy glasses and the whisperings of a moustache emerges from another room and comes over, hand outstretched.

'Mrs Smith, I'm Dr Keane.'

Honor holds out a hand and hopes the doctor will not notice that underneath the tweed Oxfam trousers she is wearing floral DMs, it having slipped her mind that a professional outfit might require more professional shoes.

'I'm terribly sorry but it's rather a busy day. I've only got a few minutes. If you could make an appointment to come back...?'

'That's fine, it'll only take a few minutes.'

She watches Keane fluster.

'Well, I suppose...'

'That's so kind of you,' Honor says, sweeping into Keane's office before she changes her mind. 'My daughter Nevis was – is – Satnam Mann's flatmate. Went with her in the ambulance. I wanted to see you because, obviously, she's very shaken by what happened and I want to be sure the university will keep an eye on her. You haven't spoken to her, I suppose?'

'Not yet. As I said, it's all been rather busy.'

'Nevis left Satnam on her own Sunday evening so she's blaming herself for what happened.'

'I see.'

'I'm trying to understand why Satnam might have done this so I can reassure my daughter it wasn't her fault and hopefully to prevent other similar things happening in future. That's what we all want, isn't it?'

'Of course, Mrs Smith. But since none of us is able to speak with Satnam directly, our position at the university is to support her parents. They seem pretty convinced that the episode was an accident.'

'Satnam took a ton of pills and drank a bottle of vodka then walked out of her apartment in Kingsdown and ended up two miles away on the suspension bridge trying to climb the suicide barrier. What part of that story sounds like an accident?'

'Perhaps she took a taxi, we don't know.'

A taxi? This is crazy. Why is Dr Keane even talking this way?

'But that doesn't make any sense.'

Keane stands, her face flushed. 'I'm sorry but I am very pressed for time.'

'Why are you insisting on something that's patently untrue? My daughter was there.'

'My point exactly, Mrs Smith. Why would anyone intent on ending their life ask someone to call their friend to come and pick them up?'

'It wasn't like that!'

'Were you there? No, I didn't think so. We're very used to

students in stressful positions and we'll offer your daughter all the support we can but you need to allow us to do our jobs.' She stands, brushes herself down with a hand, and gesturing to the door says, 'Now, please, if you don't mind, I have a great deal to be getting on with.'

Chapter 19

Nevis

Nevis wakes to the sound of oil barrels being moved in the backyard at Cod's Plaice. She rubs her eyes and checks the time. The strange thought rises up that everything that has happened since the incident on the bridge has been part of some sinister waking dream. Pushing herself from the bed she goes out into the hallway and, taking a deep breath, lets herself into Satnam's room. The space still buzzes with an odd energy that Nevis can't quite put her finger on. The only way she can think of it is to imagine that someone has dropped a stone and the dying tremor of the last ripple is still reverberating through the walls. Or perhaps the walls themselves are trying to speak. She feels sweaty and panicked. She wonders if she's losing it. Am I going mad?

Backing from the bedroom and closing the door behind her she moves quietly and swiftly through the flat, checking each room in turn, looking round corners and behind the doors, like a kid checking the bedroom for monsters. There is something but she cannot work out what. Her head feels sluggish and unrested and in her belly a fluttering has started up. She wonders now if she's eaten since last night. Perhaps coffee will help. But the moment she enters the kitchen area, she feels it again. Not a smell exactly, nor a change in the light, something more like presence, a thickening of the air, as if someone has only an instant before left the room. She holds her breath and waits for the feeling to pass then reaches for the kettle.

The caffeine hits hard and for the first time in a few hours normality sets in. She remembers now that her wave modelling coursework is due and she's nowhere near finishing it so she takes her mug over to the table and reaches for her laptop to tap out a quick email to Mark Ratner requesting a deadline extension and is startled to see an email from the Dean.

Nevis, in view of recent events, it may be a good idea for you to come in and discuss your academic progress. Would 4 p.m. today be convenient?

She types out a reply, her fingers trembling on the keyboard. The Dean! She's been to his lectures, of course, and sat in seminars with him, once even had a face-to-face tutorial and nearly died of fright. He told her she was talented, which made her heart burst from its box, and he'd be watching out for her but he had never taken any more interest in her after that. Whenever she had seen him, either at lectures or, more usually, rushing along the corridors in the mathematics building or in the Deanery, she'd tried to catch his eye in the hope that he would remember his undertaking but he never so much as glanced her way. The prospect of being together with him in a room in her current weird, disconnected state to discuss something other than mathematics is so daunting it makes her throat hurt. But she can hardly say no and so she replies and presses 'send' and the email whooshes off and she sits in the stillness of the room for a moment, conscious that her life has already changed in ways that she may not ever come back from. Maybe that's what the feeling is about. It's not the flat that has changed but something inside her that has subtly and irrevocably altered, in the same way it did back in the summer, when she found the letter. Perhaps life consists of such moments, she thinks, until a person is so changed that she no longer recognises herself. Perhaps that's what happened to Satnam.

She turns on her phone. There is a text from Honor that feels surprisingly welcome.

How are you?

She texts back OK but stops short of a suggestion to meet. The discovery of the letter broke something between them. In the first few days afterwards she looked for ways to approach Honor and tell her what she'd found and what she felt about it but she could never quite summon the courage. And so she said nothing but watched herself filling up like a boat overwhelmed in a storm, bailing so hard that she could no longer feel where she ended and the hurt began, wishing away the days until it was time to go back to Bristol and she could right herself and forget the discovery for a while. The scheme worked. Once she was back and fully engaged in her coursework, the letter lost some of its power and neither seemed so vital nor so urgent. The hurt crystallised and a little of it turned to anger, which made it more bearable somehow, but she hadn't gone home at Christmas, afraid of blurting out something that might sink them both. As the months passed it became harder and harder to broach the topic. And so it floated through her inner world, like a great iceberg, a still, silent thing to be steered around and at all costs undisturbed.

Anxious now not to remain alone in the flat, she packs her laptop and a notebook in her daypack and makes her way to the bus stop outside the chippy and there waits for the bus to the campus. A woman lifts her tiny dog from the seat beside her and places it on her lap.

'Are you a student?' the woman says, smiling.

'Yes,' Nevis says.

'At the old university?'

'No, Avon.'

'Wasn't it one of yours who caused that ruckus on the bridge on Sunday? I heard they had to close the bridge to traffic for hours. You youngsters these days never think about anyone but yourselves.'

The little dog begins to growl. The woman does not speak to her again. A little further on, the bus stops to change drivers and the whole journey takes longer than it would have done to walk.

Chapter 20

Cullen

The bleep of the internal phone jolts Cullen awake. Asleep on the job, not like him at all. All those disturbed nights dealing with Amanda and last night, when he did finally drop off, a series of frantic, scratchy dreams. When he looks up his eyes fall on the Victorian etching of his alma mater that he'd put up on the wall beside his desk. Somewhere in the recesses of his mind he hears his mother's voice, all those years ago, as he left their tiny, rented flat, hot-eyed and miserable, to walk to the freshers' orientation. *Don't wipe your nose on your shirt sleeve.* A fifteen-year-old kid in a college built for adults. The memory makes his heart shrink a little. He comforts himself by imagining the feel of her fingers drawing through his hair. *My darling little boy.*

There comes a knock on the door.

'One moment.' He checks his watch, remembers the pre-arranged meeting and brings up Nevis Smith's file on his screen. Strange, quiet thing, otherworldly almost, but intensely academic. The only dead cert for a first in mathematical biosciences in the year. A gifted mathematician but otherwise of interest only in so far as what she might or might not know about Satnam Mann.

He wonders if Nevis Smith has Satnam's phone. Not that he's overly worried about it. No more than a four out of ten, but you never know.

Cullen arranges his features into an expression of repose and calls, 'Please do come in!' The door slides open and the girl enters. She looks tired and strung out.

'Take a seat. Can I get you a coffee?'

She comes over to the desk, sits down in the visitor's chair, lays her rucksack on the floor by her feet as if offering it protection at the same time as Cullen rises to get the coffee. She does not smile and in the fragility of her composure he senses bewilderment and guesses that all this high emotion has been difficult for her to process or perhaps to understand. Keane has told him that Nevis's mother has been in touch, worried about her daughter.

Placing a cup of coffee beside her he resumes his seat. 'How are you doing?'

'I'm OK.'

'Rather shaken up I should imagine.'

She bites her lip and with some reluctance says, 'I'm fine. Like I told student welfare, I'm, you know...' She tails off.

'We are very concerned about Satnam's welfare, obviously, but also about you,' Cullen continues. 'I'm sorry to put you through it again, but could you help me understand what happened that day? I'd like to understand for myself, to make sure we find the best way to support your studies. You are such a gifted student and I wouldn't want this to set you off course.' He waits until she has absorbed this, before going on, 'Start from the beginning.'

'I woke up at 8.36 a.m.'

He holds up a hand to stay her and offers up a reassuring smile. 'Maybe not *literally* from the beginning. Perhaps from earlier that evening, say?'

'Oh,' she says, sounding surprised, 'Well, OK then.' She goes on to relate how she and Satnam had had an awkward conversation and Nevis had gone to the library only to return a few hours later and go straight to her room. At that point Satnam's door was closed and there was no light on and Nevis assumed she was asleep. The phone call had come out of the blue.

'If I hadn't gone to the library...'

'You mustn't blame yourself,' he says, then picking his way, adds, casually, 'You say you had a difficult conversation?'

'Yes, Satnam told me she wanted to leave Avon.'

Cullen's pulse quickens. He blinks hard to try to steady himself. 'Any idea why?' he says, his voice hard and splintery.

She shakes her head and he hears himself breathe out heavily.

'So no idea what might have precipitated this, then?'

'Not really.'

He closes his eyes, drinking in the surge of freedom coursing through his body. Thank Christ, I'm in the clear. *Nevis doesn't know.*

'Good...' He stops himself and rephrases, 'I mean, naturally, you probably had other things on your mind.'

'Yes.'

He observes her quietly for a moment or two as she sips her coffee.

'And what's on your mind now?'

She looks up, worried. 'I'm scared it might happen again.'

He frowns. 'Why would you think that?'

Nevis launches into a long explanation of suicide contagion most of which Cullen is already familiar with. He nods along and every so often interjects with, 'I am aware,' but the girl keeps on all the same. By the end Cullen is left wishing he'd never asked. The girl simply did not seem to realise that he no longer wanted to hear her rambling explanation. Absolutely no off button on her. Such an oddball.

'We're here to ensure the safety of all our students,' he says blandly, smiling and doing his best to get her attention but he can see she has drifted off somewhere.

A few moments pass, then, suddenly looking up from her coffee, Nevis says, 'I'm hoping to run some models. My aim is to determine the likelihood that another student might do something similar, based on the probability that the spread of suicide ideation – via various means of communication – increases as the number of suicides rises. I think I might be able to determine a threshold condition for a potential epidemic. Once I've got that, then the total probable size of an epidemic can be calculated. But it means I might be late with my coursework on deep vent modelling which is supposed to be handed in to Dr Ratner in…' she checks her watch '…forty-five hours and twenty-seven minutes.'

'Are you all right?' Cullen asks, almost genuinely concerned.

She bites her lip again. Oh, now Cullen sees it. She is doing her best to keep herself together. He supposes that the maths helps somehow.

But first he needs to find out what else she knows.

'Let's not get ahead of ourselves. To go back to Satnam, you have no ideas about what led up to this? What made her say she wanted to leave? Family problems? Workload? Boyfriend? Nothing on her phone?' He holds his breath.

She shrugs. 'She had a boyfriend, Luke, but she broke up with him months ago. Since then she's just been focusing on her work. She goes to the library a lot. Except...' She tails off. A bead of sweat rises up on Cullen's forehead. He wipes it away.

'Except what?'

'I'm there 24.66 hours a week on average and I haven't seen her there.'

'I see.' He doesn't like the direction the conversation is taking. He wants Nevis to tell him what she knows without raising questions of her own. 'As you might know, Satnam took a catch-up class with me last summer. I've been seeing her on and off since then to make sure she stays caught up. I can attest to her increased output. She'd been working hard.'

'Oh, OK.' Nevis looks unconvinced.

'But if we had her phone?' he goes on, with the most casual tone he can muster.

'It's passcode protected.'

'Do you know where it is? There was a suggestion it had been lost.'

'Oh.' She compresses her lips and falls silent.

He changes tack again. 'You've probably also heard that Satnam's parents are saying what happened was an accident?'

'Yes,' she says.

'And what do you think about that?'

'Probability close to zero.'

'You are aware, I suppose, that an amount of Ritalin was found in Satnam's blood? A great deal of alcohol too.'

She nods.

'From what I understand, a combination of that particular drug when taken with alcohol can lead to all kinds of mental confusion, hallucinations even. Satnam might have thought she was going somewhere quite different from the bridge.'

He watches her make a mental calculation and then the lines on her face appearing. 'If it was an accident why would she have taken so many pills? And she doesn't usually drink, or not much anyway.'

'I don't think you've quite understood,' Cullen says, pressing the point. 'The studies I've read show that delusions can come on very rapidly and at low levels. It's the combination rather than the quantity that's the important parameter here.' He observes her face as she considers this, sees the mental effort tighten her jaw. 'It's perfectly possible that she washed down a couple of Ritalin with a vodka shot just to enhance her studies and the effects of combining meant she lost track of her consumption, so she just kept taking them. I think that's what her parents meant when they said it was an accident.'

'I don't know,' Nevis says, looking unconvinced.

'Really? Because that seems the most plausible explanation to me,' Cullen says. 'We've had similar cases before.' He picks up Nevis's coffee cup and, sensing he's got as much out of her as he can, and done a good job planting the idea – which would absolve her of the guilt she clearly feels – that the whole incident was an accident, offers her a closed smile to signal that the meeting is at an end.

'Should I wash that up?' she says.

'That won't be necessary.' Tina will oblige. 'You'll let me know if you come across anything that might shed some more light? Probably best to go through me rather than student welfare.' He cracks open his lips. 'I'll have a word with Dr Ratner about getting you a coursework extension. One of us will email.'

'Which one?' she says.

'Does it matter?'

'Yes.'

'Then it'll be me. I'll email you.'

He waits until she has gone then closes his eyes and blows a sigh of relief. That went as well as it could. For now the ship is off the rocks. He'll need to keep an eye on Nevis Smith in case the weather turns.

Chapter 21

Honor

When Honor next passes by the *Helene*, Alex, who is sitting in the cratch having a smoke, waves and shouts, 'Everything OK?'

'Lovely thank you!' Damn, her hair is a bird's nest and she'd been hoping Alex wouldn't spot her. What a beautiful city Bristol is, but this determined rain... Does it never stop? Or not rain even, more like mist. It licks her hair into the most terrible frizz. She pushes it back, then immediately regrets the action, remembering that it was covering a hole in the shirt she'd bought from Oxfam which she hadn't seen until she'd left Lea Keane's office. And then there are those tweed trousers with the floral DMs. I look sad and a bit mad, she thinks, sighing. About right then.

Alex puts out his cigarette. 'Fancy a coffee?'

Oh absolutely, Honor does, but she can't, not now, not looking like this and not with all this on her mind.

'Probably should be getting on,' she says. 'But another time would be lovely.'

'Need anything for the work on the boat? As I expect you've discovered there's not a lot on the *Halcyon*. Hobbyists, not serious boat people.'

'Yes, yes, thank you.' She keeps all her own tools out of sight of prying eyes on the boat and only puts them in the van to transport them to and from a job. She can't bring herself to tell him that she hasn't thought about the boat yet.

Alex is standing on deck with his hands on his hips. 'I've got a load of stuff here you're welcome to use if you want to take a quick look?'

He holds out a hand and to her surprise – because she is always so meticulous about no special treatment, has found over the years of working on boat engines that it's the only way to be taken seriously in that world – she takes it and steps on board. He has a toolbox and supplies cupboard in the stern beside the pump.

'So,' he says, 'anything useful?'

She casts an eye over the box. 'I'm not sure. That rachet spanner? And some marine sandpaper. I won't really know until I start.'

'Well feel free to use whatever you want.' He turns and gestures towards the saloon. 'Now, how's about that coffee after all?'

He moves into the saloon, pulls out a spare chair and invites her to sit beside the wood stove before turning his attention to the galley.

'This interior is gorgeous,' she says, admiring the gleaming wooden floorboards and the fitted shelves stuffed with books, the glorious old brass ship's light beside the stove.

'Thank you. It was a labour of love. Kept me sane after I was made redundant.'

'Oh, I'm sorry. I realise I haven't asked what your profession is, or was?'

'Hack,' he says, 'if you can call that a profession. Worked on local newspapers in the Midlands mostly. These days I get by doing websites, that kind of thing. Not inspiring but pays the bills.' He brings over a worn stove-top espresso maker and two cups. 'What about you? Bill told me almost nothing except that you're a whizz with boats. You mentioned a research project?'

'Yes, yes. I'm...' She finds herself hesitating, put on the spot. Should she come clean? 'I'm looking into a suicide, an attempted suicide.'

'Any particular reason?' he says, taken aback.

Ahead, in the near future, she can already see a thicket of lies and misunderstandings. Better to come clean now.

'My daughter, Nevis...'

'...named for the island or the mountain?'

'The mountain. Her birth mother Zoe's favourite place.'

'Sooo...' Alex says, sounding unsure of himself.

'Zoe was a great friend of mine and when she died, nineteen years ago, I adopted Nevis.'

'That must have been very difficult.'

'It was an easy decision but other people made it difficult.' She tells him how Zoe's parents had sued for custody, though they had never visited Nevis or even asked after her, how they'd wanted Zoe to abort her. Finally she relates the events of Sunday evening. He listens attentively, rocking very slowly on his heels, as if he were a spinning wheel onto which she was feeding twine.

'So the real reason I'm here is because I want to be close to my daughter while this is going on.'

'I see,' he says, then brightening, adds, 'Look, if you want her to stay on the boat with you, I'm sure...'

Honor shakes her head. 'Thank you, but she wouldn't come,

not now. Something happened between us. I honestly have no idea what it was, but Nevis has been really distant with me since then.'

'Oh God, teenagers,' Alex says.

She smiles and allows the expression to fade slowly. 'There's something else too.' She relates the meeting with Lea Keane. 'I can't get my head around why the university is trying to pretend what happened on Sunday was an accident.'

'Aren't they just being cautious? Especially if that's what the parents are saying. I should imagine it's all rather sensitive.'

'Could be, but there was something evasive about the welfare woman I spoke to. As if she felt as uncomfortable about the situation as I did but wasn't willing to say.' She pats her thighs and, standing to leave, says, 'Anyway, it might be nothing, but let's say I've come across this kind of thing before. Just because it's a hallowed educational institution, a university isn't above covering up a crime to protect its reputation.'

'*Crime?*' He's shocked, she can tell, but not disbelieving. Journalists must come across that kind of thing all the time. 'Well, if I can do anything to help?'

'You just did,' she says.

He stands and follows her up the stairs onto the deck. 'Come for supper later if you like. I make a none-too-shabby spag bol.'

'That would be lovely.'

'Seven then.' He takes a step back and lowers his head under the cratch. 'Oh, and, Honor, from an old hack and at the risk of teaching you to suck eggs, best not broadcast your suspicions. Not yet anyway. Universities have deep pockets and lawyers. But it sounds like you already know that.'

She smiles and says nothing.

Chapter 22

Nevis

Nevis finds Jessica Easton where Tash said she'd be: on a cross-trainer in the gym. She is thinner and more nervy looking in the flesh. Her phone is balanced on the dashboard of the trainer and she is gazing at something on the screen with a blank expression on her face. Nevis approaches, waving. Jessica frowns and slows to a halt, twists an earbud from her right ear.

'Yes?'

'It's about Satnam.'

A shadow moves across Jessica's face. She reaches for her phone, taps at the screen, and says, 'Satnam's not...'

'No. I think they'd tell me.' More to the point, perhaps, it would be all over social media.

'I thought I'd be able get it out of my head here, but...' Jessica dabs at her hairline with a small white towel. 'You're Nevis, aren't you?'

'Yes.' Nevis has seen the girl at a couple of lectures, she realises, but their paths haven't crossed otherwise.

'I heard you were at the bridge when it happened...'

Jessica says, clutching the towel. Another student approaches, gestures to the machine. 'OK, yes, sorry.' Jessica picks up her phone and steps off the cross-trainer.

The two women move away towards the edge of the room. 'I spoke to Tash,' Nevis says.

'I know, she texted me.' Twisting the towel in her sinewy hands, Jessica says, 'Look, Nevis, what exactly is it you think I can help you with?'

'I'm just trying to figure out why Satnam did what she did. Did she seem OK to you?'

Jessica looks down. 'You don't think she's going to be, like, brain damaged or anything?'

'It's possible.' Nevis has thought about this, considered the probabilities, but without coming to any conclusions. Satnam could die, she knows that much, and that is enough weight to carry.

Jessica sighs. 'I don't know what you've been told but at the end of the day, Tash was *way* out of line with how she acted towards Satnam. We had no idea Satnam would actually, like, do anything like *this*, though, we really didn't.'

'Is this about the Valentine's Day party?'

Jessica looks up, suddenly wary. 'Yeah. What did Tash tell you about that?'

'That you two had an argument about something and Satnam tried to make it better.'

'*Better*. Duh, no, I don't think so.' She checks herself. 'So Tash didn't tell you then?'

'She said she was drunk and couldn't remember. I was hoping you might.'

Jessica holds up her bottle. Nevis follows her to the water

fountain, waits while she leans in and presses the tap. 'Oh, you know, not much, chatting shit… stuff…'

'Can you be more specific?' Nevis has the distinct feeling that she's being fobbed off.

Standing up straight now, the water bottle in her hand, Jessica says, 'Tash had just started seeing an ex of mine which I thought was pretty disloyal. I mean, I would never do anything like that.' She raises the bottle to her lips. Nevis watches the cords in Jessica's neck moving. 'Satnam got in the middle. She wanted to… well, let's just say she wanted to tell this guy's wife. You know, spill the beans. But it was, like, whatever.'

'Satnam didn't say anything about being depressed or wanting to leave Avon, did she?'

Jessica wipes the back of her hand across her mouth. 'Oh yeah. We *all* wanted to leave, you know?'

So Satnam had talked to Tash and Jess about this, but not to her – not until last Sunday. She feels winded, suddenly, and sad. Over the months of their friendship she'd supposed Satnam had told her everything, all her secrets, her desires, her deepest fears. She's only just learning how much she does *not* know and the experience is baffling and painful.

'Why?'

'When our grades started falling we should have read the runes and gone home. Like after the summer and that shitty maths course we were forced to do. But it was just, like, impossible.' She has her back to the wall, pressing into its hard surface with her hands. She has pushed her sleeve up and on her skin, furred as a cat's, a side effect of the anorexia eating her alive, Nevis spots the tracks from cutting. 'Our parents would have killed us. Tash is the great hope of the family and Satnam's parents were hassling her to get married and whatever and I knew mine would go mental. They're high-flyer medic types. Dad says I'm the only bulb in the family with a dimmer switch. So, you know…'

Nevis waits for the stream of chatter to subside. 'Satnam was doing much better this term.'

'Well, yeah, for *now*. But, honestly, how much longer was that likely to last? I was doing brilliantly last term but now I'm back to failing everything.'

Feeling a sudden desire to stand up for her friend, Nevis goes on, 'But Satnam was working really hard. So why *wouldn't* it have lasted?'

Jessica's hand comes up and covers her mouth. 'Oh my God. You really don't know anything, do you?'

The conversation is beginning to feel like a dance whose steps Nevis has not been taught. Confusion whirls inside her and finding no release settles in a knot somewhere inside her mind. She watches the expression on Jessica's face harden.

'Look, leaving Avon was just something we were talking about, OK? Like a fantasy, you know, ditching it all in and going to live on a beach in Bali or whatever. Everyone was pissed. Tash was being her usual bitch-self and she and I got into it a bit. Satnam was just trying to make the peace but Tash said some harsh things to her that were totally uncalled for. It was the kind of stupid drunk-row people get into, so let's just leave it.'

'But you said it was about an ex.'

Jessica shakes her head. 'I've got to go.'

This whole conversation has been baffling. Why is Jessica

being so cryptic? What's got into her all of a sudden? What is it that she knows and isn't saying?

In an act of desperation, Nevis reaches out a staying hand and plants it on Jessica's bony arm. 'Please.'

The girl blinks and shaking her off, in a low voice, she says, 'Trust me on this, Nevis, it's better you don't find out.'

Chapter 23

Cullen

Driving home with the window down to clear his head, Cullen allows his mind to wander back to the meeting with the Smith girl. There's something about her; he can't quite put his finger on it. She brings up in him an uncanny sense of familiarity, almost like déjà vu. His mind is so distracted by the idea that he narrowly misses a red light and has to jam on the brakes. The stolid mass of the Royal Infirmary rises to his left. How did I get here? It comes to him with a jolt that he must have been driving round the city without realising it. He gazes up at the building, lights ablaze in the dark, thoughts turning to Satnam Mann. Silly girl. Even if she survives, she'll be ruined.

The lights go green. Cullen's foot lands heavily on the accelerator. The car surges forward and there is a moment, a microsecond only, when his mind empties and goes blank. At the next set of lights he feels himself come to, as if waking from a dream. Recovering himself and in full control of the car once more, he makes a left turn at the next lights and heads north-west in the direction of Clifton. Christ, he thinks, what's got into me? Am I going mad?

Shaken, he reaches across the passenger seat to open the

glove box and gropes about among all the unopened bills for the quarter bottle of Famous Grouse he keeps tucked away, remembers that the last bottle was empty and that he threw it out. Though hang on, isn't there a miniature somewhere? In goes his hand again and out it comes triumphant. He unscrews the top with his teeth and takes a swig but the whisky, rather than steadying his nerves, sends him adrift on a sea of memories he'd rather forget. In his mind's eye he is in the living room at the tiny flat he shared with his mother all those years ago, waiting for the police to arrive. He remembers Amanda producing a half-empty bottle of Courvoisier and a couple of glasses, saying, 'Here, let's have a quick snifter, calm our nerves. I've got mints for after. It'll be all right.' His jacket was still damp, he remembers, even though it was early morning and he'd been inside for the best part of eight hours and she'd put it in the dryer because it hadn't started raining until nearly midnight and they had agreed that the story for the police would be that he'd arrived back from the Mathematics Society drinks party at 10.30 and that whoever said they'd seen him later than that must have mistaken him for someone else. Earlier, when he'd arrived home, ragged and terrified, she'd stood by him while he washed his body in the shower and turned the heat up to stop him shivering. 'It's just shock,' she said. He'd been sick of course. That was nerves. She'd said, 'Oh, my darling boy, whatever it is, it's best that you don't tell me. Don't ever let me hear it from your mouth.' And so he'd had to sit with it pressing down on him, threatening to suffocate him, until after the police had finished talking to him, which, as it turned out, hadn't been for the best part of a week. But that's where his mind is now: that first morning after the incident, scared witless but understanding that his mother, without even knowing the circumstances, would come good on her promise and that when the police came she would lie for him.

Oh, my darling boy.

It had been years since he'd been that, and would never be it again, but from that day on, he became dependent on her nostalgia, on the fantasy she clung to that he had needed protecting because he hadn't done anything wrong, that she knew he hadn't, that he couldn't have, because he had never spoken of it and because he always told her everything. She found out from the police, and so was able to muster the shock and righteous rage that someone should have slandered her darling boy.

Don't ever let me hear it from your mouth.

He toughened up that night, matured overnight. He never had told Amanda what really happened. He never had to. She knew he was guilty. Why else had she put his jacket in the dryer and escorted him to the shower? Why had she helped him scrub his fingernails and throw his clothes in the wash? Why else had she lied for him?

'Oh no, officer, that cannot be because, you see, at 10.30 p.m. my boy came home and for the rest of the evening he was here, watching TV, keeping his mother company.'

What he had done, the thing that from now on they would both be forced to wipe from their minds, that had given her a power over him. From then on, he knew that he would always be in her debt and that at any time she could call it in. The truth would undo him and they both knew it. For the past two decades she has chosen to keep the secret, but never for a moment has he doubted the possibility that this might, without warning, one day change. All it would take would be a cross word, a wrong move, a slippage in his attentiveness towards her. For twenty years he has been living in the shadow of what she did for him that night. For twenty years he has known too that she did it not to save him so much as to redeem herself. She was not a woman who had birthed a monster. She was the mother of a mathematical prodigy who, out of envy, two spiteful girls had tried and failed to bring down.

He parks his gloominess in the driveway, puts the bottle back among the bills in the glove compartment and walks to the front door of the house he cannot afford. Veronica is in the kitchen with her earbuds in, humming along to music. On the kitchen island is laid out an assortment of plates. There is a smell of roasting meat.

Cullen stares at the kitchen table, laid for six, two bottles of red wine already uncorked and airing. His heart sinks. He'd forgotten. Right now, feeling as inexplicably fragile as he does, he needs a dinner party about as much as a dose of the clap.

Veronica turns and smiles. 'Hello, darling.' There's a moment's pause during which he does his best to put his face into neutral, but it's too late. She stops chopping. Her nose twitches. 'Don't tell me you've forgotten? The Grays and the Askews coming over?'

'I'm not feeling a hundred per cent,' he says, feebly.

'Don't be such a misery guts. It's only the neighbours. They'll all be gone by 10.30. Have a glass of wine and cheer up. I opened a couple of bottles of that burgundy you like,' she says, gesturing towards the table without turning round. 'Since it's a special occasion, I'll let you off your alcohol fast.'

Cullen goes over to the table. There's nothing he can do

or say to get out of the evening without incurring Veronica's wrath. And he does like the burgundy. As well he might from the price tag. He's pouring himself a glass when the doorbell buzzes.

'That's probably the Askews,' Veronica says, half turning from the sink. 'They're always early. Will you go?'

Oh God, he thinks, he can't stand the Askews. Hateful pair. He goes out into the hallway and, seeing only one figure silhouetted in the acid-etched glass, immediately senses something wrong. But still he heads towards the trouble. What else can he do? He slides the chain on the door before cracking it open. A man is standing on the doorstep. Six foot four, shaven-headed meat mountain. They are not acquainted though Cullen knows instantly why he is here.

Putting his mouth to the gap in the door, Cullen hisses, 'Please, don't make a scandal. My wife is in the house. We're expecting guests.'

The mountain tries to wedge his huge ham of a foot in the doorway. A pulse starts up in Cullen's neck. His fingers begin to tingle and he can feel his Adam's apple making its way up and down his throat like the bead of an abacus. He wants to say you can't do this, I'm the Dean, but it's obvious even to him that this is ludicrous. Instead, he slams the door, slides the chain into its keeper.

There's a pause. Then the bell buzzes again, this time more insistently.

'Are you getting that, darling?' shouts Veronica from the kitchen.

Cracking open the door, Cullen growls, 'I'll get you the money by the end of the week, OK? Only, we'll need to meet somewhere neutral. I'm not having you coming round my house again.'

The mountain laughs. He names a pub in Redland. 'Friday, seven o'clock. Don't think about not showing.' He grins at Cullen. 'I know where you live.'

Cullen shuts the door and leans against it, panting, just as Veronica appears from the kitchen.

'Are you all right, darling?'

'Bloody chuggers. And no, I'm not. As I said, I'm definitely feeling rather peaky.'

'Why don't you make yourself useful by putting out some nibbles? That might make you feel better.'

Cullen hears himself say, 'How exactly?' and immediately regrets it. The Hon. Veronica pouts. The ultimate sanction against which he, and he suspects all men, are powerless.

Dinner is a horror show. Cullen watches as one extravagant dish after another is brought out. The scallops, the salmon caviar, the hulking piece of prime rib. He sits at the head of the table doing his best not to count the money disappearing down the gullets of his hated neighbours while Stella Gray casts barbs at her husband Will for not doing his share of the night-time baby duties, the Askews humble brag about their kids' music scholarships, and Veronica, in the midst of it all, tries and fails to draw attention to her considerable culinary skills.

'Of course it's only the oboe, which is hardly the most challenging instrument in the orchestra, though he really is doing so well with his piano too.'

'Do help yourselves to creamed horseradish. It's homemade.'

'Oh no, bad for the bump. We don't want to give him any more excuses for keeping me up all night, do we, Will?'

And so it goes on. Cullen watches the first two bottles of burgundy disappear, then another two. At ten, when he can't take any more, he draws his phone from his pocket and stares at the screen for as long as it takes for everyone to notice and go quiet, then grimaces and gestures towards the hallway with his thumb. So sorry, I'll take this outside.

Veronica raises her eyebrows.

I'll pay for this later, he thinks, but never mind.

He's absent for longer than is necessary. Five pairs of questioning eyes meet him on his return.

'Not another suicide, I hope?' Will Gray says.

Cullen hasn't mentioned Sunday's events to Veronica though she is clearly the source of the gossip. It hasn't been in the traditional press and Veronica disdains social media. Has she been listening in to a phone conversation? Or snooping in his email? Or worse still, helping herself to his phone? He glares at Veronica who meets his hostility with a good portion of her own.

'I have no idea what you mean by "another", Will,' he says to his neighbour, 'since there haven't been any. There *has* been a burglary in the administration building, however, and I'm afraid I do need to go in.' Saints be praised, he thinks. Excellent save, Christopher, *excellent*.

'Oh what terrible timing,' Veronica says, her voice like sniper fire. 'Well, do hurry home.'

Moments later, lowering himself into the car, he feels as if he's stepping into the last helicopter out of a war zone. He turns the key in the ignition and reaches for the glove box again. If you're going to be done for drunk driving, you may as well have some fun first. Not that this is any kind of fun. But it's at least tolerable. He backs the car out of the driveway, intending to head over to the university not to deal with the burglary because, as everyone inside the house already worked out, he lied about that, but to be in the familiar fortress of his office surrounded by his expensive coffee machine and the etching of his alma mater.

To his surprise, at the end of the street he turns away from Avon towards the centre of the city, driving through the still-clogged streets, past groups of students on their way to the clubs. He knows where he is going, knows too he wouldn't be going there if he weren't wrecked but cannot seem to stop himself. Swinging into the car park on Upper Maudlin Street, he cuts the engine and sits for a moment to compose himself. What he's about to do is probably a bad idea but it feels too late to turn back so he gets out and stumbling through the automatic doors finds himself in the main entranceway of the Bristol Royal Infirmary.

The quiet of night-time illness is immediately soothing. He goes over to the hospital map, remembering Lea Keane mentioning something about Pine Ward. Following the directions, he takes the lift up two floors, walks through a couple of sets of swinging doors and along a cucumber-coloured corridor lined with cheerful artworks to the ICU's nursing desk. Reduced night staff, no one around. He stands leaning an elbow on the counter, feeling disorientated and rather bilious, and waits. That second bottle of burgundy was probably a mistake. Time passes in slo-mo. Eventually a voice says, 'Can I help you, sir?'

He turns and sees a woman in her thirties, tall, slender, dressed in navy scrubs.

'I don't know,' he says, feeling suddenly confused.

'Are you here to see someone?'

Yes, yes, of course, that's it, he thinks. I'm much drunker than I realised.

The woman is close enough to be able to smell his breath. Her nose twitches. He wants to explain the reason for the drinking, to tell this tall, slender woman with the kind eyes everything, but he doesn't know where to begin. Pulling himself upright, he lurches back. I'm too drunk for this, I should just leave, he thinks, but even as he's having the thought his mouth is saying, 'I am the Dean at Avon University.'

The nurse says kindly, 'I'm going to have to ask you to leave.'

Yes, this is the sensible course of action, he needs to leave, he can see that now, and quick, before he loses it or makes a tit of himself. Or worse, says something he will regret. It was stupid to come. Absolutely crazy. He has no idea what he was thinking. He *wasn't* thinking, was he? He is drunk, that's the problem. He is a bloody stupid drunk.

'We don't want to have to call security,' the slender woman says, sounding much darker, almost threatening.

His world is spinning. He has no idea how to stop and get off. 'I don't think I'm very well,' he says.

The slender woman places a hand on his elbow and begins to lead him towards the swing doors. 'You'll need to report to triage in A&E.' Her tone has changed completely. She knows I'm drunk, he thinks. She despises me for it and I don't blame her. I despise myself.

She waits with him until the lift arrives. His face burns all the way down to the ground floor. What a fool! What a bloody stupid idiot! He makes his way back to his car and slumps into the driver's seat. When he comes to someone is knocking on the driver's side window.

He blinks, shaking himself awake and turning his head to the window sees a hefty man in uniform peering in.

'Time to go home, mate.'

Chapter 24

Honor

Honor reaches the meeting place half an hour early, edgy and apprehensive, as if, instead of having coffee with her daughter, she's arriving for a job interview. In a way, she thinks, she is doing exactly that. Whatever she has done to offend Nevis has led Honor to this meeting, here, in this café, with her last £50 in her pocket, feeling as if she is having to reapply for the job of Nevis's mother. And perhaps she is. Maybe that's how it always works between young adults and their parents. Or perhaps this is peculiar to adoptions. Sometimes, not often, Honor wonders what it would be like to have had biological children of her own, to be able to see in her offspring, intimations of herself. She might have done, had Zoe not died. Then again, perhaps not. Being Nevis's adoptive mother has been the greatest privilege of her life. Everything good in Honor's life has flowed from being Nevis's mother. Without Nevis she might have remained in the Welsh Marches, hated by the locals and unable to summon the strength to leave. She had left a broken woman and in the society of bargees and boaters, she had discovered the first real peace she had ever known. People had been dizzyingly kind, lending her tools and equipment, bringing round plants and wood for the stove and even, when times were so tough she wasn't sure that she and Nevis would be able to continue on the water, cooked food and store-cupboard rations. And it was a great gift for Nevis too. For all the damp and freezing winters, the cramped quarters and the constant financial insecurity, growing up in the community of bargees was the greatest experience Honor could ever have bestowed on any child.

She pushes the door of the café open and steps into a warm, cheerful, old-fashioned place. The table in the corner looks cosy and she can see both ways down the street. Odd to be nervous. Silly. Whatever this is between them will pass, won't it? It has to because, Bill aside, they only really have each other.

At the counter she orders coffee.

'Anything to eat with that?' asks the server, a young woman wearing dungarees.

Mention of food makes Honor aware that she has not eaten since the spag bol with Alex yesterday evening and now it is nearly lunchtime. It's easy to forget about such things when you're on your own. When Nevis was still very young and the pain of losing Zoe was still as raw as a beating, she would sometimes go for days without food. She would feed Nevis always, spoon the pulpy mess into her mouth, watch the little smile of pleasure come to her smooth, blameless face but she would not give that to herself. She had thought that those days and months and weeks and years of punishment she took at her own hands had come and gone, that she had dealt with them and moved on, but perhaps not.

'Just the coffee,' she says. 'I'm meeting my daughter here, but I'm early.'

'Oh, that's nice,' the young woman says sweetly, adding, 'You go and sit down and I'll bring it over.'

Moving to the corner table she takes off her coat and hangs it on the back of the chair wondering why she said such a thing. What does the woman at the counter care? Sometimes, she thinks, I don't think I've quite mastered being on my own. But there will be time. A lot of time.

She sits and waits and tries not to fidget. There are some leaflets and freesheets strewn about but she doesn't feel like reading them. A few moments later the server brings over the coffee.

'Like your fleece,' the young woman says. 'Purple's a good mum colour.'

Honor hadn't wanted to be a mum. She hadn't *not* wanted it either. At nineteen she hadn't given it much thought. In the weeks after Nevis was born, while Zoe was still alive, and they were living in the caravan, she'd done what people now call co-parenting. The caravan was so tiny that there hadn't been much choice in the matter, but she'd actively wanted to be involved. Nappy changing, feeding, bathing, getting up in the night and soothing of tears and screams, all this she had done, none of it the same as if she had been Nevis's mother. The buck still stopped at Zoe. Until Zoe was no more. And when that happened, motherhood had been thrust upon her in a way it never would have been had Nevis been her biological child.

A person less prepared for the role of adoptive mother to a three-month-old baby would have been hard to imagine. Honor had only begun to wash her hair regularly the year before and was still squeezing her pimples. Her parents, Jim and Tillie, had been too busy getting off their heads to worry about teaching their child to wash. Honor was a hippy kid, left, more or less, to fend for herself. She learned how to open a can of beans not long after she learned to walk, but it was only a month after she became Nevis's mother, via the chance remark of a social worker who had come to see how 'mum and baby' were settling down, that she discovered that washing behind your ears was considered an essential part of basic grooming. It was a steep learning curve and she had been forced to scale it while grieving for her friend. Bringing up Nevis had been the best, the most joyful and the worst and the most terrible, thing she had ever done. For the most part, it *was* done. Or had been, until the incident on the bridge brought into stark relief just how vulnerable Nevis is and how much mothering there is still left to do.

She spots her daughter moments before she enters, alerted by the long shadow and the sloping, lilting walk. Moments later Nevis has spotted her and is approaching.

'Hi. Is that new?' Nevis says, pointing to the fleece. She looks even more anxious than she did on Sunday night.

'Yeah, I mean, not new, but...'

'...new to you, which is as new as anything gets in your world.'

Oh, she thinks, with sinking heart, so it's going to be like this, is it?

'I'll go and get a coffee. You want another?'

Honor holds her hand over her mug. 'No, darling, thank you.'

At the word 'darling' Nevis blinks and a fragile, awkward smile appears. You can't bring up the rift or hurt or whatever it is, Honor says to herself, watching her daughter's back move towards the counter, not unless it's what Nevis has come to talk about. It wouldn't be fair, not now. So you must talk about anything else.

In a few moments Nevis returns carrying a cup and takes a seat opposite her mother.

'How is Satnam?'

'I assume she's the same. The student welfare office said they'd let me know if there was any big change,' Nevis says, rubbing her right eye with her fingers.

'You look a bit tired.'

'My sleep app says I slept six hours and eighteen minutes, so I'm fine, just, you know...' She takes a breath. 'I don't need you to be here, you know that don't you?'

'I know you're very capable and competent, if that's what you're asking.' All the same, Honor thinks, it was you who asked to meet. Besides which, I do need to be here. I need it very much. 'I've got paid work here now though, a refurb on a boat down in the Floating Harbour. It'll take a couple of months.' Honor picks up her coffee and drains what remains in order not to have to look at her daughter. The work is not paid and is unlikely to take as long as she has said. It has always been so hard to lie to Nevis precisely because it has always been so easy.

'But you're not going to want to come round all the time, are you?'

The sting is small and teenager-shaped but painful still. Honor says, 'Of course not, but you can come to the boat whenever you like. There are two bedrooms.'

Nevis has stopped listening, her face turning inward, the colour drained out, the strain apparent in a tightness around the eyes, a pulse at the jawline. 'Everyone at Avon's talking about it. It's all over the university chat rooms and on social. Everyone knows I was there on the bridge. I go into the library, students I don't even know pass me messages. What if people start to say I could have stopped her?'

So here it was, the reason she had got in touch. Part of her was still a kid in need of a mother's reassurance.

'Have you spoken to student welfare so they can put a stop to that stuff?'

'They're useless.'

'Someone else at uni then?'

'I'm speaking to *you* about it.'

Honor sinks back, despondent. What she hears is that she has failed, that there are other, better mothers out there, who would have been more suited, who would have known how to deal with this, and that in spite of this, she's got the part, because no one else showed up to the audition.

'Social media isn't your friend and the people who are doing the gossiping aren't your friends either.' She wonders why the university is letting this pass.

'I only have one friend.'

'You have me.'

Nevis falls silent, considering this a moment. 'I found something I want to show you.' She removes some printed paper from her daypack and puts it on the table. Honor reaches for it, turns it over in her hand, scanning the pages. 'Satnam's essay on data integration in bioinformatics.'

'Is it one of the ones you helped her with?'

Nevis shakes her head. 'No, she never asks me to help any more, not even with the maths. She only finished this one a couple of weeks ago. I found it under her bed.'

'Oh.' Honor is unsure where this is going.

'The point is, she told me she got a first for that paper but the calculations are full of errors. No way that paper was worth a first.'

Still perplexed. Why is Nevis bringing this up now?

'Could you have misheard?'

'No! We had a conversation about it. She kept saying how chuffed she was.'

Honor takes a breath. It sounds like what Nevis needs right now is reassurance.

'But, darling, everyone occasionally stretches the truth a bit to make themselves look better.'

She notes the scowl on Nevis's face and kicks herself. Why can't she get it right with Nevis? 'I shouldn't have showed you. I knew you wouldn't get it.'

'Give me another try.'

Nevis nods. 'I spoke to a couple of Satnam's friends but they got funny with me, like they knew something about Satnam that I didn't.'

'About her state of mind? Or something she did?'

Nevis shrugs. 'I'm not good at picking up that stuff.' Nevis bites her lip, considering this for a moment before deciding to risk it. 'I'm going to go back and see the Dean.'

'That sounds like a good idea, if you're worried about it.' Honor is struggling to put all this together. 'Do you think Satnam could have been cheating? And got caught out?'

'No, of course not!' The flare of outrage on Nevis's face is hard to bear. 'Forget it, all right, it doesn't matter. I just thought… never mind.' She snatches up the sheets of paper, puts them into her backpack, closes the zip. 'I've got to get going now.'

Honor watches her daughter disappear. Again. Whether Nevis's real reason for coming to her was to get her opinion of Satnam's paper or to talk to a friend or be comforted by a mother, she'd failed in all these things. Something has happened to my daughter since Satnam went to the bridge, Honor thinks, something new and very grown up and rather sad and I shall probably never know what.

Chapter 25

Cullen

Cullen is walking by the library when he spots Nevis Smith emerging from the lift. He stops and smiles.

'How are you, Nevis?'

'OK, thank you.' She is red-faced. Shyness he thinks, but who knows. An odd one. Hard to read. He is hoping very much that she hasn't got wind of the embarrassing escapade at the hospital last night, though if she has, he has already concocted a defensive strategy for dealing with it.

'I got your email about coming to see me. I have a spare moment now if you like.'

He waits while she consults her phone. 'I have a seminar group with Dr Ratner in forty-seven minutes.'

'Oh, well, I don't suppose we'll be that long, will we? Shall we go to my office?' Her eyebrows raise enquiringly. An unworldly girl, but beguiling in a funny sort of way. Something intriguing about her at least. After their last encounter he had been left with the strong sense that she hadn't told him everything she knows about Satnam Mann and this concerns him.

They walk down the corridor and through the swing doors

to the Deanery in silence, Nevis following awkwardly a couple of paces behind. He opens the door and waves her in.

'You look a little tired,' he says, going round to his side of the desk.

'So do you,' she says, perching on the edge of the visitor's seat. He glances at her, trying to gauge where that remark came from but her face is an open book or an empty plain, depending on your point of view.

He lets out an awkward laugh. 'At my age everyone looks tired.'

'What age is that?' she says.

He finds himself laughing. Either the girl is a complete innocent or she is a monster. He hopes the former. Easier to manage. 'I always think age is just a number.'

She frowns and closes her eyes for a moment and then, in a soft and puzzled voice, says, '*Everything* is a number.'

'Indeed,' he says, steepling his hands. She amuses him. Reminds him of himself at fifteen, a boy with a single-track mind, newly arrived on campus, wildly clever and not a little clueless. 'Now, how can I help?'

'It's about Satnam.' He catches her glance and holding it notes in those clever hazel eyes pain and perhaps a touch of wariness.

'I see. You've heard that her condition remains the same. Serious but stable. We'll have to continue to hope. Are you getting the support you need?'

'No.'

'Oh,' he says. 'Well, we should contact student welfare.'

'I mean I don't need any,' she says, hastily.

He looks at her for a moment. There is something rather

amazing about her. Perhaps she is that very rare thing, he thinks, a person who speaks her mind. What does she know, he wonders, and how much of what she knows does she really understand?

'Perhaps a different kind of support might be more helpful?' He smiles.

'Like what?'

'How does a coffee sound for a start?'

She returns the smile and nods. Not entirely without a sense of humour, at least.

Standing, he goes over to the coffee machine, slots in a capsule and taps the 'make' key. 'Was that why you asked to see me? Because you were finding student welfare unhelpful?'

'No,' she says, bluntly, 'I came to see you because I found something.'

'Oh?' As he walks back to the desk with the coffee cup it is hard to prevent his hand from shaking. He takes a seat and pushes the coffee towards her, waits for her to put it to her lips before saying, 'What kind of thing?'

'One of Satnam's essays. It's on data integration in bioinformatics. She must have printed it out.'

A lump catches painfully in his voice box but he manages to keep the smile on his face. He swallows, hard. No cause for alarm just yet.

'Oh?' he says, in what he hopes is a casual tone. Not that she'll notice, he suspects, though it never hurts to put on a good show of ignorance. 'If you give it to me, I'll make sure Dr Ratner sees it. You focus on your coursework.'

'It's been graded,' she says.

'Really?' he says, with a feeling of foreboding. 'I don't recall marking it myself.'

'But you teach the bioinformatics module.'

'I do, yes.' An anxious thread spirals its way up his spine.

'She told me she got a first.'

'I see,' he says, his throat closing. He slides the paper from the desk and takes a cursory look to buy some time. He has no need to remind himself. The second year undergrad proof, a stochastic differential equation for a transcriptional regulatory network in *saccharomyces cerevisiae*, simple brewers' yeast, and below it several lines of code enabling the calculation to be done from numerous different sample sets, both neatly typed and heavily annotated in red pen.

'Are these Dr Ratner's corrections?' he asks, puzzled. Who corrects papers by hand these days?

'No, they're mine. You don't have to look very hard to see that the maths is all wrong. So is the coding.'

Cullen scans the page, checking Nevis's corrections, aware of her gaze on him. Yes, of course. That would seem contradictory and odd. He imagines Nevis taking the paper to Ratner or even to Keane or Madeleine Ince, the same innocent, wide-eyed enquiry on her face. No, that won't do. Something in his head resolves and clarifies. He takes a few deep breaths and reminds himself that he is the Dean.

'Oh that's *right*, I remember now, she *was* having trouble with a few of the concepts. I gave her a couple of review sessions.' Handing back the paper, he says, 'Evidently this is an early draft. I do recall handing a batch of papers to Dr Ratner, so I expect the final draft was among that batch. Gosh, well spotted!'

He watches her soften. She is thinking, applying logic, weighing up the probability of his explanation.

'Don't worry about it. Easy mistake to make.' He smiles, reassuringly. 'But if you're concerned, why don't I call Dr Ratner now and ask him to confirm.'

'It's all right,' she says.

'Good then,' he says, checking his watch and standing to show her out. He feels recklessly exuberant now, almost grateful. Out of the woods, though perhaps not yet the forest. He'll have to continue to keep an eye. She's clever this one, and unlike most nineteen year olds, methodical. Patiently exacting. 'You know what?' Her head snaps up at the question. 'You already have my work mobile. I'm going to give you my new personal mobile number. Just in case you need to speak to me. About anything. Day or night.' He watches a delicate, girlish smile appear on her face. 'How's that?'

Chapter 26

Cullen

Cullen is just finishing Veronica's dinner of langoustines when the doorbell rings.

'Oh blow,' Veronica says. 'I was hoping that we could spend the rest of the evening getting frisky. Whoever it is, can't you get rid of them?'

'I'll do my best,' Cullen says, praying not to find the goon at the door wanting money. He'd managed to stave him off with his last few hundred but it was only a matter of time before he'd be back again. At least now, finally, he has a plan.

He moves into the hallway and sees a slender shadow through the etched glass. A woman? He checks his watch. Late.

His heart falls at the sight of the Vice Chancellor, Madeleine Ince.

'Chris, I'm sorry it's so late, I've just come from some awful fundraiser dinner. Can I have a word or two?'

'Of course. Please come in,' he says, graciously, waving her into the living room. A remarkably attractive woman, he thinks, even now. Maddy had loved him more than he'd loved her all those years ago when they were involved, before either of them ever came to Avon. But he sometimes wonders what it would have been like to have married Maddy rather than Veronica.

'I'll just tell Veronica you're here,' he says. 'Can I get you a coffee? Glass of wine?'

'A whisky if you have any.'

'Of course,' he says. Another point in Maddy's favour. Veronica only ever drinks wine.

Leaving her sitting on the sofa, he hurries back into the kitchen.

Veronica is not happy about the visitor. 'Oh God, can't you tell her you'll see her in the morning?'

'No. She's my boss in case you'd forgotten.' He's never told Veronica that he and Madeleine had a thing together. She wouldn't like it, not through any sense of jealousy or possessiveness, but for the simple fact that Maddy is now his boss and Veronica is a traditionalist, in this respect as in many others.

They walk back down the hallway together, Cullen carrying a little tray on which is balanced a small ice bucket and a jug of water.

'Madeleine, what a pleasure,' Veronica says, clasping her hands around the Vice Chancellor's.

'I'm sorry it's so late, Veronica. I'll try not to keep Christopher long.'

'Nonsense, Madeleine,' Veronica says, a little too brightly. 'Stay as long as you like. I've got the clearing up to do anyway.'

Cullen waits and feels his diaphragm move once more.

'What's going on, Maddy?' he says, with his back to her. He takes out two highball glasses and a special occasion bottle of Macallan from the mahogany cupboard, then opens the drawer beneath, looking for the silver stirrer, his eyes alighting instead on his mother's diamond and gold bracelet, which he'd lifted from behind a bank of lacy handkerchiefs in her bedside table earlier that evening, while she was quietly sleeping. The bracelet was an heirloom from Amanda's mother but needs must. Making an early claim on his inheritance is all it is. God knows, he's earned it. In the unlikely event that Amanda even misses it, he can always float the theory that someone in the home must have been responsible. One of the carers, perhaps, or another resident. But he'll cross that bridge when he comes to it.

Pouring a finger of Macallan into one of the glasses and four fingers into the other, he drops into each glass two cubes of ice and, rebuilding his best smile, turns back into the room, bracing himself for whatever Maddy has to say.

'I got a rather worrying call from Lea earlier,' she says, taking the proffered glass. 'I don't know if you're aware that her daughter, Jackie, works as a paramedic at the Royal Infirmary?'

Oh bloody hell, thinks Cullen.

Her eyes flash to the door and her manner suddenly softens and for an instant he's persuaded that she's the Maddy who still carries a torch, the Maddy he can twist around his little finger. 'Chris, what is happening to you?'

'In what sense?' he says.

'In the sense that you apparently showed up at the infirmary at some ungodly hour last night, six sheets to the wind and demanding to see Satnam Mann.'

'Ungodly? It wasn't even ten.'

She fixes him with an even look that sends a shudder through him. 'Is that your best get-around? Or is there a better one coming down the pipe?'

'She's been on my mind, obviously.' He checks the door. God, please don't let Veronica come in, not now.

'She's been on everyone's *mind*.'

'I was under the impression that her parents had requested a visit from a representative at the university. I undertook that task. It was Lea who asked me if I wouldn't mind.' A day ago, an hour, a minute even, he felt nothing for Lea but a healthy contempt. If you'd asked him yesterday, he would have said he would rejoice if she got the sack. Now, he'd quite cheerfully bury the bitch alive.

'Late at night? From someone who gave every impression of being drunk?'

'I wasn't *drunk*.'

'It was reported that you smelled of alcohol.'

'Godssakes, Maddy, a man can have a glass of wine with his supper, can't he?'

Ignoring him, Madeleine goes on, 'Because, if alcohol is the culprit, there's help out there. You'd have to step down from your role as Dean and take a sabbatical, but we'll do everything we can to support you. I doubt I could swing full pay, though.'

'We?' he says.

'The University. The Board of Governors. You know how highly they think of you and I have always, *always* supported you…' she tails off.

He feels himself stiffen. 'I suppose the Board of Governors knows how lucky they are to have me. Second most cited pure mathematics PhD of 2003. They remember that when it suits them.'

'Really, Chris, there's no need for this. You're talking to *me*, Maddy, not the Vice Chancellor now.'

'Don't bring ancient history into this, it's unbecoming. In any case, I haven't got a drinking problem so this discussion isn't going anywhere.'

Madeleine stands. 'Perhaps we *should* continue this tomorrow after all.'

He feels himself going to the door, blocking her way. 'Oh no you don't. You came here to say something, so say it! Spit it out! I'm losing it, is that it? I'm a mess. My behaviour is inappropriate. God help any of us if we dare to be *inappropriate*.'

'I think it's best if I go now, Chris.'

'Oh no, no, no. Not before you've got it all off your chest. Which, by the way, I always considered very disappointing. My friends used to call you Maddy Flatty.' His voice comes back to him as a series of sludgy, strangulated sounds, like a recording played at the wrong speed. He thinks, what the hell am I doing?

Madeleine is ice cold. 'Now you're just embarrassing yourself.'

Yes, he thinks, I am in the process of making what will possibly become the second biggest mistake of my life. Pull yourself together, Cullen. Maddy is your *ally*. He steels himself and in a single breath, says, 'Oh God, that was an unforgivably stupid thing to say, absolutely idiotic. I apologise unreservedly.'

'Hmm.' Madeleine eyes him askance. 'Very well then,' she says eventually, sitting back down.

He reaches for her hands but stops himself mid-air. He knows her well enough to understand that any attempt at coming closer will be rebuffed. There will be some kind of retaliation for his earlier remark. He lowers his voice to a whisper. 'Between you and me Veronica is driving me nuts with this pregnancy obsession.'

Her voice comes back at him at a perfectly modulated hiss. 'You have always been able to count on me, and you can count on me now, but if you put my position on the line, Christopher, you will find that my loyalty is volatile. Put it under enough pressure and it will evaporate.'

'Listen, Maddy,' he says imploringly, holding up his hands in a gesture of surrender, 'Veronica and I had a tiny disagreement. I took off in my car to cool down and found myself at the infirmary. It was a spur of the moment thing, a misjudgement I see now.'

'Just don't push it,' she says, stepping through the door. In the hallway, she stops and turns. 'Odd, you recounting tales of friends, Christopher, because I don't recall you *having* any.' At the front door she says, 'Give my regards to Veronica.'

Once he's seen her out, he leans his back on the door, shuts his eyes and does his best to steady himself. Quit drinking and stop making such a bloody mess of everything! Come on, Cullen, get yourself together. There'll be a solution to this, to all of it.

Moments later, Veronica reappears from the kitchen wearing a quizzical expression.

'What's wrong? Why have you got your face in your hands?'

He jerks upright and stiffens his spine.

'Nothing. Just tired I suppose.'

He watches her approach him with what she hopes is a seductive swing of the hips. 'Not too tired to muster those troops, I hope, darling?'

He fixes his face into a semblance of a smile, and thinks, When in God's name will this all end?

Chapter 27

Nevis

Nevis opens her eyes. It takes a moment for her consciousness to catch up, leaving her blinking into the darkened room as that part of her rises as if from the ocean bed, fighting its own weightedness, coming to the surface in spite of itself. She'd been in the middle of a dream which has already escaped though she's aware that it featured kingfishers and that they had been nesting so it must have been around Easter time. Her mind shoots back to an evening a few years ago. Easter was late that year and there were still a few days to go before the end of the school term. She blinks, the dream replaced by the memory. Her mind brings up the date. 27th March, a Tuesday, Nevis was sixteen. Honor had been out at a London Boaters meeting, which was unusual because Honor never went anywhere. She'd promised to be back by eight but had texted to say everyone going on to the pub afterwards and would Nevis mind if she went too? Nevis did not mind. So long as she was on the water she did not feel alone.

It was late when Honor finally pitched up, maybe just after midnight, and the canal was shrouded in that deep lonely dark that, in London, was unique. Nevis had woken to a cry and gone out to discover her mother, four sheets to the wind, fumbling around in the cratch for the hatch keys.

'Ssshoory to wake you.'

Nevis let her mother in and saw to it that she got down the steps into the saloon safely since whatever she'd drunk had gone to her legs, which wobbled about like a colt's. Assuming her mother would want to go directly to bed, Nevis directed her towards her room, but Honor wanted to sit up a while and watch the water so Nevis helped her to her armchair in front of the dying embers in the wood burner, laid a blanket over her lap, and went over to the kettle to make her a cup of chamomile tea. By the time she returned with the tea, only a matter of minutes later, Honor was asleep but she woke with a start when Nevis laid a finger on her arm.

'Let's get you to bed.'

Her mother peered at her through glassy eyes and Nevis saw her lips open with the beginnings of a smile. Then in a voice still cracked with sleep Honor said, 'Zoe? Is that you?'

The pain was as shocking as a knife to the heart. Her own mother, at least the only mother she ever knew, mistaking her for a dead woman, the ghost in whose shadow Nevis had always lived, always knowing that not a day went by when Honor didn't wish for Zoe's company. Nevis wanted to say, it's me, the stand-in, the understudy, the placeholder, the body double, the fraud, but no words came. Instead, she watched as reality hit and tears began to spiral down Honor's cheeks.

'Nevis, darling, of course it's you!'

And then the words came out in a rush, tumbling over one another, and Nevis heard herself say, 'But you wish it wasn't, don't you? You've always wished it wasn't.'

Time seemed to stand still. Nevis saw Honor's eyes widen into dark pools and her shoulders begin to shake and covering her face with her hands, in a voice that seemed to come up from the depths of the canal itself, Honor said, 'Never, *ever* say that again,' and Nevis knew she had gone too far, that she had touched a nerve so tender and raw that to touch it again would break them apart.

Over the days that followed Honor back-pedalled and apologised and begged for forgiveness, but the knife she had thrown had stuck, and still awaited the arrival of some force strong enough to remove it. No such force appeared and the discovery of the letter in the book of Greek myths a few years later only dug the knife in deeper. Her heart still felt so heavy that she sometimes thought the only reason she was still alive was that the blade had staunched the bleeding.

Awake now and heart thumping from the memory, Nevis sits up and, groping for her phone on the bedside table, glances at the time. 2.40 a.m. Hears a doorbell ringing, realises that it's hers. Who is at the door at this hour? Drunks? She takes a deep breath. Early morning jitters, her mind still part stuck. Ignore whoever it is and go back to sleep. A moment later the buzz comes again and this time, as she throws off the duvet, she sees her phone silently flashing a new call. She sits up and does her best to quell her pulse. It's fine, just sit here a moment until you can think straight.

Another buzz. The phone lighting up with another call. You must go, she tells herself, because whatever it is, it is already happening, the equation has already been written, the parameters set. She gets up, unlocks her bedroom door and stands in the hallway adjusting to the dim light coming in from the window in the living room where she forgot to draw the curtains. Still half asleep she shuffles to the video entry and presses the link button. Nothing. Just the thin light in the entryway.

'Hello?'

A face appears but so distorted she can hardly tell who or what it is. The voice is like a vixen wailing for a mate.

'Let me in.'

Nevis presses the green entry button and moments later the door slams shut and there comes the sound of footsteps on the stairs. She goes to the door and opens it. A figure bolts into the hallway and bends over to catch her breath, resting her hands on her thighs, her chest heaving.

Tash.

Nevis slides the door chain into its keeper, acutely aware of the adrenaline prickling her skin. Tash is speaking but the words spew between great gulps of air and Nevis cannot understand what she is saying. She feels the cold shock of spit spray landing on her cheeks then hears another voice, her own this time, shouting, 'Not Satnam, not Satnam!' Her hands have come up over her ears, trying to block the sound. There is a death and she cannot bear it.

'What are you talking about?' Tash's eyes as wide as saucers, not comprehending, her grip on Nevis's arm so hard now that the pain has broken through the panic.

'Satnam is gone!'

'No, no, it's not Satnam, it's Jessica. Jessica has thrown herself off the bridge.'

Chapter 28

Cullen

He'd woken with a hangover. At breakfast Veronica again asked him what Madeleine Ince had wanted from him so urgently last night. He repeated what he'd already said, that there had been an ongoing security issue following the break-in. The fact that she'd asked twice suggested she didn't believe him, but she'd decided not to pursue it, which was really all that mattered. Maddy had fired a shot across his bows but he was reassured that, so long as he behaved himself, she would help escort him through the current rough waters. There was no one better to have on his side.

The arrangement meant he could, at least temporarily, turn to other, very pressing matters, namely the getting of hard cash. The thug awaited payment, his visits to the house a clear threat. Cullen had managed to allay Veronica's fears for now, but even Veronica wouldn't swallow the broadband story for long. Maddy's support has at least bought him some time. Leaving the house shortly after breakfast he gets in his Volvo and drives through Clifton past the infirmary and Broadmead towards Temple Meads station until, reaching Lawrence Hill, he checks along the road for a parking space, slows into second gear and flips the indicator to signal left. In the eight years he's lived in Bristol he's never been here, though it's only four miles from Clifton. Not his kind of place. Everything is smaller and meaner, from the shops and pavements to the spaces for the cars.

He squeezes the Volvo between a Ka and a Fiesta, switches off the radio, checks the time on his watch, scopes about for the correct building number and, not seeing it, gets out. His eyes float over cheap homeware shops and takeaways in search of three golden balls indicating the entrance to S. Harold & Sons, a family-run pawnbroker which he hopes will be more discreet than the big chains.

Spotting the sign, he heads down the street, fiddling with the gold and diamond bracelet in his pocket. You couldn't really call what he's doing stealing. Doesn't he pay the majority of his mother's care home fees? Does he ever think of her as pilfering from him? No, of course not. Not stealing then, more like borrowing against his inheritance. Feeling buoyed now he stops before the golden balls and rings on the bell. A voice invites him in and he finds himself in a dingy, cream-coloured hallway at the end of which is a stand-alone signpost printed with the names of several businesses. An arrow points up a narrow staircase. Taking a deep breath, Cullen begins to climb the stairs. On the first-floor landing, above a sign printed with the name of the pawnbroker, a camera blinks. He presses the buzzer. A male voice says, 'Come in!' The door clicks open and there before Cullen stands a lean man in his fifties with a close-cropped, balding pate dressed in a suit that has seen better days. Behind the man and on two sides of the room are a series of vitrines displaying mostly gold jewellery. A locked gate bars the way to offices at the back.

'Can I help you?' the man says, smiling.

'Yes,' Cullen says, fumbling in his pocket and drawing out the bracelet. 'My mother left me this. It's diamond and twenty-four carat gold. It was originally her mother's.'

'I see.' The man's eyebrows rise and, if Cullen's not very much mistaken, his eyes glaze over just a little. He's heard all this before, he thinks, and wasn't much interested then. 'If you'd like to come over here and take a seat?'

A plastic chair of uncertain vintage sits on the side facing the wall, another on the far side of the vitrine. The man waits for Cullen to sit before going around the end of the vitrine and assuming a place of his own. On the countertop sit the tools of his trade; a weighing scale, a series of magnifiers and some other, less familiar paraphernalia.

'Are you looking to borrow on it or to sell?' the man says.

Cullen blinks. The idea that he might borrow using the bracelet as collateral and pick it up when he can pay back the money hasn't occurred to him. If he did that, the Dalek might never know.

'Give me a quote for both,' he says.

The broker inspects the bracelet, then holding a magnifier in his eye socket, makes a closer examination. Finally he weighs it, then steepling his hands says, 'This is a very good piece, but it's old-fashioned and you should be aware that we price on the size of the diamonds and the weight of the gold.'

'So if I sell it, someone will melt it down?'

'Most likely, yes,' the pawnbroker says, quoting two prices, one sum for pawning and a sum almost three times as much for selling.

He could pawn it, of course, and try to pay back the money.

But how realistic is that? Looking on the bright side, the Dalek scarcely has need for jewellery these days. Who is going to notice that she's wearing a bracelet? Most of the residents are half blind or doolally. If she knew I was in trouble, she'd probably *want* me to have it, he says to himself. Most likely she won't even notice it's gone. And if it's gone why shouldn't it be completely gone, taken apart, melted down, removed from the world, not unlike its original owner in fact. He smiles at the existential elegance of the idea.

'I'll sell it then,' he says, thinking now of the thug in the driveway.

Moments later he's bouncing back down the stairs with a wedge of twenties in his pocket where the bracelet once sat. How easy was that? Remarkably quick and with none of the sadness, the tawdriness, the seediness he'd anticipated.

Out on the street the cloud has cleared and the morning sun has broken through. See, he thinks, everything is suddenly looking rather cheerier, even Lawrence Hill. He pops his car door open, clambers in, stations his phone in its bracket and keys on the engine. Mozart caresses his ears. All is well.

He is buckling his seatbelt when there comes a text from Mark Ratner. He reads and reads again.

Jessica Easton has killed herself.

Oh shit, not this, not now.

Chapter 29

Nevis

It's late morning and Nevis needs coffee, though that probably means waking up Tash, who is crashed out on the sofa in the living room. There came a point last night when neither of them could stay awake any longer but they each didn't want to be alone. She offered Satnam's empty bedroom but Tash rejected the idea, saying the space felt creepy. Nevis only had a single bed so it had to be the sofa.

It had been a disturbed night. Nevis lay in bed struggling to sleep while lights from passing cars flickered in through the curtains and made play around the walls of the room. Everything seemed off and unfamiliar in the manner of a dream from which she could neither force herself to wake nor depart into sleep. Once or twice, she heard keening sounds coming from the living room but her body felt too heavy to heave from the bed. It was as if her body had been occupied by another soul. She told herself that she did not believe in souls, or spirits, but still the impression remained imprinted on her mind. She wondered if she was ill. A blank dawn arrived. The return of the light seemed to calm her and it was not long before she fell into a fitful sleep.

She pads into the kitchen area and sets the kettle on.

Woken by the noise, Tash appears from under the blanket, blinking. 'What the fuck time is it?'

'Just gone half past ten,' Nevis says, laying down the coffee on the table beside her.

'Oh God, I wish you hadn't woken me. I feel like shit.' She reaches for her tobacco and begins to roll her first cigarette of the morning. 'It's still true, isn't it?' she says, drawing the smoke into her lungs. She's sitting up now, dressed in last night's T-shirt and underwear, with the blanket sprawled across her knees.

'Yes.'

'*Fuck*. You looked on social yet?'

'They're saying she was on those pro-suicide websites.'

'Who's saying that?'

'Students.' Nevis takes a big mouthful of coffee, the bitterness slipping down her throat and souring her stomach.

A pause while Tash takes her first sip of coffee then a grimace. 'Shitzer, you put the entire bean harvest of a small central American republic in this?'

'The standard brewing ratio for a 0.35 litre mug is 21.3g. I usually use 26g but I do like the mug to be full right to the top.'

Putting the mug down, Tash flaps a hand in the air to signal that she wants more milk or sugar in the coffee. Nevis goes over to the kitchen and brings both. Tash is already on her phone by the time she returns.

'They're saying she was mentally ill.'

Nevis says, 'I saw her the other day.'

'Oh?'

'We talked about the photo of you and her and Satnam, remember?'

'Oh yeah.' Tash's face is sombre suddenly, lips parted, forehead furrowed into a deep frown.

'Jessica told me you and she started arguing, because you'd got involved with her ex-boyfriend. And then Satnam intervened and you got gnarly with her. She said that all three of you were thinking about leaving Avon because of your grades, and then she implied that something else was going on, too. Is that why Jessica killed herself? Is there a link to what happened to Satnam?'

Tash closes her eyes and takes a deep breath. A few moments later, when she opens them once more, they are wet. 'It's too complicated to explain. There are things you don't know about...'

'That's what Satnam *and* Jessica said.'

'It's best you don't know.'

'Seems like everyone knows something except me. What's so bad that you can't tell me?'

Tash sniffs and swallows. 'Jess was ill. You must have noticed how thin she was. She'd had anorexia or whatever as long as I've known her.'

'You two fell out because you got involved with Jessica's ex, though, right? Not about her anorexia.'

'Yeah, I guess so,' says Tash, as though it's something she's only just thought through.

'I'm confused. If Jessica had this eating disorder for a long time, why did she decide to go off the bridge now? Does that have to do with the thing I don't know about?'

'There's no logic to it, Nevis. Sometimes, people just do this stuff,' Tash says, evasively. 'People used to put their heads in gas ovens, you know that? In the old days. Then they changed the kind of gas and the suicide rate went right down. Same with the suspension bridge. They put that barrier up a while ago. It stops lots of people, makes them think twice. So I guess that must mean some people do this stuff because they're confronted with an opportunity.' She coughs and screws up her face. 'What I bet you don't know is that Jess tried before, a few months ago, before that picture you keep going on about, but she didn't go through with it. That's what she told me anyway. I don't think she said anything to anyone else. She didn't want her parents to know because they would have made her go back home and she hated it there 'cos they made her eat.'

Nevis, who has been standing all this time, takes a seat in the chair opposite the sofa. 'Did Satnam know that?'

'No, I didn't tell anyone. She made me promise not to. Anyway, I've got enough shit of my own.'

'When you sent me that email saying "Who's next?", you knew it was going to be Jess.'

'What are you *talking* about? I was just worried *someone* would be.' Tash pushes up a sleeve and displays the ladder marks on her arms. 'I need a smoke.'

'You *are* smoking.'

'Not that kind of smoke.' She lights another rollie. 'I got some in my bag. Want to join?'

'You know smoking makes you 84.7 per cent more likely to die of lung cancer?'

'No, Nevis, I did not know that. But, hey, thanks for the heads-up.'

Nevis wonders if this is snark, decides it probably is and wishes she were better at detecting that stuff.

'I have to go in a bit. I have a seminar at twelve then the

Dean invited me for lunch.' Professor Cullen had called her from his personal phone to suggest it. Said he wanted to discuss her work, make sure she was keeping up.

A cloud scuds across Tash's face. Balancing the rollie precariously on the mug of coffee, Tash lies back down on the sofa and pulls on last night's jeans.

'He's taking you to lunch? I get squeezed in between meetings. He'll want to find out what we know about Jessica *obviously*.'

'He told me he thought I could get a first, so I thought...'

'What, that you're special?' Rising and brushing the cigarette ash from her jeans onto the carpet, Tash says, 'Sorry.' The cigarette is between her lips once more as she reaches for her coat. Her eyes are on Nevis. 'I have to go now. You want my advice, don't go to lunch.'

'Why not?'

'You're really clever, Nevis. You don't need Cullen's help.' With that she pulls on her coat and picks up her backpack. Curious, Nevis follows her to the door. The Tash who first came in seems softer now and more subdued.

In the doorway she turns and, reaching out a hand, quite unexpectedly touches Nevis's face. 'Take care of yourself, doll. And remember, there's no such thing as a free lunch.'

Chapter 30

Honor

The wood burner is warming up the *Helene*, the sun is out, and Honor and Alex are eating his scrambled eggs and talking over the work that needs doing on the *Halcyon Days*. When was the last time I did something like this? Honor wonders to herself. It almost feels like a date.

'How are the eggs?' says Alex, bringing more coffee.

'Wonderful! It's been ages since someone made me brunch.'

'Any time,' Alex says, laughing. 'I do an excellent cooked breakfast too.'

'Oh!' Heat stipples Honor's cheeks and Alex, seeing this, holds up a hand and says, 'I'm sorry, I didn't mean…'

'No, I didn't think…' Honor says, trying not to sound disappointed.

A moment's silence falls before Alex says, 'How's your daughter?'

Honor recounts the sorry finale to their last encounter.

'I'm sorry. Kids can be such a worry.'

'Yours?'

'Tim, my son? He lives in Berlin. I wish I saw more of him.

His mother lives not too far from here so when he does come over, we both get a share of him.'

'Were you with her? The mother, I mean.'

'We tried but it turned out we were better at being friends. You in touch with Nevis's father?'

'No and I don't intend to be. Nevis has never met him.'

'Because?'

'Because it wouldn't help.'

'Oh, I see,' Alex says, not seeing, but backing off. 'Are there grandparents?'

Honor lets out a bitter laugh, then checks herself. 'Her birth mother's parents were a nightmare. And mine were never really "around" in the traditional sense. During the late eighties and through most of the nineties they were busy colonising Planet Rave. I was brought along for the ride, and because they would never have had any money for babysitters. Now they're on a commune in mid-Wales. More of a cult, actually. I see them once a year or so. They sort of left me to bring myself up. We were always on the road so I never had any stability, never really had any close friends until I met Nevis's birth mother, but I had a great time with my imaginary friends and it made me pretty self-sufficient. It was an amazingly free childhood, I'll say that for it, and it's left me with this anti-authoritarian streak. I want to kick out against the man without having a man to kick out against, if you see what I mean.' She looks up and smiles. 'That's probably more than you wanted to know.'

'Not remotely. Explains the boat life. All that roaming.'

'Maybe, though the *Kingfisher*'s been on a residential mooring for the last decade and a half so there hasn't been much of that. I do feel more peaceful on the water though. And you're always moving, aren't you, even if it's only on the currents or with the tide. We bargees know we can always cut loose and take off on the water. That's the biggest part of it. Not feeling trapped.' She looks up and smiles. 'I wasn't really cut out for the rat race. I haven't really made very much of myself.'

'I've had a look at the work you've done on the bulkhead. You're a very fine restorer of boats.'

'Thank you.'

'Anyway, the rat race is hardly something to aspire to. I should know, I was the rat that the phrase rat race was invented for,' Alex says.

'Were you working on the tabloids?' she asks, feeling her chest tighten. There had been a little coverage of Zoe's death in the red tops. This was before everything had gone online. It hadn't been kind.

'Oh no,' he said, reassuringly. 'Local papers mostly. Actually it wasn't particularly high-pressured. The rat bit was more about occasionally having to doorstep some mother who'd just lost her kid in a fire. I remember one poor woman turning to me and saying, "How do I *feel*? I couldn't be happier. How the fuck do you think I feel, you knobhead?" Totally deserved. Nowadays I stay away from all that. Better for it.'

'Ever married?' Honor finishes the last morsel of food on her plate and lines up the cutlery.

'Nearly, to my son's mother, but no. You?'

Honor shakes her head. At that moment Nevis's ringtone chirps and Alex bustles away with the plates.

'Hello darling?'

'Something awful happened.' There is a quaver in Nevis's voice, a stumble almost, but she is not crying. A moment passes before Honor can fully absorb the news. The name Jessica Easton is unfamiliar but distinctive enough for Honor to be sure that she would have remembered it if Nevis had ever mentioned the girl.

'Her poor parents! Why don't I come over? I can be with you in a jiffy.'

'Thanks, but I've got uni stuff to do. Avon has issued a statement on social which is, like, Jessica Easton had mental health problems.'

'Did you know her?'

'Not really, she was a friend of Satnam's or maybe not a friend but Satnam knew her better than me. She was really, really skinny so I guess it was obvious she had anorexia or something...'

'I think you can be any size and have anorexia.'

'Maybe, but that's not the point. The high-ups are trying to make it look like Jessica and Satnam aren't connected.'

'And you think they are...?'

'I'd say the probability is pretty high, yes.'

'Darling, don't you think this is all a bit much for you? Why don't you let me come round? Or you can come here if you like.'

There's a pause then Nevis's voice, sounding more resolute. 'It's OK.'

Doing her best not to sound hurt by yet another rejection, and thinking about Lea Keane, Honor says, 'Is there someone you can talk to at the university? Student welfare?'

'The Dean maybe. I've got a meeting with him later.'

'Are you sure you're all right?'

'Yes.'

With that Nevis rings off, leaving Honor poised as if on the brink of something and not knowing whether to step forward or hang back.

'Something wrong?' Alex says, returning five minutes later with more coffee.

'No, no, I mean, yes, but...' Everything Honor has seen of Alex so far suggests a sensitive, open-hearted type but they barely know one another. 'Someone my daughter knew, another student, took her own life last night.'

'That's awful. I'm so sorry.'

'Nevis is upset because the university seems to have issued a rather bald statement saying that the girl had a history of mental health problems.'

'Neither kind nor adequate in the circumstances.'

'No. I should think they're running scared. Doing whatever they can to distance themselves.'

'How is Nevis taking it?'

'She says she's OK but she sounded upset. I'll give her a call later...' She tails off and swallows hard. The skin on her face feels hot and itchy. 'Alex, can I tell you something?'

'Of course.'

'About six months ago, something changed between me and Nevis. Not the usual teenage stuff or mother–daughter stuff. It happened overnight, like a tulip going over, you know, the way the petals drop away until all that's left is the green centre.'

'And you have no idea what caused it?'

Sometimes it is easier just to tell the whole truth.

'I'm not sure. There was one evening when I came in a bit worse for wear and inadvertently called Nevis by her birth mother's name.' Alex winces sympathetically but says nothing, so Honor continues, 'I think Nevis believes I would rather she was more like Zoe. It's not true though. I never wanted Nevis to be anyone but herself. It was just an idiotic mistake.'

'We all make them.'

It is good of Alex to want to try to console her but she is not ready to be soothed.

'But that was at the end of last spring and things settled down over the summer. At least I thought they did. Nevis's friend, Satnam – the one who's in hospital – came to stay with her boyfriend Luke and we had a great time. Just before Nevis came back here for the start of the academic year something happened. I've no idea what and she won't tell me, but her attitude towards me completely changed. Like, overnight.' She feels her face prickle, the tear ducts begin to pulse. Her hands ball into fists from the effort of chasing the tears away. 'I just wonder if, I don't know, she was attacked or something and doesn't know how to tell me.'

For a moment Alex hesitates, uncertain how best to respond, then gathering himself, he leans towards her and lays a hand on her shoulder.

'The work on the boat will wait… I'm sorry, that was a silly thing to say. Of course the boat doesn't matter at all.' His hand grips the flesh where the arm meets the shoulder. 'What I really meant to say is that you might feel better if you find out.'

Chapter 31

Nevis

'Do you know Luigi's? It's only a few minutes' walk away,' the Dean says.

On the way over to the Deanery, Nevis had felt a stirring in her belly. The Dean had taken a special interest in her which could only mean that in some small way she was herself special. Gifted, if only in the mathematical realm. No one other than Satnam and, perhaps, Bill, their neighbour on the water in Hackney, had ever sought out her company. Her life had been lived in the absence of birthday party invitations and sleepovers. She'd never gone out for meals, was a stranger to a catch-up drink or a weekend get-together. Now, finally, someone had invited her somewhere, and not just anyone, but the man whose intellect and mathematical intelligence she respected more than that of anyone else she had ever met. By the time she reached the Dean's door she'd all but forgotten Jessica and felt almost dizzy with excitement.

Now, hurrying to stay abreast of the Dean as he strides across the car park towards the main campus gate, she feels the light, summery expansiveness inside her gradually fading. The Dean fills the opening space on their short walk to the restaurant with small talk about the university. Struggling to keep pace, Nevis does her best to reciprocate but she's already hopelessly out of her depth.

Before long he stops at a brightly lit doorway and pushes it open, lifting his arm to form an arch to allow Nevis to proceed into the interior. A short, wiry man comes up, smiling warmly, and greets the Dean with a vigorous handshake and hesitates as if waiting for something to happen. The Dean, returning the smile with one of his own, says, 'Don't worry, Luigi, I've got it,' and turning to Nevis with raised eyebrows, holds out a hand and says, 'Your coat?'

Nevis fumbles with the buttons, embarrassed at her hopelessness. Her earlier airiness, her sense of possibility, felt like an overlay now, a temporary concealment, like a cloud passing over the midsummer sun. All gone now, leaving her feeling like she might bake in the bright heat of Cullen's brilliance.

The Dean hangs her peacoat on a peg, then covers it with his own tweed jacket. As she watches she catches herself wondering what it would feel like to fold her own self into him, to be enveloped in his arms. Where did such dizzy notions come from? Shocked at herself and perturbed at the thump of her heart, she drops her gaze and breathes herself back to calmness while Luigi shows them to a tan leatherette banquette set into the right-hand wall at the back of the restaurant. The Dean waits for her to sit and the waiter waits for both of them, before placing the menus on the table and announcing a couple of specials. The Dean thanks him and watches him leave before turning to Nevis and in a rueful tone says, 'I wish we were having lunch in happier circumstances. The food is really wonderful.'

She nods, anxious that the phrase 'happier circumstances' is an indication that the conversation is about to head into choppy waters.

The Dean says, 'You'll have a glass of wine, won't you? We could probably both use one.'

With a wave of the hand he signals the waiter over and orders two large glasses of Chianti. They wait in silence until the wine arrives. She is aware that he is looking at her but manages to avoid his gaze, afraid of embarrassing herself by her girlishness. Is it possible he finds her attractive? No, she can hardly dare to imagine that's it. Admires her perhaps, is impressed by the byways of her mind.

'You seem a little unsettled,' he says, smiling kindly. 'Hardly surprising in the circumstances. We've had news from Satnam's parents this morning. She's stable, so that's a good thing.'

'Yes,' she says, touched by his concern but torn, too, by his assumption that Satnam is the cause of her anxiety because the fact of the matter is that in the last ten minutes she has almost – but not quite – forgotten her friend.

When the wine appears, he raises his glass. She reciprocates, and gulping down half the contents, allows herself a moment of fantasy. Here they are, a couple of mathematicians joined together by their appreciation of the perfection of algebra and geometry.

He opens his mouth to speak and she braces herself, hoping that whatever is coming next, she will be able to meet it. The Collatz Conjecture or perhaps – she blushes at the thought – the Kissing Number Problem.

Instead, he says, 'I expect you've heard about Jessica Easton? Nothing stays off social media for long.'

She catches his eye briefly then tilts her head away so that he will not see her anguish as the world comes crashing back in. Is this why the Dean invited her to lunch? To talk about a dead girl?

'Yes, I heard.'

'You knew her, I suppose? It's very sad. The timing...' he stops himself and directs his gaze downwards as if scooping up thoughts lying on the floor. 'Of course, we knew she was ill, but why she chose this moment is a mystery.'

Nevis presses her lips so tight it feels they might burst from their skins, like two sausages, and reaches for her wineglass. She thinks, please don't make me talk about this. I don't know what to say.

'Oh, you've nearly finished your wine. Let's get you another.' The Dean waves to attract the waiter's attention and points to her wineglass.

She waits for the wine with her hands in her lap, head bowed. The food hasn't yet arrived and she's already gulped down a large glass. He will think she's a boozer.

'So then, Jessica,' he begins.

She wishes he'd leave the subject. 'I didn't know her very well.'

'It's so difficult for the parents when they have nothing to go on,' Cullen says, ignoring her response. 'I don't suppose you know whether she left any kind of communication. A letter, or, I suppose, more likely these days, a text message or an email?'

The waiter returns to take the food order. She glances at the menu.

'Nevis?' the Dean says, with one eye on the waiter.

'Oh, I... I haven't really looked.' There is panic in her voice.

Cullen's eyes fall back to the menu. 'The spaghetti arrabbiata is rather wonderful here.'

'OK,' she says. The only spaghetti she knows is Honor's spaghetti bolognaise. She'd cooked it that evening last summer, when Satnam and Luke came to stay; before the letter, before the incident on the bridge, before Jessica's death, before everything mad and weird and inexplicable. The Dean orders two portions of the spaghetti and a side salad and another two glasses of wine. At that moment his phone pings. He picks it up and inspects the screen, then puts it down again.

Clearing his throat he says, 'You were saying, before, that Jessica and Satnam were friends.'

Did she say that? If she did, she has no memory of doing so. Why is he interrogating her like this? Didn't he say he wanted to talk about her work and also to tell her something? Was this the something? If only she understood better what was expected in this kind of situation.

'I'm not sure.'

'Oh, but you *did* say,' he says, smiling, his gaze not following. 'I wanted to ask whether you'd managed to get into Satnam's phone? We thought it might be useful, you know, to understand what might have been going on in Jessica's mind. The two of them almost certainly had some kind of correspondence, given they were friends, like you said.'

'Yes. I mean, no, I still don't know the passcode.' She wonders whether she should mention what Tash had told her about Jessica's previous attempt to kill herself but decides not to. This whole situation has left her feeling confused and anxious, not knowing whether it would be right to pass on something that might not be true. In such situations, she thought, perhaps it was best to say nothing.

'I see,' Cullen says now. 'It might be a good idea to leave the device with me. I can pass it on to the parents. As a matter of fact, I mentioned it to them and they did say they would love to have it.'

'Yes, yes, of course.'

'No hurry. Next time you come into the university. Later today or tomorrow will be fine.'

The food arrives. Nevis picks at the pasta and tries not to flinch at the spiciness of the sauce.

'Do you like it?' he says.

'Yes,' she says, doing her best to conjure a smile.

'*Arrabbiata* means angry.' He fixes her with a steady look and, returning her smile, in a gentle voice continues, 'Sometimes, when someone makes a suicide attempt, the person's loved ones can sometimes feel quite terrible anger, almost rage really.'

'Oh,' she says. Her head is suddenly rather swimmy. Is that the wine?

His eyes have been on her all this time. 'It can be terribly unproductive, that kind of anger. It can lead people to do very destructive things.'

'Oh but...'

He lifts a hand to silence her but there is still a smile on his face. 'Here's what I think. I think no one would blame you in the least if you were feeling quite a bit angry. Or if not angry, then very upset.'

'They wouldn't?'

'No, in fact they'd think how brave you are to acknowledge it.'

A kind of flustered silence falls between them. Not long

afterwards the waiter, returning for the plates, asks if either party would like a dessert.

The Dean says, 'Not for me, but I'm sure this young lady can fit in a tiramisu.'

Nevis demurs but the Dean orders anyway. Waiting until the waiter is out of earshot, Cullen leans in and says, 'I hope you know, Nevis, that you are an exceptional mathematician, without question a candidate for a first, and I'd like to help you fulfil your potential.' Cullen finishes his wine, observing her so intently that she has to look at her feet and pretend to be somewhere else. The skin on her face begins to redden. That someone like the Dean could show such an interest in *her* and think she has potential.

'But that means that we have to work together to make sure this thing with Satnam doesn't derail you.' He taps two fingers on the back of her hand and oh God, she could burst. 'So I think you should tell me what's troubling you. Your friend in hospital, obviously, but deeper than that.'

She sits back in her chair feeling the breath in her body, sensing that the time has finally come and that the Dean will not only listen but he will understand. Taking a deep breath through her nose she opens her mouth and begins to speak, starting with what Jessica had said about the row at the Valentine's Day party, leaving Natasha out of the picture, and going on to say that she had found Satnam crying and saying she wanted to leave and how she, Nevis, is someone who likes clear lines of thought and this has all become a bit of a jumble in her head and left her unsure what to think.

Once she's finished, to her surprise, he reaches out and takes her hand in his as if he were placing something very precious in it. There is something so shocking about the feel of her hand inside another, larger and masculine, that she does not think to pull away. Perhaps she does not want to pull away. She is not thinking about Jessica or about Satnam now. She is thinking about him, the touch of his palm in hers, the pulse in his fingers, the brush of the hairs on his arm on her wrist. The moment lasts a few seconds but leaves her feeling deliciously bewildered.

'Look,' he says, 'there's absolutely no point in speculating about what might or might not have been going through Satnam's mind. The important thing is to stay strong and try not to let any of this get to you. Stay away from social media and keep your distance from anyone who tries to push you off course.' He sets his glass aside and dabs at his mouth. She watches his lips. 'Speaking of which, haven't I seen you and Natasha Tillotson together in the last couple of days? You were in the library, as I recall.'

'Yes,' – she hadn't spotted him there, 'but I've only got to know her very recently. Since…' She tails off, realising that she hasn't mentioned Tash's emails and wondering if she should, then deciding against it. From what he just said the Dean thinks Tash might come into the category of people it might be best to avoid right now. Besides which, there is no need to resort to tittle-tattle or idle gossip. The Dean would think less of her if she divulged anything that wasn't relevant or made Natasha look bad.

Expecting that to be the end of the matter she pushes away her tiramisu and finishes the double espresso the Dean ordered with her dessert, but to her surprise, the Dean is not done with the subject. 'Take it from me, girls like Natasha can be very destabilising. Besides, I'm not sure how much longer she'll be at Avon.' He taps the bulb of his nose with a slender finger. 'But I didn't tell you that. So let's focus on you getting that first and set aside everything else for the moment.'

Nevis is at once curious and flattered. To be trusted with the Dean's secret! To have prior knowledge of something that perhaps only Natasha and the Dean know. Not that it's any great surprise. Hadn't Jessica said that she, Natasha and Satnam had all been thinking about leaving back in February? Wasn't that what the row at the Valentine's Day party had been all about?

The Dean catches the waiter's eye and flicks his chin for the bill. They wait in silence while he deposits a small fan of banknotes on the table. 'Shall we go?' he says, and without waiting for an answer, rises from the booth. She gets up and walks back under the arch made by his arm at the doorway and into the daylight. It is warm and the lunchtime shoppers are out.

'Well, I'll leave you here,' says the Dean, at the entrance to the campus. 'Remember what I said. Put all of the events of the last few days out of your mind. Don't think about it and certainly don't waste your time gossiping about it. You are so special, Nevis, you have such a great future ahead of you. It would be a shame to put any of that in jeopardy, don't you think?' He turns to go and thinking better of it, spins about on his heels to face her, raising a finger in the air as if testing the direction of the wind. 'I almost forgot. Satnam's phone. I'll be in meetings, but you can leave it with my secretary. No hurry. Next day or two will be fine.'

Chapter 32

Cullen

On his way back to the office, Cullen keeps his head down, anxious not to be accosted by anyone wanting anything from him, chewing over the lunch in his mind, pleased to have secured to his satisfaction a full understanding of the limits of the Smith girl's knowledge and to have made such an obvious impression on her. She knows almost nothing of consequence, of that he is sure. Satnam had evidently never confided in her and Natasha and Jessica had chosen to tell her very little either. He considered he'd done a good job of putting her off the scent. And although it would make him feel better to have Satnam's phone in his possession – he believed in the belt and braces approach – he thought the device was unlikely to present much of a threat. The Manns still seemed to think it had been lost somewhere between the bridge and the ICU. It was a little odd that Nevis hadn't told them that it was in her possession, but perhaps it hadn't occurred to her. She seemed an unworldly creature. Nevis hadn't made any effort to crack the passcode so she evidently didn't believe that there was anything on the phone worth looking at. All in all, the lunch had made him feel better, more secure. The phone would soon be in his possession and, so long as he wasn't stupid enough to pull another stunt like the one at the hospital, Maddy would support him. Mark Ratner could be contained with threats if nothing else. He'd find a way to get the loan shark off his back, Veronica would get pregnant, and the Dalek would die. The only real threat to his future – and his sanity – might be Natasha Tillotson. What he really wanted to do was find a way to get rid of her before she started making trouble. The clock began ticking down on Natasha's future at Avon the moment Cullen saw her getting into Ratner's car. The affair was one thing. In normal circumstances he'd have found a way to feign ignorance, but the fact that he'd caught the two of them in the lab that night and that Ratner was insisting on maintaining his connection to her made that impossible. Natasha knew that he, Cullen, knew about the affair and had chosen not to do anything about it. She didn't know why but then nor did Ratner. Which was why he'd called an emergency meeting with the girl to 'discuss her performance'.

It was hardly an unreasonable request. Natasha Tillotson had proved herself to be one of the worst students the department had ever had the misfortune to recruit. Three months after her arrival at Avon Cullen had more or less given up on her. Her work was always late and she seldom if ever completed the required reading. At the end of her first academic year she was put on notice. Then something strange happened. After Cullen had caught Natasha and Ratner *in flagrante* he'd checked the girl's academic records, hoping to find an excuse to get rid of her, and spotted a disturbing pattern. So far as Cullen could see, she was still the same lazy, unmotivated student of only average intelligence she had always been but in the last few weeks, he noticed from checking the records, she was routinely coming top of the class. Which didn't make any sense unless someone was giving her a leg up.

That someone was very likely to be Mark Ratner, who also happened to have begun an affair with Natasha in the last few weeks. Evidently, he had been doctoring Natasha's grades hoping that no one would notice, and no one would have done, if Cullen hadn't caught the couple cavorting half naked in the biosciences lab and had taken it upon himself to look up the girl's records.

At the time Cullen had decided to let the infraction go, thinking it better not to draw attention to failings of over-sight in the department that were ultimately his responsibility. There were other reasons for staying under the radar too. But Jessica Easton's death makes it inevitable that all eyes will be on the department for a while and the conduct of staff must be seen to be 100 per cent above board. Time to sweep the department clean of corrupting influences. Which means Natasha Tillotson. The girl simply has to go.

Making his way to a dull meeting room with a suspended ceiling and a whiteboard, he offers a brief greeting to the occupants and with no apology for his intentional lateness, takes a seat at the head of the grey conference table.

He waits for Keane to stop nervously scrolling through a file of papers. Then opening his laptop and resting his elbows on the table he turns to Natasha and says, 'Has Dr Keane explained why we asked to see you?'

Natasha Tillotson nods but does not look up. He cannot tell whether she is nervous or defiant but it makes no difference to him either way.

'I've explained the Fit to Study assessment,' Keane says, with her customary delight in jargon. Turning to Natasha, in a bright voice she adds, 'We're here today to help you succeed.'

Cullen thinks he detects an eyeroll from the girl.

Cullen drinks his coffee and tries to block out the sound of Keane enthusiastically relaying the support services available to Natasha. Cullen has already informed Keane that it's almost certainly too late and the best solution all round is for Natasha to leave. Had Keane checked Natasha's academic records, which she may well have done, she will have spotted a student in considerable academic peril and will most likely take the same view. Had this been the end of the academic year, it would have been too late to have corrected Ratner's overestimation of his paramour's academic prowess but Cullen has seen to it that Natasha's myriad failures have been faithfully recorded. Indeed, he might even have tweaked the odd, marginal, grade downwards. A kindness in the long run. Girls like Natasha don't belong in academe.

As Keane chatters on, he leans back and allows his mind to drift back to lunch at Luigi's and most especially to the troubling remembrance of Nevis's hand in his. The gesture had been a calculated attempt to keep her close in order to get her to tell him what he wanted to know, but her response to his touch and, more to the point, perhaps, his own response surprised him. Until that moment he'd never once thought of her in any sexual way at all. Yet there was some palpable electricity between them that he found shockingly exciting.

His reverie is interrupted by Keane saying, 'So, over to you, Professor,' catching him off guard. He glances at Natasha who appears shell-shocked. Perhaps she thought that her little tryst with Ratner would protect her. He is ready with an intervention should she attempt to use it as leverage. Or even to speak of it. This is between him and her and Ratner. Keane doesn't need to know.

'Thank you, Dr Keane,' he says, buying himself a moment to collect his thoughts. He turns to the laptop and peers at the screen as though he's been chewing over Natasha's case. 'I've looked at your grades.'

He watches Natasha's face brighten. She thinks she's in the clear. What a little fool. 'Let's see, the last two pieces of coursework... 28 per cent on the cell dynamics module, *18* per cent for biochemistry.' He puts the emphasis on the word eighteen and raises his eyebrows to indicate a rueful awakening. In fact, the figures were as laughingly simple to downgrade as they had been for Ratner to inflate. A few keystrokes earlier this morning and it was done.

'But...' The girl's eyes flick to Cullen's face and flare, though whether she's beseeching or trying to warn him he neither knows nor cares. If she has any sense, she'll go quietly. If she doesn't, then Cullen will have to use other methods of persuasion. The only reason she's hung on this long is because Mark Ratner has an appetite for blow jobs from pretty girls.

To his surprise, Natasha's eyes flare again and she sits bolt upright, her hands slamming on the table. 'Why are we even doing this? Your students are throwing themselves off bridges and you're sitting here harassing me. I know exactly why Jessica Easton killed herself,' Natasha says with a steeliness that sends a spear into Cullen's heart. She narrows her eyes and for a minute Cullen feels his mouth go dry. He stares at her with an intensity designed to scare. She does not give way immediately. For a few moments they are locked in a battle of wills, then, thinking better of crossing him, she blows air out of her cheeks and folds her arms over her chest.

'It's that kind of language...' Cullen says.

'Very unhelpful,' Keane agrees, crossing her legs over one another.

'It's our responsibility to set up each student to succeed,' Cullen goes on, trotting out his pre-prepared speech. Natasha has just unwittingly made all this so much easier. 'We were undecided as to what to do but I'm now of the strong view that you'd be better transferring to another, less demanding, university. I would be happy to recommend a few places and see to it that you got a good reference.'

Natasha stares at Cullen. He meets her eye impassively. Suddenly she looks away, biting her lip, but says nothing. The penny has dropped. He, Cullen, is cutting the girl a deal. She has understood that the price is her silence.

'We'll give you a week or so to think about it,' Cullen says.

Keane pulls out a printed form, ticks a few boxes and makes a few notes, and it's over. Cullen watches her tidy her papers and put them in her bag, and then she stands to leave, brushing down her floral dress with her pudgy, sweaty paws.

Cullen turns his head to Natasha and raises a finger. 'Why don't you stay behind for a few minutes and we can have a think about a more suitable place for you?' The Tillotson girl says nothing but makes no attempt to get up. Turning back to Keane. 'Lea, I'll see you tomorrow.'

'Absolutely.' Holding out a hand to Natasha, Keane says, 'Well, goodbye, Natasha. I wish you well in your new academic home.' Natasha blinks and without taking the hand looks away.

'Take out your phone,' Cullen says, once Lea Keane has left the room.

Natasha reaches into her pocket and places her phone on the table. Cullen picks it up and checks the off switch.

'I know what this is,' Natasha says, petulantly. 'A fucking ambush.'

'This is the best deal you'll get. Do you hear?'

The girl says nothing.

'You transfer to another university. We'll send you on your way with a glowing reference. If you work hard, you'll still be able to graduate.' She opens her mouth to speak but he silences her with a glare. 'Otherwise you will find your grades steadily decline and by the end of the year you will be forced out. No references.'

Natasha's mouth is set in a thin line of defiance but her eyes are blurry. 'You knew what you were getting into,' he says. 'You knew it wouldn't last.'

A sob bubbles up from somewhere deep in the girl's chest.

Cullen leans towards her and reaches for her chin, cupping it momentarily in his hand. 'Use your head.' The words bring an inner smile. Christ, as if that isn't what she's already been doing. 'What I mean is,' he says, correcting himself, 'use your *brain*.'

'You are a pig, you know that, *Professor* Cullen? You're nothing, an oink, a pig.'

He smiles, amused. 'Have you, I wonder, read *Animal Farm*? At school perhaps?'

She creases her brow, a puzzled expression on her face.

'Oh you should, it's a marvellous book. There's a pig in the story by the name of Napoleon. Clever fellow. Has a way of getting what he wants.'

Chapter 33

Honor

Honor, who has been sanding the bulkhead, feels the weight distribution of the boat change as someone climbs on deck of the *Halcyon Days*.

'Hey! Can I come down?' Alex's voice.

'Of course.' She had been hoping it might be Nevis. Removing her work gloves, she moves into the saloon and sees a pair of legs in jeans before Alex appears carrying a file in one hand and in the other a tray of plant cuttings.

She says, 'You're just in time for tea.'

'Excellent.' He puts the cuttings down on the table and slides onto the bench. 'I brought you some geraniums. I always do some for the homeless encampment. People seem to appreciate them. Last year, we made some raised beds at the back, behind the bivvies, and grew courgettes and tomatoes. Council turned a blind eye. Anyway, I thought if you were going to be here for a couple of months, you might like a few. If you keep them inside, they'll be flowering in a month.'

'How kind of you,' she says, reaching for the geraniums and fingering the velvety leaves between her fingers. Alex *is* kind, she's noticed that. It's rarer than it should be, kindness, compassion.

'How are you getting on with the work?'

The kettle begins to growl. She reaches for a couple of teabags, drops them in some none-too-clean cups, hopes Alex won't notice. 'I had a quick look at the consumer unit earlier. It would be a good idea to get a marine electrician in to look at the RCD. Something about it doesn't look right. Bit of a fire risk. I'd do the basic electrical stuff myself but I'm reluctant to mess with the consumer unit on a boat I don't know.'

'OK. I'll call my guy. He's usually booked up so it might have to wait a week or so.'

'No hurry,' she says, washing her hands in the kitchen sink and putting on the kettle.

'I can give you a hand with the sanding and painting if you like.'

'Thank you but don't feel you have to...'

'I'd enjoy the company.'

She brings the tea over and sits. 'No biscuits, sorry.'

'You've had other things on your mind. Me too, actually. I told you I used to be a local reporter, didn't I? When you mentioned the response at Avon I was reminded of this investigation into a series of copycat student suicides at Midland University, oh, must have been a decade ago. Four or five deaths, all boys, all studying law and all within a few months of one another.'

Alarmed, Honor holds up a staying hand. 'I don't think we're there yet.'

'No, but hear me out. Midland University initially said they couldn't have done anything to intervene because they didn't know how the students had died but it later turned out they'd sent a representative to the coroner's hearings after the deaths and knew perfectly well. They ignored the fact that they had a suicide contagion on their hands and then they covered up the fact that they'd ignored it.'

'Why?'

'One, it looks bad. Two, it puts off kids from applying. The uni doesn't get its pick of students, they struggle to keep up in the results tables, so they fall some more in the ratings, so their funding gets cut. And on and on in a Darwinian struggle for survival. The students are just collateral damage.'

'I know how that goes,' she says, thinking that this is all beginning to feel like history repeating itself.

'You were there?'

'No, no, somewhere else.'

A pregnant pause follows, which Honor feels no obligation to fill. It's Alex who breaks the silence. 'You know, it's odd, how we tell our kids that university is the best days of their lives, as though there's nothing more in adult life to look forward to, and then we wonder why the kids who struggle feel hopeless. They're looking at their lives and thinking, if this is as good as it's ever going to get, I won't bother, thanks all the same.

'What happened at Midland didn't just impact those kids and their families. The ripple effect was enormous: neighbours, friends, a whole generation of students most of whom didn't even know their dead compatriots, staff at the university. It rocked the whole city.'

Honor's not sure where this is going. Taking a deep breath, Alex goes on. 'When I was a reporter, it was all about access and authority, who had access to people in power and the authority to ask them difficult questions. If you didn't have those, you couldn't write the piece.

'You're the parent of a student at the university. That gives you authority. The high-ups can't just brush you off in the way they might a student. And Nevis has access. She knows the right people to talk to. If there's something fishy going on...'

'Did I say that?'

'Not in so many words.' He looks up and, reading the uncertainty in her face, flashes her a soft smile. 'Look, maybe I'm just a cynical old hack. I'm just saying, there's form for this kind of stuff, a cover-up if you like, and if you two *did* want to look at it, you'd be a great investigative team. Mother–daughter private eyes. Make a good TV show don't you think?' His tone is light and conciliatory now.

She leans back and takes a sip of tea, enjoying the conceit for a moment, letting it bed in, before adding, 'That presumes we're on the same side. Which, at the moment...' She tails off, not wanting to delve into her sadder feelings.

'And at least one of you would need to be a drunk with a penchant for over-complicated sex,' he says, lips cracking into a broad grin.

It feels good to laugh. She lingers on its tail end and waits for Alex to break the atmosphere. Eventually, when the last laugh has been had, he says, 'Granted, I can be a paranoid bugger, but something's amiss.'

'I think I can pretty confidently say that Satnam didn't take a massive overdose of Ritalin and drink most of a bottle of vodka by accident.'

'Hmm.' Alex draws a piece of yellowed paper from his file and places it on the table. 'I found the original press cutting about the Midland Uni thing. It appeared in the *Midlands Observer*, written by my ex, and the mother of my son actually, Anne Devlin, who also happened to be my colleague at the time. Like I said, it became a big scandal locally though it didn't make much play in the national media. God knows why. How many dead kids does it take?'

She picks up the clip and scans it. 'Says that Ritalin was "involved" in at least one of the cases.'

'Wasn't there a scandal about Ritalin back in the noughties? Kids being diagnosed with ADHD and massively overprescribed as I recall.'

Just then a draught flusters the geranium cuttings. She pulls the tray over to the other side of the table where the air is warmer and still and is aware of Alex's eyes on her. 'I remember that. They say it's easy to get it on the street now. Students take it to stay awake for essay deadlines.'

'Ah yes. In my day it was speed. I guess there's always something.'

'But you have to take a lot for it to be seriously damaging. It's not a drug you're likely to accidentally OD on.'

Another pause follows while the two of them take this in. Then Alex says, 'I looked through my notes of editorial meetings. Anne did some digging and discovered that all the students were taught by the same academic, a professor on the verge of retirement called Arthur Reynolds. I googled him. A while after the suicides some allegations of sexual assault emerged. The university allowed him to retire. There was a court case but Reynolds died before coming to trial. There was some suggestion on the web that he'd killed himself, but I couldn't confirm that.'

'I sense you're going somewhere with this...'

Alex holds up his hand. 'Guilty as charged.' Leaning his weight back and rocking gently on the back legs of his chair, he goes on. 'Listen to this. Professor Reynolds had a young female academic working under him at Midland who'd been his PhD student. After he took retirement, she became head of department. Anne interviewed her and she was mentioned at our editorial conference but none of that interview made it into the final piece, not least because she was absolutely adamant that Reynolds was innocent of any wrongdoing and didn't appear to be terribly upset about the deaths of the boys, which I remember thinking was odd at the time, particularly since they were students in her own department. There was no suggestion that she was involved in any of the sexual assaults, but if you think about it, she had to have known about them. Reynolds was a prolific predator and she worked very closely with him for a number of years and did very well from her association with him.

'Anyway, the moment I saw her name I had a feeling that I'd come across her more recently. Nothing I could pin down but I'm used to going with my gut, so I checked her out on Google to see what she'd been up to. Turns out her career took a meteoric rise after Reynolds, though so far as I could see she didn't do any of the things that academics generally do to get ahead, like publish or appear on TV or whatever. I was right about her name being familiar though. I've seen it from time to time in the local rag here in Bristol.'

'And?'

'She's the current Vice Chancellor of Avon University. Madeleine Ince.'

Chapter 34

Nevis

They meet at a 'Spoons near Broadmead. Tash is almost unrecognisable, her face puffed and raw, her body alive with nervy energy. Before her sits a pint, half drunk, another emptied glass beside it. She's wasted.

'I know I look like shit,' she says. 'So do me a favour and don't look, OK?'

Nevis takes off her jacket, drapes it round the chair, studiously avoiding checking Tash out. 'You want another drink?'

'Yeah, go on. Pint of Abbot's.'

Nevis waits at the bar, pays with her phone and picks up Tash's pint and a half of Guinness for herself. As she walks from the bar she finds her thoughts turning to the Student's t-test, devised by William Gosset, a mathematician at the turn of the twentieth century and an employee of the Guinness Brewing company, to describe the probable error of a mean in different sized samples of hops. Wonders if the Dean knows the test, decides that yes, given its ubiquitousness, he must do. Considers raising it with him over their next lunch, thinks about where the Dean might take her and is aware, suddenly, as she places the pint glass on the table, that Tash is saying, '…so the bastards are trying to get rid of me.'

'Bastards?' Wasn't this meeting to talk about Jessica?

'Yeah, the Dean and that bitch in student welfare. They are practically forcing me to transfer somewhere else.'

Tash holds her head between her hands and begins to sob. William Gosset is chased from Nevis's mind now and replaced by the lunchtime conversation with the Dean. So this is what he'd meant about Tash not being at Avon much longer. He already knew he was going to ask her to leave. *Girls like Natasha can be very destabilising.*

Tash looks up from behind hooded lids and reaches for her beer, takes a long pull and, catching Nevis's eye, in a wobbly voice says, 'You have to promise me you won't tell anyone. I know you won't, that's partly why I wanted to meet.'

'I promise,' Nevis says.

'I've been having an affair with Mark Ratner. He told me it was over.' She puts a finger up to her mouth and tears off a strip of nail, spits it onto the floor. 'I texted him, I called him, though I'm not supposed to and he hasn't got back to me. And now Cullen and that bitch Keane are trying to split us up.' More tears. 'I'm so fucked up about it all. I think I love him. I don't know what to do.'

Nevis sits with her hands in her lap. A moth flutters dully in her chest. She can see Tash is upset, obviously, but if this were a mathematical formula, it would not have the requisite Boolean constants. There is too much conditionality. What is she supposed to say? The Dean comes to mind, or rather, the remembrance of his hand, the hairs on the wrist, the delicate nail beds, the tips of his fingers sitting on her flesh. What if the Dean made a move? She'd say yes wouldn't she?

Nevis takes a couple of gulps of Guinness, buying time, and wipes the back of her hand across her face. Tash is sitting up straight now, no longer tearful but with some dark energy that Nevis cannot interpret.

'I'm not going quietly. I'm going to tell *everything*.'

'About the affair?'

She fixes Nevis a penetrating stare. She seems oddly calm, as though a tap has been turned off in her head. 'No, dummy, I mean about *everything* that's been going on.' Clasping her arms around herself and rocking on her heels, Tash opens her lips to say more, then thinking better of it, retreats, her eyes glassing over, lips tight.

A young couple sweeps by laughing, and on the next table a man delivers the punchline to a joke. More laughter. Nevis is conscious that something important has just been said but she is not sure what or why. Tash is looking at her, head tilted to one side, like a wary bird. They sit there like this for a few moments, before Tash pipes up: 'You don't know, do you? You still haven't clocked it.'

'You could tell me?'

Tash shakes her head. 'Like I said before, it's best you don't. You're not like us, Nevis. You're good, or not good, exactly, maybe just innocent. I don't think you'd understand. In any case, there's nothing to say. Mark got bored of Jess and started up with me.' Her face is filmy and unreachable.

Mark Ratner with Jessica and with Tash? The thought of it makes Nevis's stomach turn twice. Ratty Ratner the love rat. How could Tash love a man like that?

Tash picks at another nail. She is sitting back now, with her eyes closed, tears running down her cheeks. 'I'm scared, Nevis.'

'Of Mark Ratner?'

'No, idiot. I'm scared of ending up like Jessica.'

Chapter 35

Cullen

Cullen plugs in the entry code and lets himself into the nursing home. A blast of warm, stale air hits him. As he moves through the hallway the stench of lilies on the turn hits his nostrils. Maura comes out of the office and greets him with a worried smile.

'I'm sorry to have to call you so late.'

'I'm glad you did,' he says. After what Veronica has just told him, he means this in more ways than Maura will know.

'We offered her a sedative, but she wouldn't take it. She's in her room.'

'I'll go and see what I can do,' he says.

It is gone midnight and the corridors are dimly lit, though for Cullen the route to Amanda's room is so familiar to him that he could find her room in the pitch dark. Sometimes he even walks it in his dreams or, rather, in his nightmares. He knocks and, getting no response, lets himself in. Amanda is sitting in her armchair with her eyes closed, but not asleep. She's had her hair done again and looks like nothing so much as an overripe peach whose skin has become furred and mouldy. He goes towards her and sits himself on the stool in front of her armchair.

She opens her eyes. 'Oh, it's you.'

'They told me something was wrong and you wanted me to come. Do you want to tell me what the problem is and why it can't wait till morning?'

A text pings onto his phone. Cullen takes the device out of his pocket and looks at the screen. He feels himself shrinking. Veronica.

Don't be long darling. I've put a bottle of champagne on ice.

She made the announcement over a very expensive dinner. *Isn't it gorgeous? You're going to be a daddy and I'm going to be a mummy!* Women with their demands. Do they ever stop? Cullen does not want to be a daddy. He doesn't want to be a son. Right now, all he wants is to be left alone to get a good night's sleep.

'It's late, Mother.'

'You can't expect me to sleep in this den of thieves? I might wake up with nothing left at all.'

At the mention of the word 'thieves' Cullen feels his whole body contract.

'My bracelet has gone. The gold and diamond one that was my mother's.'

'You've probably just misplaced it.'

'Have you any idea what that bracelet is worth?'

'I can guess,' he says. He does, in fact, know precisely what the bracelet is worth.

'They've stolen it. The so-called carers. They're all foreigners, you know. I always knew they couldn't be trusted. And now one of them has taken the only thing that ever meant anything to me.' She begins to cry.

Maura appears in the doorway. Amanda points an accusatory

finger. It strikes Cullen then that his mother is drunk. Absolutely pickled.

'Now, Amanda,' says Maura, sadly, 'I'm sure it will turn up.'

'That's what I said,' Cullen says, grateful to have back-up. 'I'll bet it's here somewhere, Mother,' Cullen says, hoping this will satisfy her and knowing, in his heart, that it won't. 'Have you looked everywhere?'

The Dalek snorts. 'What do you mean, *everywhere*? In case you hadn't noticed, this room is the size of a shoebox.'

'It's possible that a resident took it by mistake. A few of the residents do wander and they sometimes get confused,' Maura says. 'If that's what happened, it'll turn up.'

'I am not staying in this place a moment longer to have foreigners stealing my things,' Amanda says.

Cullen cannot let this pass. If Amanda starts along these lines, he'll be asked to move her. He considers, for a moment, telling her his news, but, seeing as it will inevitably mean he has less time for her, she will like it even less than he does. Instead he says, 'Now, now, Mother. Let's have a proper look tomorrow.' When he turns in the hope of seeking Maura's approval, he sees that she has already gone. Cullen can't blame her. I wish I could disappear, he thinks. Better still if the Dalek suffered some catastrophic malfunction, imploded from the inside, say, or fell apart. Falling apart would do.

'I brought some of that sherry you like,' he says, pulling a bottle from his bag. 'Why don't I wash up those glasses and we can have a quick one.' He watches his mother's face brighten momentarily and, picking up two glasses from the table, he goes into the bathroom. How easy it would be, he thinks, to put something in her drink now, something to ensure that she forgets about the bracelet, Rohypnol, perhaps, or mirtazapine. They must have loads of that kind of stuff in the locked cupboard where the drugs are kept. He catches himself in the mirror and does not feel guilty about the mirth in his eyes. Why stop at Rohypnol? What about strychnine or cyanide? If only he knew where to get such things.

He could use a wholesale quantity. There are one or two people, besides the Dalek, who he wouldn't mind seeing dead right now. Mark Ratner for one. Natasha Tillotson for another. Now, he thinks, there's an idea.

He emerges from the bathroom with a smile on his face.

'Now, Mother, let's have that drink. We'll sort everything else out in the morning.'

Driving back through slack, blustery rain, Cullen wonders if his life will belong to himself ever again. He parks the car in the driveway, gets out and goes towards the door. At least there is no thug lurking in the bushes this time. He owes that to his mother's bracelet. What would she do if she found out that it was him who'd taken it, he wonders. Would she take revenge? Might she be vengeful enough to spill the beans?

Veronica appears from the kitchen and plants a kiss on his face.

'How was Amanda?'

'Oh, you know.'

Veronica musses his hair. 'Forget about the old witch and come into the drawing room.' She has always called the living room the drawing room, without ever knowing how much he hates the affectation. He's not a fan of 'old witch' either, not when it comes from Veronica. A man's wife should not belittle his mother. It's one of the unspoken rules. But he's not going to say anything because he never says anything because she's the Honourable Veronica Fanshawe-Drew and he's a belly-crawling coward. God, I hate myself, he thinks, following his wife into the living room, where a bottle of vintage Krug sits in an ice bucket.

'Pop the cork, darling. I suppose it's a bit naughty of me to have any, now we're expecting. Still, a glass won't hurt, will it?'

As he moves to the table, he watches Veronica's expression change from glee to concern.

'Christopher, you're shaking! Are you quite all right?'

Chapter 36

Honor

'**P**ermission to board!'

Honor peers through the quayside window of the *Halcyon Days* and sees Alex clutching a large paper bag. She presses 'send' on the text to Nevis then looks up and, smiling, waves him in, taking a quick glance at herself in the kettle and flipping back a strand of hair as she moves through the boat to the hatch.

'I bought croissants. They're still warm.' He holds out the bag, smiling. She takes it, their fingers momentarily touching, and, feeling a blush rising to her face, turns away, hoping he cannot see it.

'How lovely! Take a seat and I'll make us some coffee.'

She fills the kettle and gets the coffee from the fridge, pulls a couple of plates from the rack, puts them on the table and notices his clothes: a smart Aran sweater, pair of cords and leather walking boots. Up till now he has always been in his boatman's uniform of denim overalls.

'You off somewhere?'

'Well yes, actually. I thought you might like to come?'

'Oh?' she says. Is he proposing they go on a date?

'After we talked about all that newspaper stuff, I gave Anne a call, realised it was ages since we'd seen one another. She invited me – us – for lunch. You fancy it? She's in one of the villages near Bath. I thought it might be a nice drive.'

'There's a lot to do here,' she says, getting up to make the coffee. While filling the cafetière she pulls her phone across the counter, presses to see if her text has been answered and, in a moment of preoccupation, pours boiling water over her finger.

At her cry Alex jumps up and rushes over. 'What happened?'

'I was being stupid.' She holds out the reddened digit. He takes her wrist between two fingers and draws her gently to the sink. Cool water flows over the reddened skin.

'You can't work with that hand for a few hours anyway,' Alex says, turning her wrist gently to change the flow of water over the finger. 'Please say yes. It's a lovely drive, the weather is gorgeous and I know you and Anne will get on. She's looking forward to meeting you.' He watches her face and, seeing the clouds scudding across it, pushes the point home. 'And you can ask her more about that Midland thing, now you've got a connection to it.'

'Connection?' Honor starts and pulls back. What has he found out? For a moment she forgets to breathe.

'Madeleine Ince, remember?' he says, looking puzzled.

'Oh, of course,' she says, letting the air fill her lungs once more.

'Please say yes. I've just joined one of those car-share schemes, so we can go in style.'

'Or in Gerry.' He cocks his head which makes him look rather charming. 'My van.'

'Well that would be lovely.'

'I'm a terrible driver.'

'Ah, well, perhaps lovely's the wrong word. An adventure. Who doesn't love one of those?'

An hour later they are on their way out of the city. The rush-hour traffic has subsided and now the usual clot of cars and buses lurches fitfully towards the motorway. At the second roundabout Gerry stalls and they miss the lights. Drivers behind toot their horns irritably.

'I did warn you.'

'Nonsense,' Alex says, doing his best to sound unconcerned as the van sets off once more and briefly mounts the kerb. 'You're a marvel.'

She turns to smile. Moments later, as the van veers towards the kerb again, she returns her attentions to the road.

'Oh yes, I do see,' says Alex. 'A very *creative* driver.'

Once out of the city, the talk turns to boats and the loveliness of spring and at last, as they turn onto a series of ever narrower roads on the outskirts of Bath, they circle around to Anne.

'I'm so glad you two will get to meet.' Something about the way he says this, with a tinge of nostalgia, prompts Honor to say, 'So why...'

'...did we split? Water under the bridge. Oh, you need to turn left here.'

They swerve onto a country lane bounded on both sides by blossoming hawthorn. Honor rights the van and glances in the rear-view mirror. If only my hair was less unruly. I look like a labradoodle during a dog groomers' strike.

'Yesterday, when we were talking about the thing with Reynolds and those boys,' he says. Her eyes flick to him. 'You seemed to suggest that something similar happened when you were a student. You said you'd tell me sometime.'

'I did.'

They drive on in an awkward silence for a while. She thinks, can I really face this?

'It's right at the lights, by the way,' he says. Honor can feel his eyes on her.

'It was a long time ago, and I'd like to be able to forget it really.'

'But you haven't. And you can't.'

'Is it that obvious?'

What was there to say? My best friend Zoe, the love of my life really, was raped by someone who got away with it because he was needed to save the reputation of a rich and ancient institution. What had the detective told her? If only Zoe hadn't been so drunk. If only she hadn't walked back from the party with him that night. There was so little real evidence, they said, no proof. Zoe couldn't even remember, not really.

But Honor remembered. Honor saw. She *saw* Zoe, through the crack in the door of her dorm room. She saw him on top of Zoe, frantically at work even though Zoe was obviously passed out, her arm as floppy as a rabbit's ear, her body unresponsive. She saw the heel of his hand on the back of Zoe's head, pressing her head into the pillow and, for a moment, a glimpse of his face in profile picked out in the light coming in from the corridor. She'd shouted and pushed on the door which moved an inch then sprung back from the safety chain. She saw him freeze, could almost hear the panic going through his mind. He thought he'd closed the door. He *had* closed it, secured the chain on the inside, thought he was safe from prying eyes, but evidently the latch had been on and a draught or perhaps the movement on the bed had clicked the lock open and the door had swung just far enough for Honor to see some of the horror that was going on inside. She screamed, 'Get off her!' and tried to curl her hand around the door to reach the chain. His head snapped up so that she could no longer see his face and she heard the rustle of the mattress moving and Zoe's arm moving with the momentum, her hand half open, the fingers soft and mobile. And she'd shouted, 'Let me in you bastard,' and charged the door putting all her weight behind her shoulder. She couldn't see him now, but she watched through the crack in the door as the mattress sprang back from his weight. And she ran at the door, jamming her side into the wood but still the chain held firm. Seconds later she saw the shower room light go on and heard the door close and she remembered thinking, he's trying to get away, and that was when she ran, along the corridor and down two flights of stairs and across the quad to the campus security office and panted out who and what she'd seen. And when the security officer came back to the room with her the chain was off but the door was closed and no one responded to his knocking or to her calling. The officer would have left then if Honor hadn't insisted that they go inside to check on Zoe. With a sigh he reluctantly took out the master key and let himself in and they saw Zoe lying on the bed, passed out, alone, the thick smell of alcohol in the room.

'She's just pissed,' he said. 'Ain't no one else here. Wasting my time.'

And that was what he'd say to the police, two weeks later, after Honor had finally managed to persuade Zoe – against all the advice from her tutor, the dean of studies and the student welfare office – to go with her to the police station and report the rape.

We have a witness who will swear the alleged assailant was with *her* from 10.30 and for the whole of the rest of the night, the police said.

You didn't like him, because he had a crush on your friend, they said. You put ideas in your friend's head. Why did no one else hear you calling out 'Get off her'? Why didn't you get help from another student in the corridor? Why did the security guard find the door closed when you said it was open? How come you didn't try to find another witness? Why are you claiming you were advised by Zoe's tutor and others not to go to the police when they all remember advising the exact opposite? Why didn't Zoe go to the police as soon as it happened? Why, why, why?

So this is how it will go, she thought at the time. On and on and on until they circle back to the version they have already decided on.

'I let down a friend,' she says now. 'I didn't fight for her. Not hard enough, or not effectively anyway. It would take too long to explain.'

'I'd like to hear one day,' Alex says. 'Turn here.' He points to a single-track road leading into a dell lined on either side with beech trees. At its lowest point, beside a stream, they come upon a small brick-built cottage with a tiny garden filled with daffodils.

'This is it.'

Honor pulls the van onto the verge and they get out. A red dog ambles over, twisting in delight at the sight of Alex. An elegant woman in her late forties appears and comes down the path to greet them. Alex gives her a peck on the cheek.

'You must be Honor,' she says warmly and, taking Honor's hand in both of hers, goes on, 'Alex has told me all about you. Please come in.' Honor smiles nervously, observing Anne's poise, the graciousness of her welcome. Is this why Alex was so keen that she come? Put her up for inspection by his ex? She's doomed if that's the case. Compared to Anne she's a scruff, a vagabond, a tomboy, a woman who's never really cared for any of the usual feminine wiles.

Anne leads them into a small, dark hallway decorated with mostly watercolour landscape paintings and, taking their coats, hangs them on an old-fashioned coat stand. They follow the dog into a cosy kitchen, furnished with framed photographs and a child's faded crayon drawings in what were once bright primary colours. On a large, scrubbed pine kitchen table sits a plate of cold meat and a bowl of salad. Beside it in a cooler sits a bottle of white wine and a small vase of hyacinths.

'Please, take a seat.' Alex waits for Honor to sit then takes the chair beside her. Anne remains standing beside them.

'First time this year isn't it?' says Alex, putting a distance between himself and his ex, for Honor's benefit, she suspects. 'How are you doing?'

'Well.'

'And how's that son of ours? He doesn't Zoom or whatever you call it nearly enough for my liking.'

'Well, you know Tim,' Anne says and, with exquisite manners, turns to Honor and goes on, 'Alex tells me you have a daughter.'

'Yes. Adopted daughter.'

'And… she's studying at Avon, am I right?'

Honor feels herself redden. 'Oh, I see Alex has filled you in.'

There's a pause until with a flourish of her hand across the table Anne says, 'It's only ham and a bit of salad, I'm afraid. The bread's good though and I've made some broccoli soup. Help yourself to a glass of wine.' Turning, she makes her way to the stove. While she busies herself at the stove Alex raises the bottle and on Honor's signal pours her a small glass and a larger one for himself and for the next few minutes Honor and Alex sit in solemn silence at opposite ends of the kitchen table, Alex fondling the ears of the red dog, both conscious, Honor is sure, of what was said in the car only a few moments ago.

Anne brings three bowls of green soup to the table, distributes them in front of each of their places and pulls up a chair. The conversation turns to Bristol, then to Bath and to other local matters. Chit-chat. When the plates are finished, Anne rises once more and brings out of the fridge a large bowl of berries and a jug of cream and, coming to the table, says, 'Alex mentioned that you're interested in the copycat suicides at Midland?'

'Yes,' says Honor, glad to have the silence broken. 'A few days ago my daughter's best friend tried to kill herself then another student in the same department threw herself off the Clifton Suspension Bridge. The university seems to think that the first was an accident and the second a one-off. The head of student welfare was very evasive with me. And I'm worried, obviously, that they haven't put in enough safeguards to stop it happening again. It doesn't fill me with confidence to know that the woman responsible has form in covering up suicides among the student population, or, at least, not taking them very seriously.'

Waiting until she has decanted the berries into cut-glass bowls and handing round the cream, Anne says, 'I found my old file in the attic. Alex, darling, will you make us some coffee and I'll go and fetch it.'

At the word 'darling' Alex swallows and, flushing, lays his napkin down and rises from the table. 'I'll put my best man on to it.'

Moments later, Anne returns with a cardboard file and, sitting, begins leafing through a pile of handwritten notes. 'Back then I did most of my notes the old-fashioned way, in a reporter's notebook. I can show them to you but they won't make a lot of sense unless you read shorthand?'

Just then Alex returns carrying a tray on which sits a full cafetière, three mugs and a carton of milk.

'There was quite a lot of stuff that didn't make it into the paper because I couldn't substantiate it. Things were so different back then. People didn't talk about sexual assault in the way they do now. It seems students were always having affairs with tutors and no one batted an eyelid unless something went terribly wrong. Which, obviously, in this case, it did.'

She scans her notes for a few minutes, flipping the pages of her notebook.

'Oh yes, I remember now. The suggestion was that Reynolds had somehow persuaded or coerced several male students into sexual activity. All that only came out later, after the boys died. Reynolds denied it, of course. I'm not sure he was ever even questioned by the police.

'Midland University first insisted that they didn't know the boys had killed themselves, though I later discovered that they'd sent a representative to the coroner's hearings, so evidently they did know and decided to lie about it. Then they tried to paint the first student as unstable and mentally unwell and suggested that his death began a sort of unstoppable chain reaction.'

'You disagree?' Honor asks her.

She looks away as if rerunning the events in her mind. 'Back then my view was that the university created a culture in which predators like Reynolds could operate because they knew that the university would collude to cover up their criminal behaviour. So they were every bit as culpable as Reynolds. That's still my view.' She starts and recovers herself. 'Oh, how rude of me not to offer you more coffee.' Lifting the cafetière from the table, she goes on, 'I'm assuming this is of interest to you because you think something similar could happen at Avon.'

'I think it's possible, yes. At least, the copycat suicide bit. As to why the two girls at Avon were driven to take their own lives, and one succeeded, I have no idea. You didn't have any proof that the suicides were as a result of Reynolds's activities?' Honor says.

'Well, no. We couldn't ask the dead boys, obviously, and none of them left any kind of suicide note. But people often don't. I do remember someone at the Samaritans telling me that. She said that people who are driven to kill themselves have often already got beyond the point where they can share their shame or even name it. They only know that carrying it has become so intolerable that in their minds the only way to put an end to it is to put an end to themselves.'

A chill comes over Honor and a sick feeling of familiarity. She'd heard this too.

'There were a lot of rumours swirling around. But Reynolds had been good at covering his tracks. We did find one student, a boy named Gary Bond, a friend of one of the dead boys, Michael Fincher, who said that Michael had told him that he'd been raped by Reynolds and we confronted Reynolds but, obviously, he denied it.'

'Were the police ever involved?' asks Honor.

'As I recall, Michael Fincher's parents went to the police after Gary came forward, but Reynolds was dead by then and they didn't get any cooperation from the university either. To be honest, I don't think there was any appetite to pursue Reynolds even when he was alive. The Finchers aside, none of the parents of the dead boys really wanted to bring a complaint. It was too awful and too painful and there was probably some concern that their boys would be labelled homosexual. There was still shame or public opprobrium attached to being gay, and in those days, the assumption was that if a boy had "allowed" himself to be raped then it must be because he was gay. Men like Reynolds get away with rape because they know that their victims aren't likely to report it. Back then even more than now. It was the perfect storm of privilege, denial and homophobia. He might have exploited the fact that the boys were over eighteen and officially adults so it would be easier for a predator to hide behind a fiction of consent, but if you think about it, those boys really had no choice in the matter. Reynolds was entirely responsible for their academic futures. And there was also the terror of being exposed. The shame of what had happened. It probably didn't help that Reynolds was a lawyer, incredibly well connected, and nobody wanted to accuse him outright, even after his death. So the whole thing died on the vine.'

Alex is shaking his head.

'Oh, and Reynolds had an accomplice of sorts. A young woman who worked in his department. Fiercely clever, wildly ambitious. I interviewed her but the story moved on and I didn't follow up. As I recall, she was his PhD student and protégée. I'm guessing that her career depended on keeping him sweet. He might have promised her something particular, a promotion maybe, in exchange for her loyalty, but if he did, I never managed to find any evidence of that. I've no doubt she knew about it though, or that she lied to protect Reynolds. Can't for the life of me remember her name. It'll be here somewhere. I'd love to know what became of *her*. Quite the piece of work.'

Anne shuffles a paper and, catching Alex's eye, says, 'I know that look. You're about to tell me, aren't you?'

'Yes. Her name was Madeleine Ince.'

Anne snaps her fingers. 'That's it!' Her gaze lights on Alex then Honor, then back to Alex. 'What?' The eyes blading left and right. A sudden intake of breath and something between shock and excitement scudding across the elegant features.

'Good God, I can see it in your faces. You *know* her, don't you?'

Chapter 37

Cullen

Cullen finds himself at the sticky table in the corner of the saloon bar of the Rose and Crown. He and Mark Ratner meet there sometimes to discuss academic matters away from the distractions of campus.

Cullen catches the barman's eye and signals for another round. Another double will settle his nerves.

'Oh come on. How did you think this was going to end? You were having sex with her on campus. I walked *in* on you, remember?'

'I'm not likely to forget it.'

'Natasha has to go.'

'I said I'd sort it.' Ratner's hands are trembling as he says this, Cullen notices.

'But you didn't.' Cullen blinks back his irritation.

'How did you find out about the grades?'

'It wasn't difficult, Mark. We both know that the girl was on the verge of being kicked out, before you decided to start sleeping with her. I brought up Natasha's file and checked her record. She's a poor student, with no aptitude, no drive, no head for academics, barely scraping a pass, suddenly starts getting firsts in her coursework. You weren't exactly subtle about it. I'd have let it go if it hadn't been for your last paramour deciding to jump from the bridge.'

'Why do you say that?' Ratner's eyes are suddenly etched with panic, his face an untamed mess of blotches and muscle tics. He, Cullen, can feel his fear spilling out into the air between them. There is something to be enjoyed in watching him. What a fool the man is to imagine that he could keep his affair with Jessica Easton a secret.

'Jessica Easton was a nutjob. Unstable. That was why I got rid of her and that was why she killed herself. It had *nothing* to do with me. Natasha Tillotson is completely different, much more...'

'...malleable?'

'Pragmatic, reasonable.'

'Which is why you need to get her to accept my offer. The point is to rectify the situation in a way that best protects all of us. Natasha Tillotson can transfer, complete her degree in some less-exacting institution where she'll be allowed to scrape through and in a couple of years, she'll have forgotten all about this little episode. And you and I will have the luxury of being able to forget all about her.' He takes a breath to calm himself and continuing in a measured tone says, 'How do I make myself clearer? Your career is on the line, Mark. Your marriage too, I shouldn't wonder. Your wife can leave you, I couldn't give two hoots, but you impact me or the reputation of my department, I'll take you down myself.'

Ratner, chewing on his nails now, says, 'I'll work on Natasha. Just give me a bit more time.'

Cullen downs his second whisky chaser and calls for another. 'We don't have time.'

The barman comes over with the drinks. Cullen picks up his whisky and downs it in one. He watches Ratner's fingers sliding nervously up and down his pint glass. A sly smile comes on Ratner's face. Cullen senses exactly where he's about to go, the fool.

'You haven't exactly been an angel yourself.'

'Grow up, Mark. You sound like a silly little schoolboy in the playground.'

'If I wanted to, I could...'

Cullen holds up a hand. 'I wouldn't finish that sentence if I were you. Just make the Tillotson girl keep quiet and do as she's told.'

Cullen pushes back his chair and taking his jacket turns and walks as quickly as he can out of the pub and into the car park. Before he's got as far as the car, Ratner's voice reaches him.

'I saw you at lunch with Nevis Smith the other day.'

Cullen turns and shakes his head. Ratner is standing only a few feet away, working his hands together. 'And?'

'And pot, kettle is what.'

This time Cullen lets out a belly laugh. The man is preposterous. 'Nevis Smith is my eyes and ears, you moron. She's my spy, my useful idiot. She tells me everything I need to know about what the students are saying. I wouldn't be at all surprised if she doesn't already know about you and Natasha.'

Ratner comes closer. 'Natasha says Nevis is investigating the incident on the bridge last Sunday.'

Cullen lets out a snort. '*Investigating?* We are talking about the same nineteen-year-old oddball with zero confidence, I assume.' An eyeroll as he repeats the word 'investigating' doing his best to give the word the requisite tone of contempt.

233

He feels something unstable rise up in him, like a great elevator whose cables are about to snap. Leaning towards him, he says, 'Hear this. I don't give a damn what your little tart says. I'm getting rid of her, you understand? And if you give me any more trouble, I'll get rid of you too.'

'I'd like to see you try.'

Even as his legs are propelling himself forward Cullen is thinking, don't do this, don't let him get to you, but it is already too late. He is grabbing Ratner's shirt at the neck and shaking him. Ratner pulls back, a look of shock on his face, and there is an instant when Cullen tells himself that it is not too late to stop now, that no real damage has been done. Then his fist makes contact with Ratner's cheek. Ratner lurches back, his hand coming up to the injured part. His eyes are stormy. He is considering whether to retaliate and for a moment the two adversaries are freeze-framed, pumped up with shock but powerless to move. Then the moment passes and Cullen sees Ratner slump and turn, hurrying towards his silver VW, muttering darkly to himself, checking to make sure there are no witnesses to this little lapse in judgement. Ratner won't tell. He'll be too ashamed. All the same, it was stupid, stupid, stupid. I should go back to the office. Act normal but pretend I've got some urgent work and can't be disturbed. Get Tina to hold all my calls and appointments. Drink some coffee, maybe have a quick snooze on the sofa, put myself back together.

Mark Ratner has driven off now. Cullen walks over to his Volvo, presses the electronic key and lowers himself into the driver's seat. He leans his hands on the steering wheel, inspects the swelling already coming up on the knuckles of his right hand where they made contact with Ratner's face. He shuts his eyes and, taking a deep breath, reaches automatically for the glove box, takes out the quarter of Bell's and empties it into his mouth.

A moment later he is on the road and making his way towards the Downs and the Avon campus. It is raining now, the wind coming in off the Atlantic and chucking it on the windscreen like some crazed artist working his paints. He slows for a red light ahead. It is then that he spots a woman walking up the street carrying an umbrella. His eyes flick to the windscreen. Time ticks on. The light seems to be taking an age to turn. Behind him, cars begin to back up. Mahler plays on the radio. It irritates him, this symphony. He's about to change the station when his eye is drawn by a sudden movement in the rear-view mirror. He checks back. A gust of wind has inverted the spokes of the woman's umbrella and in that split second he sees a face he hasn't seen for a long, long time. He feels himself go limp, as if the bones in his body have been plucked out. From somewhere outside of himself he can hear a car horn blaring. He can't tell whether he is hitting the car horn or whether there is a frustrated driver behind him. Blinking, he checks back in the mirror. The woman is battling with the umbrella now but there is no mistaking those features, the dip of the shoulders, the angular tilt of the head. He pulls in to the side of the road, blindsided now, his eyes on the woman as she walks along the road. He shakes his head and blinks and the woman has gone.

Something is happening, Cullen says to himself, the tension running from him like drain water. I'm seeing things. If I'm not careful I might lose my mind.

Chapter 38

Nevis

It is gone 10.30 by the time Nevis comes off her shift at the chippy and already a frost has begun to settle on the branches of the trees whose leaves are still not out yet. It feels sometimes like everything is in a coma. Back at the flat she takes a shower to rid herself of the smell of frying batter and stale oil but there remains a chill in her bones that can only be chased away by tea. She moves into the hallway and glances briefly at the door to Satnam's room then turns and makes her way to the kitchen. Putting on the kettle, she suddenly finds herself overtaken by an overwhelming desire to break something.

Perhaps it's me I want to break?

On an impulse she crosses the living-room floor and goes back into the hallway and stands before the door to Satnam's room and knocks.

'How could you leave me? Now I have no one. *No one.* Everyone else always lied or only told part of the truth. I always thought you were different. Why didn't you tell me? Why did you keep me in the dark? Wasn't I good enough for your secrets? Didn't you trust me?'

Silence.

The kettle begins to whistle.

She goes into the kitchen and, reaching for a mug, notices Satnam's phone sitting on the counter where she has kept it on charge since the night on the bridge. What secrets might it hold? I suppose I should take this to the Dean. He asked me to, so that he could give it to Bikram and Narinder. As she picks it up, she is struck by a thought. What does it matter who has it since no one can open it?

She holds it to her ear, listens into the void, thinks of Satnam lying in her hospital bed and waits for a response, but, of course, there isn't one. Feeling foolish, suddenly, she puts down the phone, makes her tea and goes over to where her laptop is sitting on the coffee table in the living room.

Opens it and stares at the equation:

$dx/dx=rx(1-x)-x$, where r–c/e

The average persistence of local populations. The secret to the origins of life. A week or so ago the formula would have struck her with its brilliance and precision. She would have sat down with it, as you might an old friend, and listened to what it had to tell her. But now she is distracted, overcome with the creeping sensation that something bad is about to happen. This must be how animals feel sensing the first intimations of an earthquake, she thinks. Tash comes to mind. The photo at the Valentine's Day party. Tash and Jessica, vying for the same man. Didn't Jessica say as much? What if that man had been Mark Ratner? But Satnam? Where is she in any of that? So much she has yet to know or understand.

Picking up her own phone, she sends a text to Satnam, Wake up! She watches Satnam's phone light up briefly with the notification, then sends another to Tash.

You OK?

No response.

Silence is golden except when it isn't.

She returns to the equation, doing her best to follow the elegance of it. The Dean comes to mind. That hand on hers, the warm living pulse of it. Oh to be solved! To have all your loose ends tied up. To be complete. What a thought. More wonderful than the secret to the origins of life. The secret to *her* life.

Restless, she gets up and goes back to the kitchen, thinks of making another cup of tea and cradles the kettle with her hand until the heat makes her pull away. Another equation comes into her head:

$$Q_{10} = R_2 / R_1$$

Temperature coefficient. The only equation, Satnam had once laughingly told Nevis, that she could ever remember. An equation with four integers. 1021. Nevis feels her heart begin to tick and the hairs on the back of her neck stand to attention. She reaches for Satnam's phone.

Wake up!

The seconds it takes for the passcode screen to come into view feel endless. Then, all of a sudden, there it is. *Enter passcode*. Carefully, with a shaking hand, she taps in the numbers 1021. And waits. And blinks. And listens to the percussion of her pulse. An elastic fragment of a second that stretches almost to breaking point before the homescreen opens on an image of the stars dotted with icons. Her whole body is trembling now, her heartbeat rackety and wild, and she locates the message icon and taps. The white message screen appears. For a moment her eyes are too busy to see anything. Blinking away the blur, she scrolls down to messages. Tash,

Jessica, Luke, 'Home', one or two other familiar names plus a couple she doesn't recognise. She scrolls, flips back to the night of the Valentine's Day party. Not to the night of. Not yet. That feels too big.

A text to Jessica and Tash, 8.28 p.m.: We're all in this. It's time to say something. Can we talk, maybe later, at the party?

Talk, yes. Didn't Jessica say something about this? They fell out about Jessica's ex. Or about leaving Avon? Nevis remembers two versions and the distinct feeling that neither was quite the truth. In any case Satnam said something at the party that Jessica found unhelpful, she said. An odd word, but then the whole conversation had been odd. She recalled Jessica's hand on her mouth, genuinely surprised that Nevis didn't know. But what was it that Nevis didn't know? If only she'd asked. If only she had insisted on knowing. Tash knew but Tash wasn't telling. I should be brave, now, she tells herself. It's time to be resolute. To stick to the course. You know how this plays out. It is a question of resolving the equations, line by line, until there are no more equations and nothing more to solve.

The next line in the solution. She screws up her eyes. Behind them, in the deep red of the retina, is the span of the bridge leading into the void.

The phone lies in the palm of her hand.

Sunday, that terrible night, is the swipe of a finger away. She can literally reach out and touch it.

Touch it, Nevis. Connect.

A blue text box appears and in it a line of white text.

To Luke, 9.57 p.m.: Can I come round? Unanswered.

And then, to a number Nevis doesn't know, 10.25 p.m.: Had enough. Can't live with this. Unanswered.

A message sent to a stranger, though, evidently, not a stranger to Satnam. Nevis scrolls down, checking for a recurrence of the same number and does not find it. A single message, then, in a desperate hour.

Samaritans? Some other suicide prevention hotline?

She taps the number into Google. And waits. Nothing comes up. She checks the phone log for calls. No number, but something at least, a call from a withheld ID. Seven minutes and twenty-three seconds. It's enough to say what needed to be said. *Had enough. Can't live with this.*

But what? Her mouth is dry and scratchy. She needs to know and hardly dares to find out. The fingers hovering over the screen seem not to belong to her, but still they move, as if held up on puppet strings. She goes back to the message screen and touches the number. Three icons appear: Audio, FaceTime, Info.

Picking up her own phone, she takes a deep breath, and taps in the number.

Chapter 39

Cullen

Cullen waits in the loveseat in the VC's office while Madeleine finishes up her phone call. A power move, he thinks, Maddy getting back at him after he'd been stupid enough in his cups to insult her the other night. Time to make old Cullen eat some humble pie.

He takes out his phone and pretends to read the screen but his head is pounding and he wishes that he'd gone to the Deanery first and retrieved one of his miniatures from the desk drawer to put in his coffee. It's too late for that now. Sometimes his whole life feels like a missed boat. If only his worries would subside or his head didn't hurt so much. If only he felt better about Veronica and Amanda. If only he didn't feel that he was slowly going mad.

It was he who requested the meeting, eager to get the VC's ear before Ratner got the chance to turn the bruises left by Cullen's fist to his advantage. An accusation of assault would look very bad. He, Cullen, has already been issued with a warning, after all. A disciplinary measure at best. At worst, dismissal and another black mark on his CV. What would he say to Veronica? The stakes have risen exponentially since the announcement of her pregnancy. Not that he particularly wants the baby, but he does want Veronica and, more importantly, he wants the *idea* of Veronica.

He checks himself. There are certain things he has had to put to one side for now. His debts, Veronica, the baby, the Dalek and, above all, the unnerving sighting of a remnant of his past walking along the pavement last night. This is the time for focus. The battlelines have been drawn. The only possible course of action is to strike first. Which is not without risk. He must make his move with skill and delicacy. There are various ways Ratner could retaliate. He, Cullen, has been up most of the night anticipating them. But now, this morning, his focus must be wholly on his professional survival. And that requires outmanoeuvring Mark Ratner.

For the moment, at least, he has time on his side. And knowledge. So far as he knows, Ratner is not yet aware of Cullen's various difficulties. Still, he will need to put his case in such a way as to make it undeniable. So long as he plays his cards right, turns on the charm, promises to be a good boy, he thinks Maddy will come round and stay loyal.

She has made time for him in her busy schedule which is a good sign. And she's making him eat shit by keeping him waiting and this, too, is, in its way, a cause for optimism. He turns his attentions back to his phone, but it's no good, he can't focus. Oh, for that drink and a long sleep! He sits and watches his leg jiggling nervously. For God's sake calm down. Closes his eyes and lets Maddy's voice wash over him as she speaks on the phone, until he is suddenly alerted by a name.

Maddy is talking about Nevis Smith. In an instant, he's

tuned in, his body poised and leaning towards the desk in order not to miss a word.

'As I said, Mrs Smith, it sounds remarkably like you're trying to threaten me and I don't appreciate it. If there were a "contagion" as you call it, I can assure you I would be the first to know. But there is no such thing happening now or likely to happen in future and I must inform you that if you continue down this path, the university authorities will feel duty-bound to question whether Nevis is a suitable student for Avon, notwithstanding her grades. None of us wants that, do we?'

Maddy rolls her eyes and placing a hand over the mouthpiece of the phone mouths the words, *I'm sorry*.

Sorry not sorry.

Cullen waits, braced now for bad news, as Maddy continues, 'I've no idea what prompted this archaeological escapade, but we do not deal in ancient history.'

There is a pause while Maddy listens to what her interlocutor has to say. A tinny buzz issues from the phone but from where Cullen is sitting no words are distinguishable. What he wouldn't give to hear the other side of the conversation.

'As I'm sure you know, since you seem to have spent considerable effort in digging up the past, I was in the law department before taking on this role and I happen to believe that people are innocent until they are proven guilty. You would hardly expect me to recall events from nearly two decades ago, but what I do remember very distinctly was that there was never any evidence that Professor Reynolds was in any way responsible. In fact, just the opposite. And yes, I am aware that times have changed. We have an extremely robust sexual harassment policy here at Avon, as you'd expect from a university whose

Vice Chancellor is a woman. Now, if you'll excuse me, I'm terribly busy.'

Maddy cuts the call and sits for a moment with her eyes closed, thumbs hooked under her cheekbones, fingers kneading her temples.

'Shall I ask your assistant to fetch some coffee?' Cullen says, trying to sound helpful.

Maddy looks out from between her hands and straightens herself upright, a look of mild surprise on her face, as if she had forgotten the presence of Cullen altogether.

'No, no, it's fine.'

'I couldn't help overhearing, I hope you don't mind. Nevis Smith is one of mine.'

'Oh yes, of course. Her mother is a terrible pest, one of those women who spends five minutes googling and thinks that makes her better equipped to do your job than you are. She's been calling the student welfare department pleading for her daughter to get special treatment. She's claiming we haven't taken what happened to Satnam Mann and Jessica Easton seriously, which is nonsense, obviously. She really doesn't know what she's talking about.'

Cullen, who has been listening to this with mounting alarm, swallows hard and says, 'What has this to do with Reynolds?' The remnants of that scandal were still being whispered around Midland University when Cullen arrived, a few years after his own disgrace at St Olaf's. He did not engage with it, afraid that to do so might contaminate his own, slowly healing, wounds.

'As you might remember, Reynolds was my mentor and, incidentally, one of the most brilliant legal minds in academe. Whatever Professor Reynolds might or might not have done, his achievements in advancing legal thought deserve to be protected.' She looks up and catches Cullen's eye, giving a sorrowful sigh. 'A great mind exists beyond trivial notions of morality. It's our last defence against Planet Stupid.'

High-mindedness is all very well, Cullen thinks, but it doesn't make a dent in the mortgage. He waits for Maddy to stop talking and leaves a respectful pause before saying, 'Should we be worried?'

Shaking her head and waving the question away, Maddy says, 'Just keep an eye on Nevis Smith for a while, to reassure her mother.' Brightening, she goes on, 'Now, that's not what you came to see me about.'

'No,' he says, nervously. 'Though it's not good news I'm afraid.' He has been thinking about this conversation half the night. It won't be easy, but it has to be had now. Any later and he runs the risk of Ratner cooking up his own version. 'Since you brought up our robust policy on sexual harassment... Not that this is harassment, necessarily, but...'

He sees Ince look up, a small bead of alarm in her eyes.

'I discovered very recently that Mark Ratner has been carrying on with one of our undergrads, Natasha Tillotson. Of course I immediately insisted that Mark put a stop to it, but it appears that he did not.'

Maddy's brow is furrowed and her lips are pressed together so hard that the skin above them blooms creamy white. This is harder to brush aside than the petty concerns of Nevis Smith's mother. 'I assumed all that nonsense had stopped after Mark got married. Is the girl a problem? Might she bring a complaint? That's all we need right now.'

'It's more of an academic matter.' He opens his laptop.

'If you're about to show me something, you'd better come closer,' Maddy says. Cullen moves over to sit in the visitor's chair at the desk.

'You look rather tired, Christopher,' Maddy says calmly as he nears, but with a hint of reproach. 'I'll ask Alison to fetch that coffee after all.'

'I was scratching my head over this most of last night,' Cullen says.

'That must be how you came by that abrasion on your face,' she adds, pointing to a spot on his cheek. 'I couldn't see it when you were sitting on the sofa.'

Cullen raises his finger to his face and feels a roughened patch. Did Ratner get him? If he did, he has no memory. All he can recall is the moment his fist made contact with Ratner's cheek. Gathering himself and, forcing a smile, he says, 'Lazy razor work.'

Ince returns the smile and, gesturing to his right hand, says, 'Been shaving your knuckles too?'

'Oh, that,' he says, as casually as he can. 'Loose paving in the driveway. Lucky not to break anything.'

She lets this pass and, with a raised eyebrow, says, 'You were saying...'

'It appears that Mark has been doctoring Natasha Tillotson's grades.'

Maddy's face darkens. In a strained voice, she says, 'You have any evidence of that?'

'Take a look for yourself.' He swivels the laptop and waits while Maddy peers. 'Natasha was barely scraping along the bottom, and suddenly she's getting good two-ones, firsts. Besides which, I confronted Mark last night and he admitted as much.'

Maddy is staring at his right hand now. 'I see,' she says quietly. 'And you've only just noticed this?'

'Obviously, otherwise I would have come directly to you.' He resents the rebuke from a woman, particularly from a former lover, however distant their affair. And this is the second in as many weeks. It makes him think that Maddy isn't as reliable a champion as he'd assumed. It's everyone for himself when it comes down to it.

'No one on the outside would be able to prove any of this, presumably?' she says now.

'I doubt it.'

'Well that's something.' He watches Ince drumming her fingers across her mouth, which is something she does when thinking through a problem. Otherwise, her expression is, as always, a calm, matt surface.

'There's more.'

Maddy sits back and blinks.

'Mark was also involved with Jessica Easton.'

Maddy lets out a groan and puts her head in her hands before recovering her poise. 'How much of this did you know when I came round to your house the other evening?'

'Nothing, obviously, or I would have said,' Cullen says, hoping the lie lands.

'I'll admit I'm worried about you, Christopher. First the thing at the hospital and now this mess. How could you have missed this with Mark?'

This, he thinks. This is exactly why I kept the whole thing under my hat. She always *was* such a busybody even when we were together. Especially then.

She presses her lips together, fingernails drumming on her

cheek, lost in thought for a while, then straightening herself upright in her chair, says, 'I wish we could let this one slide, for all our sakes, but unfortunately we're exposed. We'll have to find a low-profile way to deal with it.'

'I put it to Natasha Tillotson that she transfers elsewhere with a nice reference to keep her quiet,' Cullen says. He doesn't mention Tillotson's absolute rejection of his idea. He still hopes she'll come round. If she doesn't, he has another, more drastic, plan in mind.

At that moment Alison enters with a tray on which sit two cups, a cafetière of coffee, a jug of milk and a bowl of sugar and some sugar biscuits and Cullen finds himself hit by an unexpected wave of sadness. If it hadn't been for that one mistake all those very many years ago, he could have been where Maddy is now, sitting behind a grand desk in a fancy office passing judgement on her 'inferiors'.

'What about Mark?' Maddy asks.

Cullen adopts a thinking pose, as though the idea is only just coming to him. 'Just off the top of my head here, but how's about something like this? Ratner agrees to resign with immediate effect "for personal reasons" and signs an NDA and we guarantee a reference? I believe Thirsk is recruiting at the moment. I could put in a word?'

Maddy drums her fingers on her chin. 'Leave it with me for now,' she says, finally.

Returning to his office but finding himself too tense to focus on his work, Cullen tells Tina to cancel his afternoon appointments and drives to the Fig Tree in Clifton where he downs four whisky and sodas before heading home.

He arrives at the house not long after Veronica has returned from shopping and his heart immediately sinks at the sight of the swag bags from silly, overpriced baby boutiques lined up along the kitchen table, like a drumbeat to his failure. Veronica is nowhere to be seen but from above him comes the muffled sound of footsteps.

He moves out into the hallway and shouts up the stairs, 'Hey, I'm home!'

Veronica comes down the stairs. She is six weeks pregnant, the thing inside her is no more than the size of a pea and she is already cradling her abdomen in a way Cullen finds irritating even in women who have something to show. She knows nothing about the pawnbroker's ticket, of course, or the unanswered demands from the bank accumulating in the glove box of the Volvo, and he will never be able to tell her, especially now. Of all the things he seems to have – job, house, a mother who loves him, and a small version of himself growing in the womb of his trophy wife, the car is the only thing he truly loves. And what has he done with the thing but make it a vehicle for his shame? The unpaid bills, the demands, the quarter bottles of whisky, hidden away out of sight but never for one moment out of mind. How easy it would be just to drive off the cliffs at Clifton Downs or Leigh Woods.

He shakes himself free of the thought, and of the mood, remembering how clever he is being, how close to ridding himself of Natasha Tillotson, Mark Ratner *and* his debts. Going over to Veronica, he gives her a peck on the cheek and to his surprise feels her stiffen and back away. She is not smiling, he realises now, and her face is uncharacteristically stony.

'I see you've been shopping. Did you just get back?' he says, wondering if the source of her irritation is that he is home rather earlier than usual, before she has had time to hide her purchases.

'No, I have been back some time, but I've been rather busy.'

What on earth does Veronica have to be busy about? he wonders. Other than shopping and preparing dinner parties she doesn't actually do anything.

'I have some questions for you, actually. I only hope you have the answers.'

The calm of a moment ago leaves in an instant and he suddenly feels himself seized by a panic that not even booze or pills can take away. He reaches for the familiar solidity of the table next to him. The room seems pixelated and hazy like the Rubik's cubes he used to play with as a young teen to pass the time while he hung his head out of his bedroom window in the hope that his mother would not smell the smoke from illicit Marlboro Lights.

'So a gentleman phoned just now asking for a Mr Fanshawe-Drew. I explained that Fanshawe-Drew was my name, not yours, and the gentleman seemed surprised. He was calling about unpaid credit card debts. It appears you have taken out a credit card using another name.'

'Not another name, darling. Your name. Just as you have credit cards in my name.'

'Men do not refer to themselves by their wives' names unless they are trying to hide something,' Veronica replies, stiffly. 'I wondered how many other names you have been using so I went into the filing cabinet in your study.'

'That's private! You don't have the key!'

'It is possible to unlock almost anything with a nail file and a bobby pin. What is going on, Christopher?' Her face is beseeching now.

'I'm not sure what you mean,' he says, desperately playing for time.

'Oh,' she says. 'Aren't you now?' She turns her back and plucks a piece of paper from the kitchen counter. 'How do you explain this?'

He takes the paper from her and buzzes his pockets for his reading glasses though he can see well enough already to know that she has found his change of name certificate.

'That was forever ago,' he says, and it was, actually, or as forever ago as matters. There is a before and after in Cullen's life that Veronica doesn't know about, must never know about, particularly now, when they are both on the cusp of parenthood.

'I feel I don't know you any more. I always assumed Cullen was your father's name and after the divorce your mother reverted to Salter. Now there's this Christopher Mulholland person. So, who are you? Who am I having a baby with exactly?'

'Darling, this isn't nearly as complicated as you're making it out to be. Mulholland was my stepfather's name. When my mother married him, she decided to change both our names to Mulholland. After she divorced my stepfather she went back to Salter, which was her maiden name, and I chose to revert to my birthname, Cullen.' All this is true, more or less, though not entirely the point. Still, he hopes it will be sufficient to placate Veronica who only ever really wants to know that her world is safe and cosseted and free from awkward truths and responsibilities. He fully expects the petitioning for a nanny to begin soon. How else does she expect him to pay for her on an academic salary other than with a little light credit card fraud?

'Why didn't you ever tell me any of this?' she is saying now.

'It's not really relevant to anything is it?'

'Well it might be,' she says, petulantly. 'And in any case, it doesn't explain why I found a credit card bill in the name of Christopher Mulholland.'

'I expect I had an account in that name and never got around to changing it,' he says, hoping she will grow tired of questioning him. 'But darling, you really shouldn't have been going through my things.'

'It just seems so odd and furtive somehow that you would never even tell me your name used to be Mulholland.'

'Because it didn't, not really, well only for a few years anyway. And if you must know,' he begins, thinking up a smaller lie as a cover for the larger one, 'there is a need to cover a small, temporary period of financial embarrassment. A tiny, tiny loan. Using Mulholland gives me a little wiggle room.'

'But that's fraud isn't it?'

Cullen looks at the heap of shopping bags on the table and senses it would be catastrophic to bring them up right now.

'It'll all be fine, I promise.'

'Well good, because I don't think you should be stressing me out with this kind of thing in my condition. It's simply not fair.'

'By the time the baby comes everything will be absolutely shipshape, I promise.'

'Well all right,' she says, pouting. 'But another thing...'

'Yes?' He smiles sweetly, doing his best to disguise his rising irritation.

'There was a bottle of Valium in the medicine cabinet.'

'Was there? I didn't know.'

She presses her mouth into a moue and, in a scolding tone, says, 'Don't give me that, Christopher, and don't think I haven't noticed it's not there any more.'

Chapter 40

Honor

'I called Madeleine Ince,' Honor says. 'I know you said to wait, but...'

'How'd it go? You look like you could use a stiff drink.' Alex picks up two glasses, throws in a couple of ice cubes and brings them over with a bottle of Jameson's. The TV is on with the sound turned down and there is the smell of something cooking in the oven.

'It was a shitshow. I completely mishandled her.' Though she was embarrassed to admit it she'd screamed at the Vice Chancellor. It was so unlike her but the rage she'd been keeping at bay for years had come roaring and ballyhooing to the surface. Men like Reynolds. Men like... She stops herself mid-thought. Don't go there. Not now. 'She's only interested in saving face. But if Avon doesn't launch some kind of investigation into what's happening, try to get to the root cause, I'm worried this is going to continue. And who'll be next? By the end of the conversation she was threatening to kick Nevis out of the university.'

'Fuck,' says Alex, putting down his glass. 'If you'll pardon my French.'

'It's like whatever happens, however many students start

jumping off bridges, they're just going to keep on denying there's a problem.'

'They have a lot to lose. Reputationally.'

'They'll have a lot more to lose if a suicide contagion takes hold. How will they explain that away?'

'My guess is they're not thinking about the future.'

'Have you spoken to Nevis about it?'

'No. Perhaps I should. I'm absolutely sure that Nevis knows something. She's just not saying what. But things are so difficult between us already and I don't want to provoke her into cutting off contact. Not now.' She feels the heat rising up into her face. Act in haste repent at leisure. Wasn't that what Zoe used to say? Not that Zoe took much heed of her own advice, did she? She sighs deeply.

'You don't think Nevis would do anything...' He tails off.

'That's the thing. I don't know.'

She watches Alex go into a small cupboard beside the wood burner and bring out a small pack of loose tobacco, some papers and a baggy and, balancing the paper on his knee, begin to roll a joint.

'This was a fortieth birthday present. Three years ago and I haven't opened it. Now seems like it might be a good time,' Alex says.

He passes her a slender, neatly built spliff and holds out the lighter. She lights and takes a deep breath of smoke which catches and spasms into a rolling cough.

'Taste of my childhood,' Honor says, righting herself.

'Ha!' Alex pours them both another drink. For a moment there is a meeting of eyes before Honor looks away. Something happened on that trip to Bath, Honor thinks. She has spent so much of her life stuck in the mud at the riverbank but on that trip she looked at Alex, still bravely navigating the currents midstream, and saw someone that, at some distant point, when all this was over, she might love.

'There are two things I've been keeping from Nevis which I think could really impact on her stability, on her sense of identity, on everything, really. All these years I've told her that her mother died in a traffic accident, but that's not true. Zoe killed herself. But I haven't been able to tell Nevis that without telling her why. And I'm afraid telling her why might destroy her. But now, with all this going on, and, you know, they say suicide runs in families.' Her chest is vice-tight now and her breathing is coming in short pants, like a dog in the sun. She manages to blurt it out just before her throat seizes. 'I'm scared, Alex.'

A moment passes. Rising, Alex moves closer and quietly lays his arms around her. 'We'll figure it out.'

She takes in the warm, spicy man scent of him and closes her eyes. The seconds go by, then the minutes. Oh how good this feels and how necessary now. 'Thank you,' she says, lifting her head from its spot on his sweater and opening her eyes. Behind Alex the TV continues to flicker. An image catches her eye. She holds her breath and, pulling away, says, 'There, on the TV. Turn up the volume.'

His face registers her alarm. He turns and freezes. His eyes are on the screen now too. As he reaches for the remote a woman's voice can be heard saying:

Police have cordoned off the northern section of the Three Lakes nature reserve and are appealing for witnesses. At this time they are unable to confirm the identity of the dead woman and are not commenting on the cause of death.

Chapter 41

Honor

Alex wants to come with her but this is something she has to do on her own. She thinks of calling a cab but decides in the end that it will be faster in Gerry. It is a crisp evening, the streets long clear of rush-hour bluster and traffic fumes, nothing impeding the journey but the odd traffic light. As she climbs the hill into Kingsdown, the solemnity of the moment hits her. In the next few minutes everything she has worked for, her hopes, her fears for the future may well collide. The bonds between mother and daughter will tighten or irrevocably break and it is for this reason that her legs feel emptied as she walks towards the entrance to the flat and her finger shakes as it presses the video entry phone. A call and a text have both gone unanswered. She waits, hardly daring to breathe. Finally there's a crackle and a voice says, 'What are you doing here?' It takes what feels like forever for Nevis to buzz her up. She closes the door behind her, waiting for the click, then treads over a pile of junk mail and heads for the stairs. What she sees on the second-floor landing makes her gasp. Nevis stands waiting for her, clad in a dressing gown, with her short dark hair plastered, dripping to her head, looking so much like Zoe all those years ago, pulled soaking from the river, that it is as if the two have become the same person.

'You've seen the news on TV about the body at Three Lakes?'

She nods. Her voice is a whisper. Honor catches her daughter's eye for an instant before Nevis looks away. Even as a little girl she never did like anyone to notice when she'd been crying. 'Someone texted me earlier.'

'They didn't name the dead woman on the TV.'

'That's why no one watches TV news any more.'

Honor follows her daughter into the living room, the girl keeping her back to her.

'Do you want some tea?' The same flattened tone, one hand absent-mindedly rubbing the groove at the back of her head.

Honor wonders if she dare approach. 'I want to know if you're OK. Do you – did you – know her?'

'Natasha. She was a friend of Satnam's and the other girl, Jessica.' There is something so resigned, so sad in her daughter's voice that it is as much as Honor can do not to break down.

'Oh Nevis, my love.' Her daughter stiffens and sways a little. A shudder passes through her body and becomes a tremble. An arm reaches for the kitchen counter, the hand fumbling for a spot to settle as she tries to steady herself, her whole body shaking as though an earthquake were happening beneath only her feet.

And then she goes down.

Leaping forward Honor stretches out her arms and manages, just, to stay the fall but she cannot stop it. Their bodies are entwined, now, each flailing but also clinging to the other. Honor feels herself land first, her thigh hitting the floor with a thud, Nevis landing an instant later, her right leg coming down hard on Honor's shin and for a moment they are there, slumped in a shocked heap, together.

'Nevis darling, are you OK?'

'Yes, are you?' Nevis rubs a spot on her upper arm.

'I'll be fine,' Honor says, too shocked to feel any injury.

They begin to untangle themselves, Nevis standing first and reaching out a hand to help Honor. They brush themselves down. Leading her daughter to the sofa Honor takes her daughter's hand and notes that the shaking has stopped.

'Rest there and I'll fetch some tea.'

When she returns some minutes later with the tea, Nevis, arms clasped around her legs, feet on the sofa, is gently rocking herself. Her eyes fixed on the middle distance, she does not immediately register the tea or her mother. In the dim slant of the light in the room her face appears sheeny with tears. Honor slides onto the sofa beside her. For a long while mother and daughter sit in silence, gathering themselves. At last, Nevis says, 'I'm sorry.'

'Don't be. None of this is your fault, my love.'

Nevis's neck snaps round to look at her. 'Isn't it? The fact is I left Satnam on Sunday evening when I could have stayed. The fact is Jessica told me she was in trouble and Tash said she was afraid of ending up like Jessica. And the fact is I could have done something, I don't know, intervened in some way, but I didn't. I didn't do anything about any of it. Everything was there, all the numbers. I failed to add them up.'

'Maybe there's nothing *to* add up?'

Nevis shoots her mother a look of incomprehension. 'Everything *always* adds up. I'm just not quite sure how. Tash told me she was having an affair with one of the tutors,

Mark Ratner. She and Jessica must have had a fight about it. Jessica said the fight was over her ex and that she was upset that Tash had taken up with him. It's possible that she was referring to the tutor. The university found out anyway somehow and they were trying to make Tash leave but Tash didn't want to go. She told me she was going to talk to them.'

Honor sits back, trying to take this in. 'Did anyone else know about Tash and Jessica and this Mark Ratner fellow? Another student? Anyone outside the university?'

'I think maybe Satnam did. She sent Tash a text suggesting they talk about something at a Valentine's Day party all three of them were going to. That was where Tash and Jessica had the fight. I think it's possible Satnam wanted to out Dr Ratner and either Tash or Jessica or perhaps both of them didn't want that to happen.'

'Because?'

'Tash told me she was in love with him. Maybe she thought if it came out into the open the affair would have to end or the university would kick her out. Jessica told me that all three of them talked about leaving Avon but they all felt under pressure from parents or whatever to stay.'

'We need to go to the police, Nevis.'

'And say what? You have to have proof or it's just someone saying something. Right now, the variables and assumptions we have, the range of possibilities is infinite and it's not as if it's, like, illegal for a tutor to have an affair with an undergraduate.'

'Well it should be.'

Nevis bites her lip. 'Satnam sent a text to someone just before she went to the bridge saying she'd had enough. I've called and texted the number and it's no longer in service. Pretty sure it wasn't Tash or Jessica though, and I know it's not Mark Ratner's number because he called me once when he was held up in traffic and late for a tutorial so his number's still in my phone. Unless he's got more than one phone. Whatever, that number was live on the Sunday that Satnam went to the bridge. And now it's not.'

'Whoever that number belonged to must have been in a hurry to distance themselves from it.'

Silence falls and in the stillness Madeleine Ince's words come rushing in to Honor's inner world.

The university authorities will feel duty-bound to question whether Nevis is a suitable student for Avon, notwithstanding her grades.

At the time the remark seemed odd and hostile but Honor had grown used to fending off harsh judgements of her daughter's quirks. She hadn't seen it as a threat. But that is exactly what it was. She can see that very clearly now. Carry on sticking your nose into this and we'll see to it that Nevis's education will suffer. But what if the deaths of Tash and Jessica and the near death of Satnam are only the start? What if there are others? What exactly is Madeleine Ince trying to hide?

'Nevis, I want you to pack a bag and come and stay on the boat with me,' she says, suddenly, impulsively. 'There are two bedrooms. I won't expect you to be in for meals or anything like that. You can just come and go.'

Nevis tilts her head, curious, wanting to know where this sudden shift in tone has come from. Honor wants to say, *I am afraid for you. I do not trust whatever is out there, forces you are too young to understand. And I am afraid of what you might do.* But she knows she cannot.

The heat of their bodies together, on the sofa, has a shocking intimacy to it. Honor hasn't felt this close, this conscious of the delicacy of the moment, for as long as she can remember. Her knee is touching Nevis's now, her body angled away, anxious not to approach too close, too soon. The desire to protect stronger than the fear of rejection, she says, almost in a whisper, 'I know I've hurt you. I am not asking for forgiveness. But I am asking you to do this for me.'

Nevis's breathing softens and stills. Slowly, Honor swings her body, angling herself towards her daughter, and when Nevis makes no attempt to increase the space between them, Honor reaches for her hands and carefully, exquisitely sensitive to any resistance or stiffening, leans towards her daughter until their foreheads are touching, each warming the other's cheeks with her breath.

In a whisper Honor says, 'I am sorrier than I can say. About Satnam, and Jessica and Tash. About us. About all of it.'

'I know.'

They make their way through the darkened, rainswept streets. Honor parks Gerry at the side of the street near the Redcliffe bridge and, escorting her daughter through the fencing and along the towpath past the homeless encampment, past the quiet calm of the narrowboats beside the bridge, the gentle slap of the water against the retaining walls of the quay, they arrive finally at the *Halcyon Days*. Alex has kept the fire going and made up the spare bed.

'Your mother texted me with the news about your friend. I'm so sorry.' He holds out a work-roughened hand and lays it on Nevis's shoulder and, to Honor's astonishment, she makes no attempt to shrug it off or back away. 'I've made hot chocolate if you'd like some?'

'No, thanks, I'll go straight to bed.'

Honor shows her to her room, helps her unpack and returns to the saloon to find Alex sitting on the sofa. Beside him two mugs let loose thin steam spirals. Across the water on the western quayside a couple strolls hand in hand.

'How is she?'

'In a lot of pain and feeling vulnerable I think, not that she'd tell me that. Maybe she'll find it easier to talk to you, once she knows you a bit better.' She turns to him. 'I know I do.'

A faint smile plays on his lips then fades into the solemn moment. 'Look, I didn't want to say while Nevis was here, but there is news. Anne called earlier to say she's tracked down Gary Bond, the student whose friend, Michael Fincher, took his life during that suicide contagion at Midland. Gary's middle-aged now, of course, but she's spoken to him and he says he's willing to meet us.' He takes her hand and runs his thumb along her palm as if he is reading her future. It's just a private moment, so intimate, somehow, that it takes her by surprise.

He says, 'Are you sure you want to pursue this?'

They sit in silence watching the play of light on the black water. Then she turns and in the dim light thrown from the table lamp catches something solid and dependable in his face.

'Yes, if you'll help me.'

Chapter 42

Honor

A new sun is smudging the sky as Honor rises from her bed. Wrapping a robe around her shoulders, she creeps out into the saloon and cracks open the door to what is now Nevis's room just enough to feel her daughter's presence without waking her. In spite of the terrible situation there is a wholeness to the morning now. She closes the door, lights the wood burner and heads to the kettle. Her first coffee of the day is drunk, as always, as she sits in the rocking chair waiting for the stove to warm the air and watching the water sparkle as the sun burns off the clouds. Her coffee drunk, she returns to the bedroom and pulls on her tweed trousers, giving them a cursory brush with a damp palm, reassured by the repeating sound of Nevis's snooze alarm. All is as it ever was. A mother and her teenaged daughter.

At 7.30 and Nevis not yet surfaced, Honor texts Alex. Breakfast here?

Not long after, Alex appears, with a loaf of still-warm bread bought from one of the bakeries in Harbourside and in a few moments the boat begins to fill with the smell of warm, buttery toast. Nevis emerges in her pyjamas, blinking back the light reflected off the water, clutching her phone and scratching her head and for a brief, too painful moment Honor thinks about the parents of Jessica and Natasha, waking up this morning without their girls.

'How did you sleep, darling?' How she wishes she could take her daughter in her arms.

'Any news?'

Nevis shakes her head and, frowning, slumps onto the sofa. Honor hands her daughter a mug of coffee. 'Thanks,' says Nevis, her attention still on the screen.

'How are you feeling?'

'Oh you know, like shit.' Still she doesn't lift her eyes from her phone but her tone is less fragile than it was last night, more resigned, with a hint of something else. Defiance perhaps or fear?

'Alex brought fresh bread,' Honor says. Nevis doesn't appear to have noticed him sitting at the kitchen table. She looks up, her eyes lighting briefly on the visitor, then dropping back to her phone. 'Oh, hello.'

'No update on what happened at Three Lakes?'

'Not on the local news site, or on the *Bristol Journal* page. They just say a body's been found. They don't even mention her name or that she was an Avon student.'

'And you're absolutely sure it's Tash?' Honor says.

'Of course I am. It's all over the internet,' Nevis says, sounding irritated. 'I tried calling her number last night but it just went straight to voicemail and now her inbox is full. I guess everyone else had the same idea.'

'Don't they have to be careful about reporting suicides?' Honor says, addressing herself to Alex.

Nevis's head jerks up. 'Who says it was a suicide? It could have been an accident; it could have been anything.'

It is such a surprising thing to say that for an instant Honor is stunned into silence.

'You're right, of course, Nevis,' Alex says. 'The police haven't ruled anything out and there can be all kinds of reasons for stopping the press from naming the victim. The paper might even have decided to protect the family's privacy, but I think it's more likely that they don't want to piss off the university. The local press is clinging on by its fingernails at the moment and Avon will be a major advertiser for them. The classifieds, the jobs pages, not to mention a source of stories.'

Honor goes over and sits down beside her daughter. 'Have you thought about what I said last night? About going to the police.'

'There's no point.'

Slapping his thighs and rising from his chair Alex says, 'I should be off. Lots to do.' Addressing himself to Honor, he adds, 'Ten o'clock OK for us to go over and see Gary?'

'I'll come to the *Helene*. And thanks for the bread.'

She watches him go then turns back towards her daughter to find her sitting with her feet on the sofa, arms around her knees, as if trying to squeeze herself small.

'Who's Gary?'

'Work thing,' Honor says.

'So why is Alex coming? Is he your boyfriend now or what?' The sharpness of the tone is surprising. Nevis shifts her position. 'Sorry.'

'That's OK.' Honor moves over to the sofa and sits beside her. This is all too much for any young woman. She gets it. The anxiety and confusion, the constant drumbeat of guilt and the fear that there may be no answers and that at some point you might have to stop looking for them. Reaching out she picks up her daughter's hand. Nevis does not pull it away.

Honor says, 'Look at me.'

Nevis twists her head and eyes her mother sceptically.

'There is *nothing* you could have done. Not for Satnam or Jessica or Tash.' Nevis takes a deep breath and sighs. Her mother goes on. 'For some people dying is the only way they're able to make sense of living.'

Chapter 43

Nevis

She waits until Honor has left before texting Luke, then sits back and stares out across the floating world, taking comfort in the familiar, gentle, elemental slap of the water on the steel of the hull and in the busyness of the water birds breaking the cool, green surface. A cormorant, spooked by a fish leaping out of the water, startles her back to wakefulness, its crack, crack backfiring into the air. If Satnam were a water bird she would be a cormorant. She has the same simple elegance, the same air of self-possession and mystery. Jessica would have been a sandpiper, with her nervous, darting energy, and Tash, well that was easy. Tash was a Canada goose, brash, noisy and nosy but with a generous heart and an adventurer's spirit. They comfort her, these thoughts, though the pain of them is sharp too. She thinks about Satnam, how she could have asked the simple question, 'Why are you thinking of leaving?' before heading out to the library that Sunday. About pumping Jessica for information without ever stopping to listen to the silences in the spaces between her words. And about Tash, hard-edged, bawdy, chaotic Tash. Girls like Tash cover up their fear with trash talk and cigarettes.

Three young women, three chances to intervene. She, Nevis, could have. So why didn't she? Was it cowardice? Is she so afraid of life that she's unable to protect it? Everything is so confusing now she hardly knows where to turn. When did it begin? At the Valentine's Day party or long before that, when three young women who were struggling with their mathematics met at a remedial summer class? What plans were hatched then? And when did they fall apart? And why has all of this passed her by? So many questions. So many unfinished and contradictory stories, tangles of half-truths and lies, of secrets and assumptions.

She thinks: perhaps I should go to the police after all. But if I did, what would I say? How likely are they to believe me, an odd girl who doesn't know much about the world? There is no proof of anything. Nothing concrete. I suppose I could call Narinder Mann but she wouldn't listen to me. There is a limit to what Narinder wants to know. Perhaps I should talk to the Dean? There was a moment, in the restaurant, when she imagined she could tell Christopher Cullen anything. What will I do, how will I feel, if I discover that he already knows? Or doesn't know and, like Narinder, doesn't want to hear?

I know nothing, she thinks. I trust no one. Except, perhaps, for Luke. This is why she has asked to see him. It's either an act of desperation or an act of hope. The hope is that she will be able to air her suspicions, her fears, her bewilderment, her pain without Luke fussing or offering false reassurances. She hopes he won't pressure her to go to the police or the university authorities or, worse, try to rescue her because, if she knows anything for sure right now, it's that Luke is as confused and uncertain as she is. And, perhaps, as wounded too. On the other hand, she is desperate enough to think that Luke might be able to help.

And so she waits, counting the water birds to pass the time. Ten o'clock, 10.15. At 10.30 she finally hears a bike rattling down the quayside. Moments later, Luke's voice calls her name and as she goes up on deck to greet him, her heart is growing lighter, the space inside her clearing as if a fog were lifting.

'I had to mend a puncture, sorry. Should have texted you but I thought it was probably just quicker to get it done.' She'd told him in the text that she was staying with her mother. Didn't say why.

Looking around, Luke gives a low whistle. 'Nice gaff.' Directing himself to her, says, 'Anyway, how are you? Fucking awful about Tash.'

'You didn't like her much.'

'No, but still.'

'You want to come down into the saloon? I've made coffee.'

He takes a packet of cigarettes from his pocket. 'I need a smoke… if you don't mind.'

'I'll fetch it up here then,' she says.

When she returns balancing a mug in each hand, he's most of the way through his first cigarette. Squinting at her through the morning sun, in a concerned voice, he says, 'Did you see it coming? With Tash I mean.'

'No. Did you?'

He shrugs and looks away. 'To be honest, I'm not sure how to answer that question. I only really knew her through Satnam. It always seemed like she was trying a bit too hard to be the cool girl. Plus I used to think she was a troublemaker. I feel bad about that now. I think maybe she was just troubled.'

269

'Have you been on campus?'

'Yeah, I swung by on my way here to pick up some coursework. Why?'

'Are they going to call a meeting or something?'

Luke blows out his cheeks and shakes his head. 'Dunno. I guess they'll send everyone an email if they plan on doing that. Everyone's talking about it though, obviously. Other students. Wondering who'll be next. I even heard that some of them were taking bets which is pretty sick, you ask me.'

He sits in silence, finishing his cigarette while Nevis tells him what she knows, about Jessica and Tash and Ratner, how Tash was convinced that the university was trying to get rid of her, the row at the Valentine's Day party, then finding Satnam's coursework, taking it to the Dean who said it was Ratner who'd marked it up. Wondering now whether Satnam too was involved with Ratner. Maybe even sleeping with him to help her grades.

By the time she's done, Luke has grown wide-eyed, his focus intense, the stub of his cigarette slowly burning unnoticed between his fingers. He slumps back and rubs his free hand across his face, reddened now and blotchy.

'She texted me on the Sunday night. It must have been just before she went to the bridge.' He starts, suddenly, as the hot ash makes contact with his flesh and flicks the offending stub out across the water.

'I know. I got into her phone.'

He screws his eyes shut and slowly shakes his head. She does not read faces well but there is no mistaking the shadow of regret and shame contouring his cheeks.

'Then you know what she said,' he says, quietly. 'And

you'll know she asked me to call and I didn't.' Luke hangs his head and picks at a fingernail. 'Obviously I'm gutted about that. It's why I didn't tell you before. But I was angry with her, you know? Texting me saying she'd made a big mistake, like I was just supposed to forgive her for cheating and take her back.'

'You think that's what she meant by a mistake? That it was about the two of you?'

His eyes swing round to meet hers, a glaze of incomprehension. She goes on, 'What if by mistake she meant her involvement with Mark Ratner? Maybe she wanted out.'

'I hadn't thought of that.'

The water of the Floating Harbour is dazzling in the sun now and from behind the boat a flurry of honking comes, and a Canada goose appears, heaving its huge bulk from the water on frantic wings. She turns her attentions to Luke, watching him observing the bird.

'Amazing, aren't they?' he says.

'Yup. So clumsy lifting off. Their flight is one of the great wonders of the world though. The ones at the back honking to encourage the leader. Flying in V formation gives them 71 per cent more range than flying alone.'

They fall silent for a moment, taking this in. The cigarette in Luke's hand glows red in the breeze. Eventually, Nevis says, 'Satnam called someone, a number that wasn't in her contacts. Whoever it was called back. They spoke for quite a while. The number's since gone out of service.'

'Ratner?' Luke pinches the remains of the cigarette between his forefinger and thumb, winces a little at the burn, and drops the stub in his pocket.

'Could be. If she was thinking about blowing the whistle on him. I would think the average guy would go to some lengths to protect his marriage and his career.'

'Don't you think you should give the phone to the police?'

'How would that help?' Nevis says. 'No one's committed a crime.'

'So far as we know.'

She gestures to his mug. 'Want a top-up?'

'No, thanks. Mind if I have another smoke though?'

Nevis watches Luke pull a cigarette from its packet, and waits for him to light it before saying, 'I think the uni must have known something. It's no coincidence that they were trying to get Tash to leave. If it had come out that Ratner was sleeping with students and inflating their grades that would have caused quite a scandal. They didn't want her causing any trouble. Who knows, maybe they were trying to get rid of Jessica and Satnam too?'

Cocking his head to one side and squinting at her, Luke says, 'I saw an older bloke leaving your flat one time. Maybe it was Ratner.'

Nevis's mind reels. 'When?'

'Like a month ago maybe? It's kind of awkward to admit this, but sometimes I used to hang around outside. I missed Satnam and it somehow made me feel better. I don't know, maybe I was hoping she'd see me and realise that she'd made a mistake and get in touch. Or maybe I wanted to find out who she'd cheated on me with. So there was...' he scrambles for the word, '...*ambivalence*, isn't that what they call it? But then I saw him coming out of the flat and walking to his car. I thought, so that's him, the guy she left me for.'

'Did you get a good look at him?'

'Not really. It was dark and he was walking pretty quickly to his car. He had an older bloke's coat on. And a kind of dad walk.'

'What about the car? You see that?'

Luke nods. 'A bloke is always gonna look at another bloke's car, especially if he's sleeping with your girlfriend. Ex-girlfriend.'

'And?' She is hoping he will say it was a silver VW Passat MK7, 2013 model, because she has observed in the past that this is the model driven by Mark Ratner.

'Like I say, it was dark so it's hard to be precise but I'd say black or dark grey or maybe midnight blue.' A dark crease appears on his brow. 'Trying to remember the make. Nah, it's gone.'

He pinches out his second cigarette and stands to leave. She goes over to the cleat and pulls the bow rope to bring the boat closer onside. He waits for her then leaps onto the quay. She waits for him to recover his balance and shouts over, 'Hey, Luke, one thing?'

'Yes?' His eyes are expectant.

'You said some students were taking bets about who'd be next?'

He shakes his head and thumbs towards Redcliffe Bridge. 'I should be going.'

She watches him take off along the quay, his tall frame gradually diminishing.

A goose lands with a loud splash not far from the boat.

'It's me, isn't it?' Nevis says out loud, to no one in particular. 'They think I'm next.'

Chapter 44

Honor

The drive to Tewkesbury to see Gary Bond takes them through pretty countryside, newly spring minted, the sky the pale blue of birds' eggs. Honor is at the wheel, Alex in the passenger seat beside her. I miss the country, Honor thinks, as they pass the lime green smudge of hawthorn hedges on either side. Perhaps when this is all over I could take a trip through the navigations and canals of the Midlands as far as Kendal and the Lakes, picking up work refurbing boats along the way. Nevis could visit. Alex might even come. We could take our time. There would be no more hiding, no more secrets. We would keep moving and leave the past behind.

Google Maps leads them to a new-build house, half-way down a cul-de-sac in an estate of similar new-builds on the outskirts of Tewkesbury. Legoland, her dad used to call these places. 'Don't expect visits from your mum and me if you end up in Legoland,' he'd say. Honor didn't end up in Legoland but they never visited anyway.

A man in his forties answers the door. Red-haired with weathered skin and fragile, searching eyes. Hams for hands. Honor introduces herself and Alex and, conscious of the delicacy of the situation, explains why they've come, avoiding any direct mention of Reynolds or the suicides.

As Gary listens his expression hardens, then softens once more. Finally, in a voice hinting at relief, he says, 'I wasn't surprised when Anne called. Not really. I knew someone would come eventually.'

He shows them to a cosy living room where, on a cushion by the sofa, a large dog lies gently snoring.

'Don't worry about Hector the Protector,' Gary says, showing Honor to the sofa. 'We went on an eight-mile walk earlier. He won't be giving anyone any trouble for a while.'

He offers up an uncertain smile, suggesting tea, and leaves the room to make it. When he returns, they make small talk for a while about the journey, the house, the floods of a decade ago before moving on to the events at Midland University.

'It's difficult to talk about, even now,' Gary says. 'Suicide is, well, it's not something we're very good at dealing with, is it?'

'We're very grateful,' Honor says. 'And no, we're not.' She has her own difficult stories but this is not the time for those.

'For a long time after my friend Michael died, years really, it was like I was trapped underwater. I used to have dreams about being on the riverbed and not being able to make it to the surface. I saw a counsellor and realised I was literally trying to drown my sorrows.'

'Did it work?' asks Alex, simply.

Gary shakes his head. 'You're always left trying to answer questions there are no answers for. And the feelings. Anger, then guilt, then back to anger again. People talk about this stuff a bit more now but back then nobody did. I haven't. I mean, I did a bit at the time, to that journalist who put you in touch with me, Anne, but not really.'

'I want to ask you about Madeleine Ince. Can you talk about that?' Honor says, treading carefully.

'Yes, you said on the phone. Madeleine was Reynolds's protégée. Older than us, obviously, but not by much. She did a lot of Reynolds's teaching for him, covered for him. The old bastard was always pissed.'

Honor reminds him that Madeleine denied knowing anything about the abuse and sees Gary's eyes flash and his face redden.

'Well she would, wouldn't she? It was so easy to lie and get away with it back then. Nobody wanted to believe anything was going on because if they accepted it was happening then they'd have to do something about it and if they did something about it then they'd have to acknowledge that it had been going on a long time. But there's no question that Madeleine knew.'

'And you know that because…?'

'Because I have proof. At the time I had a voice recorder that I used to record lectures and I took it into a tutorial with Reynolds. I still have it but…' He takes a deep breath, then reaches down and begins to stroke the dog, unable to go on.

'It would help if you could tell us what's on it.'

Taking a deep breath and sitting upright once more, Gary says, 'Like I said, I sort of knew this day would come. Reynolds would … what he would say was that he wanted to pleasure you, only it wasn't pleasurable. It was awful, but you couldn't say no because he would threaten to ruin your academic career. He would usually lock the door to his office but, this time, it was late, and I guess he forgot, and Maddy burst in on us, and, I remember this so clearly, the shame, but also the hope, because Maddy saw us and she said "Oh" and I thought, he's

276

been found out now, so everything will change, but he just said, "Maddy, as you can see Gary and I are busy being naughty, aren't we, Gary. You've caught us with our pants down." Then he laughed and said, "So if you don't mind?" So she left and he carried on. He had no idea my recorder was on, obviously. But the saddest thing, in a way, was that Madeleine saw what was happening and she turned her back on me.'

'Did you tell anyone?'

He bites his lip and shakes his head. 'That's what's so sad. None of us did. We didn't even tell each other. The victims. I didn't know it had happened to Michael until after he died. I remembered him saying how much he hated Reynolds. It's so difficult to explain, but you wouldn't have known what to say. You were so alone. I was scared of getting kicked out of the university. And Reynolds was our personal tutor, so he would have been the person to tell. And what if I had told? He could have just denied it. And Madeleine would have backed him up. In fact, I think she did. It was a stitch-up. And anyway, who would have believed me?'

'And Madeleine never said anything to you about that incident?'

'Nothing. I avoided her. I was just so, you know, so humiliated that she'd walked in on what Reynolds was doing. When you told me you wanted to talk about her, I went up into the attic and dug out some photos. I found one of her. I guess it must have been at one of the faculty drinks parties. You want to see it?' Without waiting for an answer he reaches out for an envelope lying on the coffee table and draws out a photograph of a young woman with dark hair and a broad smile punctuated at either end by dimples. Something about the image is familiar, though she has never met Madeleine Ince, only had that one disastrous phone call with her.

'She's very pretty,' Honor says, returning the photograph to the table.

'Yeah. A lot of us had crushes on her. Which somehow made what happened even more excruciating. She had a boyfriend, a postgrad, quite a bit younger than her, so that was a bit dodgy too. He was, like, this maths genius...'

Honor feels her breath quit. At that moment the dog, sensing some tension in her, wakes and looks up, cocks his head.

'Chris or Christopher as I remember. I think he was, like, the same age as us, so eighteen, nineteen, and she was in her mid-twenties.'

'You remember his last name?'

Gary taps his fingers on his chin and stares into the middle distance for a moment. 'I'm not sure. Mulholland was it? Something like that.'

Honor feels the blood drain from her limbs. The world billows and flattens. On the chair opposite, Gary bobs forward, as if poised to leap up and catch her.

'Are you all right, Honor?' asks Alex.

She nods, unable to speak just then, and, reaching for the photograph of Madeleine Ince on the table, picks it up and inspects the long dark hair, the giant, dimpling smile. The resemblance to Zoe is so uncanny it takes her breath away.

'I'll make some more tea,' Gary says, hastily disappearing into the kitchen and returning, moments later, with mugs, a teapot and a carton of milk on a tray and, laying it down on the table, says, 'I'm wondering why you're interested in all this? It was all so long ago.'

Alex's eyes dart to Honor, waiting for her to speak.

'We think there may be something similar going on, in another university, perhaps, though we're not sure.'

She watches Gary slump back and heave a deep sigh. Holding his head in his hands, he says, 'It never stops, does it? These universities care more about their reps than the people they're supposed to be serving. Young people. Vulnerable people.' He looks up, his eyes bright with tears, jawline trembling with emotion. 'It never leaves you. Never.'

'I do know,' Honor says, softly, and in an impulse reaches for his hand and squeezes it, saying, 'We're going to try and stop it, Gary. What you've told us today, what you've shared, that's going to help enormously.'

Gary blinks but does not answer.

Later, on the drive back to Bristol, Alex says, 'So what *was* that back at Gary's house?'

She looks straight ahead and in a calm voice says, 'Unfinished business.'

'You want to tell me? It's another hour to Bristol.'

She checks the time on her phone. It is nearly three o'clock.

'Can I think about it?'

He does not answer. She reaches for her phone and texts Nevis. On way back R U OK?

'Why are you smiling?' Alex says.

She catches herself. 'Oh yes, I was, wasn't I?' She explains why, how Nevis would call her text abbreviations OPT, for old person text. 'She's always on at me to use predictive text.'

There's a pause. Outside the country slides by.

'I'm glad you're feeling better,' Alex says finally.

'I'm not, not really.'

'It's still nearly another hour to Bristol,' he says.

How to explain that all of this has stirred up in her a wayward, almost savage desire for revenge. It burns in her, white hot and rageful as a wildfire. She closes her eyes and takes a deep breath. In nearly twenty years she has never told anyone the whole story. There never *will* be a good time, she knows that, but there might not be a better time either. Steeling herself, she begins:

'When I was Nevis's age, I had this friend, Zoe. She was the only real friend I'd ever had. We met as students studying classics at St Olaf's. We loved each other, Alex, I mean really loved each other. Zoe was the sister I never had.' She swallows hard, pushing down the grief.

'Nevis's birth mother?'

'Yes. When we were in our second year, the university let in a mathematics prodigy, Christopher Mulholland...'

'...the guy Gary was talking about?'

'The same. Really young he was, like fifteen or sixteen, brilliant but still a minor, so his mother came with him. He was obviously completely under her thumb. She used to humiliate him in public. It was horrible, really. Anyway, most students just ignored Christopher but there were some who teased him mercilessly, bullying, I guess. And there was this group who sort of took him as their mascot. They were mean actually, but either he didn't care or he was so desperate to fit in that he took it. Zoe was on the edge of this group, but she was kind to him and paid him attention because Zoe was like that. Maybe it was inevitable, given how lonely he was, but he developed this terrible crush on Zoe. She had no interest in him sexually – to us he was still a kid. Everyone except me thought it was funny, you know, laughable, even sweet. But I saw the way he used to look at her, the way he would pierce her with his eyes. To me there was something off about him, something creepy.

'Towards the end of our second year, Zoe and Christopher ended up at the Maths Society's annual do. I wasn't feeling well so I didn't go. Everyone was drinking tons and some genius thought it would be a good idea to ply Christopher with vodka. Zoe said he got sick and she felt bad for him so she offered to escort him home. They had to pass by her rooms on the way to the place he stayed with his mum. He begged her to let him sit for a while in her room and sober up. He said his mum would kill him if he came home drunk. So she made them both some coffee and everything began to get really swimmy and odd. It could have been all the drink that night but Zoe could take her drink so I've always believed that Christopher slipped her something. She didn't remember anything else, but I do.'

'You were there?'

'I was in bed in my room which was on the same floor, but I had to get up to pee and the bathroom was down the corridor. There was a light on in Zoe's room. Not the main light, but, like a bedside lamp. I called her name and when she didn't answer I tried the door. Christopher had obviously thought to put the chain on but it wasn't locked so it swung open just enough for me to see Zoe lying unconscious with Christopher on top of her and—' She stops. 'I can't tell you how many people I had to relate that story to afterwards. Police, the university security, the university authorities, Zoe's parents, my parents, lawyers. It was like it became the only story ever told.' She looks up at him and sees a pair of kind eyes looking back. 'But I haven't told it for a long, long time.'

'Don't go on if you can't manage it.'

'No, it's OK, I want you to know. When I saw what was happening, I shouted to Zoe through the crack in the door, but she didn't respond. I think I said something like, "Get off her," and I saw Christopher freeze. I tried to curl my fingers around the door to slide the chain but I couldn't reach it, so I took off. I was in a panic and I couldn't think who to tell. It was late, there were no staff around. I ran around campus until I found a security guard at the gate. I had to explain what I'd seen to get him to agree to come. Eventually he did. By the time we got back and he let us in, Zoe was still on the bed, unconscious, only now she was alone.'

'The security guy just shrugged and said, "She's out of it."'

'I went over and pulled the duvet over her then I raced after the guard. I said, "Aren't you going to call the police?" and he said, "She's completely pissed. What did she expect?"'

'So you called the cops?'

'Not then, I was too afraid. I thought they'd take the same view as the security guard.' Her eyes prickle. 'I know I should have done. Instead I sat and waited in her room till she came to. She couldn't remember anything, of course. It would have been easier, better even, not to have told her. Except that, I know now, she would have found out eventually. Back then I thought everyone had the right to know the truth about their lives. I believed in justice, transparency, all that idealistic stuff. And so I told her and I found out the hard way that it's not true, what they say, about the truth setting you free. The truth didn't set Zoe free. It destroyed her. I destroyed her.'

Alex's head swings round and his face is surprisingly fierce. 'Don't say that.'

'It's how I feel sometimes.'

She thinks better of saying how she had nearly destroyed herself with her hatred, her desperate need for revenge. How she would lie awake and restless at night for years afterwards picturing herself waiting outside his home and following him to his place of work, thinking up schemes of how she would call him and text him and in a thousand ways make herself known to him so that he would never have a peaceful day, would never be free of her or the fear of what she might do. How all those feelings came rushing back in a dark, unstoppable surge tide, the moment she heard his name.

'Bystander guilt. It's a thing, but the reality is that Mulholland raped your friend.'

'Yes.'

'What happened to him?'

'On the night? He went home. The next day I told Zoe what had happened and tried to persuade her to go to the police, but she didn't want to. I suggested we go to the Dean then and Zoe said OK. So we went and told the Dean what had happened and she said it would be impossible to prove so it would be best all round if we didn't say anything.'

'And you didn't?'

'We were nineteen. We were scared of the gossip, the shame, of not being believed or of being believed and losing our places at St Olaf's. We knew they would do whatever they could to keep Christopher. Taking him on at such a young age had made national news. He was their prodigy and their publicity machine. He made them look exciting, relevant, prestigious.' Her eye travels to her phone. Still no reply from Nevis.

'So you never told anyone?'

'About a month later, we did. Zoe changed her mind and we went to the police. They questioned Mulholland but his mother gave him an alibi. Said he was with her from 10.30, which was absolutely not true. It was too late by then anyway. There were no forensics, nothing. A week later Zoe dropped out of college. A few days after she left, I went too. I didn't want to stay at St Olaf's without her. Neither of us told our parents. We found a place in a squat and lived there for a few weeks, drinking and doing our best to blot things out. I got work doing odd jobs for this farming couple way out in the countryside and they let me and Zoe live in a caravan at the bottom of one of their fields.'

Her thoughts are interrupted by a ping on her phone. A text from Nevis. Sorry battery out. Heading back to the boat now. The message reminds her, if a reminder were necessary, that there are limits to how much of the story she can tell, and that, even now, she has a duty to protect Nevis from the truth. And if Nevis cannot know, then no one else can either.

'And Mulholland?' Alex says now.

'I bumped into him in the street, not long afterwards. He looked grey and depressed which I was pleased about. He told me he was leaving St Olaf's. My fault apparently. He spat at me, actually, said he'd get his own back one day. After that, neither me or Zoe ever saw him or spoke about him again. I hadn't heard his name in two decades till Gary mentioned it.' She looked across at Alex and wondered how she could convey the depth of her hatred for Mulholland, how the ticking impulse she had thought was long since dormant had been awakened now, and would not quiet until she had got her revenge. Mulholland hated her as much as she hated him and she knew that such darkness as existed between them could never be eliminated while they both lived. No matter how much light was shed on it, the shadow, the stain of their hatred would remain in the world. For she and Christopher to be truly free of one another, to be released from their mutual haunting, one or other of them would have to die.

Chapter 45

Nevis

Nevis is on the sofa on the *Halcyon Days*, considering how she might motivate herself to return to her coursework. Her essay on oceanic population has been in for a couple of days now but she has yet to settle to anything else. Luke's revelation has left her feeling restless and queasy the way food poisoning can do. If the visit of the older man to their flat had been innocent then surely Satnam would have mentioned it? Who was he and what was he doing? A dark car seems to rule out Mark Ratner, whose own vehicle is silver, though it's also possible that Luke misremembered the colour of the car he saw, or even that Ratner could have been driving some other car, his wife's perhaps? She imagines it wouldn't be hard to find out where he lives and pay him a visit, check to see if there is a dark coloured car on the drive or parked outside, even confront the man himself? He would deny any affair, she was pretty sure of that, and he might report her to the Dean. But perhaps that would be worth it?

Another possible course of action is to go to the Dean direct. Though it seems unlikely that he would believe her, on the evidence of a selfie and an essay and the casual observation of an ex-boyfriend. And if he doesn't believe her, what then? In his eyes she would be guilty of making serious and unsubstantiated claims against a colleague. What would that mean for her academic career at Avon or anywhere else for that matter? She has come to value his esteem, almost to rely on it, and the lunch at Luigi's gave her the sense that her respect for him was reciprocated. So what if he did believe her? Would he be able to muster the university to act? They had, after all, continued to claim the incident on the bridge had been an accident and that Jessica Easton's death, while tragic, was unconnected to Satnam's actions. There had been no official response to Tash's fate as yet or at least Nevis hadn't seen any. How would they pass that off? It would be so easy and not untrue to claim that Tash was unstable and a drug user; or that she had been devastated by her friend Jessica's death; or that she was not coping well with being asked to leave. Would suicide contagion be enough to explain it? After all, Tash had lived through a spate of copycat suicides earlier in her life. Hadn't she voiced her concern that the incident on the bridge might spark others? It would be guesswork but added together the guesses might well be enough to appear definitive. So why was it that, for Nevis at least, they failed to add up? Satnam had wanted to come clean, Jessica said. Satnam had told Nevis she'd had enough. She had been willing to expose Mark Ratner in order to rid herself of him. But Jessica also said that Tash was against Satnam speaking out. Why? Because she was damaged enough to think herself in love with her abuser? Or because to expose Mark Ratner would create more trouble than it was worth, and might even prove dangerous? Whatever the facts of the matter, it all comes back to Mark Ratner.

Her phone rings, interrupting her thoughts, and flashing 'Satnam Home' on the screen. Her heart leaps as for a split second it seems possible that Satnam is on the other end of the line, then the realisation hits that it's much more likely to be either Narinder or Bikram, bearing important news. She closes her eyes and does the best she can to gather herself before taking a deep breath and taking the call.

Narinder's voice says, 'Nevis?'

'Yes, I'm here.'

'My daughter is waking.' There is a long pause. 'The nurse said she asked for you. They said it would help her to wake up if you came, so I have agreed.'

Nevis can feel the corners of her lips turn upwards. Her pulse knocks out a rhythm in her wrists. A sob rises up and catches in her throat. She has hardly dared to hope for this and now it is happening.

'Can I come right now?'

'That is why I called.'

Pulling on yesterday's clothes, she thinks about hailing an Uber, checks the traffic on her phone and decides it will be quicker to run. She leaves a note for Honor and ten minutes after the phone call she is on her way.

Nurse Becky is standing at the nurses' station in her scrubs poring over a screen. She recognises Nevis immediately.

'Oh, sweetie, you're here!' She explains that Satnam's condition remains very fluid. Earlier this morning Satnam showed signs of waking so the hospital called her parents. The decision was made to take her off the respirator and let her breathe on her own again. Bikram could not leave the pharmacy but Narinder came down right away and is with Satnam now.

'To be honest,' Becky says gently, lowering her voice, 'she might have spoken but it might also have been moaning. I *think* she called for you, but it really wasn't clear. She hasn't said anything since. It sometimes takes people a while to come round after being in a coma. In any case, I thought she would want to see you.'

Nurse Becky provides directions and, as Nevis is about to turn away, Becky stops her and in a whisper adds, 'Her mum is still saying it's all an accident. Probably best if you don't argue with that right now. Nothing to be gained.'

Nevis walks down the corridor to Pine Ward with her heart in her mouth. At the curtain, she calls out. Narinder's voice answers, 'Come in.'

Satnam's mother is sitting beside the bed with her hand resting on her daughter's arm and looks up when Nevis pushes back the curtain and enters. Her face seems expressionless to Nevis. That's probably just me, thinks Nevis, I'm not good with these things. Her friend is lying on her back with her eyes closed, no longer intubated and breathing softly but giving no sign of being awake.

'They say she can hear,' Narinder says, 'but I do not believe it. I have spoken to her but she does not respond.'

'Can I try?'

Narinder seems to consider this for a moment before nodding and getting up from the chair by the bed. She hovers in the corner of the cubicle. She seems dishevelled and worn, not unlike the homeless people who congregate in Broadmead of an evening. Since the incident on the bridge, Nevis has felt very alone, but now, she can see, she is not. Satnam's condition, her actions, have taken their toll on those who love her.

Nevis sits and lays the back of her hand on her friend's cheek. From the corner of her eye she sees Narinder stiffen but she does not say anything.

Satnam shows no sign of reacting, but feeling a softening in her friend's body, Nevis reaches out and takes her hand, which is papery and covered, now, with a light bloom, like dust. From the bed comes a soft sigh which could be nothing more than a breath.

'I miss you,' Nevis says simply. 'I understand more about what you said to me on Sunday night now. But I love you and I want you to know that we'll find a way out of this together.'

Silence falls, broken by Narinder.

'You see, she doesn't know you're here.'

But Nevis, remembering the sigh, says, 'I think she knows.' She strokes Sat's hair in the casual, rhythmic way she always did when they were sitting on the sofa together watching rubbish telly. She watches Satnam's face, the quiver of the eyebrows, the tics playing around the jawline.

'She's speaking,' Nevis says.

Narinder's face opens. 'You heard something?'

'Not with words.'

Nevis watches Narinder slump back, disappointed, then turning to her friend, leans in and twists her neck around so she can lay beside her cheek to cheek. Something is happening, as if Nevis and Satnam have plugged into one another. Suddenly, she can feel Satnam's breath, her heartbeat, the thrumming of the neurones in her brain. *She is trying to tell me something.*

Nevis rights herself. 'What are you wanting to say?'

But there comes no reply.

'That's enough now,' Narinder says. 'She's tired.'

On her way out of the hospital, Nevis stops to look at the cafeteria table where she sat with Sondra waiting for Honor to arrive what seems like months ago now. In the short time since then she has become a different person. Anguish for that younger, more innocent self curls like a dead leaf inside her. No question but she is older, wiser and more cynical. She walks through the revolving doors into the car park, preoccupied with those thoughts until in her pocket her mobile phone buzzes and interrupts them. A text from Luke comes up on screen.

Just remembered. The older man's car? Dark blue Volvo.

She stops in her tracks, feels her legs weaken, a sharp rap to her brain as if someone were knocking on it, thinks someone *is* knocking on it. A dark blue Volvo. Her legs are trembling now. A passer-by stops. 'Are you OK?'

'Yes, yes, thank you. I've had a shock is all.'

It is more than a shock. It is what Satnam was trying to tell her. It seems so obvious now.

The man leaving their flat that night wasn't Mark Ratner. It was Christopher Cullen, the Dean.

Chapter 46

Nevis

The Dean ushers Nevis into his office, shows her to a seat. He is smiling without his eyes. He looks ashen and old now, she thinks, nothing like the man who laid his hand on hers over lunch at Luigi's. A part of her wonders how she could have been so innocent, so gullible. Another part hopes that she is wrong. This is what feeling torn must be like, she thinks, laying her jacket over the chair.

'A coffee perhaps?' he says.

'No,' she says.

For a moment he looks taken aback then his face resumes its soft, fake smile.

'I'm sure you won't mind if I have one?' He turns his back to her and goes over to the coffee machine. He has sensed something's up, she realises; he's puzzled and trying to buy himself some time. A moment or two later he returns to the desk carrying a cup delicately by the handle.

'You seem upset. Is this about Natasha?' he begins.

'In a way.'

'A tragedy for her family. The student had a lot of problems, as I think I mentioned to you. Only the other day she came to me and Dr Keane at student welfare, saying she thought she'd have to leave Avon because she wasn't coping. Unfortunately some students are just not able to apply themselves with the necessary rigour.' He takes a sip of his coffee and says, 'Are you sure I can't get you something? Tina made some rather wonderful biscuits.' He reaches behind and, picking up a small tin, swings his chair back to the desk, prises off the lid and offers up the tin.

'No thanks.' She thinks she can smell alcohol on his breath.

'Watching your figure I suppose?' he says, withdrawing the tin and fixing her with a steady gaze. 'No need to, believe me.' He reaches out a hand and makes contact with hers. She can feel his heat, the suggestion of sweat on the pads of his fingers.

Part of her wishes to be conciliatory, to find a way past what Luke has told her about the car and what Tash said about who it was who had orchestrated her downfall, but something about that smell, the sugary biscuits and the waft of alcohol, brings her to her senses. The words rise up and she can no longer keep them back. This is why she's come after all.

'Did you visit Satnam in our flat?' The words come out flat and tarnished sounding.

She watches the frozen pond of his face. A crack appears. When he smiles it's a fixed grin, like a jack-in-the-box clown.

'Why would I do that?' he says, in a tone suggestive of concerned, professorial enquiry. It's fake, she thinks, the regard, the flattery, the attention. It's all a sham. It was right in front of me but I didn't see it. The man I looked up to is at best a liar and a drunk. At worst he's something else too. Something more sinister.

'How are you feeling in yourself, Nevis?'

The change in him is so unmistakeable that even she can sense it. His body has stiffened around the edges, like a slice of cheese left out on the counter too long. He is drying up, curling, turning in on himself. Before she can say anything, he goes on. 'This thing with Natasha must have come as a big shock. I wonder whether you are coping. I've been thinking that perhaps the best thing for you would be to step down from your studies for the remainder of the academic year. Perhaps take a year out to regroup?'

'This really isn't about me.'

'I'm afraid I have to disagree. Your essay on oceanic deep vent modelling, for example. Well, why don't you tell me what you thought about it?'

'It was fine,' she says, perplexed, doing her best to think back.

'This is what I'm talking about, you see...' the Dean says. He blinks at his screen and with one hand swivels it around so that Nevis can see her file for herself. He is pointing at a tiny line of script three-quarters of the way down. 'Yes, yes, here it is. Oceanic deep vent modelling. Thirty-two per cent. A fail by any measure.' He looks up. 'We understand that the last few weeks have been rather unsettling, but we really do feel that it would be best for you to take time out.'

'But you said...'

'Well never mind. This is what I am saying now. If we can make this quick? I've got rather a lot on.'

Nevis swallows and tries to clear her head. Her neck begins to prickle and goosebumps spread across her arms. The smell of alcohol hits her nostrils once more. *Play him at his own game. Think about Satnam.*

'I spoke to someone close to Satnam,' she says.

Cullen blinks. When she doesn't go on, he says, 'And?'

'This person saw an older man leaving our flat a few weeks ago. He says the man got into a dark blue Volvo.'

Silence falls. Cullen watches her steadily.

'And?'

'I think that was you.'

She watches the small muscles in his face twitch but the expression remains the same. A terrible stillness settles over the room and, in a very calm voice, Cullen says, 'Have you any idea how many dark blue Volvos there are in a city like this? I really think I should call student welfare. Evidently, you are not coping.' She watches him reach out for the phone and in a blink she has slammed her fist down on the back of his hand. The handset clatters onto the desk.

'You have become rather paranoid, Nevis. I'd say borderline delusional. If you were your usual self, you'd understand just how much trouble I can get you into.'

Shame sits on her skin like a rash. She wants to dive into a shower and scrub it off and make herself clean. She knows now that she has no future at Avon, that to carry on this conversation might well ensure that she has no future at any university, but none of that matters. She is thinking of Satnam now and how she can beat Christopher Cullen.

He stands and goes over to the door and calls for Tina, then he turns and comes to sit in his chair once more. He is no longer looking at her and, she knows, he will not respond to anything she says.

'Ms Smith is just leaving,' Cullen says to Tina when she comes to the door.

Nevis rises from her chair, sensing that everything hangs on these last few moments. She had come seeking an explanation but that no longer seems necessary. What she is after now is proof. That's what the Dean's always taught her, isn't it? Without proof you have nothing. She pulls out the phone from her pocket, and standing calmly, she says, 'Just before Satnam Mann went to the bridge she texted someone. Whoever it was blocked their ID and called her back. They spoke for seven minutes and twenty-three seconds. More than long enough to have a conversation. I called that number back.'

Cullen lifts his hand, as if to stop her. His face is crumpled now and a peculiar, dead shade of pink.

'Ms Smith is leaving. Please show her out.' Alarmed by his tone, Tina hesitates. 'Now!' Cullen says. Her face stricken, Tina advances towards Nevis. Before Tina reaches her, Nevis has pulled out her phone and is tapping at the screen. She feels a hand on her elbow as Tina tries to lead her from the room.

'Call student welfare,' Cullen says. 'The student is very unwell. She needs a psych evaluation. And cancel all my meetings.'

The phone on Cullen's desk begins to buzz and spin.

Chapter 47

Cullen

After Nevis leaves, his heart tick-tocks like a clockwork toy that has been wound too tight, the breath pulsing and whirring. One minute he feels as though he might drown in his own air, the next that the air will all be squeezed from him. Sweat begins to bead on his forehead and his hands are shaking, his throat swollen and sore. He puts his elbows on the table to steady himself, dumps his head in his hands and takes a few deep breaths, attending to the rush of air, following it with his mind as it leads him out of the dark chaos of his firing neurones into the half-light of thoughts.

I am fucked, he thinks.

His mind goes back twenty years to the knock on the door and the voice crying, 'Zoe, Zoe!', to the flit from the bathroom window, the frantic run back to the flat and to his mother. He knew he was fucked then, too.

Pull yourself together and stay calm, he thinks. That was what Amanda said to him.

Easier said than done.

He takes a breath, opens the drawer of his desk and, taking out the quarter bottle of Bell's, takes a swig. The whisky goes down like a pat on the back.

I can do this, he thinks. Stay calm and think straight.

He reaches for his phone, removes the SIM card and scopes about the room for some scissors. Not finding any, he goes through to Tina's desk, locates a pair there and carefully stashes the cut pieces in his trouser pocket. You foolish man, he thinks, to be so easily outwitted. He has an urge to run but knows there is nowhere to run to. He is cornered. The only way to get out of this is going to be to show Nevis Smith his teeth the way he did Natasha Tillotson.

All is not lost, not yet.

He scribbles strict instructions not to be disturbed on a Post-it note and sticks it to Tina's screen. He needs time to think straight, doesn't want her returning from student welfare and asking questions.

Locking his office door behind him, he moves back to his desk and starts cooking up a plan. Time heaves and billows around him unregarded. He will no longer allow himself the luxury of being scattered and panicky. From now on his mind will be a laser beam.

Later, he has no idea how much later, a knock comes on the door. At first, he thinks the sound is coming from his head. Only Tina's voice brings him to.

'What is it?' he says, more irritably than he'd intended.

'There's a phone call for you, Professor.'

She never calls me Professor, he thinks, distancing herself from me already, the coward. All my allies falling, one by one.

'Did you not see the Post-it? No phone calls, no meetings.'

'It's Veronica and she won't take no for an answer.'

'All right, I'll take it. Did you manage to get Ms Smith to go to student welfare?'

298

'No but she promised to go home. She seemed to have calmed down a lot, she didn't give any sign of being ill.'

He takes a deep inhalation. Nothing he can do about the girl now. At least she's off campus. He swivels the screen back to its usual position and scrolls down Nevis's student records to the appropriate text box and types in 'Student made several appointments for welfare consults which she did not keep. Student welfare reached out but student was non-cooperative. Faculty confirmed that student had been underperforming and seemed depressed and anxious.' Keane will welcome the intervention, he thinks, since it covers both their backs. In any case, he'll square it with her later. He is about to close the file when his eye is drawn to a familiar name. Under next of kin. He peers and re-reads and peers again. The words grab hold of him like a sickness. That name. Can it be the same one? Frantically he taps out of the university database and searches for Nevis Smith's social media feeds. Sparse; the girl evidently doesn't use social much. He searches for images, and up pops a photograph of Nevis on the deck of a narrowboat with a broad grin on her face and a plant pot in her hand. Standing beside her also smiling is a familiar figure from his past. So he was not mistaken. He feels his shoulders tighten, his belly turning over. So it *was* Honor Smith he'd passed by in the street the other day. Not some ghost set free by his own dark impulses. A real-life woman, the mother of Nevis. He sits back and bites his lip, hears himself snort. So, Honor Smith, still out to get him, too cowardly to come forward herself, using her nineteen-year-old daughter to set him up, to exact her revenge. Well that explains everything.

They won't be smiling when I've done with them.

The light on his desk phone blinks, and his mind zooms back into the present and Veronica. All the difficult, demanding women. He picks up.

A voice thunders, 'What's going on? I just tried your mobile but it's saying the number is unavailable.' He can't decide whether she's angry or afraid.

'I dropped my device in the sink,' he says in an emollient voice. He'll get a new SIM card tomorrow.

'You need to come home right now,' Veronica says coldly.

'If it's that salesman again…' he says, carefully.

'No, not that. I'll tell you when you get here.'

Moments later he is ducking in and out of traffic, his mind abuzz, gears raging, heading for the outer edge of Clifton and the Georgian house he cannot afford. He parks in the driveway and takes a nip of Dutch courage from the glove box. He's pretty sure that if it was a problem with the pregnancy she'd be sounding hysterical. Instead her tone was at first anxious then coldly matter of fact. It's either Amanda, he thinks, or something about the name change again. He waits for the whisky to settle his nerves then gets out of the car. The wind is blowing. As he strides towards the front door, he can feel clean air being sucked into him, the skin on his face taut and prickly with it. He raises a hand to his cheek and feels a warmth there that is not rain. From some distant place in his memory his mother's voice says, *Wipe those tears away and stop being such a baby.* He brushes his cheek dry and strides towards the door which opens even as he puts a foot on the first step up. Veronica appears looking stony-faced. He moves in to kiss her cheek but she backs away. He knows then that the only way is forward, into whatever fate awaits.

'You'd better come in and explain yourself.' That chilly tone.

In the hallway he shakes the outside air from his coat and hangs it carefully on its usual peg, Veronica all the while standing before him, blocking his entrance into the kitchen, where they would usually do most of their talking. She has on one of her smart dresses, as if she has been to a meeting.

'Let's go into your study. You'll see why in a minute,' Veronica says.

Cullen hesitates. 'Uh-oh, I've a feeling I'm going to need a glass of whisky,' he says, doing his best to lighten the mood.

Veronica fixes him with a look of contempt.

Cullen feels himself rise to the bait and does his best to tamp his indignation. *All my allies falling.* Doesn't a man have a right to expect his wife to be on his side? His head is pounding.

She turns and walks through the study door, the as-yet modest convexity of her belly catching the fabric of her dress.

'Take a seat,' she says, gesturing to the grey sofa where Cullen likes to catnap when he should be marking papers. He sits, expecting Veronica to follow suit. Instead, she walks around his desk and takes a seat in the leather chair as if this were a police interview and he the suspect.

'If it's about the man in the driveway, I've sorted it. He won't be bothering you again,' he says, doing his best to sound confident and alpha.

'I told you on the phone, it isn't,' she says, leaning her arms on the desk and interweaving her fingers.

'Whatever it's about, I'm sorry. I apologise. Things have been rather difficult at work lately.' Her expression brings him to a grinding halt. It's not going to matter what he says. His eyes light on her perfectly polished fingernails. His stomach drops. 'Why are you dressed like that?'

'Like what?'

'As though you've been to a business meeting.'

She compresses her lips and closes her eyes. 'This isn't the order I wanted to do things in, but if you must know, I went to see a solicitor.'

'Why on earth...?' He feels himself lurch back in shock. What is this all about? He has a sudden urge to stop the clock, get back in the car and just drive.

'Please, Veronica, I don't want to lose you,' he says. He needs her now, his last ally. 'Whatever it is, I'll change, I'll be different.'

She meets his eye with a thunderous look. 'I found something. You'd hidden it rather well which is why, I suppose, I didn't see it before. But the solicitor advised me to gather information. So that's what I did. Helps that you're a little careless about where you hide your keys, Christopher. The envelope is still in the drawer. I couldn't bear to leave it out.' She draws out a large manila envelope and pushes it across the polished surface towards him.

Cullen screws his eyes so tight that he's seeing white spots. He knows what this is, but he does not want to know. His whole life hangs from a spider's silk. The spider is hiding out somewhere, waiting for him to weaken. His only defence now is to stall for time and act as though he were the wronged party. His eyes spring open. 'Wait,' he says, swallowing hard and doing his best to bring out a commanding tone, 'what were you doing rooting through my things?'

'What was *I* doing?' Veronica says in an unbelieving tone.

'What's this?' She holds up a tiny, scraggy piece of newsprint, something he didn't recall having kept, but immediately recognises.

'It was a long time ago,' he says.

'*Rape?*'

'No, no, Veronica. You've got the wrong end of the stick.'

She reads, 'Boy questioned by police in alleged rape case is mathematics prodigy Christopher Mulholland.'

'That was a malicious allegation. Entirely without foundation, which is why it never went any further. I was never charged or even cautioned. God, you can't hold that against me. I was *fifteen.*'

'Is that why you changed your name?'

'Years afterwards yes. Those allegations tailed me for *years*, made my life a misery and sullied my name even though I was entirely innocent.'

'I found this, too.' A flash drive dangles on its lanyard between them. 'Evidently, not all your secrets are ancient history.'

It hits him with a terrible gut punch. There is a moment's pause. Cullen feels as if a team of contractors is digging out a basement in his head. There is banging and noise and dust everywhere. Rising to his feet, he sidles over to the table, snatches up the drive and returns to the sofa.

'I can't believe you actually went through all my flash drives,' he says, weakly.

'There are *more*? Tell me, were these designed to humiliate me or to humiliate this girl, or both of us?'

'You're not going to believe this…'

'You're probably right about that.' She is staring at him with one eyebrow raised. He has never, until now, quite appreciated just how formidable his wife can be. 'I recognised her face from that undergraduate Christmas party you gave for the department. Though I had to look twice. Remarkable resemblance to Madeleine Ince. She's like a very young, Asian, version of her, which I suppose was part of the attraction.'

He takes a deep breath. 'Her name is Satnam Mann.'

'Oh, the girl in hospital in a coma. Well, that puts a spin on things, doesn't it?'

'Listen, Veronica,' he says, doing his best to sound authoritative still. 'I didn't go anywhere near Satnam Mann. She's a scam artist. I go to the office one morning and this is in my pigeonhole, some lame attempt to blackmail me,' he says adding, 'She's not even my type.' This last he recognises is probably a step too far.

'You're a terrible liar, Christopher. I realise now that I only believed so much of what you told me because I was overprotected and naïve.'

'I swear on my mother's life,' he says. 'The girl took those pictures herself. She was threatening to post them to you unless I gave her better grades. Obviously unhinged, or she wouldn't have tried to off herself.' He stands and goes towards her with his arms outstretched in a beseeching gesture but she flaps him away.

'Why didn't you tell me?'

'I didn't want to take the risk that you'd believe her. Some of these girls are terribly messed up. They want attention. I think they sometimes believe their own lies.'

Veronica is perched on the edge of the desk with her fingers pressed to her mouth, listening, assessing whether or not to believe him.

'Honestly, Veronica, it's been awful.'

She looks up and catches his eye then shakes her head sadly. 'It's perfectly obvious from the angles that she couldn't have taken those pictures herself.'

'So someone else took them, an ex-boyfriend, whoever, I don't know. I swear I've never had anything to do with her in that way. She's a mixed-up kid. Avon is full of them.'

Veronica heaves a deep sigh. 'Perhaps you could help me to understand why she would try to kill herself if she was at the same time blackmailing you?'

Cullen shrugs.

'I'm also struggling to comprehend why one of the images features your brogues and your blue Liberty print tie, the one I gave you a couple of Christmases ago, on the carpet in the background.' She continues to stare at him. 'I've made copies, in case you're wondering. They're with my solicitor.'

'Solicitor?'

'Yes, someone Daddy's used. He's the best apparently.'

'The best at what?' Cullen says, horrified. He feels as if he's sliding down the slippery bank towards rushing rapids, the spray already stinging his face.

'Divorce.'

'You didn't think to talk this over first?' he says. 'Please, Veronica, we have so much to lose here.'

'I've decided Bump and I will be better off by ourselves. I don't know what's been going on, Christopher, and I really don't want to know. The doctor said I shouldn't be having any stress at all. No strange men on the driveway or a husband turning up drunk or leaving the house in the middle of a dinner party, no name changes and *certainly* not this.' She raps on the envelope. 'I'm going to go back to Mummy and Daddy for a while. Until things are resolved.'

'Things?'

She leans back and, crossing her arms, says, 'Let's have a civilised conversation about next steps, shall we? I suggest we start with you telling me exactly who it is I am divorcing, Christopher Cullen or Christopher Mulholland? Or perhaps there are other Christophers I don't yet know anything about?'

Chapter 48

Nevis

She waits for Luke at the far side of the campus by the bike store. Her phone chimes. Honor. She picks up.

'I got your message. Is everything OK with Satnam?'

'They're going to put her under again.' She thinks about what she knows. 'They say she's out of danger but I'm not so sure about that.'

A herring gull lands on the rails beside the bike store. Her mother says, 'Nevis, are you OK?'

'Yup, fine.' Why does Honor do this? All the fussing, making Nevis feel that she's not trusted to take care of her own business. 'By the way,' she says, deflecting, 'you are aware that the stove on the boat needs looking at, aren't you?' The metal has separated from the plyboard underneath the heat shield. A moderate fire hazard.

'It's on my to-do list.' Her mother sounds anxious and distracted. She's been that way ever since she went with Alex to see a guy about some work, preoccupied by something she doesn't want Nevis to know. 'I'm concerned about you,' she says now.

'I'm not a kid.' She is tempted to say, *I am not* your *kid*, but stops herself. Things have actually been a bit better between them since she moved onto the boat.

'I know, I know. I was just thinking, that location finder you told me about? The one on your phone that lets someone else know where you are? I'd feel better if you'd turn it on, just while all this is going on.'

'Really?' She does her best to quell her exasperation. Honor has always been a worrier. Still, better that, she supposes, than a mother who doesn't care. She spots Luke approaching from the student union. No time to debate her mother now.

'I've got to go. I'll turn on location finder. For now. For you.'

They finish up the call.

'What's so urgent?' Luke says, a cigarette bobbing between his lips.

'I went to see Satnam.'

She watches him freeze. He blinks as if pushing back tears.

'She's breathing on her own. It looked as if she might wake, but they're saying she might not be ready yet and they're talking about putting her back under.'

'I went to the uni chapel, on the Monday after what happened on the bridge. I've never been in there before. I don't even know if I believe in God. I just wanted someone to talk to.'

'I know,' she says, then taking a breath, 'We're going to the police, Luke.'

The cigarette drops from Luke's mouth. 'What?'

'The man you saw leaving our flat. I thought it was Mark Ratner but it wasn't. It was Christopher Cullen. We're going to the police to tell them.'

Luke is waving his hand in the air. 'Hang on... Satnam was involved with *the Dean*?'

'I think so. They had some kind of arrangement. Swapping sex for grades.'

She watches Luke's face contort in shock. 'No! Why would you even think that?'

'Because it's what Ratner was doing with Tash and Jessica. And because the Dean tried to do something similar with me. Taking me out to lunch, telling me I was in line for a first. Only in my case I don't think he was trying to get me into bed. I think he was trying to get me onside so I wouldn't ask awkward questions about Satnam.'

There is a pained expression on Luke's face. 'But Satnam would have told you, wouldn't she?'

'I think she wanted to protect me from it. Looking back I realise she was trying to tell me on the bridge. She'd got in too deep. She said she'd had enough.'

'Enough of what though?'

'The situation. Think about it. One minute she was struggling with her coursework, coming to me all the time to help her, and then all of a sudden it stopped. That wasn't because she got better at the maths. I saw her paper, remember. It was full of errors. I assumed her grades were improving because she told me she was working really hard, putting in the hours in the library, but I was always in there and I never saw her. Not once.'

Luke yelps and shakes his finger where it made contact with the business end of his cigarette. He says, 'None of that sounds like Satnam.'

'I know, and that's why we didn't see it.'

'You think the guy she said she cheated on me with was the Dean?'

'Most likely. But I don't think she ended it with you because she didn't want to be with you any more. I think she just felt too ashamed.'

Luke groans. 'I really loved her, Nevis. I still do.'

'She told me something else, and I just didn't connect the dots till it was too late. This is going to be hard to hear, but I still think I should tell you, because then you'll understand.'

Luke nods an OK.

'Last summer, after her parents found out about you, they found her a match, some guy from Birmingham. She refused to meet him. She wanted to be with you. At the start of the academic year she came to an agreement with her parents that, if she began doing better at uni, they would let her graduate and find a job. She was afraid that, if she had to drop out, she wouldn't be able to resist the pressure they would put on her to get married.'

'So she made sure she wouldn't have to? Didn't she tell you on the Sunday that she was thinking about leaving Avon though?'

'Think about it. She was trapped. She couldn't live with doing what it took to remain at Avon, and she didn't want an arranged marriage. By transferring to another university she was hoping to free herself from her situation. But I think that, by the end, she'd just decided that the world was better off without her.'

As Luke takes this in, his mouth contorts and the flesh of his cheeks reddens. I should comfort him, Nevis thinks, slinging an arm awkwardly around his shoulders.

'What Jessica told me was that Tash had started dating an ex of hers, a married man. At the Valentine's Day party, the one where Tash took that selfie with her and Satnam and Jessica, Satnam threatened to make trouble, to "spill the beans" Jessica said. I'm wondering if Satnam was about to blow the sex for grades thing out of the water? But the whole situation actually suited Tash. She might already have been in love with Ratner by then anyway. So she felt threatened by Satnam. I honestly think Satnam wanted to do the right thing, but Tash wouldn't let her.'

The warmth of his body seeps through her peacoat. A few weeks ago she would have hated this. Too close, too much contact. But that is the past and, as someone once said, the past is a different country.

'If she did do that stuff with the Dean, it was done for the best of reasons, Luke. Because she wanted a life of her own. We all deserve that, don't we?'

Luke is sitting very quietly now, staring out across the dimming sky.

'When Satnam wakes she'll tell the truth, she'll give Cullen away.'

'I wouldn't be surprised if he has a plan to make sure that Satnam *doesn't* wake.'

'Nevis, that's mad.'

'Is it? First Jessica goes, then Tash. Why wouldn't Satnam be next? The university would continue to deny any responsibility. If pushed, they could blame suicide contagion. That way it's just a sequence of events, a dark chain reaction, no one's fault, just one of those things.'

Luke takes a minute to consider this, then throws his cigarette on the ground and grinds it with his foot. 'Fuck.'

Chapter 49

Cullen

He rises from his bed unrested, passes Veronica's dressing room and sees the empty spot where her hairbrush usually sits.

I have been a fool, he thinks.

All night he has been turning over the implications of a divorce; the loss of Veronica and his child. He loves Veronica. More to the point she is his route out of all the old ignominy, his ancient obsessions. The mad visit to the hospital seems like years ago now, his fixation with Satnam an odd, strange delirium that he can now clearly see was merely a replaying of the old stuff, the odd, unwelcome reprise of a greater, longer lasting obsession, his first, last and singular love. He'd seen something in the girl the instant she arrived on campus, had picked her out from the gaggle of lanky boys and giggling lasses. She was only moderately pretty and no intellectual and – though you couldn't ever say this in today's world – he wasn't generally drawn to ethnic girls and yet he found it hard not to look at her. He had been so puzzled by his attraction that it was easier just to deny its existence. And so it went under the radar where it should have stayed. He made sure she was never in his seminar groups and kept his distance at faculty events.

It was months before the problem of her magnetism resurfaced at the remedial maths class he'd run during the summer. His growing fixation unsettled him terribly. Still though, the class was short and he was able to restrain himself, in part because his attraction remained such a puzzle. It was Veronica who'd nailed it at the faculty Christmas drinks party. His wife was the first to remark on the resemblance between Satnam and Maddy Ince. And when he looked closely, he could see it too. From that moment two things happened. First, his obsession grew, even as he understood that, just like Maddy, Satnam would only ever be a poor stand-in for Zoe. Secondly, he became aware that Mark Ratner was screwing his students. Which meant that, so long as Cullen was discreet, there was no reason he shouldn't join in the fun. Ratner wasn't likely to snitch on him.

It was he who had first suggested an arrangement. Taken Satnam to lunch at Luigi's, laid out in some detail, without actually using the words, how she could sleep her way to a first-class degree. There were conditions. He demanded absolute discretion. If anyone else so much as suspected anything, the deal would be over. Secondly, during their encounters he would only ever refer to her as 'Zoe'. When she demurred, he piled on the pressure by taking her coursework grades down a notch or two. At the same time, he believed, her parents were also pressuring her to give up her studies and marry. When she finally conceded he waited until she slept and took a few 'glamour shots' in the room at the Travelodge as insurance. He didn't for one moment consider where their affair would go or when it might end. He was living a fantasy that had to be realised. For the first time in years, decades perhaps, he felt truly alive.

All that is over. The bubble has burst. He recognises that. Veronica is his only future now. Not his one true love, but no matter. Perhaps for a man as sensitive as Cullen there can only be one great love affair in a life. With Veronica there might be a future in a life where all too often only the past has seemed real. There might be some solace to be found in a normal life with a wife and, soon, a child. He could clear his debts. Ask Veronica's father for the money. The imminent arrival of a grandchild would make it impossible for his father-in-law to say no. Veronica is my only ally, he thinks. The one person who will stand by me. Without Veronica I am condemned to live with the ghosts of the drowned and the dead.

Perhaps there is still a chance to win her back? If she has spared her parents the ugly details, they may yet root for him. True they never really gelled but with a child on the way perhaps they might see the sense in their daughter remaining with her husband. Perhaps I could lay it all out before her and beg for her forgiveness? He thinks about it. She will see, she will understand. Yes, that's it. I will go over to her parents' house now and I'll take her out somewhere fancy. I'll revisit the old days in Manchester, the times we were both happy. I'll mention the house, how much she longed for it, remind her that we were happy there for a while and that we could be happy there again. I'll lay it all on the line. I'll say, 'It wasn't my doing. I was seduced into it, drawn into something much bigger and darker than myself that I did not recognise and was powerless to resist.' Quick, quick, yes, that's it, that's exactly what I'll do.

Feeling unexpectedly buoyed by this thought, he hurries out into the hallway, grabs his coat and picks up the keys to his Volvo, too absorbed to notice the shadows of two people through the milky glass of the front door until he is almost upon them. Who can this be? Not thugs collecting debts, as he has staved them off for now with the proceeds of his mother's bracelet. Oh of course! It is a couple of carers from the nursing home, come to tell him regretfully of his mother's death. Ha! Little do they know that the moment they are gone he'll go straight to the cellar and open the bottle of twenty-five-year-old Macallan he has been saving for that very purpose. He stops for a moment, his hand on the door, feeling strangely hollowed out. Odd how you can hate someone but not quite enough to stop loving them.

He takes a breath and opens the door to find a man and a woman, both in their thirties, conventionally but inexpensively dressed, standing on the front path, just shy of the doorstep, wearing serious expressions. The man steps forward and introduces himself. Cullen hears the word 'detective' and nothing more. The woman opens her mouth but he cannot catch anything she says at all, for the loud buzz in his head. What he does understand is that both the man and the woman are expecting to be let inside.

'I wonder if it can wait? I have an appointment to get to.'

Shakes of the head. Lips resolutely pressed. He senses that there's no way out of this one without looking as if he has something to hide. Which he does, obviously. When the police officers promise they don't need much of his time, he fakes a smile and waves them in, hoping that whatever it is they want they'll be quick about it.

'We'll go in here,' he says, ushering the officers into his study and inviting them to sit.

'Lovely house,' the woman says, looking around.

'Yes. Regency,' he says.

'Must take quite a bit of upkeep. Tough on an academic salary,' she says. There is something in this, he thinks, a suggestion that the police may know more about his financial dealings than they are letting on.

'My wife has family money,' he says, doing his best to sound unrattled though his whole body is battling to remain calm. He coughs. 'I don't mean to rush you, but perhaps we could get on to why you came?' He has already considered his moves and decided that at this point a feint is what's required. 'I'm guessing it's about Satnam Mann?'

The policewoman's head snaps round. 'Why would you think that?'

'Oh, I assumed you'd come with the news that she had sadly passed away.'

The two police eyeball each other in a way that makes Cullen feel slightly panicky. 'I mean, because I am the Dean of the faculty.' The woman frowns as if struggling for comprehension. Desperately playing for time, he says. 'I'm sorry, I didn't catch your names?'

'I'm DC Linda Worsley and this is DC Mo Hassan. We're here about another of your students, Natasha Tillotson, the young woman who was found up at Three Lakes. Just a few routine questions.'

He takes a step back and tries to shake his hand free of pins and needles without the police officers seeing. For a moment he feels he might suffocate.

'About what?' he says, doing his best to seem genuinely baffled. Somewhere nearby he hears the sound of a car alarm going off. 'I mean, of course, absolutely, whatever you need, naturally.'

'We're wondering how well you knew her?' This from DC Hassan.

'Natasha?' he says, as if momentarily forgetting. 'Not well, I'm afraid. An average student, a bit unstable as I recall. One of the unhappy ones.' He wonders whether to say that she'd been asked to leave then decides it's best not to give away anything he doesn't have to.

'Can you tell which of your students are unhappy?' This from DC Worsley.

'Not always, but Natasha seemed the anxious type, you know, the sort who might have to take something to steady herself, get through the day.' He is thinking on his feet now. 'You'd be better off talking to my colleague...' he corrects himself, '...*former* colleague, Mark Ratner. He had more to do with her than I did. My role as Dean means that my teaching load is lighter and I generally focus on my area of expertise.'

'Which is?' asks DC Worsley.

Why are they asking me this, he thinks, they must know already, surely? All it takes is a quick google.

'The application of mathematics in the life sciences. Statistics, probability, modelling, that kind of thing.' He leans back in his office chair, feeling suddenly rather more at home.

Looking up from his notebook DC Hassan says, 'Can you tell us about the last time you saw her?'

For an instant Cullen's mind toggles back to Zoe. He blinks away the thought and takes a deep breath, staring at the ceiling in a simulacrum of remembering, then looking first at Hassan and then at Worsley, he says, 'I'm not sure when that would have been exactly. Oh, wait a moment, yes. We were obliged to hold a fitness to study meeting with her.'

'We?' asks DC Hassan.

'Yes, the head of student welfare, Dr Lea Keane, and myself. When a student is struggling academically, we request a meeting to talk about how to improve things. Unfortunately Natasha had proved herself to be unsuited to the rigours of Avon. As I remember, we suggested a transfer to another, less academically exacting, course at another university. She wasn't very happy about it. I hope we didn't inadvertently set the stage for what was to come, but I'm afraid that, these days, quite a few students come to us who really aren't well suited for the academic life.'

'And Natasha was one of those?' asks DC Worsley.

'Yes,' Cullen says, decisively, then when neither of the pair responds, he goes on, 'I can show you her academic record if you like. Very poor.'

Another exchange of looks between Hassan and Worsley. What are they plotting? The thought suddenly arises that they may have spoken with Nevis Smith. But they wouldn't be minded to believe anything she said, would they? Hassan and Worsley are probably not the sharpest tools in the box but even they would see Nevis's claims for what they were – the delusions of a girl with a crush on her teacher. His mind steps back to that lunch at Luigi's. He blinks to rid himself of the memory. Focus, that's what's required here. Outwit the enemy.

'You might have come across the phenomenon of suicide contagion, officers?' He pauses long enough for the word officers to bed in. 'Unfortunately this is what I believe was going on here. Natasha was a good friend of another of our students, Jessica Easton. As you might know, Jessica very sadly took her own life a couple of weeks ago. Before that there was another incident, very likely a suicide attempt, by Satnam Mann, who was also a friend of the other two. It starts with one student and spreads to their friends. There was another incident of it, if you remember, at Midland University a good while back now. Four or five suicides that time, I believe. And a plague of copycat suicides in America in 2015, as I recall. Shocking but very difficult to predict or prevent. Studies…' he tails off, wary of sounding rehearsed.

'We are aware that copycat suicides can happen, yes,' says DC Hassan. 'But…'

Cullen raises a hand to continue. So long as I'm talking, he thinks, they can't do anything. Can't arrest me or even ask me questions. He takes a deep breath. 'It goes without saying that after Jessica…' he searches in his mind for a delicate expression '…*left us*, the university did all it could to reach out to anyone who knew her, other students, her friends…' He fleshes out the university's student welfare policy, its reputation for student satisfaction. Before him, the police officers listen in respectful silence, nod, occasionally glancing at one another. This is going very well, he thinks, very well indeed. 'So, as I say, you'd be better off speaking to Mark Ratner,' he says.

The police look blank and say nothing, which is unnerving. Eventually DC W— the woman anyway, he can't recall her name – cracks a slow and unconvincing smile and says, 'Your *former* colleague.' She checks her notes. 'Dr Mark Ratner. He's heading to Thirsk, we believe.'

Cullen blinks, and coughs to buy himself a little time. Have they already been looking into Ratner? He is sure that he hasn't mentioned Thirsk. They must already know it. Who else have they spoken to? Feeling very rattled indeed, he takes a deep breath. Nothing for it but to talk his way out of this one. 'If you must know, I think Dr Ratner may have quite a bit to answer for. He is, shall we say, quite one for the young ladies.' Be careful, he thinks, you don't want to incriminate yourself here. 'I don't know for sure, but it's possible that he had an eye for Natasha and for Jessica. It's not unknown for Mark to go off piste, as it were.'

'Off piste?' asks the woman.

'Dalliances,' Cullen says. 'The university discourages them but they're not a sackable offence, or at least, not if there's been no academic benefit to the student as a result. The heart wants what the heart wants and all that.' He lets out an indulgent little chuckle. 'Unfortunately there was some suggestion that Mark had allowed his personal preferences to affect his impartiality, began to alter his paramour's grades, which is why we decided, on balance, to let him go. Evidently Thirsk believes in second chances in a way that more exacting institutions don't.'

DC Hassan smiles pleasantly while his colleague remains buried in her notepad.

'Lovely house,' he says, 'Big. Just you and Mrs Cullen here, is it?'

'Yes,' Cullen says, shifting on his seat. 'At least, my wife, who prefers to go by her unmarried name, by the way...'

'Which is...'

Cullen suppresses an internal smile. This will impress them. 'Well, officially she's the Honourable Veronica Fanshawe-Drew.' He's about to go on and explain that Veronica is pregnant, when DC Hassan says, 'You and Mrs Cullen both seem unusually fluid about your names. Let me see...' He consults, or pretends to consult a notebook. 'Didn't you originally go by Mulholland...?'

'Yes. That was my stepfather's name. Cullen is my birth name. I changed it by deed poll back to Cullen after my mother and stepfather got divorced. It was a long time ago.'

'Hmm. According to our intelligence, you would have been...' DC Hassan hesitates and checks his notebook once again '...six when your mother and stepfather divorced. Quite precocious to change your name by deed poll at that age.'

'Well, um no, it was...'

'And you appear in your student records as Christopher Mulholland.'

'Well, yes, I mean, that was still my *official* name but I was calling myself Christopher Cullen even then.'

'Though none of your records indicate that. But let's proceed. I'd like to know when Cullen did become your "official" name... Was it after your conviction for credit card fraud? Or following the incident of alleged rape at St Olaf's University, which is near Ludlow I believe?'

Christ, he thinks, doing his best to hold himself in. They've done their homework.

'That was dropped,' he said. 'A storm in a teacup. I was never even charged.'

An idea bubbles up. He flicks his eyes first to one officer then to the other, sees that they are attentive and launches in. 'As a matter of fact, I'm glad you raised that. Because the woman who made that malicious and vindictive accusation – which was wholly without merit – happens to be using her daughter to spread outrageous lies about me *as we speak*. I am being harassed. This is what all of this is about.'

The two police eyeball one another. 'Professor Cullen, if you have a complaint to make about this person, you'll need to come down to the station and we can deal with it there,' DC Hassan says.

For a moment he thinks that this is just what he'll do until a small voice inside stops him. Suppose this is a trap to lure him down to the cop shop so they can put him in a cell?

He clears his throat. 'As I said, I have an appointment to get to.'

'We won't take any more of your time than we have to, then, sir. Just a few routine questions.'

'Very well,' he says, graciously, adjusting his position in the chair.

'You mentioned earlier that Natasha might have had a drug problem?' DC Worsley says, checking back her notes and reading carefully, '"The sort who might have to take something to steady herself, get through the day."'

'Yes, yes, you know, Valium or something like that.'

'Did you *know* she was taking Valium? Did she disclose that to you?'

'No, no, as I said, I didn't really have much to do with her. It was more of a thought, really. A guess, you might say.' He smiles. 'Just trying to be as helpful as I can.'

'We appreciate that,' DC Worsley says. 'There's something else you can help us with. Do you remember what you were doing on Thursday, sir, the 3rd of April that would be?'

The day Natasha Tillotson went missing.

'As I said, officers, Mark Ratner is the person you want to speak to. I'm pretty sure he was…'

'We've spoken with Dr Ratner. He was in Thirsk on the 3rd and 4th attending an interview.'

'Oh, well then, as I said, I can't help you.'

'We think you might be able to, sir,' DC Worsley says. 'We think you might be able to tell us why your car, a dark blue Volvo...' she rattles off the licence plate number, '...the same car as is currently in the driveway, was caught on CCTV in the Three Lakes area at 9.23 p.m., very close to the time it's estimated that Natasha allegedly committed suicide?'

'Look,' he says, 'if this is about Nevis Smith...'

'Why would it be about Nevis Smith?'

'As I said, I am the subject of vindictive harassment from one of my students and her mother.'

'If you want to make a complaint about that...'

Cullen cuts him off. 'What exactly are you after?'

'What might we be after, sir?'

'I've told you what you need to know.' He is feeling flustered and irritated now. What can he say to get these irritants to buzz off? 'These girls were copycat suicides. There's no *allegedly* about it. Natasha Tillotson was unstable and a Valium user. As for me driving around in my car, I have no recollection of that at all.' He thinks of Veronica. Even if she doesn't want him back, he will always be the father of her child. She's always hated scandal. She won't want to see him getting into any trouble. If he plays his cards right, promises her whatever she wants, the house, everything, then surely she'll back him. Just as Amanda did all those years ago. 'My wife often drives my car, so I expect that was her.'

'We'll ask her, sir, obviously. She's not here?' DC Worsley says.

'No,' he says, panicked. He cannot allow the police to speak to Veronica before he does. 'She's visiting relatives for a few days but I can ask her to get in touch with you when she gets back if you like?'

Worsley smiles and says nothing. Do they know more than they're letting on? What if they've already spoken with Veronica and they've just caught him out in a lie? He feels his tongue catch, the roof of his mouth dry as sandpaper, his legs jiggling so that he has to press his feet hard into the carpet so as not to let it show. He tells himself to bloody well calm down. They haven't got anything real or they would have arrested him, wouldn't they? He was too careful. Though was he careful enough? How careful do you have to be to cover up... something like that? He cannot bring himself to say the word. So long as it remains unnamed, he can pretend it never really happened except in the dark recesses of his mind. A fantasy.

'Well,' Worsley is saying now, shifting in her chair, 'we don't want to take up more of your time than we have to.'

'Thank you,' Cullen says stiffly, rising.

The two police officers exchange glances. He notices the woman nod briefly to the man. So there it is, they haven't got what they wanted from him. No confession, nothing like that. There will be no arrest.

With mounting relief he leads them down the hallway to the front door.

'One thing,' DC Worsley says, standing her ground. 'I'm wondering how you could be so sure that Natasha Tillotson had taken Valium?'

'Students take uppers and downers all the time.'

'But you were quite specific, weren't you? And you're right, as it turns out. Natasha did have Valium in her blood, but the tests have only just come back from the toxicology lab so...' DC Worsley side-eyes her colleague '...that was a pretty good guess, now, wasn't it?'

Chapter 50

Cullen

Cullen shuts the front door and reaches for the wall to steady himself. He takes a deep breath before stumbling into the living room and going over to the drinks cupboard, then decides that now would be a good time for that bottle of Macallan after all. The still deep of the cellar is as comforting to him as death. Finding the bottle, he comes back up into the living room and takes a long swig, waiting for the burn to do its job. He thinks about calling Maddy Ince. A week or two ago he would have. Now, he's not so sure. Maddy has always been about Maddy.

He's standing in the narrow hallway again now, the whisky bottle clasped in his hand, feeling the world closing in on him. He can't think straight. His head is screaming. Fleeing might be an admission of guilt. Staying might risk arrest. What to do? Has he ever felt this alone? He is on a frozen sea in a tiny boat. He takes a swig and lets the alcohol burn some sense back into his brain.

The only person left in his world is Amanda. The moment this thought comes to him he sees the sense of it. Right now, like a dying soldier slung over barbed wire, he needs a mother, any mother, even one as disastrous as Amanda. But what does he want from her? Advice? Love? Courage? Maybe all of those things. But mostly hope, he thinks. I need hope to be able to carry on right now. Will he get it? Who knows, but there's no one left to ask. He puts down the bottle of whisky, thinks better of it and picks it up again, swipes his keys from the hallway table and goes to his car. A fifteen-minute drive brings him to Wychall's. He parks, inexactly, in the visitors' area and walks across the threshold into the blanketing heat of the nursing home. In the office off the hallway, Maura gives him a cheery wave. He proceeds through the living room, past the Christmas cactus and the hand sanitiser dispenser, through the double doors into his mother's cucumber-green corridor.

He finds Amanda in bed with what she claims is a terrible headache, watching a rerun of a baking show on TV. He pulls up a chair beside her and pretends to be engrossed for a few moments.

'Mother, I wonder if you'd like a whisky? It might help clear that headache.' He feels mildly tipsy but not drunk enough to be able to summon the courage to tell her what is going on. 'I bought a bottle of Macallan.'

Her head spins around ninety degrees and creases her brow into an anxious inverted V.

'I thought you'd been drinking. I can smell it,' she says. 'I suppose you realise it's not yet dinner time?'

He slips the bottle from under his jacket.

She gives him a testing look. 'What is going on, Christopher?'

He removes the stopper cork and, emptying Amanda's water glass into the plastic orchid, pours her a very large serving. Adds just the right amount of water, not from the plastic jug, but from the tap in the bathroom.

'Oh, that's much too much,' she says, glugging down half. He watches her smile and drift into an internal reverie, humming very softly to herself, and finishing up the whisky. 'You really are a very good boy sometimes,' she says, returning to the present. She holds out her glass. 'I suppose I could have just a little more.' He fills it, his heart quickening now. Any minute now he will tell her.

A knock comes on the door and a carer pops her head round.

'Oh, you've got a visitor, Amanda.'

'We're just having a lovely chat, aren't we, Mother?' he says.

Amanda side-eyes him. The carer smiles broadly and backs out of the room. Cullen goes over to the door, closes it and, with his back to Amanda so that she cannot see, turns the lock.

'Mother, I need to tell you something,' he says.

'Do you?' she says. 'I wonder if it's just better if you don't.'

He moves over to the bed, takes the remote control from her bony fingers and switches off the show.

'Put that back on!' she barks.

'No, Mother. I have something to say. It's important.'

'In that case, give me another whisky,' she says, petulantly.

He fills her glass and watches her take one elegant sip before reaching for a plate of biscuits on her bedside table and taking a nibble on one, wrapping her tongue around the crystals of powdered sugar left at each corner of her lips.

'I do so love a shortbread,' she says and with a smile still playing on her mouth, she leans back against her pillows, closes her eyes and lets out a murmur of pleasure. Cullen lights on the call button at Amanda's bedside. He puts her glass on the bedside table and slides the call button out of reach.

'The police came...' he begins but she lifts a staying hand, her eyes still firmly closed.

'There you go again, you see, always ruining things. You never had the slightest regard for timing, Christopher.'

'Mother, I'm in trouble and...'

She lifts an imperious hand. 'Please, Christopher, don't go on. I am too old and tired for this. Didn't you hear me say I have a headache?'

'*Please*,' he says, feeling the hope tremble inside him like a wild bird. 'Without you...'

The hand comes up again. 'Christopher, if you continue to assert yourself in this way, I shall call a carer to escort you out.'

He feels his legs go from under him, manages to make it, just, to a tub seat by the window. All the old feelings of injustice rise like dark birds disturbed in the act of picking clean a carcass.

At that moment there's a knock on the door. He goes over to unlock it. A carer appears with a supper tray. He waits in silence, his heart pounding, lest his mother betray him. Once the carer is gone, he says, '*I* ruined everything?'

Amanda opens a single eye and looks at him with measured disdain. 'Yes, you disappointed my expectations. First you made me lie for you. I have had to carry that lie for twenty years, Christopher. I could have gone to prison for bailing you out of your sordid teenage enterprises. And the thanks I've had is to be abandoned here, in this terrible place. Now you have stolen my bracelet, the only thing I had left of my mother. Don't think I don't know it was you.'

'If this place is so terrible, you won't mind leaving it,' he says furiously. An idea has surfaced in the way a bruise surfaces, purple and green and ugly. And like a bruise he is compelled, somehow, to keep pressing and pressing, the pain spreading through his limbs into his deeper parts. His mother's eye pops open, ominously. He has woken the spider and she is unfurling her spidery legs, readying herself.

She blinks at him. Is that a hint of fear in her eyes? Or a glint of triumph?

'I am ready to unburden myself, Christopher. I am sick of hiding and lying for your sake.'

His mind freezes. He hears a voice hiss, 'What are you talking about?' and realises it is his own.

'You always told me she let you, that girl, all those years ago. You said she didn't mind. But she couldn't stand you. I saw you together once, in the gardens of the college, you sidling up to her like a whipped dog, her recoiling from your presence, repelled. I could smell it on you that night, your disgusting lust. She *let* you? Ha! You had your way with her and then expected me to lie for you. I had to shut up and lie or wave goodbye to every hope I had. To all my dreams and aspirations for my child, my only son. But even after I'd saved you, you couldn't keep it together, could you? The snivelling self-pity. Oh poor me, child genius, undone by a minor indiscretion. Boohoo.' Her eyes narrow and gleam. 'Well now someone else can know about your dirty little secret. I'm ready to finally release the poison I've been carrying around all these years and let someone else know the truth, that my son is a rapist and a thief, a weak, disgraceful creature, a source of nothing but shame.'

There are no thoughts now, only pure instinct. In an instant he is reaching behind him for the large cushion on the chair, then he is upon her, pressing the soft down into her face. He feels her grow rigid with shock or perhaps fear and then begin to thrash. The sound of her choking makes him retch but still he carries on. He hears himself say, 'Don't make this last longer than it has to, Mother.' When eventually she grows stiff again and then floppy and still, he removes the cushion. He cannot bear to look at her face to check if there is still breath coming from her lips. Instead he grabs a plump wrist and holds it, waiting for a pulse which, to his relief, never comes.

Replacing the cushion, he sits himself in the wing-back chair by the bed and, reaching for the supper tray, takes a few bites of a nondescript sandwich, washing it down with another swig of Macallan. He picks up the tray and stands to leave. At the door he does not turn but in a quiet voice says, 'Goodbye, Amanda.' Then he goes back to the nursing office and finds the care worker who came in not long before.

'I've left her sound asleep,' Cullen says. 'She ate her supper. We shared a few whiskies.' He passes over the tray.

'Hopefully she'll sleep through till morning now then,' says the carer. On the room board a light begins to flash. 'Oh, I have to go to this resident,' she says and, turning and nodding, adds, 'See you next time, Mr Cullen.'

From the home Cullen drives up to the Downs from where he can see both the bridge and the gorge on the other side, where Natasha Tillotson's body was found. In his head he can hear his own words, the advice he'd given to Natasha as he'd driven her to her death. 'You are ruined. You have brought this on yourself. You have nothing left to live for. There is only one honourable way out and it is beautiful in a way, to give yourself up to the air and to the water, a pure thing, one final act of love.'

There will be time to free himself. Before he does, there is an old score to settle.

Chapter 51

Nevis

A flashing light wakes her. She rubs her eyes and blinks away her dream. The curtains are still open and she is dressed and lying on top of the duvet. It's cold, too, the air bringing a damp chill off the water. She reaches for the phone and notes the time. Just after 10 p.m. There are a couple of check-in texts from Honor and a voicemail from Stavos at the chippy. The voice says: Γεια σου υπέροχο which is what Stavos always says. She thinks it means, hey lovely! But maybe not. Most likely not, since she has just remembered that her shift at the chippy should have begun four hours ago. That has never happened before. Texting Stavos back. Really sorry missed my shift. Not feeling well. This is true and not true.

She scrolls down, sends her mother a brief goodnight text and, putting her phone back on its charger on the bedside table, changes into her night-time uniform of T-shirt and leggings and slips under the covers, wanting the day to be over, hoping that in sleep what to do with what she knows about Cullen and Ratner will become clearer and she will wake with a course of action in mind. The phone buzzes with another text. From

Stavos, this time. No worry. You feel better I hope. A man come to your flat. He wait outside long time.

Inside her something pings and snaps. She supposes it could have been Luke. Texting back What he look like? She waits, biting her lip, for a response.

It arrives moments later. I don't know sweetheart. Stavos not into men :). Tall, thin, not so young. He say he has important message about your flatmate, so I tell him you are at the boat.

The Dean. She is sure it is him. Why he would be looking for her so soon after their unpleasant encounter at his office she does not know, but there is something ominous about the visit. She could tell the university authorities her suspicions about him, and about Mark Ratner too. The sex for grades, the dismissal of girls who threatened to speak up or wouldn't toe the line. Her growing conviction that Satnam was involved with the Dean and that he had something on her, something so bad she couldn't live with it. She could tell them that the Dean had groomed her in order to find out how much she knew about his involvement with Satnam. Cullen and Ratner would cover for each other, as men caught with their pants down so often did, and, she suspected, Madeleine Ince might support them. She'd seen Ince and Cullen laughing together more than once and seeming more than usually familiar. Then again, she could go directly to the police. But who would listen to a geek with a reputation for not quite getting it when it came to human interaction? Who would believe *her*?

She goes to the hatch and tests the lock, then checks that the windows are shut and pulls the curtains on the quayside, leaving the lamp on the table in the saloon switched on. A text arrives from Honor to say that she and Alex will be back before long. They'd wanted her to come to dinner with them but she'd needed the time on her own. Plus it felt awkward given how obviously taken with one another they are. Now though she almost wishes she'd tagged along. There's a feeling of unease, an unsettling. Something seems off. No idea what exactly. Her body trying to tell her something. She checks the hatch lock again, peers out of the windows onto the black water, then closes the curtains and sits nervously playing with her phone and, suddenly remembering her mother's earlier request, turns on location sharing. Not that she's going anywhere. She decides, on balance, that it might be easier if she's already in bed by the time the lovebirds get home. An early night might be all she needs to feel more herself. Checking the logs on the burner she heads for bed once more, undressing this time and pulling on her pyjamas. Within moments she is asleep. When she opens her eyes again the white light of the streetlamps is still blading in from a gap in the curtains. She listens out for a minute or two and, hearing nothing, turns, pulls the duvet over her head but she cannot settle. Her legs keep moving and her head feels awash in white noise. She tries to settle herself with deep breathing but that only seems to make things worse. Her nostrils feel scratchy and her eyes are beginning to sting. Some new knowledge is making its way to her sleepy brain. It takes a second or two to form and then suddenly, whoosh, she is sitting bolt upright, her nose going crazy, a fizzy feeling in her palms which she knows to be adrenaline.

Somewhere there is smoke.

A soft thump starts in her right temple and fear rushes in as if on the tide. All around her the air begins to move, an almost imperceptible quiver but growing now and in the darkness she can see something curling up from under the door like a snake. The wood burner, she thinks, feeling panicky all of a sudden. I forgot to close the door to the wood burner. That's a first, she thinks. Having grown up on a solid fuel heated narrowboat she's always been particularly vigilant. And hadn't she spotted a fault in the backplate? It's because I've been so distracted, she thinks, I'm not thinking straight. Leaping from the bed she rushes out into the saloon and stops in her tracks. The door to the wood burner is shut tight. Through the glass she can see the logs smouldering. She takes a deep breath. The burning smell is powerful now. She turns and frantically scopes around the saloon, then moves to the stern, checking the shower room and Honor's bedroom. It's only there, turning, that she sees the yellow flicker of light on the black water. The wind blows up, sending a thin veil of ashy smoke across the window. The whole of the engine compartment is on fire.

Chapter 52

Honor

On their way back from the restaurant to the van Alex's phone rings. He unzips his jacket pocket. They take a few paces together and then he stops dead, his face is ashy, the jawline ticking, the eyes raw, mouth tightly compressed.

'What's wrong?' Honor says, alarmed.

'We have to go back to the boats.' His face turns to hers but he will not look her in the eye. 'It'll be quicker if I drive. I know the shortcuts.' He holds out a hand. 'Give me the keys.'

They are off, at tremendous speed, ducking down a side street and into an area of office buildings. Several times she asks why they are having to rush but he will say only that there's a possible problem with the boat and that everything is most likely fine and perhaps it might be a good idea to call Nevis, before returning his attention to the road. So Honor calls but gets no response. 'Probably asleep,' she says out loud. Alex doesn't answer. The city, which only a few hours ago seemed small, its outlines visible from the high places, the lights petering out into the darkness of the hills around, has lost its shape and billowed outwards. She wishes she had a giant's legs

335

and could straddle the roads and the lights and roundabouts and one-way systems.

At Queen Square she smells it, seeping in through the ventilation system, a spicy, acrid taint on the air, the sky a sinister pinkish hue. There are sirens now too and the whump of a helicopter. Alex is driving round, looking for somewhere to park, finally giving up and pulling the van in beside a parked car. They both leap out and, not stopping to lock up, rush across the wide green space of the square in the direction of Redcliffe Bridge. The smell is terrible, the air scraping at the throat and thick on the lungs. At the top of the bridge there are already police cars stationed and a group of uniformed officers is diverting the traffic, whilst others tape off the area to secure it. At the far, eastern end of the bridge, a police van blocks entry to traffic and there is a line of people strung along the barrier that side whose bodies appear to be turned to the east. Lights are being set up but they're not on yet. On the inside of the barrier Honor can just see the twirling lights of fire engines. From where she is standing on Welsh Back there is too much billowing smoke to make out the source of the fire but it appears to be somewhere on the water. She thinks of the brazier and the circle of bodies warming themselves beside it. Her head ticking, she surges forward towards the police cordon.

A policewoman holds out her hands to stop her.

'No one on the bridge, I'm afraid.'

'Is the fire by the tents?' Honor is bent over, trying to catch her breath.

'I believe it's on one of the boats.'

Oh God, Honor thinks, remembering the back panel of the wood stove on the *Halcyon Days*. Why hadn't she fixed it?

'We have... We live on one of the narrowboats. My daughter...'

Alex has caught up now. 'Is everyone safely on shore?'

'Impossible to say at the moment, sir,' the policewoman says. Holding up a hand to answer her radio, then turning back to Alex and Honor, she says, 'I'm sorry, this is an ongoing situation. I'm under instructions to keep everyone here until further notice.' She leans into her radio again and straightening herself to full height says, 'The information I'm getting is that the affected boat is called *Hal's Days*?'

'*Halcyon* – that's ours! That's our boat. My daughter...!'

Honor feels herself surge forward and then trip. Alex's hands are on her, pulling her back.

'Honor, they won't let you go.'

She feels herself struggling but it's hopeless.

'It's OK,' he says, talking into her ear. 'It's OK. I want you to promise to stay here on the bridge.'

She pulls away and looks at him. He nods encouragement. He has shed his coat already and is kicking off his shoes. He is going to go off the bridge into the water, she thinks.

'No!' she says.

'Stay here.'

The policewoman has seen him. She is heading his way. 'Sir!'

'It's all right,' he says, yanking at his shirt. 'I know what I'm doing.'

'Alex, no!'

She can hear the policewoman calling for back-up.

From the water comes a surge and then a rumble. There is a tremendous pain in her ear followed by a muffled roar. A sickening yellow light fills her field of view and for a moment she cannot breathe. She reaches up and scrabbles to wipe away the searing, sticky hail raining down on her face. She scrambles about for a purchase on something but it is like trying to find a shadow in the dark. Her chest aches now, lungs feel that they might explode. There are no more thoughts. There is nothing.

Chapter 53

Cullen

Cullen has been waiting for this moment. For hours now he has watched the comings and goings on the boat from an abandoned graffiti-strewn shed on the quayside which, judging from the smell, some of the people in the encampment have been using as a toilet. But no matter. He was nauseous anyway. Adrenaline does that to a man.

Killing Amanda felt nothing like killing Natasha. The Smith girl will be next. Could murder be growing on him?

He waits for the harbourside to settle into its night-time routine, the gulls sail off to wherever it is they pass the night, the water birds find safe moorings on the pontoons, the brazier at the homeless encampment softens to a glow, the encampment's inhabitants retreat to their tents to get shelter from the rain.

It has been years since he has felt this alive. Come to think of it, this is the most alive he has ever felt since he was a child. Which is not to say that his death wish has gone away. On the contrary, it leers over him like a great dark cloud waiting to disgorge its contents. That's a good part of the feeling of aliveness.

The only important thing about death, he thinks, is that you have to choose it before it chooses you. The only good death is the one you control. He is not afraid. He believes in the purity of death. The sanctity of release. When his time comes, soon now, he will thumb his nose at life and go gentle into the good night and for a few seconds or microseconds he will be happy.

A pigeon sails by his little window on the world. The lights have gone out on the *Halcyon Days*. Nevis is alone. He knows this because he has been watching the boat for hours now and he saw her mother leave. It would have been easier, in a way, to have killed the two of them. But this is better, more exquisite, for what could be more terrible to a mother than the death of her child? To leave this world knowing that he has taken from Honor Smith the two people who truly gave her life meaning. What a sweet sensation that will be!

It would have been so easy to have satisfied him. He was an easy kid to satisfy. When he was hungry he took a biscuit, when he was tired he went to bed, when he was bored he played computer games. He had wanted love too but Amanda had met his longing with a kind of haughty contempt. The story she'd spun was that she'd adored him up until the point that he had disgraced her, and for years he'd believed her, blamed himself. Only now does he see that this too was one of his mother's self-serving lies. The focus of her love had always been booze. She'd never really loved him. She'd deprived him of what every child has a right to expect. And so the longing for love twisted and turned inside him like a broken cobweb. When he wanted to love Zoe, to take possession of her, to feel her from the inside out, didn't he have a right? If she had only said yes to him, he could have taken what he wanted. She could have given it to him and got on with her life. He would soon have tired of her. Instead she denied him and denied him and then set him up to fail. What happened was her fault for refusing, not his for wanting.

He has no expectations of being reunited with Zoe in death and realises only now that he does not care. It was never Zoe who interested him, only the idea of Zoe, of all the Zoes, the young men and women he met at St Olaf's and then here at Avon who burst with life, while he, the boy wonder, the genius, felt dead inside. He would put himself in their company only to see something of their light diminished by it. They were the sun and he only ever the shade. They were life – the name 'Zoe' literally *means* life – but the only thing that ever lived in him was death. I see now, he thinks, that I took an ordinary girl and transformed her in my mind into someone magical and special, someone worthy of my obsession. She would be the light to illuminate my darkness. Oh, what a fool I was.

Still, he doesn't blame Zoe for his downfall, even though she engineered what had happened, offering to escort him home, allowing him into her room. And yes, he slipped her something in her coffee but he didn't understand what he was doing, not really. The phial had been given to him by one of the third-year students at the Maths Society party who'd seen how he followed Zoe with his eyes. The student sidled up to him, slid the phial into his pocket, and laughing, said, 'That one is way above your pay grade, mate. You want some action you'll need to slip this in her drink.' He'd winked and put a finger to his lips. Later that evening Cullen noticed him standing with another student, looking at him and laughing. They considered him comical, his love for Zoe a puppyish crush. It made him burn inside, as if someone had made him swallow bleach. Well, he thought, I'll show them. And what harm had he done really? Zoe couldn't even recall what had happened. It was Honor who had stirred up the trouble. The jealous bitch. He'd seen the way she looked at Zoe. Why persecute him, a fifteen-year-old boy, who barely knew what sex was, and had never been told that you had to ask someone for it and doesn't believe that even now. Women are vixens. They never think twice about taking what they want when they want it but bleat like sick lambs as soon as the tables are turned. Zoe caused him pain but it was Honor who ruined him, who turned up at his door and bothered his mother and harangued St Olaf's until the university had no choice but to ask him to leave. He had been ruined by a single malevolent spirit.

It's payback time. Revenge is the only way to close the circle, to leave the world a tidier, more orderly place. To solve the equation of his own misery. It would be too easy to kill Honor. This way is better, more creative. Solving an equation is, after all, as much a demonstration of the beauty of the process as it is about finding the right answer. There would be nothing to stop him sneaking onto the boat and cutting Nevis's throat. But where would be the skill or the beauty in that? Revenge, he realises, has its own logic. It is very much like mathematics in that regard. No wonder that he finds both magnetic.

The rain has ceased but the wind is up now and he is suddenly aware of the tap-tapping of the buddleia where it has invaded the roof and reached down into the interior. He staked out this abandoned outbuilding. No time like the present, he thinks. It is dark and there is only the most rudimentary CCTV. Everything on the water is quiet. At the encampment things are livelier since the rain held off. Someone has stuck a few broken pallets in the brazier and a drum circle has started up, enough noise to give him cover. Most of the encampment's occupants will be drunk, or high on something, he thinks, in any case too dazed to notice what is happening on the water until the smokescreen is up and he and Nevis are long gone.

He removes from its holding bag his birding rifle and slides out of the shed onto the quayside. Beside him, on the Floating Harbour, the boats perch like sentinels on the water. He makes his way quickly and quietly to *Halcyon Days*. The blinds are drawn, the lights off. There is a roof light but someone has laid a pile of two-by-fours across, a few pots of creosote lined up beside, from some renovation project, he assumes. All to the good. Creosote will burn up a treat. He hops onto the cratch and under the cover. It takes him less than a minute to reposition the pots in front of the hatch. Once he sets the light, that exit will quickly become a wall of flame. He takes out his lighter, and the remains of his bottle of Macallan. Lowering himself very gently into the transom he waits for the gentle movement of the boat to settle.

All he has to do now is wait for the smoke to seep into the boat's interior. When she opens the aft hatch and sees him, he will act the rescuer. If he's lucky she might fall for that. And if she doesn't, she will try to get as far away from him as she can. She might race for the bow hatch and, if she does, she will find her exit blocked by flaming paint tins. She might try the skylight but she will not be able to lift the two-by-fours. She might scream for help but she won't be heard above the din of the drum circle. She might try to hide but before too long the smoke on the boat will flush her out. All he has to do is to show her the rifle. She's unlikely to fight back; if she does, he's quite prepared to knock her out.

He has already determined the back route they will take through an industrial lot and a broken fence to where his car sits waiting. By then the boaters and the people at the encampment will be too distracted by the fire to pay them any mind. With any luck, they will be across the bridge and at the cliff on the other side in twenty minutes. Cullen has marked the spot where Nevis will fall. He will make her remove her shoes and her jacket and leave them stacked tidily by the cliff edge. There will be no skid marks or broken branches or signs of struggle. In a matter of seconds it will all be over. They will think that she set fire to the boat and went to be with Natasha and Jessica. There will be no evidence that her death was anything but one in a regrettable and tragic series of suicides. Honor will find out the truth eventually. And with any luck the truth will kill her. Not quickly and easily, the way Nevis will die, or the way that later he too will leave the world, but slowly and painfully, week by week, year by year until all that is left of her is an agony of regret and guilt. By the time they find Nevis he will have reached St Olaf's. He will jump from the same bridge as Zoe two decades ago. He will enter the water where she entered it, will feel its cold embrace just as she did. He will rejoice in the brilliance of his revenge. His death will make the papers. Honor will find out, he will make sure of that. He will leave a note and sign himself Christopher Mulholland. He will take Honor's daughter from her. Honor will never be able to visit the places where her daughter and her best friend died without thinking of him.

Chapter 54

Honor

For a few moments after the explosion everything is a blur. A fiery ash rains down and pricks her skin. She blinks dust from her eyes but still she cannot see Alex. People dart by but she does not hear them. The world is a confusing rush of lights and dust and movement. As her head begins to clear a single word surfaces. Nevis. She hears herself scream, 'My daughter! Where's my daughter?' And then her legs are carrying her fast towards the bridge. Her body collides with another. Arms clamp around her shoulders, holding her back. She struggles and kicks out wildly but the arms are too strong. A voice says, 'Calm down. You have to stay behind the cordon.'

'My daughter Nevis is on that boat,' she says, coughing up ash.

The arms do not let up. A voice says, 'The fire crew are doing all they can.'

'My daughter!' She can feel the heat of the fire in her lungs. Her voice is a scream now.

A policewoman approaches, holding a hand to her ear. Remembering Alex suddenly, Honor says, 'I was with a man, Alex. Where is he?'

'The guy who tried to jump in? We've put him in the back of the van over there. For his own safety.'

The policewoman turns away and whoever is holding her loosens their grip. There is shouting. Instructions are barked. She hears another voice saying, 'I am Yolanda Graham from family liaison. The first responders are doing everything they can to establish whether there is anyone on the boat.'

'Please,' she says, her heart screeching, like a car in too low a gear. 'I have to get to her.'

She feels herself being spun around, a woman's arms around her now. Is this Yolanda? I can't think straight. I can't... Her heart is beating so fast now she feels it will explode from her chest. Her breath seems to snap, everything is happening too fast, her head is fizzing and buzzing.

'You need to come with me,' the voice is saying. Yolanda has her firmly by one elbow, the other hand slung across her shoulder. She feels her hands covering her face, the smell of sweat and ash on them.

'I can't see,' she says.

The voice says, 'You don't have to see, I've got you, just come with me.'

Her legs stumble forward, her body following on, the pressure of the hand on her elbow, the arm around her shoulders.

She hears a car door open and feels herself being pressed down. The door closes and for an instant stillness falls, then in a blast of warm, sooty air, Yolanda appears beside her. She removes her hands from her face and blinks into the light from the street.

'We're in one of the patrol cars. You're quite safe. We're not sure whether there is anyone on the boat, but we're doing our best to find out.'

From the radio come bleeps and crackles and the sound of voices.

She is trembling now, her whole body shaking. Someone, Yolanda she supposes, has put a crunchy silver blanket over her.

'You're OK, it's just shock. Try to breathe slowly.'

A knock comes on the window of the driver's side. The glass slides down. A policewoman in uniform is bending towards the car. Beside her stands a man with a blackened face.

'This gentleman thinks he saw your daughter on the quay-side.'

She stops breathing, the shaking stops. Sirens blare in the background. Every cell in her body is still now, waiting.

The policewoman steps aside. The man with the blackened face peers in.

'I saw a girl jumping from the boat. She was coughing but she was all right.'

Honor gasps out the words, 'My phone!'

'In your pocket,' Yolanda says. 'I can see it.'

With quaking hands Honor inspects the screen. No response to her calls, her texts. She has to think very hard to remember the passcode, her fingers shaking on the virtual keyboard. Calling Nevis's number. Voicemail.

The man with the blackened face is standing beside the uniformed officer and speaking but she cannot hear above the sound of sirens.

'She was with a man,' shouts the uniformed officer.

'Did he get a look at the man?' asks Yolanda.

The uniformed officer turns his back to them for a moment then, swinging round and leaning into the car, says, 'The witness says he saw the girl and the man jump from the boat together but he didn't catch sight of the man's face.' She lays her arms on the door and lowering her voice says, 'He's had a drink or two.'

Honor sits back, trying to think straight. The police radio crackles, '...active search for Professor Christopher Cullen, also known as Christopher Mulholland, in connection with the deaths of Natasha Tillotson and Amanda Salter, believed to be his mother. May be armed.'

Mulholland. She feels the breath quit her body, goosebumps rising, a terrible cold like ice water in the veins. She hears the words 'No! Stop!' in her head but finds herself unable to speak. Seconds pass in which she can hear nothing but the blood thumping in her forehead. Hands clamp her mouth so hard it is painful. She knows they are her own hands but at the same time it seems they are someone else's. Words chase through her mind but her head is so full of noise she cannot catch them. A disembodied voice says, 'Are you all right?' She does not answer, holding her breath now, doing her best to steady herself. Cullen, Mulholland, Cullen, Mulholland. A drumbeat. A call to action. It takes a moment to put the pieces together. Mulholland? After all these years?

In connection with the deaths of Natasha Tillotson and Amanda Salter, believed to be his mother.

The thoughts are a frantic jumble in her head. Mulholland. Zoe's rapist, Madeleine Ince's partner during the time of the Midland suicides, Mulholland becoming Cullen. Cullen the Dean.

Oh my God, Nevis! The way she's spoken about him, her tone fan girl soft.

Who'll be next?

Nevis seen leaping from the boat with a man.

No! Not Mulholland. Not now.

In a second, she springs from the car. Yolanda's voice trails behind. No time to stop and explain. A helicopter buzzes overhead. Every sense sharpened by adrenaline. She scopes about, thinking of Alex, desperately seeking the man with the blackened face and suddenly spots him on the opposite side of the road, hastening towards Queen Square.

'Hey, hey!' She has to scream to make herself heard above the sound of the helicopter blades. The man stops, the yellowy whites of his eyes like beads in the light from the streetlamp.

'The girl you saw is my daughter.'

'I told the copper everything I know.'

'Please.' She wants to grab him, shake him down. 'Please, tell me where they were heading?'

She watches his eyes sink in thought. *Quick, quick! There's no time for this. There's no time.* Her breath is coming in fits and starts. She watches him clocking it, alarmed. Please not now, not now. She holds herself still so as not to alarm him, watches his jaw relax.

'You could try behind the shit shed. Abandoned boat shed down there in the undergrowth. Hole in the fence back there, you can get into the industrial park. Spare wood there sometimes for the brazier. Didn't want to say nothing in front of the police in case they tell the owner. Handy, that hole in the fence.' He tips his head towards the scene of the explosion. 'Police cordoned off the whole area though. They wouldn't let you through if you was the Queen.'

'Thank you, thank you.' She can drive around, hit the streets. She pivots and walks away, briskly, feeling for the van keys in her pocket, not wishing to arouse anyone's interest. Last thing she wants is the police getting involved. No time for that. The moment she is out of sight she breaks into a run. The van is where they left it. She jumps in and starts the engine and is about to pull out into the road when she hears her own voice from earlier this evening asking Nevis to turn on share location.

I'll think about it.

She pulls out her phone, taps in her passcode, goes to settings.

And there it is.

Nevis's phone. A blue dot moving too fast for Nevis to be walking. They must be in a car, she thinks. She watches as the blue dot comes to a halt then starts up again, heading through the streets of Clifton towards the suspension bridge.

Chapter 55

Honor

The van screams into fourth gear, as she jumps through a red light, one eye on the road, the other on the blue dot. They're on the bridge now. She hears herself cry out as the blue dot slows to a halt. *They'd have to climb the suicide barrier... too hard to finish that thought.* There is time. The road ahead is clear. She checks in her rear-view mirror for blue lights, floors the accelerator through another set of lights. Eyes blade to her phone. Feels her breath explode from her chest. The blue dot has begun to move steadily over the span and out onto the other side. Now it is anyone's guess. She is closing the gap is all she knows. She swerves onto the approach road to the bridge, willing the driver's side window to lower more quickly, one hand on the steering wheel, the other fumbling in her pockets for the bridge toll. *Please let there be change!* Remembers Nevis teasing her, saying that no one uses cash these days. And there they are, tangled in the seams of her trousers, two £1 coins. She slams on the brakes at the barrier, throws the coins in the hopper, notices the 40-mph speed limit sign but does not wait to see if the booth is manned. The cameras will catch her. Accelerating onto the bridge she finds herself suspended above the gorge and heading for the lights around Leigh Woods. Checks the speedometer, lifts her right foot and jams the accelerator. An APNR camera flashes twice as the van speeds by, hits sixty-five, seventy, rapidly catching up with the car ahead, she swerving at the last minute to avoid it, the blaring horn of the driver behind her already fading. Driving crazy enough to alert the cops.

On the other side of the bridge she slows and checks her phone. The blue dot is moving more slowly now too. They are no longer in a vehicle, she thinks, but on foot. They have entered the woods on the cliffs overlooking the gorge. One eye on the road, the other on Google Maps. There is an entrance to the woods just up ahead and beside it a car park. She turns off the road towards the woods, switches off the car lights, navigating from Google Maps and the reflection of the bridge lights on the water. Just before the entrance to the car park, she pulls onto the verge and cuts the engine. Takes a moment to compose herself. No longer panicky or flustered now, the blood burning hot in her veins, powered by a terrible, immutable rage. Thinks, you got Zoe, Mulholland, but you will not get her daughter and you won't get me. I have thought about this moment, fantasised about it even, for years. You have no idea how hot and for how long the desire for revenge has burned in me.

All those years ago, at St Olaf's, he said he would get his own back. No one could say he hasn't been patient. He has planned this. The blue dot is a breadcrumb trail. I'm coming for you, Mulholland.

Jumping from the van she strides around to the back and flings open the doors, using the torch on her phone to check the small store of work tools she keeps stashed there. A torch, a length of rope, a roll of strong tape, a toolbelt and a Stanley knife with a new blade. She straps the toolbelt around her waist and drops the tools into their various compartments then makes her way to the car park where a blue Volvo sits alone. She approaches, cautiously, and moving close, takes out her phone. She dials 999, and when a voice answers, gives Mulholland's name and location and hangs up. There's no time to explain. The police will put two and two together. Mulholland will know they won't be far behind him. Listening for movement or, better still, voices, she scans the trees searching for specks of light. They are somewhere in the darkness a few minutes ahead of her, but where? He will kill Nevis if he can, but he won't make his move until she has found them. He will want to see the whites of her eyes. He will want to think he has finally destroyed her. She begins to creep along the forest fringe, using the railway line which skirts the edge of the gorge as a guide. The wind is up now and the moon appears blue behind scudding clouds.

Believed to be armed.

All these years he must have hated her and longed for revenge. To be in that man's life all that time. To have been part of his thoughts. She'd never imagined that the boy who spat at her in the street and swore he'd get his own back would ever see it through. But here he is. For her own part, she'd thought of him rarely. The years had passed in a busy blur of motherhood and work. She'd googled him once or twice and found nothing. She had always dared to hope he was languishing unregarded in some distant prison or that he had taken his own life. He'd changed his name and managed to walk away from his past.

On those occasions that she had thought about him it was always like looking into a deep dark well inside herself and it had unnerved her. She knew if ever she saw the bastard again she might kill him. She just never expected to put her conviction to the test. He wants to draw it out, this fight between them. He wants her to suffer, to prolong her anguish. But her mind is absolutely clear now. If he's prepared to use her own daughter as bait then he'd better be prepared to die.

A light flickers through the trees. She takes a breath and heads towards it. Zoe, she thinks, I could use your help. She moves forward along the path, the thin moonlight creeping through the still-naked branches of the trees enough, just, to keep her on track. Ahead the torchlight flares and fades like the spark of a firefly. The pulse drums in her temples and at the back of her brain, and her breath comes in fits and starts. The only sounds around her are those of the forest, a sinister rustling and the odd screech of a night bird. Is that you, Zoe? I hope so.

She moves through the clearing and comes out onto a chalk cliff. She can see them now, two figures hugging the sky, standing on the railway tracks overlooking the gorge. A rifle glints in the moonlight. There's no way to know if they've seen her. She drops the torch she's clutching in her toolbelt and, holding her hands above her head so that Cullen can see she's unarmed, shouts, 'I'm here, Nevis.' She watches them shift and turn.

A voice says, 'Hello Honor.' Mulholland. The voice has matured but she'd know it anywhere. He is wearing hunting gear, as though he were going on a country shoot for pheasants but the rifle in his hands is aimed at Nevis. His face is twisted into an awful grimace. Beside him Nevis seems frozen, barely registering Honor's presence. 'Do come and join the party,' he says, glibly. She wonders if he has gone mad.

Creeping closer, her hands in the air, she says, 'It's not Nevis you want, Christopher. It's me.'

He beckons her over. 'Let's talk awhile.'

She is a few metres away now, close enough to be able to see their faces, blue in the moonlight. Mulholland looks odd and crazed, the whites of his eyes like those of an animal caught in a snare; raging, unpredictable and with nothing left to lose. Nevis is beside him, hands held out unsteadily in front of her, her body stiff and angled away. She swallows hard and gasps a little. But she is not crying and there is something about the way she is holding herself, tensed and poised for action, which suggests to Honor that hope hasn't left her.

'You killed your mother, Christopher. I overheard the police radio. As weird as it might sound, I get it.' He frowns and shakes his head. Still she presses on. 'I used to feel for you, in the early days, when you first arrived at St Olaf's, so much younger than the rest of us and so uncertain of yourself, so much in her shadow, living *her* dream. I know she gave you an alibi, that night after the Maths Society party and I know that because of that you would never be free of her, never become your own person. If that were me, I think I'd have wanted to kill her too. But Tash? What could Tash have possibly done to have deserved to die?'

'She got in my way. She was a tittle-tattler.' He cocks his head towards Nevis. 'Just like your friend in the hospital. She didn't understand that is the line you cannot cross. I gave her plenty of warnings but she always knew better. Natasha had a good death. A great deal of Valium and a little push to send her on her way. She had no idea what was coming. As for the other one, Jessica, I had absolutely nothing to do with that. She did the job for me. But I would have done, believe me. These women, *girls*, happily sold themselves for better grades. Why should I think anything of them when they thought so little of themselves? Listen, a man who can kill his mother can kill anyone. *Anyone.*'

'Let Nevis go. You don't hate her. You hate me.'

'That's plenty.'

'You told me once that you loved Zoe, do you remember?'

At the mention of Zoe's name he gives a start as though all this time he has been in some kind of dream that he is only just waking from.

Nevis's eyes flare and she begins to tremble.

'Zoe was the only woman I've ever met who was worth anything. Every woman I was ever with after Zoe was a stain on her memory. You couldn't *bear* that I loved her, could you? You had to get in the way. You with your ruinous jealousy. Your hatred. You could have said nothing that night. Zoe would never have known. It was you who kept at her, on and on, with your stupid, sentimental version of "justice". You ruined your best friend. It was because of what you did, not what I did, that she took her life. You killed her. And now you come to me, thinking you can make terms, do a deal. Well I don't deal with the devil.'

Honor takes a step towards him. She has been hoping not to have to say the unsayable. All these years she has kept the secret from her daughter because she was afraid that it might kill her. But Christopher has left her with no choice. There is

356

no other route out of this. Telling the secret might be the only way to save her now.

'Look at Nevis, Christopher.' Mulholland glances at the figure beside him. 'Look at her jawline, her eyes, the contours of her mouth. Who does she remind you of?'

Mulholland looks away. She watches his nose twitch, his chin crumple, the implacable look of confidence give way to something more troubled.

'Nevis, tell Christopher who Zoe Jeffers was.' Believe me, she thinks, this is not how I wanted to tell you, this is not what I'd planned.

There is confusion scribbled on his face.

In a tremulous voice Nevis says, 'Zoe was my birth mother.'

'And when were you born?'

Nevis splutters out the date.

Honor watches Mulholland's eyes turn inwards. He blinks and checks himself, then turns his head and stares at Nevis.

The air is thrumming now. A helicopter nearing.

'What's going on?' Nevis says, in a pleading voice this time.

'Tell her, Christopher.'

Mulholland doesn't speak. She watches the rifle go slack in his hands. The thrum has become an insistent buzz now.

'It makes no difference,' he says, his voice hoarse with pain. 'The only person that ever mattered to me was Zoe.' Turning his face to Nevis he bellows, 'How could you betray your only true mother? This woman, this pretend mother, has brainwashed you. There is no *honour* in this woman...' he is pointing now. 'Only envy. Your mother didn't die in the way you think she did. This woman *killed* her.'

Nevis blinks and swallows hard, turning first to Mulholland

and then to her mother. Honor watches her begin to shake, her shoulders fold in on themselves. The fingers of her right hand come up to her mouth as the words form, too terrible to say out loud.

The silence between them is thick and murky. Who will break it? What is there to say? A howl starts up and becomes a roar. Nevis rising to her full height now, her teeth glinting in the moonlight. Mulholland tightens his grip on the rifle.

Honor takes a breath in. She thinks, now is the time. If not now, then never. She sees Nevis staring at her, trying to make sense of Mulholland's words and, opening her mouth, she says, 'Remember the kingfisher, my darling, when she left the Ark, turned blue by the water and orange by the sunrise. She was the first, the bravest.'

The sun will rise here too. There will be a new day, a new beginning.

The 'copter is shaking the tops of the trees.

Is that the sound of sirens in the distance?

And then, in a flash, it happens. From the tracks comes a roar as Nevis launches herself through the dusty blue air and at the enemy. Her feet jam into Mulholland's belly. He buckles then stumbles back over the railway track, arms windmilling in space, his legs twisting under him. Honor sees the spark as the barrel of the rifle hits the tracks, hears a thud and the unmistakeable crack of bone snapping on metal as Mulholland goes down. For a moment Mulholland reels yelping in pain and reaching for the rifle tries to stand and then Honor, leaping towards the prostrate figure, kicks his damaged leg from under him. He goes down again. She steps forward, raises her boot and stamps down hard on his rifle arm. Mulholland roars with pain and loosens his grip on his weapon. In a split second Honor lunges forward and kicks the gun away and, catching her foot on the side of her leg, sways and feels herself falling, seeing the earth coming up towards her, swinging her body and landing with a thud just shy of the tracks. Again Mulholland tries to stand but the broken leg hangs from his hip like a used paper bag and, as he struggles to get his balance, Honor scrambles forwards on all fours and grabbing the rifle with one hand pushes herself to stand. Fighting the urge to be sick, she lifts the weapon in her arms so that it is primed on Mulholland. How much of her life has been leading up to this moment.

'You have no idea how to use that,' Mulholland says.

'Try me.' She smiles to herself. As a girl, she was taught by Jim how to shoot the rats that hung around the Traveller encampments. Said it was kinder than laying down traps or poison. A girl doesn't forget the lessons of her father.

Nevis is standing just behind her. She reaches back behind her, feels the tips of Nevis's fingers reach out to touch her, says, 'My brave girl. Are you OK?'

No reply.

Without taking her eyes off Mulholland, she moves her body and out of the corner of her eye sees her daughter, struggling to catch her breath, a haunted expression on her face.

'What he said, just now, I want you to know it's not true.'

Nevis compresses her lips and turns her head to the sky, watching for the helicopter. Confused and in a state of shock, Honor thinks, and who can blame her for that. For herself, though, there has never been a time when her mind was more clear, more settled, more determined on its course.

To Mulholland she says, 'We're going for a stroll.'

The man lets out a groan and shakes his head, his hand going to his twisted, hopeless leg. She watches him panting from the pain.

Her voice strangely calm now, she says, 'Get up.'

Chapter 56

Honor

He staggers onto his one good leg, hand grasping the air for the support that isn't there, skin slick, eyes rolling wildly in his head. He knows he is defeated now, she thinks, but he'll not go down cleanly. He cannot physically destroy her now but he will do everything to deprive her of her reason to live. She must be alert to his tricks, that keen intelligence which once, many years ago, she almost admired. She holds the rifle to his back and directs him to the far side of the railway track near the lip of the cliff, Nevis following on behind and crying out, 'Where are we going?'

Her daughter's voice sounds very distant, as though it were reaching her from the past, the way a star's light beams down from centuries ago.

'Not far.'

The voice again, more insistent this time. An edge to it. 'I don't think we should go any further. We should wait for the police.'

They come to a standstill, Mulholland quiet now, his shoulders shaking, his breathing laboured. She is surprised by how little pity she has for him.

'Move to the edge,' she says. 'Take a good look over.' She waits for him to comply. 'It's a long drop into the night. You're going to feel it.'

He grimaces, a small, strangled laugh escaping from his lips. 'I stopped feeling a long time ago. It didn't agree with me.'

'Then you won't mind.'

'Not really, though I would have preferred to do it on my own terms.' From under hooded lids his eyes go to Nevis. 'Your daughter might, though. Only she's not really your daughter, is she?' His eyes close and his body slumps like an emptied sack. 'If she belongs to anyone it's to me, her father.'

She feels Nevis tense. So, he has worked it out. Done the maths. Well, he is a mathematician. She supposes it's more surprising in a way that he never found out before, wasn't curious or just didn't want to know. Nevis's soft sobs creep into every corner of her being.

She says, 'It'll be all right, darling, I promise.' This is not how Honor wanted her daughter to find out, not something she ever wanted her to know. He will pay for this too. Taking a step closer to him, she says, 'Turn and face me and keep your hands where I can see them.'

He hops about, unsteady on his one good leg, and stares at her, his face growing dark and waxy as if he were already slipping into death.

Tilting his head in Nevis's direction, he says, 'Why did you never tell her?'

'Because she didn't need to know.'

The ticking of the 'copter blades, a thickening throb in the ear.

She watches him slump as if defeated then think better of it, straightening himself upright, a last act of defiance.

Honor flicks her eyes skywards. 'They're coming for you, but you know that,' she says to Mulholland. 'Men who murder their mothers don't do too well in prison.'

He does not answer.

'This is a way out,' she says. 'A way to escape the shame.'

'How funny.' He laughs, bleakly, until the laugh hits pain and fizzles out. 'That's what I said to Natasha.'

'You're a monster.'

His face twitches and he shakes his head. 'They knew what they were getting into. All three of them. A pact with the devil.' His eyes go from Honor to Nevis and back again. 'And here I am.'

Silence falls. Beside her Nevis appears frozen. As for Honor, she can no longer distinguish between the whump of the 'copter and her own heart. He has said it, finally. It is said.

All around them the trees sway in the downdraught. Soon the 'copter will be overhead again. She wants this over with.

'Two steps back. You won't see it coming,' she says.

His bad foot taps the ground. He shifts his weight just long enough to take a half step backwards towards the cliff, roars with the pain and falls to his hands and knees. Yes, crawl you bastard.

A voice shouts, 'Wait!' Nevis raises a hand. 'How is this man my father? *How?*'

Mulholland is looking up at Nevis, his breath short and laboured. 'They kept me from you, Nevis. *She...*' He points to Honor '...kept me from knowing anything about you. Couldn't stand to have a rival for your mother's affections on the scene.'

'*Affections?* Zoe couldn't stand you,' snorts Honor, sidestepping closer, the rifle still trained on Mulholland. She reaches out a hand to her daughter and tries not to cry out when Nevis steps away.

The ticking of the 'copter blades fades once more into the night.

Honor feels weak, the rifle suddenly an unbearable burden, something she can barely carry. All the weight she has shouldered, to protect Nevis from exactly this. The thing no child should ever have to know: the knowledge that she only exists because of an act of violence.

Nevis moves her head a quarter turn, eyes blade across, narrow, then return to Mulholland. 'I found Zoe's note, the one she wrote before she died. At the end of last summer. You left it in that book of Greek myths, the one you used to read when I was a kid. That's how I found out you'd been lying to me all these years.'

Honor blinks and swallows, a small muscle in her right eye flickering like a broken light. No wonder Nevis has been so distant. To find out that way. Of course Honor blames herself. It was she who left the letter in the book. Was it carelessness or cowardice? Is there a difference? How can she tell Nevis, now, in the midst of all this? How can she explain? Both of them so young, Zoe depressed, all three holed up in the caravan on the edge of a field, the baby colicky from the damp, by night all three in the same bed, keeping each other warm, by day Honor working shifts in the shitty café, no help, too young to know that help was possible.

At the bottom of it all, Mulholland, that malevolent presence. She wants the bastard dead, *needs* it. In the corner of her eye she sees blue lights flicker across the bridge. Mulholland is propped up on one hand, his bent leg lying limp in front. She could shoot him, but what then? Claim it was self-defence? Against a man who would have been unable to defend himself let alone attack?

'Why didn't you tell me?' Nevis cries. 'Didn't you think I had a *right* to know? All these years you telling me my mother died in a traffic accident, that she didn't even know my father's name. And now this.'

She holds her breath and swallows but the blood is screaming in her veins. 'I did it to protect you. Maybe that was wrong. Your mother loved you, Nevis.'

'Not enough to hang around.'

Ahead of them, in the dim light, Mulholland stirs and, seizing his opportunity, shouts, 'This woman is nothing to you, Nevis. You and I are blood.'

Silence.

Now is the time, Honor thinks. The truth has done its time. It will not be held prisoner any longer. She says, 'When this man was fifteen, Nevis, he raped your mother.'

Nevis steps back. '*What?*'

Honor goes on to describe what happened that night. Nevis, so still she is almost fading back into the night, stands listening. Mulholland blinks and shakes his head, saying, 'No, no.' When she is done, he says, 'Nevis, listen to your father. Your blood. There was no rape. Never a scrap of evidence. The police dismissed it. That woman…' with a shaky hand he points at Honor 'manipulated Zoe into making a complaint. She was lucky not to have been charged with defamation and wasting police time. If I'd really "raped" Zoe why wouldn't she have had an abortion?'

Nevis clasps her hands around her head and begins to sob.

Honor swallows, hard, pushing the nausea, the red rage down, down. 'This is his revenge, Nevis, I hope you can see that. He can't destroy me so he's trying to destroy the most precious thing in my life – my connection to my daughter. Zoe wanted you. From the very beginning. She always said you were the best thing that could ever have come out of what had happened.'

'I loved your mother, Nevis. She was the love of my life. Why else would this woman make these outlandish claims unless it was her intention to keep us divided? It's what she's done your whole life. Your mother took her own life, but it was this woman who really killed her. She left Zoe with nowhere to turn and kept you from your father. Well here he is now, and he is *telling* you, you were born from *love*.'

Honor gasps at the audacity of it. But how clever he is, to have been able to twist his lies into something that can sound so like the truth. How can she deny her daughter the comfort of his words? How can she insist that there was nothing lovely about Nevis's conception? The bastard has beaten her. He took Zoe and he will take Nevis if she lets him.

The blue lights have disappeared into the darkness now. If Mulholland is going to die, it will have to be soon. She owes this to Zoe, to Natasha and Satnam and Jessica.

She raises the rifle, sets the stock against the meat of her shoulder, as if she were about to shoot a rat.

She says, 'Step back, Christopher. End this. If you don't, I will end it for you.'

'Go ahead,' he says, a sharp defiance in his voice.

From somewhere in the trees an owl calls.

She takes a step towards him. The rifle steady against her

shoulder, no breath passing through her, absolute focus. I must do this now.

Something on her shoulder, a sudden sharp shock, a feeling of weightlessness as the rifle is ripped from her hands. She freezes, topples, rights herself, cries out in the dark.

The wind whips up, the owl calls again.

A voice cuts through the night, 'This is for me to do, Mum.' Nevis is standing between them, breathing hard, the rifle clasped to her chest. She is looking at the prostrate figure on the ground. Addressing herself to Mulholland, she says, 'If anyone is going to kill you, it'll be me.'

Mulholland's voice, flat, almost as if the man has already departed his body. 'Do you want to throw away your life?'

'You don't understand. I am reclaiming it.'

Honor says, 'Darling, please, he is right. This is our business. Let us finish it.'

Nevis holds up a hand. 'I'm not doing this for you, or for me. This is for Natasha and Jessica and Satnam.'

For a moment Honor is stunned into silence. She opens her mouth to speak and in that instant realises that Nevis is right. This is not her business. It never was. Her spite, her rage, everything she has felt about Mulholland over the past decades, all this has taken up precious space in her heart where it had no business being. A piece of herself closed off and unavailable. She has never been completely and wholly present. An absence in her own life. And in her daughter's. A small dense ball of shame rises up and in its place a rush of release.

She hears Mulholland bleating, 'I loved your mother.'

Nevis. 'You *raped* her.'

'I was young. It wasn't like that.'

'I choose to believe Honor, my other mother.'

Folding his good leg under himself, and pushing off the ground with his hands, growling in pain, Mulholland rises to a stand. 'One last time, I beg of you to think again.'

Nevis braces herself. 'I'm done thinking.'

A ragged silence falls.

From somewhere nearby the owl hoots again. Mulholland says, 'Please forgive me,' and in a flash he has wheeled about and is rushing towards the lip of the cliff, roaring in pain as his broken femur bears his weight. From the corner of her eye she sees Nevis raise the rifle's sight to her eye. Honor hears herself cry out.

The roar becomes a scream as Mulholland goes over.

The whump of the helicopter rotors grows louder. Nobody hears Mulholland's last moments in this world.

She watches Nevis gasp and, head in hands, crumple to the ground. The rifle drops and clatters as it lands. Rushing over and falling to her knees, Honor clasps her arms around her daughter. The wind from the rotors sweeps their bodies and lifts the hair from their scalps but they remain, each holding the other. A voice from a loudhailer instructs them to stay in place.

Landing a kiss on her daughter's head and, feeling her body as it softens into her, Honor says, 'It's OK now.' Nevis swings an arm around her mother's shoulders and reaches for her hand. And so they huddle together, fingers loosely entwined, and wait for the police.

Chapter 57

Honor

'I get tired but otherwise, I'm good,' Satnam says, helping herself to another biscuit. 'It's strange to be on the *Kingfisher* again, but happy strange.'

Honor, Alex, Nevis and Satnam are taking cold lemonade and shortbread in the saloon. They are tied up on the banks of the Avon upstream of the Clifton Suspension Bridge, awaiting a helping tide. It is afternoon and hot, the water of the Floating Harbour a burnished bronze in the late summer sun.

Honor says, 'It's a year since we were last all together on the boat. Can you believe that?'

'It's like everything in the meantime happened to another Satnam.'

Honor observes Satnam and Nevis lock eyes, their lips curling upwards, new lives already evident in their smiles.

After the fire and the incident in Leigh Woods, Honor and Nevis went back up to London to recover. But sooner than they anticipated, Nevis missed Bristol and Satnam, Honor missed Alex and after a week on the canal in Hackney, they decided to make the journey to Bristol in the *Kingfisher*, tie up a while, until they figured out what was next.

Satnam says to Nevis, 'Will you miss being a student?'

'Perhaps, if I have the time to think about it much.'

Honor will see to it that she doesn't. She has signed on for a winter berth on the Montgomery canal on the Welsh Marches where she and Nevis will stay busy during the cold and dark months giving the *Kingfisher* a facelift, and also a change of name to the *Wise Owl*. When spring arrives Nevis will head off to her placement at the bird sanctuary at Hermaness. She'll spend the summer on Unst, monitoring the guillemot breeding season. After that, who knows? Perhaps one day she might even return to her studies.

Satnam says, 'I'm going to miss Bristol but I'll be back to visit Luke.' Tomorrow, Satnam is going back to live with her parents and begin a law degree at Birmingham University. Despite the official apology from the new Vice Chancellor of Avon along with the offer of a place to study law, it has been an easy decision. 'Biochem was what I thought I *should* study. But the law is my passion,' she'd told them. There is a lesson there.

Bikram and Narinder have been very supportive of their daughter's decision. It appears that, at the prospect of a lawyer in the family, Satnam's parents have decided marriage can wait. Love, though, has a timetable all of its own. Luke is staying on at Avon to finish his degree, but it's not far from here to Birmingham and, as Satnam says, there will be visits.

'We'll keep in touch, won't we?' Satnam says to Nevis now.

'All the time, forever,' Nevis says.

A calm ease slides across the room. Outside a party of ducks quarrel on the bankside. After a few minutes Alex, who has been checking the tide tables, breaks the silence.

'We'll need to get under motor again soon.' They've been

waiting for the tide to start coming in. It'll make the journey out a little trickier but there'll be less of a risk of being swept out to sea.

It is nearly six months since the incident on the Clifton Suspension Bridge. Satnam isn't ready, yet, to step back onto the span over the gorge and may never be. But the counsellor she's been seeing has suggested going under it might help close the circle. Besides which, it'll be a chance to remember Jessica and scatter flowers on the water where she fell. No one they know went to her funeral, nor to Tash's either. Both happened far away, in their home towns and their parents either didn't think to or chose not to invite Satnam. She understands that. It would take some time to deal with the residual shame of what had happened with Mulholland but she would get there. Her guilty sense of having been the catalyst for the deaths of Jessica and Tash was more deep-seated though. That might never quite go away.

Alex stands and waits for Honor to finish her lemonade.

'You need help, Mum?' asks Nevis.

'Nah, it's OK. Alex and I have got this.'

She waits while Alex sidles by, tipping a friendly wink, and moving towards the stern hatchway. She follows on, stopping to fire up the engine. The *Wise Owl*, as she thinks of it now, shivers into life and starts to growl. Engine in neutral, she goes up on deck, pausing momentarily to register the change in weight distribution as Alex steps off onto the bank. They'd tied up facing against the ebb tide and now the water's coming in again the bow will have to be turned round: a simple manoeuvre, one Honor prefers to do herself. She looks out across the soupy brown water, gauging its speed and depth, listening out for Alex to call her to catch the ropes. Her mind drifts until she's brought to her senses by Alex, saying, 'Anything wrong?'

Turning to face him. 'No, no. Ducks taking off is all. This year's crop, all grown up already. A little miracle to watch them fly.'

She turns away from the channel towards the bank as Alex swings the ropes and waits for them to get airborne so she can catch them as they fall.

Waiting for him to step back on board she gestures to the tiller. 'You hold this a moment while I draw up the anchor?'

'Oh sure. Listen, Honor, I didn't like to say in front of Nevis, but I read in the local paper that Mulholland's wife had her baby. A little boy.'

'Yeah, I saw that,' Honor says, busying herself with the anchor chain.

'You planning to tell Nevis?'

'Soon, yes. She's got a half-brother out there, she has a right to know.'

'Something else. An old contact in the news business rang and asked me to write a long piece.'

'About?' She watches the anchor appear from the water.

'About how a child prodigy became a rapist and got away with what he did because he was brilliant and an asset to an ancient institution which valued its reputation over the welfare of youngsters in their charge. I'll keep Zoe's and Satnam's and Nevis's names out of it. I'll write about how institutions continue to turn a blind eye to the Mulhollands and Reynolds of this world, and the folk who cover for them. Young women and men at the start of their lives are still dying of shame because they have run out of hope, because they can't see a way forward, because they don't think they'll be believed.'

The riverbank throws up a green smell. Ahead of them the distant span of the Clifton Suspension Bridge glints in the sunlight. 'That'll be a powerful piece.'

She stands, brushes a fallen leaf from her trousers, and, going over to him, pushes her fingers into the spaces between his. He eyes her watchfully. For a minute nothing seems to move, then he says, 'I was thinking of taking the *Helene* cruising in the spring. Maybe I'll make it as far as the Welsh Marches.'

'I'd like that.' She puts the engine into gear and steers the boat into the channel.

Not long afterwards they are motoring into the shadow cast by the bridge. Everyone is on deck now, Alex and Honor taking turns at the tiller and the two girls, faces to the sun, talking. Honor watches them and smiles to herself. Nevis does talk these days, or more than she used to, anyway.

Not far from the bridge, Nevis stands and makes her way alone towards them.

'Hey, Alex, would you mind going to the bow and sitting with Satnam? She doesn't want to be alone when we go under the bridge.'

Alex stands and, doing his best to cover his surprise, says, 'Wouldn't she rather you be there with her?'

Nevis shakes her head. 'She already asked me once, remember? She thinks that's enough for anyone. And I agree.'

Nevis waits for Alex to move then takes his place beside her mother. Together they watch Alex's back swaying as he makes his way along deck. A companionable silence falls between them, broken by Nevis.

'If the Dean hadn't jumped, Mum, would you have pushed him?'

Honor takes a while to think about this.

'No. I wanted to, but I wouldn't have shot him either.'

'Why?'

'It would have played right into his hands. Mulholland didn't care about his own life. He only cared about stopping me living mine. And besides which, he was your father.' Turning to her daughter, she says, 'Would you have pulled the trigger?'

'And let him determine the course of the rest of my life? Absolutely not.'

A flock of Canada geese whirrs by, underwings in shadow, the stragglers honking encouragement to those ahead of them, burdened by the keen edge of the wind. Bewitched, Honor and Nevis watch the birds as they sail in V formation high above the bridge and grow smaller as they near the sea, disappearing at last.

The fast, brown water chops around the boat. The engine hums and churns. Up at the bow, Satnam leans on Alex, her body small and shrunken, clasping firmly in her fingers the white lilies she will scatter at the spot where Jessica fell.

Nevis reaches for Honor's hand and, squeezing it, says, 'I think I see why you didn't tell me about him before. I wish you had, Mum. I wish you had told me years ago. But I understand.'

'Thank you,' Honor says, her eyes burning. 'Take the tiller now, darling. Take us wherever you want to go.'

Author note

Two Wrongs is a work of fiction. Avon, Midland and St Olaf's universities are invented institutions. The characters and events in this novel are imagined. Any resemblance to any real-life person, event or institution is entirely coincidental.

Acknowledgements

My heartfelt thanks to everyone who worked on this book with special mention to the dedicated teams at HQ and HarperCollins, Rogers, Coleridge & White and Sayle Screen, and to booksellers (especially the indies) everywhere. Emily Kitchin, you are a dream to work with. Thank you to Jeremy White and Lynn Keane for being there. And a very big thank you to readers, bloggers and book enthusiasts. You make everything possible.

Turn the page for an exclusive extract from the
gripping and shocking psychological thriller
from bestselling author Mel McGrath…

Available to buy now!

I

Cassie

2.30 a.m., Sunday 14 August, Wapping

I'm going to take you back to the summer's evening near the end of my friendship with Anna, Bo and Dex.

Until that day, the eve of my thirty-second birthday, we had been indivisible; our bond the kind that lasts a lifetime. Afterwards, when everything began to fall apart, I came to understand that the ties between us had always carried the seeds of rottenness and destruction, and that the life we shared was anything but normal. Somewhere in the deep recesses of my mind I think I had probably known this for years, but it took what happened late that night in August for me to begin to be able to put the pieces together. Why had I failed to acknowledge the truth for so long? Was it loneliness, or was I in love with an idea of friendship that I could not bear to let go? Perhaps I was simply a coward? One day, it might become clearer to me. Perhaps it will become clear to you, once I have taken you back there, to that time and that place. And when I am done with the story, when everything has been explained and the secrets are finally out, I will ask you what you would have done. Because that's what I really want to know.

What would you have done?

Picture this scene: a Sunday morning in the early hours at a music festival in Wapping, East London. Most of the ticket holders have already left, and the organisers are clearing up now – stewards checking the mobile toilets, litter pickers working their grab hooks in the floodlights. Anna, Bo, Dex and I are lying side-by-side on the grass near the main stage, our limbs stiffening from all the dancing, staring at the marble eye of a supermoon and drinking in this late hour of our youth. None of us speaks but we don't have to. We are wondering how many more hazy early mornings we will spend alone together. How much more dancing will there be? And how soon will it be before nights like these are gone forever?

At last, Bo says, 'Maybe we should go on to a club or back to yours, Dex. You're nearest.'

Dex says this won't work; Gav is back tonight and he'll kick off about the noise.

We're all sitting up now, dusting the night from our clothes. In the distance I spot a security guard heading our way. 'I vote we go to Bo's. What is it, ten minutes in an Uber?'

Anna has spotted the guard too and jumps onto her feet, rubbing the goosebumps from her arms.

'I've got literally zero booze,' Bo says. 'Plus the cleaner didn't come this week so there's, like, a bazillion pizza boxes everywhere.'

4

With one eye on the guard, Anna says, 'How's about we all just go home then?'

And that's exactly what we should have done.

Home. A long night-tube ride to Tottenham and the shitty flat I share with four semi-strangers. The place with the peeling veneer flooring, the mouldy fridge cheese and the toothbrushes lined up on a bathroom shelf rimmed with limescale.

'Will you guys see out my birthday with one last beer?'

Because it is my birthday, and it's almost warm, and the supermoon is casting its weird, otherworldly light, and if we walk a few metres to the south the Thames will open up to us and there, overlooking the wonder that is London, there will be a chance for me to forget the bad thing I have done, at least until tomorrow.

At that moment the security guard approaches and asks us to leave the festival grounds.

'Won't the pubs be closed?' asks Anna, as we begin to make our way towards the exit. She wants to go home to her lovely husband and her beautiful baby, and to her perfect house and her dazzling life.

But it's my birthday, and it's almost warm, and if Anna calls it a day, there's a good chance Bo and Dex will too and I will be alone.

'There's a corner shop just down the road. I'm buying.'

Anna hesitates for a moment, then relenting, says, 'Maybe one quick beer, then.'

In my mind I've played this moment over and over,

sensing, as if I were now looking down on the scene as an observer, the note of desperation in my offer, the urgent desire to block out the drab thump of my guilty conscience. These are things I failed to understand back then. There is so much I didn't see. And now that I do, it's too late.

Anna accompanies me and we agree to meet the boys by Wapping Old Stairs, where the alleyway gives onto the river walk, so we can drink our beers against the backdrop of the water. At the shop, I'm careful not to show the cashier or Anna the contents of my bag.

Moments later, we're back out on the street, and I'm carrying a four pack but, when Anna and I reach the appointed spot, Bo and Dex aren't there. Thinking they must have walked some short distance along the river path we call and, when there's no answer, head off after them.

On the walkway, the black chop of the river slaps against the brickwork, but there's no sign of Bo or Dex.

'Where did the boys go?' asks Anna, turning her head and peering along the walkway.

'They'll turn up,' I say, watching the supermoon sliding slowly through a yellow cloud.

'It's a bit creepy here,' Anna says.

'This is where we said we'd meet, so. . .'

We send texts, we call. When there's no response we sit on the steps beside the water, drink our beers and swap stories of the evening, doing our best to seem unconcerned, neither wanting to be the first to sound the alarm. After all, we've been losing each other on and off all night. Patchy signals, batteries run down, battery packs mislaid, meeting points misunderstood. I tell Anna the boys have probably gone for a piss somewhere. Maybe they've bumped into someone we know. Bo is always so casual about these things and Dex takes his cues from Bo. All the same, in some dark corner of my mind a tick-tick of disquiet is beginning to build.

It's growing cold now and the red hairs on Anna's arms are tiny soldiers standing to attention.

'Shall we call it a day?' she says, giving me one of her fragile smiles.

I sling an arm over her shoulder. 'Do you want to?'

'Not really, but you know, we've lost the boys and . . . husbands, babies.'

And so we stand up and brushing ourselves down, turn back down the alley towards Wapping High Street, and that's when it happens. A yelp followed by a shout and the sound of racing feet. Anna's body tenses. A few feet ahead of us a dozen men burst round the corner into Wapping High Street and come hurtling towards us, some facing front, others sliding crabwise, one eye on whatever's behind them, clutching bottles, sticks, a piece of drainpipe and bristling with hostility. A blade catches the light of a street lamp. We're surrounded now by a press of drunk and angry men and women. From somewhere close blue lights begin to flash.

'We need to get out of here,' hisses Anna, her skinny hand gripping my arm.

They say a person's destiny is all just a matter of timing. A single second can change the course of a life. It can make your wildest dreams come true or leave you with questions for which there will never be any answers. What if I had not done what I did earlier that night? And what if, instead of using the excuse of another beer to test the loyalty of my friends and reassure myself that, in spite of what had happened earlier that night, I couldn't be all bad, I had been less selfish and done what the others wanted and gone home? Would this have changed anything?

'Come on,' I say, taking Anna's hand and with that we jostle our way across the human tide, heading for the north side of the high street but we're hardly half way across the road when we find ourselves separated by a press of people surging towards the tube. Anna reaches out an arm but is swept forwards away from me. I do my best to follow, ducking and pushing through the throng but it's no good. The momentum of the crowd pushes me outwards towards the far side of the road. The last I see of Anna she is making a phone sign with her hand, then I am alone, hemmed in on one side by a group of staggering drunks and on the other by a blank wall far too high to attempt to scale.

Moments later, the crowd gives a great heave, a space opens up ahead and I dive into it, ducking under arms and sliding between backs and bellies and a few moments later find myself out of the crush and at the gates of St John's churchyard, light-headed, bruised and with my right hand aching from where I've clutched at my bag, but otherwise

8

unhurt. I feel for my phone and, checking to make sure no one's looking, use the phone torch to check inside the bag. In my head I am making a bargain with God. Let me get out of here and I will try harder to believe in you. Also, I will find a way to make right what I have done. Not now, not right away, but soon. Now I just want to get home.

The light falters and in its place a low battery message glows. God's not listening and there's nothing from the others. I tap out a group text, *where r u?*, and set myself to the task of getting out.

Taking the path through the churchyard, feeling my way past gravestones long since orphaned from their plots, I head along a thin, uneven stone path snaking between outbuildings at the back of the church. From the street are coming the sounds of disorder. Somewhere out of view a mischief moon is shining, but here the ground is beyond the reach of all but an echo of its borrowed light and it's as quiet as the grave.

The instant my heart begins to slow there's a quickening in the air behind me and in that nanosecond rises a sickening sense that I'm not alone. I dare not turn but I cannot run. My belly spasms with an empty heave then I am frozen. Does someone know what I've got? Have they come to claim it? What should I do, fight for it or let it go?

A voice cuts through the dark.

'Cassie, darling, is that you?'

There's a sudden, intense flare of relief. Spinning on my heels, I wait for Anna to catch me up. 'Oh I'm so glad.'

She flings an arm around my shoulders and for a moment we hug until the buckle of my bag digs into my belly and I pull away. What a shitty birthday this has turned out to be. If they knew what I'd done some people would say it's kismet or karma and if this is the extent of it I've got off lightly. They'd be right.

'Have you seen the others?' I ask Anna.

'Bo was with me for a bit. He and Dex got caught up in the crowd which was why they didn't make it to the Old Stairs, then they got separated. No idea where Dex is now. He might have texted me back, but my phone's croaked.'

'I got nothing from him either.'

'You think we can get out that way?' She points into the murk. 'Hope so.'

We pick our way down the pathway into the thick black air beside the outbuildings, me in front and Anna following on. As we're approaching the alleyway between the buildings my eye is drawn to something moving in the shadows. A fox or a cat maybe? No, no, too big for that. Way, way too big.

I've stopped walking now and Anna is standing right behind me, breathing down my neck. Has she sensed it too? I turn to see her pointing not to the alley but to the railings on the far side of the outbuildings.

'Anna?'

'Thank God!' She begins waving. 'The boys have found us – look, over there.' In the dim light two figures, their forms indistinct, are breaking from the crowd and appear to be making their way towards us.

'Are you sure it's them?'

'Yes, I can tell by way they're moving. That's Dex in front and Bo's just behind him.'

I watch them for a moment until a group of revellers passes by and the two men are lost from view. From the alley there comes a sudden cry. Spinning round I can now see, silhouetted against the dim light of a distant street lamp, a man and a woman. The man is standing and the woman is bent over with her hands pressed up against the wall, her head bowed, as if she's struggling to stay upright. I glance at Anna but she's still looking the other way. Has she seen this? I pull on her arm and she wheels towards me.

'Over there, in that alley.' It takes a moment for Anna to register, a few seconds when there is just a crumpled kind of bemusement on her face and then alarm. The man has one arm around the woman's waist and he's holding her hair. The woman is upright now but barely, her head bowed as if she's about to throw up.

Anna and I exchange anxious looks.

Every act of violence creates an orbit of chaotic energy around itself, a force beyond language or the ordinary realm of the senses. A gathering of dark matter. The animal self can detect it before anything is seen or heard or smelled or touched. This is what Anna and I are sensing now. There is something wayward happening in that alley and its dark presence is heading out to meet us.

With one hand the man is pressing the woman's face into the wall while, with the other, he is scrabbling at her clothes. She is as floppy as a rag doll. He has her skirt lifted now, the fabric bunched up around her waist at the back. Her left arm comes out and windmills briefly in the air in protest. Her hand catches the scarf around her neck and there's a flash of yellow and blue pom-poms before the man makes a grab for her elbow and forces the arm behind her back. The woman stumbles but as she goes down he hauls her up by her hair. Her cry is like the sound of an old record played at half speed.

Something is screaming in my head. But I'm pushing it away. Another voice inside me is saying, this is not what I think it is, this is not what I don't want it to be, this is not real.

The man has let go of the woman's hair. He's pressing her face into the wall with his left hand while his right hand fumbles at his trousers. His knee is in the small of the woman's back pinning her to the wall. The woman is reaching around with her arm trying and failing to push him away but her movements are like a crash test dummy at the moment of impact.

'Oh God,' Anna says, grabbing my arm and squeezing hard, her voice high-pitched and tremulous.

In my mind a furious wave is rising, flecked with swirling white foam, and in the alley the man's pelvis is grinding, grinding, slamming the woman into the wall. The world has shrunk into a single terrible moment, an even horizon of infinite gravity and weight, from which there is no running away. Anna and I are no longer casual observers. We have just become witnesses.

I feel myself take a step forward. My legs know what I should be doing. My body is acting as my conscience. The step becomes a spring and Anna too is lunging forward and for a moment I think she's on the same mission as me until her hand lands on my shoulder and I feel a yanking on the strap of my bag and in that instant, Anna comes to an abrupt stop, sending the bag flying into the air. It lands a foot or two away and breaks open, its contents scattering. The shock soon gives way to a rising panic about what might have spilled and I'm down on my knees, rooting around in the murk, scraping tissues and lip balm, my travel card and phone, cash and everything else back inside the bag, checking over my shoulder to make sure Anna hasn't looked too closely at the spilled contents.

As I rise she's grabbing my wrist and squeezing the spot where my new tattoo sits. I try to shake her off but she's hissing at me now, her body poised to pull me back again. 'Don't be so bloody stupid! You don't know what you're getting into.'

'He's hurting her! Someone needs to intervene. At least let's call the police.'

My hand makes contact with my bag, peels open the zip and fumbles around in the mess. And in that moment in my mind a wave crests and rushes to the shore and the foam pulls back exposing a small bright pebble of clarity. What would the police say if they found what I am carrying? What would Anna say?

In my mind an ugly calm descends. My hand withdraws

and pulls the zip tight. They say that it's in moments of crisis that we reveal most about ourselves.

'My battery's dead. You'll have to call from yours.'

I'd like to say I'd forgotten that Anna's phone was out of juice but I hadn't. In any case, Anna isn't listening. Something else has caught her attention. On the far side a phone torch shines, a light at the end of a dark tunnel, and in its beam is Dex, as frozen as a waxwork. Behind him, in the gloom, lurks a shadowy figure that can only be Bo. If anyone is going to put a stop to what is going on in the alley it'll be Bo.

Won't it?

'Please,' murmurs Anna. 'Please, boys, no heroics.'

Dex continues to stand on the other side of the alley, immobile, his gaze fixed on me and Anna. It's at that moment that I become conscious of Anna shaking her head and Dex acknowledging her with a single nod. For a fraction of a second everything seems frozen. Even the man, ramming himself into the woman in the alley. And in that moment of stillness, an instant when nothing moves.

We all know what we are seeing here but in those few seconds and without exchanging a word, we make the fateful, collective decision to close our eyes and turn our backs to it. No one will intervene and no one will tell. The police will not be called. The woman will be left to her fate. From now on, we will do our best to pretend that something else was happening at this time on this night in this alley behind this church in Wapping. We'll make excuses. We'll tell each other that the woman brought it on herself. Privately, we'll convince ourselves that this can't be a betrayal because you can't betray a person you don't know. We will twist the truth to our own ends and if all else fails, we will deny it.

We'll do nothing. But doing nothing doesn't make you innocent.

The light at the end of the tunnel snaps off and in a blink Dex and the shadowy figure of Bo have disappeared into the darkness. I look at Anna. She looks back at me, gives a tiny nod, then turns and begins to hurry away up the path towards the church. And all of a sudden I find myself running, past the alley where only the woman remains, slumped against the wall, past the wheelie bins, along the side of the church, between tombstones decked in yellow moonlight and out, finally, into the street.

ONE PLACE. MANY STORIES

Bold, innovative and
empowering publishing.

FOLLOW US ON:

@HQStories